THE
WISH

LENA GIBSON

Black Rose Writing | Texas

ISBN: 978-1-68513-254-5
PUBLISHED BY BLACK ROSE WRITING
www.blackrosewriting.com

Printed in the United States of America
Suggested Retail Price (SRP) $23.95

The Wish is printed in Chaparral Pro

*As a planet-friendly publisher, Black Rose Writing does its best to eliminate unnecessary waste to reduce paper usage and energy costs, while never compromising the reading experience. As a result, the final word count vs. page count may not meet common expectations.

Praise for
THE WISH

"*The Wish* is a twisty, labyrinth thriller that grabs the reader from the opening page and never lets up. It's engrossing and wholly original."
–David Buzan, author of *In the Lair of Legends*

"Who has not had the fantasy of going back in time to correct one's mistakes? Gibson keeps her readers guessing as Elizabeth scrambles to find a different future than the one she already experienced."
–Carolyn Geduld, author of *Who Shall Die*

"Readers will fall headlong into this book. Even after the last page you'll be thinking about the characters, in particular Elizabeth, for a long time."
–Eileen Cook, author of *You Owe Me A Murder*

"The speculative parts of the story, the time travel and other elements, were integrated into the story line without taking it over, which was refreshing and kept the story grounded in reality. There were plenty of twists and turns that pleasantly surprised me and made the book hard to put down."
–Kirsten Schuder, author of *Inside Dweller*

"*The Wish*, a multi-faceted work of women's fiction, seamlessly blends suspense, romance and time travel in a memorable story featuring a resilient woman seeking a second chance at a happy life."
–Gail Ward Olmsted, author of *Miranda Writes*

"Lena has done it again! Another great book with so many ups and down, adding a bit of fantasy, making it a fantastic story. I couldn't put it down."
–Angera Allen, author of *Spin It Series*

To my wonderful daughters:
For Laurel, who made Christopher her book boyfriend.
For Hayley, who helped torment my main character.

THE
WISH

Chapter 1

Sometimes change is infinitesimal, slow. You don't notice its icy fingers wrapped around your throat, stealing your breath, your beliefs, changing who you are until you don't recognize yourself. I was in the middle of such a change before the accident. The slow erosion of myself, into nothing.

I hadn't been behind the wheel in two years, not since the accident. I didn't like to be reminded of those dark days. Few career women in their early thirties don't drive, but walking kept me from another harrowing driving experience. Plus, I'd discovered that I enjoyed the fresh air and exercise.

I crossed the Museum lobby and nodded to the recent hires at the Information Desk, though I'd never spoken to any of their fresh, youthful faces. I stepped into an empty elevator, heading up to the peace of my office and lab.

"Hold the elevator," came the call from across the lobby.

I ignored the request. Christopher, the conservator of our museum, raced toward the closing door, shoved his arm inside, and slid in beside me. I rolled my eyes. I'd almost escaped, but hadn't been fast enough. Trapped beside him, his heat radiated toward me and I scooched sideways. He wore running clothes and his dark, wavy hair dripped with sweat. His muscles looked hard, the kind only dedicated athletes or gym rats achieved. I hoped he planned to shower before work.

"Hey, Lizzie." He smiled, the dimple appearing in his cheek.

My teeth ached with the effort as I maintained a neutral expression. I was not, nor had I ever been, a Lizzie. I hated that nickname. My name was Elizabeth, which suited me—serious, classic, and a little stand-offish. The latter may not have suited me when I was younger, but it did now. I'd been burned too many times to let people get close to me. Life had been filled with harsh lessons.

I nodded to be polite. Being around Christopher was a constant struggle to maintain professionalism. What I really wanted to do was yell, "Leave me alone. I don't need anyone." More than anyone else, he brought out the worst in me. Why wouldn't he take a hint and leave me alone?

"Cat got your tongue again?" He leaned across me and pressed the button for his floor. "My magnificent presence has once again rendered you speechless." He winked.

The elevator ride lasted an eternity. How long did it take to get to the fourth floor?

He smirked.

I raised one eyebrow, but he knew I wouldn't respond. Even before I stopped talking, I hadn't spoken to him. Not since his brother Brandon had disappeared without a word of explanation. Why start now?

"Oh, Christopher."

His mincing tone meant to mimic my voice as he clutched his hands to his chest, caving in his broad shoulders in an attempt to appear feminine.

"You're so handsome and strong." He batted the long dark lashes that fringed his ice-blue eyes. "I'd love to meet with you after work. I don't want to be around anyone, but I find your magnetic charm irresistible."

I cast a withering glance in his direction. Other women fawned over him. He'd probably been told those exact words last week. He could have been charming if he wasn't loud and annoying. Half the time, what came out of his mouth was so full of expletives that I had to filter them out in order to listen. If I spoke, I couldn't imagine it would be to him. He'd never told me anything I wanted to know, like where the hell his brother had gone. Not that I'd asked. I'd been too proud.

Our colleagues at the museum left me alone. They were content to send me emails and receive answers the same way. But not Christopher. Christopher intruded upon the peaceful setting of my office and harassed me for details in person. He was the only person in my professional life who cared that I couldn't speak. His ridiculous remarks seemed designed to elicit a response, but I didn't give him the satisfaction.

"I'll see you later, Lizzie. I have a couple of questions about the new shipment from the Middle East, and something personal." He stepped off on the fourth floor. "I'll come chat after I've showered."

I gritted my teeth. I couldn't wait.

His tall frame strode from the elevator and he turned to blow me a kiss. Why hadn't I reported his outrageous behavior to HR? I didn't want him to know I'd enjoyed his attempt, though after he was gone, I allowed myself an amused smile. I continued to the sixth floor where my office and lab were located. Maybe I should install a punching bag in the corner and bring workout clothes. It might help after encounters with Christopher. I could work on my left-right-knee-roundhouse combinations.

I couldn't wait to get to the lab that had become my sanctuary. The lab access was through my office. One side of the room had a custom-designed, painted chart of the most recent theory of human evolution. The tree-like diagram of the origins of the human race and their relatives took an entire wall. Seeing it made me smile because it reminded me of the part of my life over which I had control.

They'd hired me fresh from grad school, where I'd received my PhD in Paleoanthropology, and three summers of co-op jobs at the Smithsonian. My job was to create and maintain a display at the brand-new museum here in Portland, meant to one day rival the famous exhibits at the Smithsonian in Washington, DC, or the American Museum of Natural History in New York City.

Scientists used to think Neanderthals in Europe and the Middle East had died out, replaced by more advanced, modern humans moving out from Africa in a single wave.

Now, scientists acknowledged that multiple waves of anatomically modern humans had interbred with Neanderthals and older populations of early humans in several parts of the world. It shouldn't have been a surprise. Anyone who'd seen certain hockey players in the eighties could have recognized a Neanderthal brow ridge. Who knew what DNA lurked within the human species, waiting for selective pressure to force the next wave of evolution? Part of my job was to bring these modern ideas into the new exhibits.

Once I would have discussed these ideas with my boyfriend Brandon over tea in my office after work or over dinner at the cozy restaurants with good food that he always seemed to locate. Or I would have chatted online with my friend Jeff. We'd been close in grad school, but my job was here and he was across the country, in New York. It had been easy to drift apart, through geography and circumstance. The biggest factor in my lost friendship had been my husband, Eric.

It was hard to maintain a long-distance friendship with someone you weren't allowed to see or talk to. I missed sitting and talking about men and movies. We'd had almost the same taste in both, but now it had been years since Jeff and I had a conversation. The gulf had become too immense to bridge. Without a friend, I talked to myself or to my cat. Ember didn't mind, she just purred. Now she was the only one to hear my voice.

After the accident, I hadn't set out not to talk. I just had nothing to say. I'd become lost in my thoughts, trying to cope with my snarled mess of feelings. Then I didn't want to speak. It took months before I realized I couldn't anymore. It had been two years, and I still hadn't spoken in the presence of another person. I hadn't been injured, but the trauma had inhibited my voice. It infuriated my therapist, Dr. Maeve Fossey. We'd been unable to find a solution. We were scheduled for another fruitless appointment tomorrow. She talks. I type.

I read my emails and replied to everything that needed attention. It took an hour, but it would ensure uninterrupted peace afterward. In my office, I was accessible, but in the lab, everyone recognized I was unavailable. Barring an emergency, everyone would leave me alone. Hitting *Send* on the final message, there was a knock at the door. Before I could escape, Christopher barged inside. He'd changed into dark blue jeans and a t-shirt, his work uniform unless he was meeting with the Board, which was the only time he wore a suit and tie.

"Lizzie, perfect." He closed the door and the room shrank. His big personality stole most of the limited space. "Glad I caught you. Downstairs took longer than expected because there was a problem with a water leak in the Modern Technology display. I expected you would have escaped by now."

I shot him a sharp look at his choice of words, so close to my thoughts when I'd heard his knock.

"I had an unusual phone call last night. Once I would have talked to Brandon, but I want your opinion."

At the mention of Brandon's name, the world closed in and it became difficult for me to hear the rest of his words. Maybe there wasn't enough oxygen in the room. I had trouble concentrating and my vision blurred. My face burned and I willed myself to keep the tears at bay. Christopher continued talking but trailed off when he realized I wasn't listening.

"I'll pick you up at seven. I'll explain then."

I wanted to refuse his invitation, but I was too upset to protest.

His expression was thoughtful, as if I'd said something he hadn't expected, though I hadn't said a word. Maybe my discomfort was written on my face.

I expected him to mimic my daze or pretend to dab at imaginary tears, but he didn't.

"You okay? Do you need to sit down?"

I shook my head. My palms were sweaty, and I crunched them into balls and shoved them deep into the pockets of my white lab coat. I didn't want to go. I couldn't spend that much time with Christopher. Trying not to be obvious, I took calming breaths.

"Look Lizzie, I wouldn't ask if it wasn't important. Please?" All traces of his usual jokes were gone.

I'd have done anything for his brother at one time—before he'd disappeared from my life without an explanation. For Christopher too.

"I know you don't like me," Christopher said.

At that, I looked up and tried to focus. Not that I didn't like *him*. I didn't want to like anyone.

His voice was quieter and less abrasive than usual. His pale blue, almost silver eyes looked sincere.

"But I'm out of options. Please eat with me."

I panicked again and shook my head. Eat? That wasn't a meeting. It sounded more like a date. I glanced down at my jeans, comfortable walking shoes, and lab coat.

"You don't have to change. It's not a date," he said, interpreting my glance.

He'd said *'Please'* twice. I couldn't recall hearing that word cross his lips before now. Maybe I hadn't paid attention. Despite my feelings, I was the slightest bit curious. I shrugged and nodded. Sighing would be rude, so I kept it to myself.

"Thanks, Lizzie. I appreciate your overwhelming enthusiasm. I'll see you at seven." His blue eyes twinkled—his good humor restored.

What had I gotten myself into? I already regretted my decision.

When he showed himself out, I moved into the lab and retrieved the most recent box of fossils to arrive. I wanted to forget Christopher, banish him from my mind. Dr. Maeve said my favorite coping mechanism was avoidance. With a hint of defiance, I opened the box and sorted the contents. Most were casts of bones or bone fragments, but one box contained original fossils from the Middle East that were close to a hundred thousand years old. The Middle East's proximity to Europe, western Asia, and Africa made it the perfect place to find evidence of mixed populations of early humans and some of the rarer species that had become extinct. This Mesolithic study was for the next exhibit I was developing.

I stayed in my lab for the rest of the day, removing Christopher from my thoughts, until my phone chimed with a notification.

"Ready?"

I didn't know he had this number. He'd never used it before, as far as I could remember. I'd changed my number because Eric used to scroll through my messages, looking for reasons to be angry. It had been easier to start fresh. This number had been for family and work only. How could I reply and get out of dinner?

Christopher tapped on the window.

He was in my office. There was no escaping.

I shrugged and rotated my neck, the muscles tight from the precision of measuring, labeling, and identifying the fragments of fossilized bone. I glanced at my phone—seven-ten. How did that happen? I was late. He'd been patient. Leaving the box, so I could resume tomorrow, I jotted a few quick notes, shut off my computer, and turned off the lights before I joined him in my office. I needed a few minutes for my brain to change gears.

As I locked the door and joined him in the hall, my unasked question about his brother returned to my mind. Something he'd said had stuck with me all day and I wanted an answer.

"Why can't you talk to Brandon?" I texted while we waited for the elevator. Once upon a time, he and Brandon had been so close.

A strange look appeared on Christopher's face. I couldn't decipher his emotions, and his usual smile disappeared.

"I thought you knew about Brandon." His voice was flat, without inflection.

He looked like he was working up the courage to tell me something difficult. My eyes narrowed. If I'd Googled his brother, I could have known, but I'd avoided even that temptation for the last five years, deactivating my accounts on social media.

"Fuck. I'll just say it. Brandon died. Four years ago."

My body sagged as though I'd been gut-punched and I used the cold stainless wall to steady myself. The taste of bile rose in my throat. All this time I'd imagined Brandon married, living his own happily ever after across town. Successful and alive. I shook my head. I'd been a bitch for thinking the worst of him.

"After your breakup," Christopher said, "He disappeared from everyone. Worked all the time. Didn't talk to anyone. Kinda like someone else I know."

I couldn't look at Christopher, but his voice continued as though from a distance. It seemed calm, which was shocking considering the topic was his brother's death.

"A couple of months after you two argued, he slipped into a coma and never woke up. At first, we had hope, but he stayed like that for a year. By the end, there were no longer signs of brain activity. We turned off the machines. He wouldn't have wanted to stay like that on life support."

For Christopher, this was old news and the pain would be more distant. Not forgotten, but squished down to a manageable level. Would my pain become dull, blunt? Today it was like twisting knives.

I rewrote Christopher's words in my mind. The argument that led to my breakup with Brandon had been minor. After that, his brother ghosted me, blocked my number, and vanished. I'd waited outside his house twice, but I hadn't seen him. Later, I'd been so wrapped up in my own problems with Eric that I hadn't heard about Brandon's coma or death. Tears pricked at my eyes and this time, a few escaped. Christopher could mock if he wanted. I didn't care. I'd cared about his brother. With partial success, I smothered my feelings so I could ignore them. Dealing with them all at once was too difficult.

The elevator doors opened at the bottom and we stepped out. I reeled—his words like blows. Coma. Dead. I'd spent all this time wondering what would have happened if we'd stayed together. How things would be different. They'd have been the same. I'd be in mourning, and still voiceless, since that was my response to trauma.

With this new grief surrounding me, the memory of the accident hijacked my waking hours. I slipped back to my moment of crisis, the flood of memories overwhelming my mind.

There was a clarity in the headlights. I discovered that in the moment with the blinding lights, screeching tires, and jarring crunch of sound, that while I didn't want to die, I was resigned. White light rushed toward where I was frozen and time stopped. When I'd viewed photos of the wreckage online, I didn't understand how anyone could have survived. As the driver, it was my fault. I shouldn't have been the one to live.

"Lizzie, are you okay?" Christopher's voice came from far away.

I nodded, numb. We walked out of the museum as I relived when I'd walked away from the twisted, mangled metal. My old life had died in that infinite moment, transfixed by the lights, and with it my voice.

Chapter 2

Christopher and I strolled a few blocks to a restaurant, the air warm in the May evening. In this part of the city, most restaurants had outdoor sidewalk patios—so many interesting places to choose from. It was a beautiful evening, ripe with the promise of the approaching summer. Outside was better. I had more space and fresh air. I could tell from his frown that he was concerned, but he'd asked to talk and I would try to listen, despite the shocking news that brought back my trauma. Once again, my mind flashed to Eric and the night that had changed my life.

As we walked through the door, I recognized where we were. I'd been here before when it had served Italian instead of Indian. The scent of rich spices filled the air, bringing me back to the present, and I inhaled their fragrance. I was starving. I couldn't remember my last hot meal. For convenience, I ate a lot of salads and sandwiches. Once more, I breathed in the heavenly aroma. I couldn't wait to eat.

A server in black pants and a white blouse led us to a quiet table in the back with dim lighting. It wasn't supposed to, but it seemed like a date. To a stranger, we might look like a cute couple, though Christopher and I were mismatched. But they say opposites attract. He's tall and I'm short. He's dark, I'm fair. His face was made to laugh, while mine was serious. I've always been the kind of person who everyone says would be pretty if only I'd smile—the worst compliment ever. Despite all those differences, from the outside, it might look like we fit. I glanced toward the door, wondering if I could bolt or if Christopher would follow.

"Still not a date," Christopher said under his breath as we sat.

The way his thoughts followed mine was uncanny. Was I so easy to read?

Our server said, "Can I start you off with drinks?"

"A bottle of red," said Christopher. "Do you have a recommendation?"

I didn't drink alcohol, so I handed my wine glass to our server and shook my head. He inclined his head and accepted it without pause.

Christopher chuckled. "Never mind. What's on tap? I'll get a beer instead. Lizzie, you want a beer? A cocktail?"

I shook my head and held up my water glass.

When our drink order was settled, Christopher said, "I didn't know you don't drink. Was it the accident?"

I started. I had forgotten that he'd know about it, but I didn't want the conversation to be about anything personal—especially not the accident—so I shook my head. It took up too many of my sleepless nights. I couldn't let it take my days, too.

He lifted my phone from the table and handed it to me. "Tell me."

"My mom drank. She died. I don't. Why are we here?" Impatience surged through my veins.

"Let's order first. I'm starving. If you're wondering what's good, it's all as delicious as it smells. Sometimes I want one of everything on the menu."

I dreaded the ordeal of ordering in person. Most of the time, I ordered takeout online to avoid the embarrassment of silent pointing, which made me feel so useless. Sometimes I wanted to talk, but when I tried, nothing came out. Dr. Maeve said that I wasn't trying. That deep down, I didn't want my voice. She said I needed to find the right incentive.

I studied my menu and flipped it closed almost right away. Christopher was staring, but I was determined not to fidget under his gaze.

"Well, Lizzie. What're you getting?"

He leaned back in his wooden chair, the picture of ease and relaxation, while I dripped with sweat, a side effect of extreme anxiety. I hoped it wasn't obvious.

I pointed to the two items I'd chosen.

When our server returned with ice water and a pint of his chosen IPA, Christopher ordered. "The lady will have the lamb madras curry and I'll have butter chicken. We need two orders of vegetable samosas, an order of naan, and a side of basmati rice."

Grateful he'd handled my order with so little discomfort, I sipped my ice water. Why was he being so considerate?

"Thanks," I texted. My tense shoulders loosened a little.

"I suppose I should explain." He took a long drink of beer, then set it on the coaster. He adjusted it to sit in the exact center before speaking. "I didn't know you were unaware of what happened to Brandon. I apologize. He'd said it was a rough breakup, and I respected both of you enough to stay out of it—give you space. It was none of my business. I thought you would've heard what happened to him through others at work. I didn't consider how little you interact with people and I'm sorry I upset you."

I shrugged, watching him play with his fork.

"I didn't handle it well at first, either. I had a rough couple of years. We all need to escape. Hence the women. Though, as you may have noticed, I quit some time ago."

I hadn't noticed. As usual, I'd only noticed things I wanted to see.

I nodded, suspicious of his motives for taking me out for dinner. He was the last person I'd date, if I dated. Which I didn't. That would require being close to someone.

Christopher took another sip. "Last night, I got a strange call. Someone called for Dr. Winters. I seldom use that name outside work, even though I have a doctorate. Then the man launched into gibberish about the serum and needing to restart human trials. He talked fast. Something about genetic enhancement."

Startled into meeting his eyes, I grabbed my phone. *'He was looking for your brother.'* I couldn't type his name any more than I could say it. My fingers felt paralyzed.

"Yeah, I figured that, but he didn't let me explain. It was a brief call. He freaked out near the end. Said he had to go, that they'd traced his line, that it was too dangerous. In the background, there was a crashing sound, then a bang, like a door had been forced open. There was a scuffle, and the line went dead."

My eyes widened in surprise and my pulse quickened. Once, I'd overheard Brandon on the phone. He'd mentioned the pressure to start human trials. I'd asked him about it later. That conversation had been our last.

"I've tried calling back, but it goes straight to an automated voicemail with no name. I didn't leave messages."

I shook my head.

"What?"

"They might come for you if they think you're him."

"Who? Brandon?"

I cringed when he said the name, but maintained eye contact.

"Give me some credit. I blocked my number. But I appreciate your concern for my well-being." He grinned, his dimple reappearing.

My heart lurched at the sight. I didn't want to like him. I'd rather ignore him.

"What I was wondering," he said. "Does any of that sound familiar? Brandon said you remember everything. So, if he mentioned anything odd like that, I figured you'd know."

I must have hesitated or looked guilty because his eyes lit up and he talked faster.

"I knew it. It's years later, but better late than never. The doctors say a drug overdose caused Brandon's coma."

I choked on my water and my hands shook as I set down the cold glass. I couldn't have heard that right. Brandon had been career-driven, health-conscious, and careful. He'd never take drugs.

I shook my head. No way. The room became too hot as my cheeks burned. A tightness constricted my chest as it sucked the air from my lungs. The restaurant became too confining. I had to get out.

"I agree. He didn't do drugs. It wasn't an overdose. His coma had to have been caused by something else. The call may be a clue. I want to solve this mystery and I need your help. Help me Obi-wan Kenobi, you're my only hope."

Ignoring the Star Wars reference, which in other circumstances I would've loved, I shoved back my chair, grabbed my phone, and ran. Christopher called after me, but I didn't listen. I made it outside and two buildings over before I stopped to throw up. I wanted to be left alone, but, of course, Christopher followed. When I leaned forward, one hand on the rough stone wall, he held my hair away from my face as I heaved. He rubbed my back and made soothing sounds I couldn't understand for the roaring in my ears. What if I could've helped Brandon, and I'd let him down?

Christopher handed me a glass of water and a cloth napkin from the restaurant to wipe my mouth. My legs were rubbery, and I shook all over.

My eyes filled with scalding tears, but I didn't let them fall. I took a deep breath and barricaded my feelings away. Since my childhood, I'd taken upsetting thoughts or feelings and visualized them behind a barrier. Sometimes it helped.

He stepped back, his hands shoved deep in the pockets of his jeans.

"I have nowhere else to turn, and I need your help. I won't say another word about Brandon tonight. I had no idea how badly you'd react. I'm sorry. Come inside and eat. You're too skinny. Then I'll drive you home, leave you alone to think."

I was a coward. I didn't know how to help, but I let Christopher take my arm and guide me back to our table. He slid a piece of gum across the table and ordered mint tea to settle my stomach. I allowed him to take this much care of me while he chattered about books and movies. He made it easy for me to just sit. He didn't ask questions or make demands. I'd walked to work, so it was convenient to let him drive me home—I could avoid the darkening streets.

On the walk to his car, I pulled out my phone to text him the address, but he said, "I know where you live. The same place, right?"

I nodded. He'd picked up his brother a few times, long ago. My heart hurt. I wanted to curl up with a romance novel and escape.

At my darkened townhouse, I got out, texted my thanks, and climbed the stairs. I wished I'd left the porch light on. I'd known I might not be home until after dark, as I often worked late. I raised my hand to signal that I was fine, but Christopher didn't drive away until I'd located my key and unlocked the door.

If I hadn't found being around him confusing, it could have been a pleasant evening. I hadn't expected to enjoy his company. I'd felt more normal than I had in a long time. The last two years had been lonely and had seemed like an eternity.

I put down dinner for my kitty and headed for the shower, wishing I could wash my feelings down the drain. It was getting too hard to keep them distant. I had so many regrets in my life and tonight only highlighted them. I'd spent years feeling sorry for myself about Brandon's disappearance, wondering what I'd done wrong. Afraid I hadn't measured up. That I hadn't been good enough. I regretted getting mixed up with Eric. Our marriage had been a disaster. I also regretted the energy I'd spent hating someone who, while over-confident and annoying, wasn't so bad.

Tonight, my house seemed quiet and too empty. My eyes grew tired from reading and I shut out the light, but the silence pressed inward and wouldn't let me rest. I tossed and turned for another two hours. Too many thoughts tumbled in my head, like clothes in a dryer. Around and around, going nowhere. My mind went where it always did when I couldn't sleep—back to the same few jarring moments.

After the accident, my boss advised me to take some time—a leave of absence was usual in these circumstances. Instead, I threw myself into my work, which became my existence. I went through the motions of living. I attended Eric's funeral, but all I remembered were white flowers and the smell of lilies. After the funeral, I avoided my family. They meant well, but despite the tragedy, it didn't affect their lives the way it did mine. My family misinterpreted my wall of numb silence as shock or sorrow. They didn't know that guilt consumed me. Or relief. Or guilt about the relief.

I couldn't remember the last time I'd laughed. It must be years, but it had nothing to do with the accident. It dated back to the beginning of my marriage, when I'd let myself slip away, becoming a cringing, fearful husk without friends. I was ashamed that I'd made such poor choices. I didn't want anyone to learn what I'd hidden the last four years, locked in the prison of my mind. The real secret was now six feet under.

In moments like this, I believed that keeping secrets had led to one thing. I was alone. I didn't have anyone to lean on, to confide in. Alone didn't have to mean lonely, but I was. Nothing seemed to fill the gaping hole inside.

"I'm still ashamed, Ember." I stroked her soft fur. She didn't open her eyes, but a rumbly purr emerged. "Eric hurt me and before that, Brandon. When you let yourself care about people, they have the power to hurt you. I don't know how much more I can take. Being alone is too hard."

In desperation, I jumped out of bed and grabbed a piece of amethyst from the top of my dresser. A couple of sessions ago, Dr. Maeve had brought out a tray of stones and asked me to select a piece to be my worry rock. I'd thought her request silly, but harmless, and had complied. My gaze had settled on the purple crystals as if they'd spoken. I had expected nothing to come of it but had taken it home. I reviewed her words as I gripped the crystals in my hand.

"All my hardest clients choose something special," she'd said. "Stones have properties to heal our minds. This may relieve your anxiety. Hold it when you're sleepless and overwhelmed."

I didn't know how it worked, but she wanted me to think of better times and believe I could get through this rough patch. I'd tossed it there weeks ago, skeptical of its use. I'd been unhappy for so long, but news of Brandon's death was the last straw.

What did I have to lose? Something had to make a difference. It was worth a shot. Tears leaked from the corners of my eyes as I stared at the ceiling and clutched the purple stone to my chest, its sharp edges etching the palm of my hand. My feelings were impossible to keep at bay at night.

With Ember curled into a tabby-sized ball of fur near my hip, I whispered.

"I don't know how to change anymore. I'm so alone."

As I squeezed the stone in my fist, I shuddered and suppressed a sob.

"I wish I had a mulligan so I could redo my life."

Chapter 3

When I woke, the air was different. A scent, a feel. Something had changed. When I opened my eyes, the first thing I saw was Ember. She sat on my chest, touching me with her cold nose, which is what had woken me. I blinked a few times, wondering if I was dreaming, but I wasn't seeing wrong. She was a kitten.

It was her. Four white feet, a crooked white blaze on her nose, and copper eyes, but she was as tiny as when I'd first chosen her five years ago. I scooped her aloft and stared at her. My mouth snapped shut as I sat up, my eyes still riveted on her small body. How could this be? She squirmed, protesting this unusual treatment, so I pulled her close and cradled her against me. She purred and nuzzled my chin. It seemed she'd forgiven me for sailing her through the air.

The sun shone in the window, golden and warm. I must have forgotten to lower the blinds last night. As the fog lifted from my brain, I glanced around again. I'd slept in my old room? The one I'd moved out of after the accident? I hadn't set foot inside this room for two years. My skin crawled whenever I considered this space. After the accident, I'd closed the door and bought new clothes, towels, sheets, the works. I never wanted to touch or wear anything Eric may have used. Had I been sleepwalking and ended up here?

That didn't explain my cat.

I slid from the bed and made my way to the kitchen, still holding a kitten-sized Ember for comfort. There were changes here as well. The kitchen seemed more cheerful than I remembered, with plants on the window and a stack of books on the table. Everything looked familiar. It was my stuff, but nothing was how I remembered leaving it.

Opening the fridge was as much a surprise as the now miniature Ember. It was full, stocked with things I liked but hadn't bought in years. Yesterday, my fridge contained half-moldy cheese, mustard, dill pickles, and an assortment of half-empty takeout containers. The hair rose on the back of my neck and it became hard to breathe. It was almost like I'd stepped into an alternate reality or back in time.

I set my kitten down, and she scampered for her kibble, her claws skittering on the laminate floor. Today should be Wednesday. I had work, didn't I? I turned on the electric kettle and went to take a quick shower, racking my brain for an explanation. The hot water helped me feel more normal, though my hair was longer than I remembered.

I staggered at the sudden realization of where I was. No, not where... when. How had this happened? It should have been impossible. My pathetic wish last night had come true. Using Ember's size as a reference, I guessed I'd traveled back in time five years. My stomach fluttered in excitement. Five years ago, there'd been no Eric and no accident. Had I erased them from my past?

Jumping out of the shower, dripping water everywhere in my haste, I checked the date on my phone. I gaped, unable to look away. May 23, 2017. Not only was it five years ago, but it also wasn't Wednesday. It was Friday. Date night, and I had less than two weeks before Brandon disappeared. My screen was lit up with red notifications, so I checked them. My stomach danced. Brandon had left two messages while I'd slept. My hands shook as I clicked the first, reading the text reminder about dinner tonight and where to meet. He'd also left me a voicemail with the same information, stressing the time. It was disconcerting to hear his voice after so long, especially knowing his fate. My hands turned ice cold, and I took a few calming breaths.

In this time, we were together, and he was alive. I could try again. I didn't have to drive him away. Maybe I could save his life. Maybe I could make myself a happily ever after. This was my chance.

"Kitty, I don't know how this happened, but maybe we don't have to be alone and miserable." My mind raced through a million minor changes in my life since 2017. The details I could improve at work. The ease with which I'd learn the software update next year. Covid. Everyone still worked at the office full-time.

I didn't know how or why, but I could redo the last five years. I twirled in my kitchen and poured hot water into my teapot with a flourish. When my phone rang, I whipped it out of my back pocket. It was Meghan. I hadn't heard my sister's voice, except in messages, in forever. I hesitated a second, my heart leaping, then touched the screen.

My happiness crashed to the ground like a meteor when I tried to speak. Nothing.

"Elizabeth? Are you there? Elizabeth?"

I tried again, willing my voice to work, but no sound emerged. 2017 me was still mute, unable to speak to people, just like in 2022. I remained voiceless.

I clenched the phone tighter and hung up. Taking a deep breath, I texted. *"Sorry, my phone is acting weird. What's up?"*

"That sux. Is Brandon coming to our engagement party? Haven't seen him in ages."

"I'll find out and get back to you."

Last time, I'd gone solo to the engagement party and met Eric. It had been a week after Brandon disappeared. I'd had no business getting involved with anyone while heartbroken. I'd slept with a stranger out of spite, which led to disaster. This time, I would avoid anything to do with Eric and take a different route. My mood soared. He would never be my husband.

• • •

Work in 2017 was much the same. I slipped into the building and upstairs without a conversation. Even before all the heartache, I'd been solitary, preferring to avoid awkward social situations. I glanced at the dress that I carried with me—the sight brought a rush of memories from the last time I had lived this day. Maybe I should have switched up my clothes. Last time, I'd gone all out and dressed in a new cherry-red dress with a cute flippy skirt and heels for dinner with Brandon. Wearing such a fun dress had made me feel beautiful. Buying the shoes meant a shoestring budget for a few weeks. I'd given up Starbucks.

While I was trying to change the overall outcome, I saw no reason to make everything different. I hung the gorgeous outfit in my office so I could change my clothes before dinner. I'd expected a proposal that night, but Brandon had disappointed.

We hadn't discussed marriage, and looking back, the possibility had all been in my head. Tonight, I had no expectations on that front and hoped to enjoy myself. Maybe I could fix our relationship by relaxing, and by being less intense. I took a few breaths to calm my racing heart. So much was riding on this dinner and fixing my relationship with Brandon. Not speaking would be weird, but if I could have a pleasant non-date with Christopher, I should be able to make an evening work with Brandon. I didn't want to cancel, so I planned to fake laryngitis.

Work flew by and soon it was time. With a smattering of butterflies circling inside my stomach, I hopped in the elevator, fixing the strap on my frivolous shoe. It stopped on the fourth floor and in walked Christopher.

"Elizabeth." He looked at me from head to toe with those stunning pale blue eyes and whistled. "Hot date? My brother's damn lucky."

My cheeks turned pink as I nodded. I'd forgotten that this Christopher and I had gotten along. We'd been friends—and before

I'd met his brother—I'd hoped Christopher would ask me out, but he never had. I froze, hoping he wouldn't notice that I couldn't speak. I would need his help to save Brandon, but I hadn't yet figured out how. I smiled, though I was worried that he'd expect chit-chat. Before my silence became awkward, his phone rang.

"Ya, hey," he said. "Sure, what's up? Ya, she's right here, on her way." He winked at me. "No nudge needed."

He was talking to Brandon.

We lurched to a halt in the lobby. I waved goodbye as I rushed out, hurrying to the restaurant. Brandon didn't like it when I was late. Despite the best of intentions, I always forgot to allot time to use the elevator and walk a few blocks. Some things never changed.

When I arrived, I stopped outside. Brandon was inside—his back to the entrance—allowing me to watch him through the window. He'd already been seated and was no longer talking on his phone, but sat reading the screen. I smoothed my hair and straightened my skirt. Squaring my shoulders and taking a deep breath, I prepared to see him again. I'd never thought to have this chance.

When I stepped up to the table, I tried to speak, hoping my attempt this morning had been an anomaly, but nothing came out. Brandon hadn't noticed my arrival or my voice difficulties. He looked the same as he'd looked in my imagination—serious and put together.

Pasting on a smile, I slid into my seat across from him, waiting for him to look up and acknowledge me. I set my phone on the table.

"You're late again." He tapped something on his phone and continued reading.

I was my standard fifteen minutes late.

I'd been disappointed when he hadn't commented on my outfit, but this time I was prepared. I chalked it up to my being late. The dress was new and cost more than I could afford, but Christopher's reaction justified its purchase. My heart sank, but I couldn't expect Brandon to be different, not yet. I couldn't expect to make sweeping changes in just one day.

"My throat hurts." I sent. *"Laryngitis."* At least he would read his messages because his phone was in his hand.

"Want to go home?" His eyes remained fixed on his screen as he spoke.

I'd just arrived, and he'd hardly looked up from his phone.

When I didn't answer, he glanced upward, and I interpreted annoyance in his steady brown gaze.

I shook my head.

They seated us at a good table, decorated with a blue and white checked tablecloth, and tucked in a quiet corner, away from the kitchen. I ordered by pointing. I was an expert, despite wishing it wasn't necessary. Throughout dinner, Brandon continued to check his messages every few minutes, scrolling back through existing ones. He was absent more than he was present. He spoke a few times, telling me the scores of the playoff games and about something he'd found funny from work, but he forgot the punchline. My lack of voice didn't seem to throw him off. Worse. He didn't seem to notice.

Twice he got calls. Both times he excused himself and spoke elsewhere, so I wouldn't hear. Had he always been so secretive? When he returned to the table, he went back to scrolling through old messages. Without my efforts, there was no conversation. With sinking feelings, it was difficult not to take his behavior personally.

Brandon signaled for the bill as I put the last bite of pasta in my mouth.

"You don't want dessert, do you?" He didn't bother looking up from his phone. He wanted to leave. No proposal and no dessert.

I placed my fork beside my knife across the plate and blinked back tears. I didn't have many more chances to save his life. A week. Two, tops. To get more time, I needed to keep him from disappearing. If I couldn't talk, I didn't know how to get his attention. This night was supposed to end up in bed, but my heart plummeted into the soles of my expensive heels. It wouldn't happen. No ring, no cheesecake, and no sex. Tonight was worse than the disappointing date five years ago.

I frowned, remembering that after this date the first time, Brandon hadn't slept over. He'd bolted before midnight, citing an early meeting. He might still.

The car ride was silent until Brandon stopped his car in front of my place and gave me an absent peck on the cheek.

"I'm not coming in. I wouldn't want to get sick." He didn't make eye contact.

His dismissiveness stung. I pasted on a fake smile and held up one finger to get him to wait while I texted.

"Meghan's engagement party. Friday after next. You coming?"

"Two Fridays? Wouldn't miss it. Tell her I promise. Wild horses and all that."

I walked up the stairs toward my dark front door, searching for my key. When I located it, I turned to wave, but the curb was empty. Brandon had gone. I hadn't realized his level of distraction had been a sign of danger, but now I wondered. What made him so worried?

Had there been signs of our breakup before? What else had I missed? I'd been oblivious.

It was too early for bed so I opened a tub of gourmet ice cream, changed into comfy clothes, and settled in to watch the movie version of Pride and Prejudice, one of my favorites. Ember waited only for the blanket to settle before scrambling up to join me, kneading the fuzzy cover with her little claws.

While I snacked, I tried to remember the sequence of events that had followed this evening. Seeing Brandon brought back memories, things I hadn't thought about for years. It had been too painful. We'd had fun together, hadn't we? Not tonight. But usually? Tonight, his stand-offishness had put me off. Had he always been that way? My gut screamed, yes. How had it not bothered me? Now, I was different. I'd been so excited before dinner, with butterflies flitting about my stomach, but had felt very little when I'd seen him. I'd expected my heart to skip and to feel swoony, but I hadn't. It had been flat and boring. No sparks. He'd been so... ordinary.

After what Eric had done, I suppose I was scarred in more than one way, more than the physical scars on my back. I gasped, pressed pause, and I ran to check. Peeling up my shirt, I peered over my shoulder into the bathroom mirror. My skin was smooth and unmarked. A sight I'd never thought I'd see again. The raised belt scars that criss-crossed my back were gone. I could wear a bikini without shame. My throat closed up with emotion. That sight alone was worth the cost of time travel.

•   •   •

Brandon was unavailable that weekend, canceling our plans on Saturday and working late, but we traded a few texts. I worked overtime at the museum. The exhibit on Human Origins was scheduled to open in a few months, and there were several major things and a million smaller ones to finish. The opening hadn't been seamless, so I was determined to improve it this time around. Sunday night rolled around, and Brandon still hadn't called, so I texted him, citing continued laryngitis. He suggested he could make dinner on Tuesday and I became more settled after the exchange.

On Tuesday, Brandon picked me up from work. I carried my overnight bag and Ember's cat carrier. She'd roamed my office for the day, swatting pens, stalking spiders, and napping on my important documents. I couldn't speak, but at dinner, Brandon made an effort. He'd dressed up and joked while he cooked. I tried not to over-analyze, and just enjoy being together. He was handsome and charming, even if a little stiff, his conversation forced. Still, I bloomed with his attention. It had been so long since anyone had focused on me or made me feel cared for. It was almost like old times.

We enjoyed a satisfying evening until just after nine, when his phone rang. My heart sank. I remembered what had happened next. He excused himself and went into his bedroom to talk. Palms sweaty and heart racing, I tiptoed down the hall and stood to the side of the door because I didn't want him to see my shadow underneath. I'd done this before. Eavesdropping wasn't honorable, but I had a reason beyond curiosity. This time, I was trying to save his life.

"We aren't ready for human trials." His voice barely concealed his frustration, like he'd explained this before.

My heart drifted lower, sliding to toe level. This was the conversation I remembered. I had so little time to change the future.

Brandon hadn't talked about his recent project. But human trials sounded experimental, downright controversial for his line of work as a toxinologist. Injecting venom into people wasn't their business. Or so I'd thought.

There was a long pause while he listened to the caller.

"It isn't safe." His tone no longer concealed his irritation.

"I realize you're the boss, but I've explained several times. The lab rats have all died. You pay me for my expertise. I'm telling you, it's too soon. It won't work and it isn't just a matter of dosage."

There was another pause. This time, a loud voice on the other end of the line shouted. I couldn't make out what the other person said, but he seemed angry.

"That isn't necessary. Don't do that. I'll work harder," Brandon said.

He no longer sounded confident.

"I don't appreciate threats." There was a pause. "Another month. Give me that long. Two, maximum. But, the human subjects have to know the possibility that it won't work. You'll need to pay them. Waivers and full disclosure. I'll work on an antidote in case we need to reverse the effects."

I shifted, and the floor creaked. He stopped talking. I held my breath and didn't move.

"I know you don't think that's important. It's just a precaution."

There was more yelling from the phone.

"You don't have to do that. I won't let you down."

The call was over, and something in the bedroom crashed. I was terrified by the violent outburst and needed to get back to the kitchen before I was caught. Taking a breath, I crept away, silent as a mouse.

Last time, I'd overheard only the middle and had slunk away. Part of me wished I'd done the same this time. Whatever Brandon was involved in sounded dangerous. Who was this mystery boss? Brandon hadn't discussed this kind of pressure to succeed before. Perhaps his boss was someone new.

I played with Ember in the kitchen, dragging a toy across the tile floor. Her tail swished, and she pounced. I flicked her mouse away. It was several minutes before Brandon joined us.

"Do you need to bring that cat with you when you stay overnight?" He slammed a cupboard door when he got a glass. Stalking to the fridge, he poured himself some water.

What a grouch. He didn't need to take it out on my kitten.

"*Ember's a baby. I don't like to leave her home alone overnight.*" We'd talked before. He didn't allow her inside the bedroom, but at least she was here.

"*Everything ok?*"

He didn't look okay. He was flushed and his usual well-groomed hair stood on end, while his forehead glistened as he glanced at his screen with a frown.

"Of course. It was my mom. There was a problem with the delivery of the flooring they chose for their place in Florida." He set the half-empty glass on the counter. "Let's watch that movie."

I let him have the lie because I didn't want to fight. I wanted tonight to have a different outcome than it had years ago. Last time we'd argued.

We watched TV, but he was no longer present. We sat on opposite ends of the couch, Ember on my lap, with no-man's-land between us. Brandon didn't pay attention to the show and shut it off five minutes before the end. I pretended not to notice. When we went to bed, he didn't touch me. He yawned, kissed the atmosphere near my cheek, and rolled away.

Sleep eluded me and I stared at his white stucco ceiling. This evening had played out the same as last time. While I hadn't asked about the human trials, and we hadn't fought about my listening when it was none of my business, nothing else had changed. For a few brief hours, I'd forgotten my extreme loneliness. This was almost as lonely as my life in 2022. I controlled my feelings, not letting them get the best of me.

When I was sure Brandon was sound asleep, I slid out of bed and slunk out of the bedroom. I snuck into the kitchen and tapped in the password on his phone. With my phone, I snapped photos of the numbers that had called him today. There were three. One had called five times. Flipping to his messages, I read everything recent. Four were from me and another couple from his brother. I shouldn't be snooping, but I did. They'd rescheduled their sacred beer night twice. At least he'd brushed off Christopher, too.

A new message arrived while I held his phone. It included a date and an address in Reno. It matched one caller. I took a picture, then marked it as unread. I would examine them later.

I returned his phone to the counter and slipped into his home office, wincing as the door creaked. My heart pounded as I froze. No sound emerged from the bedroom, so I continued. Anything could be a clue, so I took pictures of everything. I had less success with his laptop than his phone. I couldn't sign in. My heart lodged in my throat throughout my self-imposed mission, and I listened so hard my ears ached. I didn't have an excuse if I was caught.

Just before I gave up, I found a thin file in his desk drawer with his company logo. Inside were memos that mentioned results and time intervals before death for several sets of animal trials. I took pictures. When I finished, I tiptoed back through the dark apartment and climbed into bed, hoping my time away had been unnoticed. Eventually, I fell into an exhausted sleep.

The next morning, I acted like nothing was wrong, though he was distant. When he dropped me off at the museum, Ember once more in tow, I kissed him. I held back my tears, hoping it wasn't the last time I would see him. Five years ago, I wished I'd known that it was the last time. This go around, I feared the outcome, and it wasn't easier. Other than not fighting, events were about to play out in the exact the same way. How long did I have to prevent the coma and save his life?

His last words were, "Lunch on Thursday. Usual place?"

I nodded and watched his car until it was out of sight. The same final words as before. I'd tormented myself with them a thousand times.

Brandon and I had a standing lunch date twice a week. He'd canceled Tuesday but had made it up with the dinner. We'd been together for two years, but seldom spent more than two lunches, a mid-week dinner, and Saturdays together. How well did I really know him? Not as well as I'd thought. He'd kept me at arm's length and I hadn't noticed until now. I'd believed everything was rosy until it had come crashing apart. I wouldn't make that mistake again.

On Thursday, he wasn't at the usual Mexican restaurant for takeout. He didn't come and didn't text. I waited twenty minutes, hoping he'd arrive at the last minute, but he didn't. When I gave up and ate, my tacos tasted like ash. Despite my hope, it was the same.

With a familiar sinking feeling, I texted him but got no response. Not that day, or the next. I called, and the line went straight to voicemail after one ring, as though his voicemail was full or he was on the line—also signs that I could've been blocked. I didn't know what to do. It wasn't time to panic, yet. I had to give him a chance to reply in case I was wrong. I didn't want to appear clingy or paranoid. There was still a chance it could be different.

I was desperate enough that I called on Saturday and again on Sunday, to no avail. I didn't know what I'd do if he answered, but I had to try. When this had happened before, my feelings had been hurt and I'd waited weeks before going to his place. He hadn't come home. I couldn't track him down at work. His lab had tight security and I could never get past reception.

Last time I'd been too proud to ask for help, but I had to change the outcome. I couldn't let him die, so I did what I'd been too scared to do before. Desperate times called for desperate measures.

Chapter 4

I texted Christopher Monday morning.

"Elizabeth here. Can we meet? It's important."

He answered in less than a minute. *"Sure. Where? When?"*

"After work? The Starbucks around the corner. Six?"

"At six I need food. La Cocina?"

There was one near work. *"Sure."*

I arrived almost at the appointed time, only seven minutes late. The casual Mexican restaurant was festive with green and red decorations that matched their flag. In the background, mariachi music played—the atmosphere at odds with my mood. My stomach rumbled as I walked in. I hadn't eaten well since the second awful date with Brandon. The sense of impending trouble had upset my stomach. Tonight, I was hungry.

They'd seated Christopher already. His laugh reached me first. He was larger than life, with a wide smile, talking to a server. It was hard not to be offended by his cheerful demeanor. The things weighing on my mind were serious.

I slid into the booth across from him.

Ice water, chips and salsa, guacamole, and sour cream sat on the table, so I helped myself.

"To what do I owe this surprise?"

I pointed to my throat and lifted my phone. *"Laryngitis. I know this is weird, but can I talk without you judging me? It's about Brandon."*

I looked up, waiting for his answer. I didn't know how he'd react.

He frowned before he leaned forward, grabbed a handful of chips, and said, "Brandon's been acting strange. You know something?"

I nodded. It was about to get worse. I'd thought overnight about what to say, even though it would sound far-fetched. I'd tell the truth, at least some version. When we first met, we'd had a discussion years ago about an old TV show called Quantum Leap with time travel and the possibility had intrigued Christopher.

"Brandon's in trouble. He ghosted me. Blocked my number. We didn't fight or break up, if that's what he said."

"He said nothing," said Christopher. "One-word texts. No, ok, later. Mostly no." His tone was more clipped than usual.

I was relieved. I wouldn't be giving an opposing point of view.

"He's dodging my calls, giving me the run-around. Skipped beer night three Thursdays in a row." He grabbed another handful of chips.

He would notice that. *"He's in trouble, work-related. I'm going to tell you something a little unorthodox to explain how I know. Kinda unbelievable. Please keep an open mind."* I was desperate enough to try the truth with someone who also cared about Brandon's future.

"I'm intrigued. An opening like that? Now I need to hear. I'll suspend my disbelief until you're done. You're different this week, and I can't recall the last time you asked to talk to me, so you've got my undivided attention."

"I'm from the future."

He laughed out loud, the sound attracting glances to our table. My cheeks burned, glad I hadn't spoken aloud. The last thing I wanted was for others to hear what I'd said. By the time he'd stopped, our server arrived to take our order.

I grit my teeth and tried to look pleasant while I pointed to a chicken burrito.

"Can you please ask for no rice on my burrito?"

After my request and his order, our conversation resumed.

Christopher leaned forward and spoke in a quieter voice. "The future?" He raised one eyebrow. "Do you have numbers so I can win the lottery? I'll split the winnings." He flashed his dimple.

"Try to be serious. I'm from 2022. Brandon's in danger. He ends up in a coma." I didn't say he died, figuring that would be too much. The brothers were close. I remembered how I'd reacted when he sprang the news on me about Brandon's death.

"Why can't you talk in the future? This is more than laryngitis."

How had he guessed? It wasn't the question I expected. Nothing about time travel, just my voice. Why didn't he believe the laryngitis story?

I hesitated. A flood of terrible memories seeped into my thoughts.

Before me floated Eric's face in a sneer. The crack of the back of his hand across my cheek, my split and burning lip. The taste of blood in my mouth. "Liar."

I cut off the memories of Eric and focused on Christopher's words.

"You aren't sick, you're different. I figured it out the night you wore that slinky red number. Your mind has always been organized, even if your sense of time is lousy, but now it's like a brick wall."

My eyebrows shot up. My mind?

"I'm willing to believe your story, but I want straight answers." He leaned back, his pale blue eyes intent.

No signs of mirth. With those eyes, it was like he saw inside me— my private thoughts on display. I swallowed and nodded. I'd try the truth. Even if it was upsetting.

"This happened before. Brandon ghosted me. I married my rebound guy, and it was awful. We had a car accident. My husband died two years ago. I haven't spoken since the accident. Just over a week ago, in 2022, you came to me. You'd had a strange phone call. You said Brandon collapsed into a coma months after our breakup. He never woke up. You wanted my help to solve a mystery."

I looked up to see how he was taking this. I'd told him his brother had died. He'd said to be honest. My hands shook. Discussing Brandon's death made me ill.

"And?"

My stomach dropped. I'd never told my history outside of therapy. I couldn't read his thoughts from his expression. He must play poker.

"I was miserable and wished I had a redo button for my life. I woke up in this time on the red dress Friday. I want to save Brandon. You asked for my help, now I'm asking for yours."

I set my phone on the table and jumped when it rang. Christopher snatched it and answered before I could protest.

"Hey, Meghan," Christopher said.

Her name had appeared on the screen. I'd been dodging her calls. I shook my head, willing him not to say anything.

He swatted the phone away when I held my hand out. My sister was going to have a million questions about him. She could be like the Inquisition. Meghan's questions were hard to evade, and she had a limited understanding of personal boundaries.

The server arrived with our dinner-laden plates and set them on the table.

"Thanks." Christopher's hand covered the phone for a few seconds.

"Ya, her phone keeps dropping calls. She's so busy she hasn't gotten it fixed. You know how hard she works."

There was a pause while my sister spoke.

"This is his better-looking brother, Christopher. She will absolutely be there on Friday. If Brandon's too busy, I'll bring her myself. He's slammed these days at work."

Meghan spoke again, and Christopher winked at me.

I couldn't believe what he'd done. Now I'd have to go to her party.

"Well. I *am* a nice guy. Great, see you then." He hung up.

I had to pick my jaw off the floor. He'd covered my lack of voice with ease.

"Your sister's a peach." He handed back my phone with a smirk. "I just got an invite for free food."

I braced my elbows on the table, put my head in my hands, and rubbed my temples. How was I going to explain that I couldn't speak? I sighed. This is what I'd been avoiding.

"You can't skip her engagement party. Can't duck her forever. She's your sister. Tell her the laryngitis story, make it stress-related. She'll buy that."

I sat up straight to answer.

"I haven't seen her in two years. Not since the funeral. I've gotten good at avoiding. In my timeline, she doesn't know I can't speak."

"Not two years for her. She probably thinks ten days is too long. Don't you have dinner there on Sunday nights?"

I didn't know how he knew that, but I nodded. *"That was before Eric."*

"Since the accident, you mean?"

I shook my head. I didn't want to explain.

He picked up my phone and put it in my hand. He wouldn't let me off the hook.

"Almost five years. Eric didn't like when I went for Sunday dinner."

"So, you didn't go? That's stupid. What about after? How could your family let you get away with disappearing?" He spun his fork on the table.

I shrugged. They hadn't tried very hard to keep me in their lives. *"I was difficult, and they were busy."* Meghan and Andrew had been occupied with her difficult pregnancy, then with my nephew. I'd fallen through the cracks in their busy lives.

"What about your friends? Didn't they realize you couldn't talk? What did they say?"

I almost laughed. What friends? *"My closest friend was long distance. Nobody else realized, or maybe they didn't care."*

"That's just not right." He started eating his enchilada. "I don't believe nobody cared."

"I think you cared. You baited me, trying to make me talk. Said outrageous things."

"Sounds like me."

"Why do you believe me? I just told you I've time traveled." He hadn't reacted beyond the initial outburst of laughter.

"We all have secrets. If you're good, one of these days, I'll tell you one of mine."

He grinned and his dimples reappeared. My heart lurched. When he turned the charm on me, I wasn't immune. The problem was that he knew he was drop-dead gorgeous and besides, I was dating his brother.

The hardest part of the evening wasn't telling Christopher or explaining my wish, but forgetting the seriousness of the mission. I couldn't afford to forget. Helping Brandon was a matter of his life or death. I had the sense that Christopher almost believed my story and was on board. He might need a day or two to think.

Gusts of wind blew my fair hair into my face as we strolled back to the museum after dinner.

"You parked underground?"

"I walked. I didn't feel like driving." In an effort not to think of the accident, I clamped down on my thoughts.

"You aren't walking home. It's too far."

I shrugged, irritated at his high-handed attitude, not appreciating being told what to do after my relationship with Eric. *"I'm used to it."*

"C'mon. It's no big deal. It's on my way home. I'll drop you off."

Trying to decide what to do, I looked up. A homeless couple huddled next to the building in tattered sleeping bags. Catching my eye, the man smiled and rattled a container in my direction. I dumped my coin purse into my hand, and then into his tin. The change plunked into the empty can.

"Thanks, Miss." His smile revealed a missing front tooth.

"You know you want a ride," Christopher said, diverting my attention back to him.

While I hesitated, the first drops of rain splattered my face. I turned up my hand. Several more landed and I sighed. I hadn't brought my rain jacket or an umbrella. Maybe a ride would be okay; I wouldn't be behind the wheel.

"I'm driving you home. No arguing."

Christopher took my hand and led me toward the stairwell to the parking level of the museum. His warm hand covered mine, dwarfing it in size. There was nothing sexual about it, but I hadn't had physical contact for so long, that jolts of electricity raced throughout my body. Humans aren't meant to exist alone. This casual touch was one thing I missed, something I craved. A cold evening with Brandon had done nothing to help.

Christopher towed me to his low-slung black 370Z. I'd always admired the sleek look of that model.

"Get in. Still live in the same place?"

I got in and I sent him the address. The car smelled divine. Like a combination of coffee and chocolate. I breathed deep, inhaling the scent. Somehow, it seemed comfortable. Christopher sent me an amused glance.

The drive to my townhouse took only seven minutes, though it would have taken half an hour to walk. Throughout the ride I sat tense, white knuckles in my lap while the windshield wipers swished back and forth, but his driving was smooth and confident. When we got to the block, I pointed to my door. I'd forgotten to leave my light on again. I wished I had the kind of life where someone turned lights on for me, where I wouldn't always be returning to an empty house.

Christopher turned off the engine and got out with me.

I shook my head. *"Thanks for driving."*

"I'm walking you to the door. It's dark."

I could see it would do me no good to argue.

At the top of the stairs, I fished around in my purse. When I found my keys, I jingled them to indicate that he could go.

He jammed his hands into his pockets. I'd seen him do it a few times now. He did it when he was nervous or uncomfortable. I enjoyed learning that about him.

"I'm going to talk to my brother. You've got me a little freaked out. He hasn't blocked my calls, but he doesn't return them. Can we meet again soon? This week? We can compare notes."

I nodded.

I unlocked the door and turned to wave. Christopher hugged me, catching me off guard. He was warm and hard and smelled even better than his car. It signified more to me. Not only did he believe my improbable story, but I wasn't in this alone. He had an even bigger stake than I did in saving his brother.

I burst into tears of relief.

"It's okay." He held on and squeezed.

I could have lived in his hug; I didn't want him to let go.

"We can solve this together, Lizzie."

Shocked, I stepped back. *"What did you call me?"*

He looked confused and glanced at his screen. "You told me to call you Lizzie."

I shook my head. I hadn't spoken. At that moment, the name had been in my head, a memory of his taunting. That was his name for me in the future. What was going on?

Chapter 5

Once inside, I remained jittery, unsettled. I couldn't sit still. While successful, my conversation with Christopher hadn't gone as expected. I downloaded the photos from Brandon's place to my laptop, but couldn't sit long enough to examine them. Normally, I had karate on Mondays and Wednesdays. I'd joined karate in this time too, but I'd missed my classes last week and again tonight. I had too much pent-up energy, so I pushed the coffee table out of the way. In this time, I had no gear, but had signed up to start karate again. I didn't have the actual blue belt here, but I knew the kata. I'd work my way up again if necessary, depending on dojo policy.

The patterned movements of my kata brought my memories rushing back.

I'd started karate a year into my marriage after I'd taken Eric's abuse one too many times.

I remembered the night that had pushed me to seek lessons in self-defense. Eric made dinner plans for our first wedding anniversary. He wanted me to cook—for us to stay home. I would have preferred to go out, but despite his professional success, he was tight with money. So, we planned a night in. He asked me to make his favorite dessert, homemade cherry pie.

I meant to do it; I wanted to do it. I looked up the recipe and bought the ingredients, but the head of my department had asked me to stay late at work the night before. However, I'd lost track of time and arrived home after nine p.m. Instead, I would make the pie after work on our anniversary. It could bake while we ate dinner.

Putting the pie together and making the filling and the crust from scratch took longer than expected, as I'd never done it before. I wanted it to be perfect. When it went into the oven, it was the best I could do, but the top crust was uneven. Dinner became later and later.

Eric sat in the living room, drinking. He refilled his scotch three times while I worked in the kitchen. Each time he checked my progress, but didn't say a word. I became frustrated and clumsy, worried that he was unhappy, and nervous about him drinking on an empty stomach. But I couldn't make the food cook faster.

It was after eight when we sat down to eat. For several minutes, we ate while an ominous silence stretched between us. I'd known I was in trouble.

"So, who the hell is he?" Eric didn't look up from his plate of roast beef.

I didn't know what he was talking about, which was dangerous.

"Pardon," I said, as I put my fork down with a clink. "Who?"

"That's what I want to know. Who the fuck is he?"

"You must be mistaken." I stood up, trying to look casual. I needed to leave. There was an edge to his voice. It wasn't often this bad, but all the signs were there. My heart beat like a drum against my ribs.

"Just admit you're screwing around." He knocked back the rest of his drink. Looking at his plate, it was clear he hadn't eaten more than a few bites.

I didn't want to turn my back on him, but when the oven timer went off, I had to get to the kitchen. "You're mistaken. We can talk after I take out the pie." I slipped past him, my mouth dry and my palms sweating.

I struggled to breathe normally when his chair scraped backward. He followed me into the kitchen. His face was flushed and his footsteps heavy. He stood behind me, wrapped his arms around my middle, and nuzzled the back of my neck. I felt claustrophobic. I didn't want him to touch me, but I couldn't protest. This could go either way.

Either he'd turn on a dime and say how much he loved me, or I'd get hurt.

I tried not to show my tension, but I was scared. His unpredictability was terrifying.

I didn't understand. I struggled to keep the welling tears from releasing. Before he'd shown this side, nobody had ever treated me better than Eric, not even Brandon. Eric bought me little presents and called me his Baby Doll. I hated the name, but he said it as an endearment, meaning well. He liked to spend time with me and was jealous if I stayed out too long. He liked to keep me close.

But he had another, darker side that surfaced from time to time. At those times, he used his belt, called me horrible names, and invented slights. He forced me to earn his forgiveness. He claimed he was helping me. His touch made my skin crawl. He treated me like I was the one who'd done something wrong, even if I had bruises or he blackened my eye. One thing he obsessed about was that I was cheating.

By this time in our relationship, the only men I saw were at work or at the grocery store. I stopped talking to Jeff, never spoke about male colleagues, had no friends, and limited my contact with my family, so he wouldn't be jealous of the time and attention I gave them. I tried not to give fuel to his anger.

"I need to get the pie. Careful of the oven." I attempted a smile, though it wasn't convincing. He shot me a look I couldn't interpret, and I repressed a shudder. I removed the pie. Its sweet fruity smell filled the townhouse, and its crust was a perfect gold. I was proud of it, my first homemade pie. It looked amazing despite the crooked lattice. I set it on the counter to cool, the cherry filling molten and bubbling through the spaces on top. I couldn't wait for it to cool so we could try it. It smelled delicious.

"We can't eat that tonight," Eric said. "You can't keep track of time. You're not just a slut, but a worthless piece of shit. There's no way you ever get anything right. I should have known you'd screw this up."

He shattered my mood and my smile disappeared. I bit the inside of my cheek and tried not to cry. Breathing became difficult and my heart raced.

He took the oven mitts from my sweaty hands.

I didn't know what he was thinking and hadn't anticipated his next move. That was the worst. He could have done anything.

I stepped back and watched, aghast, as he picked up the pie and smashed it against the wall. It landed facedown and the glass pie plate broke. I should have run. Instead, I stood rooted to the floor, frozen. They say in survival mode, responses are fight, flight, fawn, or freeze. The last was my specialty.

"You should have baked it last night. Pie needs to cool, you imbecile."

The first blow was to my face. The second to my ribs, my breath stolen with its sharp pain. Others followed.

"I'm going to have to teach you a lesson."

I tried to get away, but I couldn't. The fear overwhelmed me. I limped for days, called in sick with the flu. Other than my trip to the hospital, I didn't let anyone see the bruises. I told the doctor that I'd fallen down the stairs.

When I went back to work ten days later, I joined a karate class. I was older than most of the other women at thirty-one, but determined to succeed. During my lunch break, I worked two days a week to make up time for my class. I sent my karate Gi to a laundry service each week and hid it the rest of the time at the office. Eric didn't know. If he found out, I wasn't sure I would survive his ire.

On the night of the accident, eighteen months after the pie incident, Eric tried to backhand my face, his patented first strike. I sidestepped, blocked the blow, and countered without thinking. It was what I'd worked toward, what I'd trained for, but when my fist connected and smashed his nose, I felt horrible. Despite my commitment to karate, I never wanted to hurt anyone. Was he the bully that night, or was I?

I was driving him to the hospital when a drunk driver smashed into our car. It had been dark and rainy that April night. Neither the paramedics at the scene of the accident nor the doctors in the emergency room discovered Eric's prior injury. On impact, the airbags had deployed and hit his face. The collision with the truck had killed him and everyone assumed that was the source of his injuries. I'd told no one the complete story, not even Dr. Maeve. We were in that car at that moment because I'd broken his nose. That was the moment of my nightmares.

I'd blamed myself for a long time. I should have been stronger and walked away the first time he'd hit me, but by then, I was isolated and alone. I didn't know where I'd go or who I could ask for help.

When I finished my practice, I repositioned the coffee table—my nerves calmed.

It was Wednesday when I next saw Christopher, this time in a professional capacity. As the museum's conservator, he dealt with different departments regarding artifact preservation in the environments where they were housed for storage and display.

After our meeting, he took me aside. "Brandon still hasn't answered my calls. Texted to say he's got an important project and not to worry. But I do. Can we meet again tonight?"

"After karate." I tried to be nonchalant, but I enjoyed saying I took karate. It made me feel tough.

"You take karate? I didn't know that."

He looked at my slight frame and said, "Let me guess: dynamite comes in small packages, and all that."

He probably thought he was hilarious, but I'd been hearing that my whole life. At five foot two, I was used to being underestimated.

"First class this afternoon. In the future, I've been training for three years."

"You any good?"

I shrugged. I didn't want to brag, but I was proud of my steady progress.

"That means yes. What belt?"

"Blue." I didn't know if he knew the sequence. It was near the middle, just before brown.

"That's impressive for three years. Remind me not to piss you off."

He was only kidding, but the blood drained from my face as I replayed the crunch of Eric's nose. I turned away so Christopher wouldn't see how that comment had cut.

"Hey, what did I say?" He turned me to face him, his eyes concerned.

I shook my head, but he wouldn't let it drop. Christopher was relentless. His mission in the future to make me respond to his gibes had shown me that.

"You hurt someone," he said.

Some of his guesses were uncanny.

"My husband used to hit me." I kept it matter of fact. *"I joined karate for self-defense. I wanted to make him stop."*

"What did you do?"

"Broke his nose." My hands shook as I revealed this bit of information. I didn't like people knowing my secrets.

"Good. Bet he didn't hit you again."

His reaction surprised me. *"Nope."* Thankfully, Christopher dropped the subject.

"How 'bout I buy takeout and bring it over? You can tell what you know about Brandon. After your class."

I hesitated, but there was no harm in letting him into my house. All I had on my agenda was watching episodes of my new favorite show, Buffy the Vampire Slayer. It was something I'd always wanted to watch. It was that or my usual fare, rom coms, and I wasn't in the mood for that type of movie. These days I preferred butt-kicking to romance.

"Anything I should avoid food-wise?"

"Peppers and onions."

"Easy. I hate onions too."

I looked up. I'd never heard anyone else say that. People looked at me like it was a weird request. I'd been alone in the onion-hating club.

"How's six?"

"Good." That would give me time to clean up and change after my class. My email to Sensei had gone about how my original one had three and a half years ago. He'd invited me to join a women-only, all-levels class from four to five p.m. I missed the class dynamic and the exercise. My email explained that I had a throat injury and couldn't speak, and I purchased a Gi.

Arriving at the dojo, Sensei Daniel suggested I stay after class to run through several katas and he'd place me in the level that was warranted. That was more than fair.

The Gi came with a white belt and I stood on the far left of the line of women with the beginners, where I'd stood when I'd first joined. It gave me a sense of déjà vu. With each belt I'd earned, I'd moved up the line. Sensei Daniel was a tall man with a craggy face. He was nearing sixty, but looked younger than his age. He was tough as nails. He could have been intimidating, but was soft-spoken and kind.

I recognized several women from 2019 when I'd joined before. They'd been my level or higher, but tonight they wore belts of different colors than I was accustomed to seeing them wear.

I was jittery about the class, but everything seemed the same as it was in 2022. My classmates were polite and respected my wish for space. I kept to myself. We bowed in and did the basics. The ritual was familiar, and I soon lost myself to the movements, which gave me a sense of peace. It was easy to leave the rest of my life outside the dojo.

After class, I stayed and ran through all my kata, starting with the beginner patterns and moving up to the ones I'd learned in the last several months. I made my movements crisp and sure. The only thing I lacked was the announcements at the beginning. I borrowed weapons: bo, nunchaku, and sais to demonstrate my abilities. Sensei raised his eyebrows at the sound of my ki-yi's. Though I couldn't speak, I could yell in my kata. At the end of our time, he bowed, welcomed me to his dojo, and shook my hand.

"You must not have had much time off," he said. "You said you're a blue belt, but I'm promoting you. You've shown brown belt level."

I bowed my thanks. My eyes sparkled with happy tears, but I blinked them back. The dojo was not a place to cry, but I was warm inside, proud of my accomplishment.

I strode through the warm evening on my way home. Summer approached with longer daylight hours. When I arrived home, it was six and Christopher was due any second. He'd have to wait. I needed a shower, so I sent him a quick message.

"Late getting home. Need fifteen minutes."

He sent back, *"LOL. I knew it. Picking up food in fifteen. Hope you like sushi."*

I loved sushi.

I set my gear on the table, fed Ember, and jumped in the shower. I'd just dressed when I heard a knock. Good timing. I threw the door open and Christopher entered, carrying two large bags of food. He'd brought enough for four people.

"How'd you know I'd be late?" I was unsure if I was grateful or offended.

"I've known you for years. You're late to every meeting, every dinner, every date you've ever been on with my brother. Trust me, I've heard about it in excruciating detail. I counted on you being late." He set the food on the table and picked up my new brown belt. "Crisp and new," he said. "Congrats."

My irritation at his comments flew out the window, and I flushed, happy he'd noticed. I enjoyed sharing my news. It was less solitary. Grabbing my jacket, Gi, and the items from the table, I took them into my bedroom to hang up later. I'd moved back into the guest room. I hadn't been able to sleep in the Master bedroom. There were too many terrible memories associated with that space.

"Plates?" he said as I returned to the kitchen. "You must be starving, too."

I grabbed plates and chopsticks and set them on the table while he unpacked the containers of food. It was hard not to stare. There must have been over a hundred and fifty dollars' worth of sushi. Regular rolls, fancy rolls with sauces, tuna and salmon sashimi, edamame, sunomono, tempura, all my favorites.

"I didn't know what you liked, so I got things I like. Looks like you approve."

I nodded.

"What's my share?" He'd paid for the Mexican the other night when I was in the washroom. It wasn't fair to make him pay this time, too.

"You're supplying free dinner on Friday."

"That's my sister. Not me."

"I'm giving you credit. Take it."

I didn't want to talk about Friday and I was hungry, so I let the subject drop. We loaded up our plates and started eating.

"I don't think I've met your sister before, have I?"

I shook my head. My hands were too busy to type when I was eating.

"On the phone, she sure talked fast. Asked a lot of questions."

I shrugged. Meghan and I were just different. She always had lots to say, and I didn't.

"You like her fiancé?" He speared another piece of sashimi and dipped it in soy before popping it in his mouth.

I nodded.

I typed before grabbing another California roll. *"Andrew."*

"And your dad? You get along?"

I nodded again as I ate a spicy scallop roll. Dad got along with everyone, but he was easy-going and went with the flow. Meghan bossed him around, but he didn't seem to mind.

"You ever wondered why Brandon and I don't look alike?"

That was out of the blue, though perhaps related to the topic of siblings. I nodded. Christopher was tall with dark hair, icy blue eyes, and a Captain America physique. His shoulders were worth admiring. My cheeks turned pink at the thought. Brandon was slim and shorter with brown hair and brown eyes. He had a scientist vibe about him, perhaps enhanced by his distracted air. He was always thinking of his work. I'd seen no similarity in their features. I'd assumed they took after different sides of the family. Meghan and I also looked little alike. I'd never met their parents, who now lived in Florida, so I hadn't been able to compare or look for family traits.

"His family adopted me when I was a kid," he said as he captured another roll.

I looked up, my eyes widening. I wanted to hear this story.

"I know," he said. "Brandon and I are brothers now, but first we were friends in elementary school. He used to look out for me. My mom split when I was little, leaving me with my dad. Problem was, my father drank, and he wasn't good at looking after a kid. He disappeared when I was in second grade. I looked after myself for about a week, but I ran out of food. I told Brandon, figuring he could bring me supplies from his house."

My heart went out to him. I related to having a parent who drank, but I couldn't imagine being abandoned. My mother had trouble being an exemplary mother, but I'd been able to count on my dad. After her death, he'd stepped up taking dual parental roles. He baked a mean batch of butterscotch chocolate chip cookies.

Christopher chewed another roll, then continued. "Brandon told his parents, and they took me in. Instead of sending me to foster care, the Winters kept me. It started out as short-term, but the state let me stay. When I was nine, they made it official. Signed adoption papers when my father gave up his parental rights. I've been lucky with how my life turned out. It could have been very different. I owe that to Brandon. If someone's trying to hurt him or mess him up, I have to help."

I'd never heard personal information about Christopher before. It made me see him in a different light. His life hadn't been perfect. It made me wonder how well I'd known Brandon that this was new information.

"The cops said Brandon's coma was from a drug overdose. We know that's wrong. There's no way." I was proud I could now type his name without trouble. I was becoming used to talking and thinking about him again after avoiding it for years.

Christopher clenched his jaw but said nothing. He speared a piece of salmon sashimi with a chopstick.

"It's something from work. He's switched his specialty to a venomous scorpion. They want to inject it into people. He said it wasn't ready for human trials, that the test subjects died."

"How do you know?" He turned his piercing gaze back on me.

I fought the urge to squirm. *"I might have overheard a phone call last Tuesday night. I might also have snooped on his phone and in his office when he fell asleep."* I grimaced, ashamed to admit this invasion of privacy. *"That's how I got your number."*

"Good for you."

I looked up, surprised at this reaction. I forwarded pictures of the files and Brandon's messages from work. *"If any of this makes sense, let me know."*

"Thanks. I'll read through them later."

It was eight o'clock, and we were taking a break from sushi when Christopher said, "What does the rest of your evening look like?"

"I appreciate dinner. You don't have to entertain me."

"No, seriously, I'm too full to move. You'd be doing me a favor. If you don't mind, I'm going to intrude for a while longer."

I found I liked his company. I wasn't planning anything exciting, another typical night in, so I pointed to the TV.

"Perfect. Anything in particular?"

I sent him a picture of Buffy.

He laughed and moved to the couch. "I used to love that show. I haven't seen it in ages. Can I watch?"

"No date tonight?" I said, surprised he was free.

"I seldom date."

My eyebrows moved skyward. There'd been a string of model-type women his future self had paraded through the office. I remembered him mentioning that he hadn't handled Brandon's death well.

"What?" he said, seeing the look on my face.

"After 2019, you date a lot. Different girls every week or two."

"Then I apologize in advance. 2017 me is boring and lame and I like to stay in. Beer night on Thursday being the exception. It's my chance to hang out with Brandon."

I looked up. Tomorrow was Thursday.

"He's canceled for tomorrow," he said to my unspoken question. "Said maybe in July. No explanation."

Changing the subject, he leaned forward and said, "So, tell me about these women. Are they hot?"

I laughed. *"Every one. Tall, blonde, and big boobs. You seem to have a type."*

"Jealous, are you?"

Annoyed, I used the remote more savagely than usual. My cheeks burned as I sensed him watching. It was hard not to compare myself to those women who were beautiful even when they didn't smile.

"I didn't know that Brandon died. None of your family thought to tell me. You seemed happy, and I was miserable. I was jealous of your life, not the women. I was angry." I hadn't thought about it much, but this seemed like the truth.

"But I'm not so bad after all," he said with a grin.

That look was irresistible, especially when his dimple reappeared.

The next two episodes were the Season Two finale, called 'Becoming.' The narrator's voice entranced me and I almost forgot Christopher was there or that he'd annoyed me. Ember crawled onto my lap and snuggled, purring.

After several minutes, Christopher said, "Cute kitten." He held out his fingers and ran them along the edge of the cushion between us. Ember, intent on their motion, twitched her tail and her small body tensed. He pretended not to look while he wiggled his fingers. She pounced. They played for a few minutes, and then, to my surprise, she climbed his shirt to his shoulder to perch. It looked like she was watching TV with us.

Christopher stayed through the second half of the finale.

"One of my favorite episodes," he said when it had finished.

"It was so sad," I said. *"She sent her true love to hell to save the world, just as they cured him. The magic kicked in and he got his soul back."*

"That's what was brilliant," he said. "If he was still evil, and she stabbed him with the sword, it wouldn't have been heartbreaking."

We sat and debated the merits of the show for another half hour, though he was careful not to spoil upcoming episodes, which I appreciated. The night had flown.

It was after ten when he stood up and stretched. I hadn't enjoyed a quiet evening with company like this in years. It hadn't felt phony or forced, and somehow, we'd eaten every bite of the food. It had been comfortable, like we were friends.

"Thanks for dinner. You're sure I can't pay for my share?"

"Na, I'm good. Thanks for the clues and the relaxing evening," he said. "I'll stop by Brandon's work on Sunday or Monday. Make him talk."

"Will his company let you in? I've never made it past reception. Security and all."

"Won't know until I try."

I walked Christopher to the door, and this time was less surprised when he hugged me goodnight. I never would have guessed he was a hugger, but it appeared he was. As I took a deep breath, I tried not to be obvious. He smelled like rich chocolate.

"There's an episode in Season Three I'd like to watch. Can I come back?"

I nodded. *"Which one? I'll let you know when I'm close."*

He grinned and started down the stairs, jingling his keys. "You'll relate to this one. It's called 'The Wish'."

Chapter 6

Friday was rainy and miserable, and I arrived at work with my feet soaked, but I'd brought spare clothes and dry shoes. Sitting at my computer, I researched bus schedules and routes to take to get to my dad's for the engagement party. I'd just about decided when I'd need to leave when Christopher texted.

"Pick u up at 6. I'll drive."

I needed to change for the party after work. *"6:30? My place?"* I didn't drive and his offer was thoughtful, so I added, *"Thanks."* He didn't make me feel like he felt sorry for me. We were becoming friends again. It was more satisfying than disliking him. That had made me feel petty. We had more in common than I'd thought.

At six forty, I was still searching for my shoes. I listened for the doorbell, knowing Christopher could arrive any second. He knew I'd be running late, but I wasn't quite ready. I was nervous about seeing Dad and Meghan in person. It had been a long time for me and I hoped I wouldn't make a fool of myself. Maybe they'd be too busy with their guests to talk much and would believe the laryngitis story. I didn't enjoy lying to them, but I didn't see how I could tell the truth.

"Maybe I should cancel?" I was alone and spoke aloud.

There was a knock at the door, and I jumped. Had Christopher heard me?

I opened the door to find Christopher wearing dark jeans and a pale blue collared shirt that matched his eyes. My heart fluttered.

They'd think he was my date—except he was out of my league. He was even too beautiful to be my friend.

"No canceling."

He didn't make a big deal that he'd heard my voice, but he must have.

I shrugged and wondered if I'd have to explain, but before I got a chance, he whistled. I smiled at his reaction. I'd worn the red dress again. I'd told myself it was too nice a dress not to wear, and I remembered his eyes from the elevator the other time I'd worn it.

"Any word from Brandon?"

I shook my head. My newly curled hair swayed above my shoulders with the movement.

"His loss," he said. "You look gorgeous. We should go. We're going to be late."

I'd worried about being too dressed up, but the look in Christopher's eyes made my efforts worthwhile.

"They probably told me the wrong time," I said, grabbing my purse.

He laughed. "I like your family already." He reached inside and flicked on the porch light with a smile. For once, I wouldn't be returning to a dark doorstep.

I sent him the address and took a deep breath as we pulled away. He was a skilful driver, alert and confident.

Christopher couldn't look at his phone when he drove, so I couldn't talk to him, but he did the talking for both of us. I'd never met a man who was so chatty.

We parked near the house, and I had a moment of trepidation. My stomach churned, and I was tempted to call the whole thing off, but Meghan would be disappointed. Years ago, I made a mistake at this engagement party. I'd broken my rule and tried to drink my heartbreak over Brandon away. Tonight, I wouldn't do that. I knew where it led. This was my chance to be better and not make the same mistakes.

I stood on the wet sidewalk staring at the house I hadn't seen in over two years when a red corvette parked behind us. The world tilted and my stomach dropped to the ground. I'd forgotten I'd have to deal with Eric. Here. Now. He stepped out of his car. I'd have to face him. I froze and Christopher looked back.

"Hey, you okay? I'll let them know about your laryngitis and we'll get you some tea."

I shook my head. I wanted to vomit. This was too much. What was I doing here?

Christopher walked back to stand beside me and followed my gaze to the new arrival. "Who's that?"

He kept his voice quiet, but his eyes were hard as granite as he watched Eric approach. Menacing, dark clouds drifted closer and a drop of rain landed on my hand.

"You here for the engagement party, too?" Eric stopped beside us.

His eyes raked over me, but he addressed his remarks to Christopher.

Christopher took my hand possessively, and I squeezed. In this time, I hadn't met Eric. He didn't know me. In this world, I didn't have scars, and I hadn't gotten him killed. I tried not to picture him bloody, green eyes staring and vacant, slumped over the airbag. Lifeless.

"You must be Eric." Christopher didn't release my hand. He was smart, and he'd figured out who this was from my reaction.

"Oh, you've heard of me." Eric's chest puffed up.

"Andrew mentioned your car," said Christopher.

Eric laughed. The sound grated down my spine. "That's right, he's jealous. Now that he's tying the knot, he'll never get a sports car. Next thing we know, he'll trade in his SUV for a minivan. I didn't catch your names?"

"Sorry, I'm Christopher and this is Elizabeth."

"That's right, the sister," said Eric. "I've heard of you. You study bones or something."

Christopher didn't release my hand to shake Eric's.

I was grateful for the support, and I didn't want Eric thinking I was available. I wanted him to be uninterested. I planned to avoid Eric all night.

"You two going in?" said Eric as he passed. "Your girl's cold."

He acted like he saw through my dress. He smirked as he headed toward the house.

"In a minute," said Christopher, "I'm waiting for a call."

Christopher hadn't made his usual polite small talk.

Christopher waited for Eric to be gone, and he put his arm around me. "You're shaking. You didn't mention your future husband would be here. I don't like how that asshole looked at you."

"I tried so hard not to think about it, I almost forgot. He'll NEVER be my husband now." Relief swept over me to say it, even in print. Did that mean I wasn't a murderer?

"An accident isn't murder," said Christopher.

Had I said it out loud? I shot him a look. I kept forgetting to ask questions about why he knew so much, but I didn't have time to ponder as Christopher's smile dazzled me.

"Imagine me as your bodyguard tonight. I'll be attentive and practice being a suitable date for all those future hot chicks."

I was supposed to laugh but couldn't. Despite my sweater, I was freezing. I took his warm hand again.

"Your sister is going to get the wrong impression if we're holding hands."

An electric current shot up my arm as his thumb rubbed the back of my hand. He could have let go, but instead, laced his fingers together with mine.

I could deal with my sister later, but I owed Christopher an explanation. The boyfriend act would do me a gigantic favor.

"Last time Eric and I hooked up here, at the party." My face burned, and I kept my eyes downcast, studying the sidewalk. The details had always been fuzzy and the night an alcohol-induced blur.

I'd had sex with him in my childhood bedroom and agreed to a date so it wouldn't be a one-night stand. The next day, Eric had called and asked me out. He'd been on his best behavior for months. We were married less than six months later. It fit the adage: marry in haste, repent at leisure. His ugly side stayed hidden until after our whirlwind romance.

Eric was the biggest regret of my life.

"I'm not judging," Christopher said. "I've done my share of stupid things. If you want me to run interference, I'll keep him away."

Meghan's arrival interrupted us. "Elizabeth, here you are. Eric said he'd met you outside. You're still almost late, even though I gave you the wrong time."

She was so close. I stepped out of Christopher's protective circle and ran the last few steps to my sister and threw myself at her, catching her in a hug. I squeezed harder than I meant to. I'd missed her for too long.

She laughed. "Don't squish me to death."

I let go and stepped back, drinking in the sight of her tousled black curls and her expressive dark eyes. As usual, she wore bright colors. Her summer dress was orange, purple, and red flowers. Before my silence got awkward, Christopher stepped forward.

"I'm Christopher. We met on the phone." He shook her hand. "Your sister has laryngitis, or she'd be thanking you for letting me invite myself. She didn't want to come alone since she and my brother are taking a break."

"Laryngitis? It's not contagious, is it?" She spoke to me. "Did you break up with Brandon, or did he break up with you? He's an idiot if he lets you get away."

I shook my head. I lifted my phone for her to read. *"Stress-related. Dr. says give it time, not to strain my voice. Brandon ghosted me. I work with Christopher, have known him for years."* That should be a lot of detail to make her happy.

"Well, let's go make you a hot tea." She turned to Christopher with questions in her eyes. I would have to explain. "Come meet everyone."

Meghan's eyes flickered as Christopher took my hand again, but she said nothing as we followed her to the house.

"Dad's been worried. I guess this is why you blew us off for dinner on Sunday and haven't called back. You could have at least texted."

I nodded and bit my lip. She was right.

The house was cozy and the cheerful sound of partygoers filled the rooms. I waved to a few people I'd met before as Meghan took us through to the kitchen. She knew I didn't like crowds. Andrew stood near the food while Dad put trays of homemade mini tarts and quiches into the oven. The scent of tangy and sweet pastries filled the kitchen.

"Found her," Meghan said. "She was hiding outside by the cars."

She stood on tiptoe and kissed Andrew, who handed her an orange drink with a purple umbrella. He wore his police uniform, though not the gun or badge—he was off duty. It was a long-running joke between them. He pretended Meghan had fallen in love with him because she loved how he looked in his uniform, but it was because he was one of the nicest men around and he adored her.

"She's got stress-related laryngitis and a new... boyfriend."

An unspoken "and some explaining to do" filled Meghan's voice.

Andrew grinned and Christopher winked.

When Dad closed the oven and turned, I gave him the same too-big hug Meghan had received. Dad was tall and blonde and squished like a giant teddy bear. It had been too long. It was wrong that I couldn't remember the last time I'd hugged them. Two years? Three? A piece of my heart that I'd walled away tumbled free.

"Christopher," he said, introducing himself.

He shook Andrew's hand, then my father's. His other hand rested on the bare part of my back, just above the waist of the red dress. His hand was warm, and I liked how it felt. I smiled up at him. We might be acting, but it felt natural and comfortable.

Meghan made tea, and I cradled the steaming mug as we circulated before returning to the quiet of the kitchen. My sister spread the word about my laryngitis, but there were few people I would have spoken to beyond a few words. I'd never been social. Part of me enjoyed this perfect excuse not to talk, even if it wasn't a permanent solution. I would have to come clean before long. I wouldn't be able to disclose everything—they'd never believe time travel, but I'd have to think of something more long-lasting. Perhaps an injury.

Andrew and Christopher hit it off. They talked a lot, and I lost track of the conversation, but in a comfortable way. It was nice to be included, and not have to try hard. Meghan circulated throughout the house but checked in several times.

"You should have told me about Brandon," she said on her pass through the kitchen when Christopher was out of the room.

I nodded, blinking back the tears that rushed to my eyes at his name. We hadn't figured out how to save him. He was going to die unless I changed something.

She grabbed my arms. "Don't feel bad about the upgrade. It might be awkward for a bit, but Christopher's great. He's crazy about you. That's a delightful change."

A stab of guilt raced through me at the deception.

"He's not exactly shy and retiring, is he?" she said.

His booming laugh filled the kitchen as he returned to my side. When I caught his eye, his smile lit up the room. My heart lurched. I didn't want Christopher to be a rebound any more than Eric had been. I wasn't looking for love or even lust. I was looking to save Brandon. I would keep telling myself any attraction to Christopher was because I'd been celibate too long. Not because he was perceptive, fun, and gorgeous.

Was this what Dr. Maeve meant by changing my reality? For years, I'd only seen Christopher's negative qualities because I'd been angry. I'd failed to see all the good.

On that note, I excused myself and went upstairs where it was quiet and I ducked into my old bedroom to think. I sat on the bed. It looked the same as it had when I'd left for Columbia at eighteen, two lifetimes ago. My dad had left my bedroom alone, and I'd never reclaimed the treasures of my childhood or teen years that I'd once considered precious. I had a job in the city and had furnished my place with new stuff.

I picked up a framed photo of our family, the three of us one Christmas when I was fourteen and Meghan twelve. I blew the dust off, thinking of that day years ago, losing myself in memories. When the bedroom door closed, I looked up.

Eric had slid into the room and locked the door. He leaned against it. He wasn't tall, but was stocky and took up space. My palms became sweaty, and I bit the inside of my cheek. There was no way I could get through him and out.

The picture dropped to the white carpet when I stood.

"I thought I might find you alone if I was patient." His look focused on my cleavage, not my face. "Do you believe in love at first sight?"

I shook my head.

"I saw the way you looked at me outside. I could tell there was a certain heat."

He was crazy. I'd been scared, not interested. I shook my head again and stepped away from the bed.

"You don't need to play hard to get, Baby Doll. I feel it too, this instant attraction."

At the pet name, my blood froze, and ice filled my veins. A human popsicle in June.

He cocked his head to the side and ran his hand over his buzz-cut hair. "I heard a rumor that you can't talk. Does that mean you can't scream?"

I didn't dare look away. He stalked toward me and I moved away, my back to the window. My heart raced and my throat constricted. I wanted to speak more now than at any point since the accident. I wanted to tell him to leave me alone. Nothing came out.

I'd seen the look in his eyes before. It was frightening because they gave nothing away. His jade green eyes were flat and showed no emotion, reminding me of a reptile. He'd hypnotize with his stare, then strike. But not today.

I swerved to the side and lunged for the door. Eric grabbed my arm. I surprised him when I stepped forward and broke his hold. I fumbled for the door. He kicked it closed when I unlocked it. He spun me around and back into the room. I flew toward the bed. He followed and held me down, whispering in my ear.

"If you can't scream, this can be our secret. I think you'll like my surprise." He flipped up the skirt of my dress and tugged on the band of my underwear while I struggled. He snapped it against me with a sting. Playing, drawing out the moment of power, something he got off on.

I should have struck when I'd broken his hold on my arm, but I'd lost my chance. I wanted to hit him, but I'd sworn never to strike anyone again. The memory of the sound of his nose breaking and of the sensation as my hand smashed into his face made me freeze. He was much stronger than I was. He kept me pinned with his tight grip. Without the element of surprise, I wasn't strong enough to break free.

I needed him off me. My stomach roiled.

Taking a deep breath, I kicked and caught him a glancing blow. A regular flailing kick, not a karate kick that would cause damage. I rolled to the side, off the bottom of the bed, and stumbled toward the window. The ABC's of self-defense went out the window. Avoid was a failure. Breathe was a failure, as mine came in gasps. Neither had I remained Calm. It was hard to focus. What next? My brain seemed short-circuited. Silent tears escaped. I had to get out of the room, but I didn't know how. The door was too far.

In my head, I yelled, *"NO!"* He advanced, backing me up against the wall as far as I could go. I shook my head in terror. *"NO!"*

"You aren't going anywhere, baby. Stay here. I've known since the moment I saw you outside that we were destined to be together."

The door flung open with a crash and Christopher stormed into the room. Fury radiated from every line of his powerful body.

Despite his position, Eric tried to bluff his way out. "Slut," he said. "She was coming on to me, dude. Your girlfriend's got a problem."

He didn't get to finish. Christopher's fist connected with Eric's face. Knocked him across the room. When Christopher lunged again, Eric ran. Christopher stood at the entrance of the door and watched him flee. We said nothing. Then the door at the bottom of the stairs slammed. We still didn't speak as I listened to the roar of Eric's car as it screeched away. His ultimate departure broke the silence.

"You should've kicked him into next week," said Christopher, turning to me at last.

I stepped back. His frosty eyes froze my blood and stopped me in my tracks.

Was it disgust in his voice or anger? My eyes filled with tears. My hand shook as I pointed to the door.

"Lizzie, I...," he started, but he got a better look at my face and stopped talking.

I wrapped my arms around myself. Without another word, he left the room and retreated downstairs. Each footstep, like a blow. I couldn't face anyone. I wanted to thank Christopher for coming to my rescue, but I'd sent him away and now I felt stupid.

I locked the bedroom door, curled up on my old bed, and wept until my pillow was a lake. I'd held back the majority of my tears for years, but the levee had broken. The sobs hurt my throat and I couldn't stop them. I cried for my old self that Eric had seduced and then broken. I cried for Brandon's death. Now I was sure I'd lost my only friend, the only connection I'd felt in years.

When my tears stopped, I remained on the bed, wishing I hadn't come to the party. I didn't know what to do. When someone knocked on the door, I didn't want to answer. My phone buzzed. I checked. It was Christopher.

"I'm sorry if I scared you. Let me in."

I didn't answer.

He sent another. *"I know you're listening."* Then he spoke aloud. "Your family has been kind enough not to kick me out, even though this looks bad. You're up here locked in your old room and I hurt my hand. I'm lucky they've waited for your explanation. We need to talk, and it's getting late."

I stood up, straightened my dress, and glanced in the mirror. Most of my mascara was on the pillowcase and my hair was a mess, the curls smashed. I smoothed my hair and tucked the front behind my ears. Better. I unlocked the door and stepped back. I couldn't look at his face, afraid of what I'd see. I looked at his shoes and tried not to cringe.

Christopher entered and closed the door. He held an icepack against his knuckles.

"I'm sorry I lost my temper." His voice was soothing and low.

I raised my eyebrow as I risked a look upward. His eyes had defrosted several degrees.

"I was furious, but not with you. You didn't let him molest you. I'm an idiot not to have just comforted you. I was too mad to realize how scared you were. He hurt you for years. You lived like that every day and I can't imagine what you went through. I have no right to judge. I wanted to protect you and was useless. You were only gone a few minutes, and the creep attacked you."

His last words hit home. I'd been thinking and had a wild theory. There'd been multiple clues, so I took a chance. *"How did you know I needed you?"*

Christopher's eyes didn't leave mine. "Yes, sometimes I can read minds. Yours less than most. Your mind is guarded, like a wall. But at times, you let down your barrier. That's why I believed you about time travel, how I knew who Eric was. I sensed your panic and heard you call for help. I've seen flashes of him mangled in a crushed car, covered in blood. You torment yourself with that, but he got what he deserved."

He slid closer. "I've seen the scars on your back, though they aren't there anymore. Your skin is flawless." He stroked the skin of my back to illustrate his point.

Goosebumps raised everywhere and tendrils of current shot through me at his touch.

"I know about our conversations in the future. You replay the moment when I told you about Brandon's death. I was a jerk to tell you like that. When I taunted you in the future, it was only because I was trying to help, to make you talk. I wanted you to scream, to tell me to leave you alone. I feel the echoes of you yelling that in your head."

I said nothing. Spider-like cracks appeared in the brick wall of my mind, threatening to crumble the mortar. He was hard to resist when the force of his personality was directed my way.

"I'm sorry future me didn't tell you about Brandon. It's unforgivable that I let you suffer alone or thought you wouldn't care, especially considering the timing.

It hadn't been all his fault. I'd been so messed up with Eric and avoiding everything that made him angry. I hadn't spoken to anyone about anything personal. I'd pushed everyone away and kept them at a distance, and I'd let myself become isolated.

"What am I thinking now?" I let the brick wall fall.

He tilted up my chin. "You're thinking that when I walk out of here, you'll be lonelier than ever before."

I nodded. I expected him to turn on his heel. I was too damaged.

Instead, he pulled me into an embrace. His solid warmth and the sweet chocolatey smell of him brought me back, thawed me. I couldn't stay behind the brick wall all the time. I wasn't just in 2017 for myself. I was here to save Brandon, but it didn't have to be so lonely. Christopher's arms wrapped around me made me warm, safe. I snuggled in closer.

If I was being honest with myself, I'd always been attracted to Christopher and missed his friendship those years since I'd pushed him away. I worried about getting my heart broken again, but tonight I didn't care.

"Will you help me tell my family what happened with Eric? Please."

"So, you accept my apology?"

I nodded. He smiled and took my hand.

We went downstairs and joined my family in the living room. The guests were gone and Meghan and Dad wore matching furrows to their brows, looking more alike than usual. Andrew's hair stood on end like he'd been pulling on it and he couldn't sit. Dad wouldn't meet my eyes. Another stab of guilt. I hoped I hadn't ruined their party.

"I'm going to speak for Elizabeth," Christopher said, "so she doesn't have to text."

Meghan looked at me, and I nodded.

"We met Eric outside. He figured out Elizabeth couldn't talk, waited for her to be alone, and followed. He tried to rape her."

"Are you hurt?" Meghan got to her feet—her arms crossed. "I don't understand. Have you met him before?"

I hesitated, then shook my head. To him, I'd been an easy victim. It had been opportunistic.

Meghan turned to Christopher. "How did you know she was in trouble? One second you were here, the next you were racing upstairs."

"Earlier, she said that he gave her the creeps. She'd been gone too long, and I got a bad feeling, so I went looking. When I got upstairs, I heard his voice."

I looked up at Christopher. When he looked down, it felt like a caress and heat infused my body.

"Do you want to press charges?" Andrew paced back and forth. "I've been drinking and am off duty, but I can get someone here. That bastard shouldn't get away with this."

I shook my head. *"I'm okay. Christopher interrupted and punched him."*

"How do you know Eric?" Christopher asked.

"He used to be my neighbor," said Andrew. "I invited him, just to be polite, when I ran into him last week. He'd asked how living together with Meghan was working out. I had no idea he was a sick fuck. I'm so sorry. You won't ever see him near us again. I want to kick him into the middle of next week. Are you sure about not pressing charges?" He frowned.

"I just want to forget about it. Sorry if I ruined the party."

"You didn't ruin it," said Meghan. "We're glad you came. I thought for sure you'd try to weasel out of it. I'm just sorry it turned rotten at the end. I'm glad you're all right."

She shot Dad a look that I didn't understand. Their reaction was odd and subdued. Shouldn't they be more upset at Eric? What was I missing?

I rested my hand on Christopher's arm.

"It's time for us to go," he said. "It was nice meeting everyone. Congratulations again, from both of us."

I hugged everyone. Only Andrew seemed angry. Dad and Meghan seemed worried, but like they didn't know what else to say. It wasn't often that Meghan was at a loss for words.

"No dinner here on Sunday." Dad wrung his hands together. "But I'll expect you both the following week."

He included Christopher in the invitation, which made me smile. Dad looked shaken about what had happened, but he didn't like to talk about feelings. He'd always been like that—emotions made him uncomfortable. He was more a hug-first-talk-never kind of guy.

"We'll be here," said Christopher with a final handshake.

This time, the car ride was quiet instead of filled with chatter. I rested my head on the back of my seat and closed my eyes, though I stayed awake.

It was late when we stopped at the curb outside my place. I was drained from my emotional outburst upstairs in my old room.

Christopher shut off the engine. "I'm considering borrowing you." He paused, then said, "I want to take you to my place and keep you." He took my hand in his.

His words were the opposite of what I expected. I raised my eyebrow. I didn't know if he saw it in the dark, but he must know I had questions. My heart skipped with his possessive words. They weren't threatening—they felt protective.

I looked up at him. His eyes gleamed with reflected light from the streetlight.

"I don't want to leave you alone tonight. You'll convince yourself that you don't deserve to be happy, or some rubbish like that. You'll try to shut me out. You'll say it's too soon, that you and my brother only ended things last week. Before you say that, I'm going to remind you it's been five years since the two of you broke up. I've also known you a year longer than he has. When you talk about him, when you think about him, you don't feel like you're in love."

He was right.

"Can I come in, so we can finish this discussion?"

His voice cracked as he asked to stay and my heart went out to him. I nodded and stepped out of his car. He took my hand as we made our way to my front door. I liked how he showed physical affection so often.

Inside, he released my hand and shoved his hands in his jean pockets. He took a deep breath and said, "Are you scared of me? Knowing I hear some of your thoughts. I try to ignore most of what people think, but though rarer, yours are focused and often a shout. They're hard to ignore."

I shook my head. Christopher didn't scare me.

"It'll be hard for you to keep secrets. Are you okay with that?"

It was scary, but the thought of someone actually knowing me and liking me anyway was intoxicating. If I let him in, it would be all the way in. I nodded.

We kicked off our shoes, and he guided me to the couch. Butterflies flitted about my stomach as I sat. I wasn't sure who moved first, but his mouth was on mine, that mocha scent that was him enveloped me. My arms wrapped around him. He was hard everywhere, his muscles like iron.

We kissed until I wasn't aware of anything in the world other than Christopher's lips, his hands, and his body touching mine. If there were kissing Olympics, he was the champion, the gold medalist. My nerve endings flickered with a fire's heat and he knocked all thoughts from my head. There was nothing left for him to read when my mind was blank—peace was bliss.

Eventually, he wrested his mouth from mine. We were lying on the couch and I lay on top of him. My lips tingled and were swollen. His icy blue eyes sparkled. One of his hands made lazy circles on my hip under my dress. So little separated us.

"Are you aware that this dress makes me want to rip it off you?" His voice was soft, but huskier than usual.

When he kissed me again, I mouthed, "Yes," against his lips. I'd worn it for him. His answer was a moan and for a second it seemed like I read his mind, too. I sensed an upwelling of tenderness. It wasn't the unadulterated lust I'd expected.

"You're certain I don't scare you? What about my temper? I might yell, but I'd never hurt you. I yell, then flash, my anger gone. I felt like such an asshole earlier."

As I kissed him, I breathed my answer against his mouth. "No." I was rewarded with another surge of emotion. His hand was gentle on my face, the other splayed across my lower back beneath the fabric of the dress.

"It's late. Can I sleep here tonight?" His eyes searched mine. "Just sleep?"

I nodded and slid off him, missing his warmth immediately. It was after one. Ember had disappeared ages ago. She'd be on the bed.

When we went down the hall, we passed the master bedroom. I'd left the door open earlier when moving more of my belongings to my new room.

"This is the guest room," Christopher said as we entered my room. He turned one way, then the other. "Isn't it?" He raised an eyebrow. "There's no ensuite. Isn't the other room larger?"

Eric used to hurt me in the other room. When I'd woken up in the other room two weeks ago, I'd moved back here, though this time I'd brought my clothes. Eric had never seen or touched them.

"Maybe we should buy you a new house," he said as I plugged my phone into the charger on my nightstand. "Somewhere with no awful memories."

I handed him a fresh toothbrush from the stash I'd accumulated from the dentist and let him get ready for bed. It didn't take long before I followed. I slid into bed with him, the sheets already warmed by his heat. I wore a T-shirt and loose shorts. His arm pulled me into position, nestled against him.

"Lizzie," he said against my hair. "I don't want those other women; I only want you."

What would we tell Brandon? I was no less determined to save Brandon, but the reason had shifted.

He answered as though I'd spoken. "We'll explain that we've been texting, like an updated version of 'You've Got Mail.'"

I giggled. The sound rose out of me, real and audible as the image of Christopher being a secret rom-com fan who used a chick flick to explain our relationship to his brother cracked me up.

The surrounding arm tightened as he said, "That's our secret, you evil woman."

For the first time in years, I fell asleep feeling safe.

Chapter 7

The next morning was Saturday, so Christopher and I didn't have to work. I laid out the clues so we could examine them together.

"Brandon's a toxinologist," I said. *"I looked it up years ago, to see how it differed from a toxicologist. He used to study medical applications of rattlesnake venom. Last year, he switched to the Arizona bark scorpion. Did he explain why?"*

"Said it would be more profitable because of the military applications. When I asked more, he said it was classified. Couldn't talk about the details. You know him, that was the end of the discussion. He's another with a guarded mind; his is impenetrable. More steel than brick."

"Military?" I tapped my top lip. *"That could be why he was scared."*

"What do you mean?" said Christopher with a slight frown. "You didn't mention that."

"That phone call I overheard sounded like someone threatened him. Wasn't himself afterward. They scared him."

"How long until he's found in a coma?" The crease between his brows deepened.

"I don't know. In the future, you weren't specific. A couple of months. Brandon told whoever he was speaking to that he could solve the problem in a month or two. Said he'd make an antidote as a failsafe."

"If he doesn't think whatever they're making will be ready for human trials by the end of the time, what do you think he'd do?" Christopher's gaze was intense.

The blood drained from my face and my hands shook as I typed. *"He'd try it on himself."*

"So, either we have to stop him from injecting himself with poison or find his antidote in case we're too late."

"He's not answering your messages. I'm blocked. What would happen if you told him specifically not to use it? Is there something you could send, some sort of coded message to let him know how important it is that you speak to him?"

"Such as?"

"A secret or an inside joke. He's your brother. What might he understand that nobody would think out of place if they intercepted the message? Something about a vacation or your favorite book or movie."

Christopher picked up his phone. He read his message aloud as he typed. *"I need to see you about our trip to Mexico."* He looked at me. "We've never been to Mexico. My biological father moved there. Years ago, Brandon said if I wanted to track him down, he'd go with me."

"Perfect."

Christopher hit *Send*.

Minutes later, Brandon replied. *"Sunday 8 a.m. The lab. I'll set it up with security. Working all weekend, but I want to talk to you, too."*

"Do you want to find your father? I'm curious."

Christopher shook his head. "I have no interest in my birth parents. Why should I? They threw me away and never looked back. The Winters are my family. I was glad to get a new name and belong to someone who cared."

Was that true, or what he told himself? He'd spoken with so little emotion, not like his usual voice. Being abandoned couldn't have left him unscathed, but I let it go for now.

We spent the rest of the day reading about the Arizona bark scorpion. I couldn't figure what was so special about it, other than it was the most venomous North American creature. Many thought of scorpions as insects, but they were arachnids, like spiders. I shuddered when I discovered the adults could grow up to eight cm in length. They were huge. I'd hate to find one by accident and was thankful that they were rare.

The question that I kept circling back to was about the possible military applications. An idea popped into my head and I looked up uses for animal venom to see what experiments were being conducted, the kinds of things Brandon used to work on. I shared my findings with Christopher.

"They use venom for treating and trying to cure cancer, strokes, and autoimmune diseases, such as rheumatoid arthritis. That isn't military applications. It's not surprising that venom is useful. Humans have used plants and animals for medical purposes for thousands of years. Traditional Chinese Medicine has used animal parts for thousands of years. Even Neanderthals knew about grinding up poplar bark as a painkiller."

I hesitated to let Christopher read my long message. When he looked up, I sent my burning question. *"What if someone wanted to make a painkiller so strong it inhibited pain? Might allow them to make a super soldier. That's military."*

"How would that work?" said Christopher.

He didn't shoot down my crazy idea.

"Animal venom evolved to target the nervous systems of other animals. It paralyzes prey. What if they're working on a way to suppress the nervous system's reaction instead, to make it resistant to pain?"

"Wouldn't they need a lot of venom?"

"Scientists don't need real venom anymore. They make it in a lab. It's safer to study because they don't have to keep animals or extract venom."

"That's unreal. How did I not know about this? I used to imagine Brandon playing with rattlesnakes at work."

An image popped into my head of Brandon juggling rattlesnakes. I enjoyed being around Christopher—he made me laugh.

"Brandon didn't talk about his work. At all. I don't know the names of anyone he works with. I'm lucky I heard about the scorpions."

We spent the better part of the day reading about venom. It was fortunate we had scientific backgrounds that helped us to read the medical papers and science journals—some of them were technical and full of jargon.

Before I knew it, it was evening and approaching dinner time. I had little in the way of food in my house. I was back to pickles and mustard, because we'd finished the bread and cheese at lunch. I also hadn't shopped since returning to this time. I would go tomorrow and do better about keeping my fridge stocked. I'd enjoyed having food at home to cook. My stomach growled.

"Pack up your cat." Christopher stood and cracked his back as he stretched.

My head shot up. *"My cat?"*

"You don't like to leave her alone at night. Ember's a sweetheart. We can bring her. I don't mind."

"Where are we going?" I lifted an eyebrow.

"My place. I'm going to feed you and we're going to watch something sappy and you're going to tell me more of your deep, dark secrets. We're having another sleepover."

"You're just deciding for me?" I crossed my arms.

Christopher laughed. "It helps when I can read your mind. All afternoon you've been wondering if we can sleep together again. I want to too."

My face flushed hot. *"That's an unfair advantage."*

He took my hand and laced his fingers through mine. His hand should have dwarfed mine, but they fit.

"I've told no one about reading minds. I didn't know how you'd take it."

He was dead serious as he traced circles on the back of my hand with his thumb.

"That's my deepest, darkest secret. Not even Brandon knows. People think I'm just perceptive or a good guesser. I try not to say too much that I learn."

That's what I'd thought before I'd spent much time around him. Although he was those things too.

He looked up. "I enjoy being around you. Most people have chaotic minds with so many thoughts jumbled together that they're hard to be around for long. It keeps me from hearing individual thoughts, but it's noisy, so I've preferred the peace of being alone. Until now."

This intense intimacy or the potential for it was unfamiliar territory. For us both.

"I'll try not to lie. But you have to be honest, too."

"I can do that," he said with a smile.

My heart fluttered.

"Can I make you dinner? I want to feed you." He flashed his dimple. "More than just pickles."

"Are you a fabulous cook?"

"I can barbeque just about anything." He laughed, a genuine happy sound.

"Will I be allowed to help?"

He grabbed me and kissed me in a way that stole my breath. I was gasping when he released me. I didn't care what we had for dinner anymore.

"I'll let you do anything you want." He reached for his phone. *"I need you in my bed tonight."*

My heart skipped a beat. The tips of his ears turned pink while I read his message. He wasn't as confident as he pretended.

I answered through my thoughts. I wanted to be naked with him, so I pictured it in vivid detail. It had been so long since I'd had sex, and longer still since I'd wanted it like this. I imagined it with his every touch. If I seemed desperate or brazen, I didn't care.

"If we start now, we won't get food," he said. "I've got steaks in the fridge. I want to feed you, then play for hours. You'll need stamina." His gaze burned.

I swallowed. Nobody had ever spoken to me like this. I was so turned on. I wished we could strip now, but he was right.

I called Ember and collected her travel supplies. Christopher's eyes tracked my every move. This was more like the lust I expected. I changed into date clothes and packed an overnight bag.

Christopher's house was a ten-minute drive from my place, situated on the hillside above the river. The house was set back from the road and private, surrounded by established trees.

"*How can you afford a place like this?*" I was envious of its solitude.

"My parents sold it to me. Gave me a deal. I love it here."

Inside had a homey feel, cluttered with the artifacts of a busy life. Sunglasses, a stack of unopened mail, and a half-full coffee mug sat on the counter while a hoodie draped over the back of one of the kitchen chairs, but it wasn't dirty. There were vaulted ceilings and a sunken living room with the mandatory big screen TV in the living room, but there was also a smaller, cozy room with a rounded wall and window seat that looked perfect for reading away the afternoon. I recognized many of the books on the shelves as recent publications, many of them non-fiction. History and biographies for the most part.

He saw my interest. "Does it surprise you I read a lot?"

He looked amused when I nodded. My old image of Christopher as a womanizing dating machine had been wrong, and I needed to let it go. I let Ember out of her carrier and put down a litter tray and her food dishes. While she explored, so did I, but only for a couple of minutes. Then I went to help with the food.

We didn't make it much past dinner. We cleaned up the dishes and when I reached for the dishtowel to dry the wooden salad bowl, his long arm snaked out and captured me, tugging me close. I'd changed into a skirt for dinner and now his hands slid underneath it, holding me against him. I slipped my hands under his T-shirt and felt his solid bulk. His skin was warm, and he radiated heat. I loved feeling his strength. I was so wet it embarrassed me that he'd notice. He chuckled and stroked me through my lacy underwear.

"You're wet and smooth," he said. "I like that."

I moaned when he slid a finger under the edge of my thong. He licked the finger that had touched me, tasted me. He leaned in for a kiss, his lips capturing mine. I trembled as he played with the lace of my soaked underwear, his touch tantalizing me.

Pausing for air, he said, "We won't make love tonight." His voice was low. His thumb stroked my lower lip, and I quivered like a bow drawn and held too long, the arrow ready.

As his words sank in, my hopes crashed. I stepped back, my cheeks flaming. Had I done something wrong? Misread the situation? I ached from want. I tried to turn away. Mortified.

"You mistake me," he said, taking in my stricken face. He tugged me closer and kissed me again. His grip was like iron and so was the rest of him. I wasn't mistaken about his need that matched my own. My knees weakened. His lips and body told me how much he wanted me. His breathing was erratic as he struggled for control.

He was impossible to resist, despite my confusion. He smelled delicious and tasted better.

"We'll make love one day soon, but tonight won't be slow and tender. I feel what you need," he said. "You need a fuck."

My knees buckled at his words. He was right. I trembled as his fingers slid beneath my underwear again. I was slippery and wetter than I'd imagined possible. Mixed into his kisses were small bites. The gentle scrape of his teeth on my neck as he nibbled his way up my throat and behind my ear was nearly my undoing. He wound me tighter and tighter. I couldn't concentrate on anything except the slow, swirling movement of his fingers, the taste, and the feel of his mouth.

"You need this. Hell, I do. I won't be gentle. I want to wreck you."

He stroked my most sensitive places, his eyes on my face, watching me react to his words. My heart raced, and he smiled when my pulse quickened. He slid my underwear off.

"I've wanted you for years," he said, his words soft in my ear. "Even when I thought we'd never have a chance, I fantasized about you."

I became a quaking mess. I'd been anticipating this all day. Sex was something I'd always wanted to enjoy, but I'd been underwhelmed. I had a feeling that was about to change. Christopher knew what he was doing and what I needed. I couldn't keep my hips still as he stroked around and around—his fingers teasing cruel perfection.

I closed my eyes, gave myself over to the feeling, and came on his hand. Before I could be embarrassed, he dropped to his knees and kissed my pulsing center. Devouring me. I'd had no one send me to the next level this way, and I came again, shuddering hard, gripping his hair to stay upright.

We still hadn't made it to the bedroom. I didn't think I could take more, but we weren't done. He could have leaned me against the counter and taken me. From the look in his heavy-lidded eyes, it looked like he'd considered it.

Christopher undressed and peeled off my remaining clothes, stripping me slowly, like he was unwrapping his birthday present, drawing out when I'd be naked. His fingers brushed my breasts, caressed my hips, and teased my heated flesh. On his knees, he kissed my stomach before he slid my skirt down. He stepped back. From the expression in his eyes, he admired my body as much as I admired his in all its glory.

"My turn." His smile was sensual.

Drunk and slow from pleasure, it took me a few seconds to understand his words. I read his smile and dropped to my knees. He leaped at my touch after I stroked his impressive cock. I ached again, longing for what he'd promised. But I could wait, let the anticipation rebuild. I licked him, starting at the base and flicking upward to the tip. I repeated this motion twice more before I took him in my mouth. Two could play this game.

He cursed as I took more and slid him in and out each time I took as much as I could. I used my hands and my mouth, wanting him as turned on as I was. I watched his face with each movement. His eyes closed, and he held the counter for support. When he grabbed my head to speed my movements, I gasped. He was so hard that I was concerned about the next part; he was a formidable weapon. I whimpered while I sucked, my sounds unstoppable.

I teased Christopher, slowing my torture each time he neared release.

"You're exquisite." His voice was husky and ragged.

His hands tangled in my hair, guiding my movement. I touched myself, and the heat built with each swirl that matched the rhythm of my mouth. His eyes watched my mouth, then my hand. I smiled.

I'd forgotten we were in the kitchen until he pulled me to my feet and led me down a darkened hall to his bedroom. Pushing me up against the wall, he held my hands over my head in one of his and slid his other into me. I should have been embarrassed by the sounds I made, but I wasn't. We moaned into each other's mouths as we kissed. I wanted this to continue forever. Flipping on the switch inside the door, he nudged me into his room and onto the bed.

He pulled my legs apart and knelt between them, once more touching me with his magic fingers. When I was close to ecstasy once more, the sweet rip of a packet came. I kept my eyes closed and my fingers busy, taking over while he paused. Seconds later, his massive, hard cock pushed inside me. I bucked beneath him, clenching tighter, uncontrolled desire coursing through every cell. I was on fire.

The world spun as I ground myself against him and cried out. Almost like pain, but pleasure spiraled and erupted like fireworks in my brain. Not yet satisfied, I pulled him deeper. With my hips, I held him where I needed him and fucked him in return. The world went dark around the edges and my vision blurred. I needed this. Not just sex, but sex with Christopher.

The sounds I made weren't coherent as I exploded again. The grand mal. This was like no orgasm I'd had before. I gave him everything, holding nothing back. I wasn't myself. I was wild sparks, heat, and light—lost for an unknown length of time. When he thrust again, I shook and shuddered. I tried to recover and participate, but he was content to do all the hard work.

He'd told the truth. There was nothing gentle. Each thrust was power. Twice he tossed me into unique positions as though I were a toy, a rag doll. Twice more I came, my limbs limp, before I regrouped. I lost track of time and the number of my orgasms. It felt unfair, but he was patient. I could stay here forever. My head was empty. In the literal sense, he'd fucked me senseless.

I'd never been with anyone that had this kind of stamina. I squeezed with a final spasm and without warning, he finally lost control. It was incredible to see and feel how far he went. I marveled at our chemistry. First sex was never incredible. Hell, no sex was like this. It was typically awkward, and I otherwise regretted its anticlimactic quality. In the past, I'd been disappointed, but this was beyond my wildest expectations. It was my best sex fantasies come true, and then some. Another Olympic gold. Platinum.

He caressed my hip as though he couldn't bear not to touch me.

"I wanted more," he said. "I could have held off a few more minutes."

I laughed and kissed him, nipping at his bottom lip. His heart hammered against mine. I rested my hand on his chest to feel its movement.

"What will we do for an encore?" His eyes closed, and he rested his forehead on mine.

I couldn't tell if he'd read my mind, or if it was how he felt. I was too blissed out to care.

Before Christopher rolled away, he kissed me again, soft and gentle—the opposite of our wild ride, but no less passionate. I'd missed out my whole life and was now spoiled for sex with anyone else. It was unthinkable. Was he as shell-shocked?

"I don't know what to say. Can I keep you? I want that every time," he said.

I laughed. Me too.

He stroked the side of my face. Perhaps he heard, or perhaps it was written on my face. We kissed again. Every nerve ending I possessed still tingled. His lips were swollen, and I suspected mine were too. He wanted me wrecked, and I was. We rested on his bed while our breathing returned to normal.

Eventually, we recovered enough to return to the kitchen for our clothes and for ice cream. He heaped the bowls with salted caramel gelato, splitting the carton between us. Settling onto the soft couch together, he pulled up Netflix and found Buffy.

"Ready for 'The Wish?'"

I nodded. His feet rested on the coffee table. I sat sideways against him, my legs on the couch. When we finished our ice cream, he threaded his arm around me and held me close. I'd never been more satisfied, both physically and emotionally.

In this episode, Buffy wondered if anything she'd done in Sunnydale made a difference, but the viewers saw what happened when an angry friend wished she'd never come to town. Without her, in the alternate version of life, her friends became vampires, Buffy was hard and cold inside, and the town became hell on Earth. The show struck a chord. Sometimes I'd wondered if anyone would notice if I disappeared, if my presence made a difference to anyone.

Looking at Christopher, I realized I was living my alternate reality, and here I mattered. I'd be content to sit with him and hang out, read, watch TV, anything. I pictured years of contentment. This was the start of something fantastic. He took my hand, once more tracing circles on my skin.

I didn't need another wish. It had been granted, but a niggling moment of disquiet intruded. I wanted to save Brandon, but what would he say about me and Christopher? For me, our relationship had been over for five years. For him, it had been a week and a half, though he was the one who'd chosen for it to end. I didn't want to hurt him, even if I didn't love him the way I thought I had. I leaned on Christopher and built up the bricks just a little, hiding thoughts of Brandon far from us. Christopher wasn't fooled, but he didn't push, and we enjoyed the rest of our night.

• • •

The next morning, we indulged in morning sex, awake early so Christopher could be at Brandon's lab for the appointed time. Leaving before eight seemed like an obscene hour to be out on a weekend. I hadn't been included in the invitation, but we thought we could try. I would go with Christopher for moral support, then we would enjoy the day. We wanted to spend every second that we could together.

The building where Brandon's lab was located was a chrome and glass monstrosity, surrounded by a ten-foot fence with triple-strand barbed wire on the top and security cameras at regular intervals. Christopher spoke into a two-way speaker by the gate. Brandon had left his name, so we could proceed through the gate.

We parked and entered the lobby. I'd met Brandon here several times, though I'd never been farther than reception. A familiar older man in a crisp blue uniform stood behind the desk.

"Miss Elizabeth," the security guard said. "Nice to see you again. Christopher too. What an unexpected pleasure."

"Hi, Paul," I mouthed, then pointed to my throat. *"I can't talk today."*

He punched our names into his computer and then looked at me, the corners of his mouth turned down. "You're not on the list. Just Dr. Christopher Winters. Is our Dr. Winters expecting you?"

I shook my head.

Christopher turned on the charm.

"She came as a surprise. He's been working so hard," said Christopher with a friendly smile. "Hope that's ok."

Paul shifted from side to side and rubbed the back of his neck. "I'm afraid I can't let her in without proper authorization."

He grimaced and looked torn. Like he wanted to help but knew he shouldn't.

"Should I call up and ask? Even if it ruins the surprise?" Paul said. "If Dr. Winters clears you, you can go."

Brandon would say no, so I put Paul out of his misery and shook my head.

"I'll wait," I texted Christopher. I pointed to the armchairs near the window in the morning sun.

"If you don't mind," Paul said.

The poor man looked relieved and I could tell he felt bad, but he was just doing his job. I smiled to let him know I wasn't upset.

"I'm fine down here. Brandon doesn't come down until I arrive because I'm always late. Paul's a nice man. Sometimes I bring him hot chocolate or brownies."

Paul scanned a security card through the reader, and a green light flashed by the door. He opened the heavy metal door. "Elevator's at the end of the hall. Your brother will meet you there with his security card. I'll take care of Miss Elizabeth."

Sitting in the sun, I sent a text to my sister. *"Feels weird that it's Sunday, but there's no Sunday dinner."*

"Tell me more about Christopher. I'm dying to know," she said.

"We work together. I've known him since I moved back to Portland. We were interested in each other before, not sure why we didn't go out. His brother asked me out first. So, we've been friends. Until now." Images of the previous night flashed through my mind. We were more than friends now. My face was sore from smiling.

"He's a good fit for you," she said. *"You're too serious sometimes. Plus, he's hot."*

"Yes, he is."

"OMG, you had sex already. That's not like you. You seem different."

"Is it like radar with you or what?" I wrote. *"I hardly said anything."*

"It was hot, wasn't it? I can tell you're smug."

"Volcanic."

"You could come to our place for dinner tonight, with me and Andrew, tell me everything," she said. *"Unless you have a better offer."*

"I think we have plans." I imagined picking up with Christopher where we'd left off last night and this morning.

"You'll have plans," she said. *"That gorgeous man couldn't take his eyes off you. I'm surprised you're on your own right now."*

I smiled as I read her messages.

"We'll be there next week." It felt good to say that. They might hope I could talk by then, but I already had the story about stress. I wouldn't

let them drift away again. My family was too important to ignore. That was another mistake I could fix.

My sister sent an emoji with heart eyes and flames on either side. *"Am I that bad?"*

"Worse. You two are repulsive and cute together. I like seeing you smile."

Twenty minutes later, Christopher returned without Brandon. His jaw was clenched, and he looked subdued, without his usual energy. Their talk must not have been productive. I smiled at Paul and left with a wave, following Christopher to the car when he didn't speak.

"Are you going to tell me?"

He didn't look at his phone when it chimed. He seldom ignored me. My forehead tightened and bunched up. He backed out of the lot and drove twenty minutes back toward town without talking. He pulled into a lot by a park. We weren't going for tea. A hard lump formed in the pit of my stomach. This park was familiar, only a few blocks from my house. It had walking trails and a pond. We sat overlooking the water while I waited for him to break the silence. The gulf between us grew wider and wider.

"Brandon was excited that I came today. He wanted to show me something. Something for you."

He paused, waiting, perhaps searching for the right words.

"He has an engagement ring on his desk," he said. "In a blue box."

I covered my mouth, choking on my horror.

Christopher continued with no expression in his voice.

"He said when this project settles down, he'll find you and beg for forgiveness. He's just too busy for a girlfriend right now. He wants to do better. He loves how undemanding you are, how little you need."

His words punched me in the gut. I struggled to breathe, the air stifling.

"I don't want that kind of relationship. Brandon and I are through."

He didn't look at my messages. I wanted to speak to Christopher. To tell him not to do this. I sensed what was coming. His words created a feeling of inevitability, the undertow of his revelations dragging us under.

"That's not love."

I tried to protest aloud, but my words jammed in my thickened throat, as though barricaded behind a dam. I was still voiceless.

Christopher shut me out. Though he could read minds, he wasn't listening. Perhaps he needed to say this without interruption.

"When I asked how that would change later, Brandon said you wouldn't mind. That you were so self-contained that you'd barely notice his absence."

His voice cracked at the end.

Christopher knew that wasn't true. I wasn't self-contained on purpose. That was a self-defense mechanism. I'd feared getting hurt if I let someone close. All my life, even before Eric, I'd kept people at a distance. Brandon and I kept each other at arm's length. We hadn't been close or intimate. I hadn't always seen it, but now it was clear. I fit a certain profile that checked the boxes for a wife: intelligent, educated, and independent. Once I might have thought that would be enough, but it wasn't. I wanted friendship and heat. I wanted Christopher.

Tears threatened. I didn't want to let them fall in front of Christopher. I wanted to be brave, but they overwhelmed me and scorched trails down my cheeks.

"Point blank I asked if he loved you."

Christopher's voice quavered as he fought for control. "He gave me a strange look and said, 'Of course. She's what anyone would want in a wife, and besides, she gets me.'"

He paused, but there was more.

"He was so excited about getting engaged. I've never seen him like that before."

"I'll say no."

Christopher still stared straight ahead. Both hands clutched the steering wheel in front of him, as if it could keep him afloat. He looked skyward and gasped for breath, as though he, too, found the air insufficient.

He looked destroyed, and I wanted to comfort him, but couldn't find the strength to reach out. He was breaking my heart.

"I didn't understand how much you meant to Brandon," Christopher said. "Or I never would have pursued you. He'll think I came between you, and I can't do that. He's my brother."

His voice broke.

"I waited too long to ask you out the first time and he asked first. I didn't want to make the same mistake and watch you move on with someone else."

He wouldn't look at me. The final words formed like bubbles rising to the surface. Inevitable that they would burst.

"I can't hurt Brandon. He was so excited to tell me he wants to marry you. You're amazing, so of course, he loves you. I can't destroy my relationship with my brother. For most of my life, he's all I've had. He'd be devastated. I'm so sorry."

I expected them, but the words still stabbed like a dagger to my heart.

"Before our relationship gets any more serious, we have to stop."

He still wouldn't look at me. For two perfect nights and the day in between, I'd been cherished and there was no going back. Brandon would never be enough. This had been real, but it was over before it had started. No matter what I said, Christopher wouldn't change his mind. Brandon was his brother.

"Maybe after enough time has passed." My last desperate grasp for hope—but he'd already slipped away. Either he didn't hear or he didn't want to answer.

We'd dropped Ember at home on the way, so I had nothing to carry. I escaped from the confines of the car. Tears streamed down my face and I couldn't speak. I sobbed so hard I couldn't catch my breath as I stumbled away.

At the edge of the park, I looked over my shoulder. His car was still parked, and he'd slumped over, his face in his hands. Building the bricks in my mind, I vowed to practice every day and keep him out. I sent one last message. He was trying to do the right thing and I should, too.

"It's for the best." The lie broke my heart.

Once out of sight, I collapsed to the ground and wept.

2017 was no better than 2022.

Chapter 8

Desolate after Christopher and I stopped spending time together, I wallowed for a few days. When I patched myself together, I forced myself to be practical. We'd had the best sex of our lives, but he wasn't my boyfriend. There'd been potential, but that was all we had—oodles of potential and insane chemistry.

I took a leap of faith and reached out to my friend Jeff back east. It hadn't been as long for him, and he answered right away, commiserating with me about my loss. His long-time boyfriend had cheated on him and they'd broken up, too. We made plans to get together later in the summer when he would come to town for a long weekend. His upcoming visit gave me something to look forward to. I'd missed having a friend and was excited to reconnect, but it wasn't like having someone nearby to talk to.

I fell back on what I always did in times of stress—I trained, worked in the lab, and read a mountain of books. In the evenings, I researched the company Brandon worked for and followed leads from his messages I'd intercepted. I emailed Benny Jacobs at the Reno address. Most nights, I read until exhausted enough to fall asleep. Sometimes I kept the nightmares at bay by concentrating on positive memories, but woke hot and sweaty with thoughts of Christopher that turned my insides to jelly.

Embarrassed after my conversation with my sister, I didn't want to explain what had happened with Christopher. I didn't want to voice that something I'd been so excited about had gone nowhere. I let my family think that a combination of work and Christopher kept me busy on three consecutive Sundays, but I noticed myself falling into the same trap as before. I was pushing them away, which wasn't my intention.

After this realization, I attended the next Sunday dinner without explaining Christopher's absence. Meghan asked, but I ignored her questions. I should've dealt with my feelings instead of suppressing them, but I was excellent at avoidance. Instead, I offered to help Meghan with her plans for the wedding next May. When she suggested I see a doctor regarding my missing voice, I shrugged. She wasn't pleased, but didn't say more that evening. She would bring it up again soon.

The silver lining to my life in this time was that Christopher had scared Eric away. That relationship was a mistake I wouldn't have to relive. I didn't expect to hear from Christopher unless it was news of Brandon's coma and he needed my help. Despite his avowal of love, I hadn't heard from Brandon either.

I avoided Christopher at work, coming and going at odd hours. Each time the elevator stopped on the fourth floor, I held my breath until I realized he wasn't there. Afterward, my heart ached, and I wondered how he was. I wanted to see him, but avoided him all the same. It must be difficult for him too. The pain in his face when I'd last gotten out of his car hadn't been hard to read.

I guarded my thoughts in the museum and found my control improved daily. I didn't know how far away he needed to be to read minds, so I didn't take chances. My cheeks flamed. Had my feelings been intrusive? At first, it exhausted me to imagine the bricks encasing my thoughts for long. It had been something I'd always done, but only for a few minutes at a time, not extended sessions. Blocking out thoughts of Christopher took practice. I couldn't turn off my feelings for him or my loneliness, but the wall helped me to cope.

Just as I had in 2020, when I first lost my voice, I switched all communication to email and made an appointment with my future therapist. I needed a note for HR that said I couldn't speak, but that I was working on recovering my voice.

I made the appointment via Zoom for a Thursday afternoon. It would be odd. Dr. Maeve wouldn't know me, but I missed talking with her, even if I was limited to the chat section.

At the appointed time, I logged in, looking forward to seeing her friendly, wrinkled face.

"Darling, you missed your last session," were her first words.

I frowned and shook my head. I had missed an appointment the day I'd time traveled and arrived in 2017. That couldn't be what she meant. That appointment was still in the future.

She shook a knobby finger at me, her unruly sunset glow curls bouncing. "Child, it doesn't matter what you're doing or where you are, you promised to keep your appointments."

I had promised this after the accident during my first appointment three years from now. In this time, I had promised nothing. We'd never met before now.

I was about to ask if she had me confused with someone else when she said, "Elizabeth, you might find this surprising, but I was trying to help. I admit, this type of therapy is unusual."

Her brightly painted eyes looked garish in the poor light of her office, and her wild clothes were as outrageous as usual, with three clashing scarves competing for dominance. She looked and sounded the same as I remembered. She'd always been unconventional, but I didn't know what she was talking about.

"What therapy? How are you helping?"

"You were miserable, and we weren't getting anywhere with our regular sessions," she said. "You were more entrenched in silence than ever, with no incentive to speak, so I sent you to the past. I thought if you saw you were the same years ago, that you don't face your problems, you'd learn that the real problem wasn't Brandon. Your problem wasn't Eric, and it wasn't from your car accident. It's not always possible to see what's real in front of you. You convince yourself of a different reality. You like being voiceless. It gives you power."

I clenched my teeth and shook my head, focusing on her revelation instead. Dr. Maeve had sent me to the past? That made little sense until, in a moment of clarity, I remembered the chunk of purple stone she'd given me, the one I'd clutched when I'd made my late-night wish. It didn't seem possible, but I was here and had to believe. I'd been so giddy at first about the possibilities, but I should have asked questions.

"I don't want to go back. But if I did, could you do it?" I was curious.

"You're not ready." Her bright red lips pursed as she stared into her camera, her emerald-green eyes seemed to expand. "Find your voice. You couldn't do it before, maybe it's possible in your past. If you decide to stay in 2017, it will be as though none of the later events happened, which is what you wanted."

"But I still can't talk."

"From your perspective, the events of your future have happened. You've lived through the trauma, and it can't be erased. Your marriage, the car accidents, they happened to you, but to no one else. You've gone back in time to a younger version of yourself. We've reset your clock to thirty. We'll see what choices you make this time. Maybe you'll wish for your old life, mistakes and all. If you return to your original timeline, this loop will disappear. You'll wake up and think it was a dream."

I shook my head. Even now, melancholy and lonely, I wouldn't give up the feeling I'd had with Christopher. He'd make me feel worth loving, even in a short time. It wasn't something I'd experienced before. I wanted to find that again. Plus, if I stayed, he might need my help with Brandon. Any day I expected to hear he was in a coma and my research would become useful.

"What do you need from me this week?" Dr. Maeve said, her voice changing to a brisk, professional tone. "I assume there's a reason you made this appointment, beyond getting one of my lectures."

"Documentation for HR about stress-related laryngitis."

"That's what you're calling it now? No longer trauma-induced selective mutism, I see." She typed something and then turned on me with a stern look.

"Anything else I should know about?"

This was an opening, but I didn't want to talk about Brandon and I couldn't talk about Christopher—it was too raw. *"I didn't go out with Eric, so I avoided the pitfall of my abusive marriage. No first date, sweet talk, or the wool pulled over my eyes."*

"That's progress and a divergence in your timeline. Was Brandon as perfect as you remembered? The one that got away?"

"I'm not in love with him anymore. I saw him and felt very little. Don't know what I was thinking. Compared to Eric, he was great, but that's too low a bar." I didn't tell her about Brandon's impending coma or the dinners with his brother. All roads led back to Christopher and my heartache.

"Until next time, Darling. Keep me posted."

I waved at Dr. Maeve as I left the conversation. She sent me the requested letter which I forwarded to HR. I didn't make my next appointment as I was accustomed to doing when I logged off. I wasn't sure I wanted to talk to her after all. I told myself I wasn't avoiding my problems. I just didn't want to share until they hurt less.

I walked home that evening by my usual route. On the way, I stopped to pick up groceries for dinner. One of my goals was to cook more for myself. I came around the corner into the produce section and saw Eric. I stopped in my tracks and my stomach lurched. My worst nightmare was in my local grocery store, holding a shopping basket. From a distance, he looked ordinary, not like an abusive narcissist. Why was he here? He didn't live in this neighborhood, unless it was a recent move.

I turned away, hoping he hadn't seen me. I circled back several minutes later, praying he would be gone. The produce section looked clear, but as I picked up a head of romaine lettuce, I sensed someone behind me and was enveloped in a cloud of Eric's too-strong cologne. He'd sauntered up behind me. The hair on the back of my neck stood up. He'd never understood personal boundaries. The voices of the other shoppers faded, and I focused on getting through this encounter.

"Elizabeth, isn't it? Meghan's sister."

His scratchy voice gave me the creeps. He should be dead. I tried to picture him lifeless.

Bile rose in my throat as I turned and nodded. I tried to go around him, but he shifted his body in front of mine. I'd have to shove to get past, but I didn't want to touch him. I prepared to drop the basket and run if he followed.

"Still can't talk, can you? That's too bad." He glanced around, scanning our fellow customers. The grocery store was dinner-hour busy with several shoppers in the vicinity. "I'll see you around."

His vicious smile turned my mouth into the Sahara. It was all I could do not to gag.

To an outsider, his words might sound friendly, but knowing him as I did, they were a threat. He didn't know me, but I knew his moods and his voice, having been married to him for almost three years. I'd learned to be hyper-aware of his movements and tone for self-preservation. He had no actual reason to talk to me in this timeline. I didn't know him. Our only contact had been at the engagement party.

His perception was that I was powerless without a voice, and therefore, intriguing. This so-called random meeting was familiar and disturbing. Chance encounters that were more than coincidence had followed the party in my old life as well. Once I'd found them cute, but now I found them frightening.

As I walked away, I broke into a sweat and willed myself not to run. Prey runs. I didn't want to be seen that way. I sensed his greedy eyes following my movement as I paid with my credit card. Goosebumps broke out and the hair on my arms lifted. I shivered. Outside, I gulped the cool evening air, trying to chase away the taste of fear. I'd held my breath through most of the conversation.

I hurried home and didn't relax until I was inside my townhouse. I locked the doors and checked that the windows were closed. Feeling silly, I did another round an hour later and checked again. I would keep the curtains and blinds closed when I was home from now on. Had he followed me? I struggled to sleep, tossing and turning as I passed another fitful night. It had been years since I'd slept well, except for the nights I'd spent with Christopher.

Two days later, striding through my neighborhood on the way to work, I was struck by an odd sensation. My skin crawled, and I sensed I was being watched. With my heart in my throat, I glanced in all directions, but couldn't find the source of the feeling. I kept a sharp lookout for Eric's red corvette, but in vain. The same prickly sense alerted me the following day. To shake the feeling, I varied my commute, finding a different route each day.

I returned home at odd hours in the evening but made sure I didn't stay at work too late. The outside light was on. I didn't want to be alone when few people were out walking. Eric hadn't shown up again, and I questioned myself, worried that I was suffering from paranoia.

Just when I was ready to dismiss my misgivings and told myself everything was normal, little things around my house went missing. First my favorite socks, then my pink thong underwear, and a book from my bedside table. I hadn't moved them, and no matter how hard I searched, I couldn't find them. Days later, the book reappeared, but without the bookmark.

Had Meghan stopped by to borrow something? She could have moved my stuff. Maybe she thought it was funny to move my organized belongings the way she'd mixed up my alphabetized paperbacks when we were teenagers, just to see if I'd noticed. I wanted it to be her, and she had the only other set of keys. The alternative was worse. Soon, something new disappeared every day. Nothing valuable, but it bothered me that so many things were lost or misplaced.

It preyed on my mind until the next Sunday at dinner, when I asked my sister.

"Have you stopped by my house? I can't find my fuzzy socks or my bookmark."

She laughed. "Welcome to the club. The rest of us lose things all the time. Forget where we put them. It's normal."

"I thought maybe you moved them as a joke. There's a bunch of things missing."

"You're making too much of this. I doubt anything is missing. Your favorite socks will turn up. Maybe the dryer ate them, that's what happens. So nice to find out that you, too, are fallible."

I asked no more questions for the rest of the evening. I hated being mocked.

I didn't bring up the missing items again for weeks, but I worried. I didn't have anyone else to talk to, and I had no proof, but things kept happening. I'd come home and the lights would be on, though I was positive I'd shut them off in the morning. Apples disappeared from the fruit bowl. At first, I wondered if I'd miscounted, but I stopped buying them so I wasn't feeding my stalker.

It came to a head the day I came home and Ember was outside on the back porch, mewing through the kitchen window. I never let her out. She was an inside kitty. I was grateful she hadn't run away, but I was now certain that someone had been in my home. None of it made sense. I was afraid I was losing my mind, and I avoided thinking about the alternative. I didn't want to consider that someone else had access to my locked house. I considered reaching out to Christopher, to tell him about my trouble, to ask for help, but we'd cut all contact and I didn't dare. I called a locksmith and had the locks changed.

Plagued by scenes of the accident, tormented by restless thoughts of Christopher, I relived the nights of Eric's abuse. He wasn't far from my mind, no matter how hard I tried to ignore it. I lost my appetite, jumped at shadows, and refused to answer the door unless I confirmed it was my delivery. I tried to tell myself it was in my head, but in my gut, I knew it wasn't harmless. It was Eric, and I was his target.

•   •   •

The next Friday was the day of the grand opening of my new exhibit on Human Origins at the Museum, my first major accomplishment. I'd have to see Christopher at the party that evening, even if I wouldn't have to spend time with him. My best defense was a gorgeous black dress and fake smile. I'd had the gown in the closet for months and twice I'd found the zipper from the garment bag undone. On the Sunday before the opening, I asked my family again.

"*Has anyone stopped by my place while I was out?*"

"Has your sock monster struck again?" Meghan laughed.

She re-enacted a routine she'd seen on a Seinfeld special about runaway socks, ones that hid against the dryer wall, waiting for their moment, then inched down the road as they ran away, heading for a puppet show.

Though I tried to remain calm, I was livid. She wasn't taking me seriously and worse, she made it hard for Dad and Andrew to consider the possibility. If things continued, I would speak to Andrew on his own. Maybe there'd been similar complaints in my neighborhood. As a police officer, he could check.

"*Will you all come to the gala at the Museum? I sent an invitation but you haven't replied. It's the official opening of my new exhibit.*"

"Sorry we haven't answered yet," said Dad. "Meghan said she'd take care of it."

Meghan had lived with him until a few months ago, when she'd moved in with Andrew. Dad always let her take charge of his social life. My face burned as I wished he'd think for himself for a change.

"We'll come if you tell us why Christopher is gone," Meghan said.

I couldn't believe she'd put conditions on their attendance. I didn't want to be alone at the party with no one to share my accomplishment.

"What happened? You two were smitten. I liked him."

"We aren't together." The pressure of tears built behind my eyes, but I willed them away.

"There has to be a reason," she said. "We've given you time, but you never tell us anything. You've gotten so thin and look tired and unhappy. Now you're jumping at every noise and looking for things in the shadows. We're worried about you. You need to stop bottling everything up inside. We should plan a girls' night."

"After the opening." I didn't want her third degree and hoped she'd forget. Maybe she'd be too busy.

I didn't want to explain, but days before the official opening when my family still hadn't RSVP'd, I gave in and sent a message to Meghan.

"Christopher and I can't see each other. Brandon had an engagement ring. Christopher is honorable. It's his brother."

"That's awful. You ok?" she said. *"Why didn't you say so before?"*

"I didn't want to talk about it. Respecting his decision. Could use some moral support. Please come to my opening Friday. Dressed up. Seven sharp? It would mean a lot."

"We'll be there. How's your voice? Did you go to the doctor yet?"

"The same. I can't talk."

"Go to the doctor again. It's been months. Laryngitis shouldn't take this long to heal. Don't be mad, but have you considered the possibility that it's in your head? What about a therapist? Maybe you need help."

I'd wondered how long it would take for her to ask again. She was a psychiatric nurse and worked at the hospital's psych ward. After what had happened with our mother, I didn't want her to think I was unwell. Maybe that was the reason for the strange look that had passed between Meghan and Dad after the engagement party. Mom had jumped at shadows and suffered from paranoia. Drinking had been her way to self-medicate.

"I have one." Although I hadn't talked to Dr. Maeve again, I would. I'd put it off, as I didn't know what to say. I didn't know how she could help with my stalker and I hurt too much to talk about Christopher.

I considered Meghan's suggestion, but a regular doctor would say it was all in my head. As far as the other stress, without proof anyone had been in my house or was following me, I wouldn't be taken seriously. I had no evidence to take to the police.

At seven, Meghan informed me she'd arrived with Andrew and Dad in tow, none of them being afflicted with my poor sense of time. They arrived fifteen minutes before I did. I changed upstairs, and it had taken longer than expected. I hadn't wanted to walk home and walk back to the gala in fancy clothes. Before my encounter with Eric, I had no fear of walking.

The reception was packed with guests, all dressed in their finest. Christopher appeared everywhere I went—his broad shoulders, his smile, his jaw. His laugh followed wherever I went. I missed him, even the idea of him. Once, the coffee and chocolate scent I associated with him drifted by in passing. I tried not to let it upset me. After three months of constant practice, my wall had become a brick monolith. I hoped.

I didn't need to worry about giving a speech, even if it was my exhibit. My boss, Mr. Brown, had agreed to speak on my behalf. He was the Museum curator and liked to hear himself talk. He droned on for a while to mark the occasion. I only had to smile and wave when introduced. Meghan and Andrew took care of the social talk, a two-person comedy show that entertained, and I stuck to them like glue so I wouldn't be alone. Meghan was the funny one, and Andrew was the straight guy. He'd deliver the naughtiest lines with a poker face, making them more outrageous than ever. Several times Meghan steered me away from Christopher, running interference, and I was grateful.

The guests walked through the exhibit, which started four million years ago with the first fossils and casts of the Laetoli footprints of the australopithecines who'd first walked upright on the savannas of Africa. They continued with Lucy and later examples, the branches of early hominids, some of whom led to extinction. It included the tool-using homo habilis, which evolved into us, modern humans. I was proud of the exhibit. We'd assembled an impressive collection of fossils and tied them into the more recent migration to North America by the First Peoples across the Bering land bridge, and by small watercraft down the coast. A gallery walk of human evolution. The story of continuing migrations.

At the end of the night, when everyone had gone, I slipped upstairs to collect my laptop and work clothes. I could have asked Dad or Meghan for a ride home, but I didn't want to explain that I no longer drove and that I used transit to get to and from Sunday dinner. There were things I hadn't shared. I ordered an Uber. It would be out front in fifteen minutes.

I headed back downstairs when the elevator stopped on the fourth floor. Wasn't I the only one left in the building at this hour? Christopher stumbled in. My heart pounded against my ribs. He was too big. The elevator became hot when he took up all the space. He'd been drinking and had a rosy glow, but even loose and disheveled, he was sexy as hell. In all the years I'd worked with him, including future ones that hadn't happened yet, I'd never seen him drunk. Until now.

I shrank against the back of the elevator, giving him room. I didn't want him, or even his clothing, to brush against me and test my control. For weeks, I'd been bracing myself for a chance meeting. I'd expected him to bring a date tonight, but I hadn't seen one. Small mercy. At close range, it was more important than ever to maintain my wall. I hoped he couldn't sense anything. Even drunk, he was beautiful and made my heart skip. I didn't want him to know how much his presence affected me.

"Can I drive you home?" There was a slight slur to his words.

"You can't drive." I couldn't believe he was considering it. *"Call a cab. Or get an Uber."* For emphasis, I repeated, *"You can't drive."* He couldn't be serious.

He glanced at his screen. "I'm fine. Just fine." He swayed as the elevator stopped in the lobby to let me out. "I don't live far." He shook his phone in my direction. "You can't tell me what to do." He laughed, though I'd said nothing funny.

"When did you get so stupid?"

"You know when," he said.

For all that he wore a charming smile, his eyes lacked their usual sparkle.

Did he mean going out with me, sleeping with me, or when he ended things? A smorgasbord of mistakes.

He held the elevator open and jangled his keys. "Coming?"

I snatched his keys and stalked out.

"Lizzie, wait up," he said as he followed me onto the sidewalk. "It happened almost two weeks ago. I wanted to call, but after what I did, I was scared."

"Scared?"

He didn't look at his phone, though it buzzed. I clenched my jaw. I hated to be ignored.

"You shut me out. All I see is a brick wall. Lots and lots of bricks."

Good, it was working.

"What happened?" He ignored the buzz again, and I held up my phone. *"I want details. I said I'd help."*

"You're so beautiful. I miss how you smell, like lemons and vanilla. Good enough to eat. And you're so smart. I can't do this without you."

He ran his hands through his wavy hair. He needed a haircut. Jamming his hands into his pockets, maybe to keep them to himself, he rocked back and forth on his heels. With his tie loosened and his shirt untucked, he was the picture of debauchery—and nearly irresistible.

His words chipped pieces of my icy heart, but most of all, I wanted to smooth down his hair where it stood on end. *"So, Brandon is in the coma, then?"*

He didn't answer and shoved his phone in his back pocket. End of discussion.

I gritted my teeth and looked at the night sky, wishing I had answers.

We waited on the empty sidewalk in front of the building—the other partygoers long gone. We had a problem. I couldn't leave him this way and I couldn't call him a cab. He couldn't walk home in this condition. His place was farther than mine. He wouldn't look at his phone, so I couldn't discuss it with him and my Uber would be here soon.

I didn't enjoy riding with strangers, but the feelings of distrust Eric had awakened meant I'd made an exception. This would be better. I wouldn't be alone. They could drop me at home, then the car could carry on to Christopher's. If he was serious that he wanted my help, we could meet on the weekend.

"We're going home tonight. Separate homes. Come over tomorrow. Tell me what happened then." He didn't so much as glance at his phone, but he would see my message in the morning. Or would he be too hungover to call?

I kept watch, but for once I was outside and hadn't felt Eric's eyes. Christopher babbled while we waited, but I didn't pay attention. I updated the car request to have two stops. When the compact car arrived, I needed assistance to load Christopher into the back. When he started talking about driving again and turned toward the building, I jingled his keys like bait, reminding him I had them. I was lucky that the Uber driver was tough and wiry. He shoved my tall friend into the back.

"It's always the big ones that drink too much." The driver looked in the rear-view mirror as he spoke. "You little ones take it easy. You're smart."

I smiled. He had kind eyes.

Christopher sprawled, taking up most of the backseat, and sat too close to me—practically on my lap—but it would be a brief ride. I returned his keys once the car was moving. He rested his hand on my bare leg and it burned. I looked away and bit my lip.

Outside my place, I nodded my thanks and paid in advance for the second stop.

Christopher leaned out the window, his arm resting on the frame. "She doesn't talk," he said to the driver. "She's a time traveler from the future and speaks a different language than us mere mortals."

The driver laughed. "That's a new one. Time travel."

Before the Uber left, Christopher flung open his door and stumbled out. He followed me up the stairs, hauling himself upward with the handrail.

"Lizzie, I have to talk to you."

"He's all yours, lady." The driver got out to close Christopher's door. "I don't think he wants to go home."

Despite his words, the man waited.

"Thanks for the ride." Christopher waved with big, exaggerated movements.

At the top of the stairs, he rested his hand on my lower back while I searched for my house key. It branded me with its heat. Electricity zinged through me.

The driver said, "You want me to come get him?"

I shook my head.

"The mean lady stole my keys and won't let me drive."

Christopher gathered my hair away from my neck and pulled it over my left shoulder, leaving the other bare. One finger traced a line from one shoulder to the other. I ignored his touch, though it shot through me everywhere.

"I'm not mean. I'm smart. You're in no shape to drive."

He ignored his phone. I wanted to strangle him. Was he doing this, so I'd lower my wall?

"Sure you're good?" said the driver.

I nodded. I appreciated that he'd stayed to make sure I was okay.

"Your girlfriend's smart, not letting you drive," said the driver. "She's a keeper."

This time, he got back in his car and left. I watched his red taillights to the end of the block. I hoped I wouldn't regret this. What should I do? Let Christopher sleep it off in my spare room, I supposed. I didn't love the idea, but was resigned.

It took forever to find my keys, even though I'd made an effort and turned my porch light on before the gala. When at last I got the door open, I pushed Christopher inside. He stumbled willingly. I removed his shoes and sent him into the master bedroom, alone. I did the rounds, checking the locks, but nothing was amiss.

Ember was asleep on my bed, curled up in a puddle of fuzz, soft and furry, beside the second pillow. She didn't twitch as I slid in next to her. I'd never seen a cat who slept so hard. She was always comatose after her dinner until morning. So much for felines sleeping with one eye open.

Though I was exhausted, my brain wouldn't shut off. I couldn't relax. I was desperate to learn more about Christopher's news about Brandon. It had made him upset enough to drink to excess. I'd been expecting news of the coma anytime for the last three months. I'd accepted that I couldn't prevent it as I was no longer in his life. Instead, I'd focused on learning ways to help afterward. I wished Christopher had answered my questions.

With Christopher in the house, I didn't dare let my guard down, at least until I was sure he was asleep. I didn't want him to know how much I yearned to be with him. It was all I could do not to slide into his bed and test his resolve. The memories of our nights together reignited. I craved his touch. He couldn't know. His ego was big enough.

The smell of bacon woke me, and I checked the time. I'd slept later than usual. Nightmare free. I hadn't realized how much safer I'd feel, just knowing I wasn't alone in the house. Following the scent, I hurried into the kitchen, hoping it wasn't a dream. Christopher had made tea and was cooking breakfast. He was dressed, but barefoot, in my kitchen. The grease popped and sizzled. He passed me a mug filled with steaming hot tea. His smile warmed me to my core.

I sat down at the table with my drink. I didn't know if I should start. What would I say?

"Look, I'm an ass," he said as he flipped the bacon. "Sorry about last night. I didn't know who else to turn to. Getting drunk and following you home wasn't how I meant to ask for help."

He cracked several eggs into a bowl and whipped them with a fork. Pouring them into the waiting pan, he said, "For all that we couldn't be together, we made a good team. You figured out that stuff with the venom. I tried to talk to Brandon about it again, tried to warn him, but he threw me out. That was three weeks ago, and he's been silent since. I feel it in my gut. You were on the right track."

I listened while I sipped my tea. My gaze followed his hands while he cooked so I could avoid his eyes. Bricks, bricks, and more bricks.

"Last Wednesday, I got the call from the hospital. They found him in his lab that morning, in an unresponsive state. One of his co-workers called it in. They called me, as next of kin." His voice cracked. "He's on a ventilator and they aren't sure he'll wake up."

"I'm sorry."

He glanced at his phone. "I know. The longer he's in a coma, the less likely he is to wake up. Or if he does, he might have a permanent brain injury."

I said nothing at first. We hadn't stopped him from injecting himself with his synthetic venom compound. We had no proof, but we suspected that's what he'd done.

"You could have called."

He shook his head. "I couldn't." He sat on the chair next to me.

"I said I'd help. I time traveled. This is one reason. Let me help."

He didn't answer at first. He was tight with worry and had dark shadows under his eyes. More than a night's worth of worry. I wanted to give him a hug. It was all I could do to stay in my chair. My heart rate increased with his proximity. Damn him. I reinforced the bricks in my mind. Imagined slathering them with extra mortar.

"Have you seen him?"

He nodded. "I went that day. It was a drug overdose, like you said."

"The drug overdose coverup by his employers. We've got to reverse it." When he didn't read my words, I slid closer and held my screen in front of his face. It put me in range and he squeezed me into a hug. I tensed, but put my arms around him and returned it, inhaling his scent. I'd missed him. The tight feeling that had lodged in my chest months ago lifted. We weren't together. This didn't solve our problem, but we could spend time together, working side by side to save Brandon. We could go back to being friends.

I let him hold me for a minute, then pulled back. *"I like my eggs dry, not burnt."*

He smiled, or at least attempted one. "Let's eat. It's the first round of my apology."

He dished up, and we ate breakfast. He broke off bits of bacon and, one by one, put them on the edge of the table for Ember to steal. It was easier to look at her than at each other.

"She's grown." He gave her the last chunk of bacon and met my gaze. "Would you come with me to the hospital? I need to confirm there's no change. I stop in to talk to him every morning. Then we can make a plan."

I nodded. Spending a few minutes talking to Brandon wouldn't change anything, but it might help Christopher feel like he was doing something. It was hard to be helpless.

"Feel like going on a road trip this weekend?" I said.

His eyebrows shot up. "A road trip where?"

"Reno."

Chapter 9

"What's in Reno? We don't need a quick divorce and I'm not in the mood for gambling."

"*A man named Benny Jacobs lives there. I found his address on Brandon's phone in May. He's an expert on venomous insects and reptiles and has a collection. I sent him an email earlier this month. He's free on weekends after five. His information might help us create an antidote. I can't synthesize bark scorpion venom or antivenom. He might supply some or know where we can get some.*"

I waited for Christopher to decide if he would come, then said, "*I didn't want to go alone and I wasn't sure how I was going to get there. I waited until after the opening at the Museum. If you say no, I'll take the bus next weekend. Down on Saturday, back on Sunday.*"

"That's a long way to go for someone who doesn't drive." He looked thoughtful.

I bit my lip and nodded. We hadn't discussed that I didn't drive. He'd been observant.

"Hours of driving."

I glanced down, my shoulders sagging. He was going to say no. That it was crazy to go that far to talk to a stranger based on a hunch. I'd tried to ask my questions by email, but Mr. Jacobs insisted I come in person.

"I can be back here and ready to travel within the hour. Can we stop at the hospital on the way?"

I looked up, surprised that he'd agreed. I'd expected to have to convince him. I wanted to jump up and down.

"Thank you." I smiled, thrilled that I would have help and support.

I hadn't given up on helping Brandon, but I had been reluctant to travel to Reno on my own. Christopher and I were better as a team.

"I can be ready. I'll let him know we're coming this weekend."

Christopher finished his breakfast and set his plate on the counter. "Sorry to leave you with the dishes," he said. "But my ride is here. Breakfast wasn't much of an apology after all. I still owe you. After I get my car, I'm going home to change my walk-of-shame clothes. I'll pick you up as soon as I can get back. That work?"

I nodded.

"Thanks for last night. I appreciate you taking care of me. I was in rough shape." He grimaced. "I haven't done that since college."

He hurried out. I relocked the door before I texted my sister.

"Can you come take Ember overnight? An unexpected trip came up. Going to Reno."

"Of course," came her reply. *"Everything ok?"*

"I think so." I appreciated that she'd agreed with so little explanation.

"You're going to need to explain everything at dinner tomorrow."

There they were, the strings. I sighed. She never changed.

Christopher returned in the prescribed amount of time. I wasn't quite ready, but he was patient while I finished. I'd showered and packed an overnight bag. As I made my bed, I found a folded note tucked under my pillow. My throat tightened, and I blinked back tears. I opened the paper to read, *"You looked fantastic in black."* I allowed myself a small smile. The writing looked familiar, but I couldn't place it. Maybe Christopher had hidden it for me to find. If he had, I couldn't bring it up. Our feelings were too raw.

Shrugging, I tucked the note into my jewelry box and finished packing while Christopher waited. Reno was too far for us to plan on driving home tonight. We'd find some place to stay.

Checking my phone, I read my reply from Benny, the critter guy. He didn't care when we arrived—this afternoon or evening, either way, he was free. He reiterated how important it was for me to see his specimens. I didn't understand the fascination with snakes, spiders, and scorpions.

Now that Christopher had showered, shaved, and changed, he didn't look worse for wear from his night of drinking, though he had a tightness between his eyes and tense set to his broad shoulders. The tension must be Brandon-related. I didn't know if I'd be able to maintain my mental shields for the ten hours I was about to spend with him in the car, but I'd do my best. I didn't want to force unwanted feelings on him. It would be unfair when he was trying to be honorable.

When we entered the hospital, I stopped. It smelled the same as it always did, a mix of antiseptic and scented cleaners to cover deeper organic smells. It triggered the memory of my last visit.

I sat in Emergency, my arm aching—likely broken—while I waited for treatment. My nerves jangled from the accident. My numb state of shock cushioned my grip on reality. I kept seeing the swirling red lights from the ambulance. My forehead cut stung from whatever the paramedics had applied. I watched while they wheeled Eric's body away on a stretcher. Visions of his angry face accusing me at impact floated in the air. They said they'd do what they could, but I'd seen his face. He was dead and not coming back. All I felt was relief and wonder. Somehow, I was still alive. I reached up to touch the cut on my forehead, right at the hairline.

I should have a slim scar, but my fingertips couldn't locate it. Another scar that had been erased.

I blinked and remembered why we were at the hospital. Christopher turned back to look at me with concern. I slapped the wall back up, certain it had slipped when my thoughts had jumped into the past. The vision had been too close to the center of my pain. He didn't know I was a murderer.

I sent him a sharp look, and he turned around, shoulders rigid. I was a jerk. Being at the hospital had to be horrible. We were here to see his brother, who was in a coma. It wasn't about me. I swallowed. Seeing Brandon wouldn't be a picnic for me either. Until a few months ago, I'd thought Brandon was my true love, the one who'd gotten away. His original disappearance had broken my heart, crushed my soul, made me doubt my gut. Proved I was right not to let anyone too close.

When I'd returned to this time, he'd been different than I remembered, colder, more clinical. Despite my efforts, he'd left me months before the coma. Maybe if I'd had more time, I could have changed his course of action. He'd left me without thought, thinking I wouldn't care. Like I hadn't mattered. For all his talk of loving me, it didn't feel like love. He'd taken me for granted. He might love some version of me, but he didn't know me if he thought I wouldn't be upset. Those years I'd spent wondering what I'd done wrong had been a waste of time.

Christopher took my icy hand, breaking my reverie. I squeezed, then let go. We weren't allowed to hold hands, but I wanted him to know I was here for him. Friends offering reassurance. He shot me a half-smile.

Brandon lay in his hospital bed, propped partially upright with pillows. There were tubes in his arm and a mask attached to the ventilator covered his face. He looked smaller, shrunken, and younger than thirty-two—the faint lines by his eyes had disappeared. Christopher sat on the chair beside the bed and lifted his brother's hand. The hiss and whoosh of the ventilator was the dominant sound in the room. I remained near the door, one foot on the threshold.

"I brought Elizabeth today," said Christopher. "We're on our way to track something down to help you. We know this wasn't an overdose, no matter what the doctors say."

He spoke in ordinary conversation tones, as if his brother might answer. He talked for another couple of minutes, telling him about a new beer he'd tried and the scores of the Mariners' game last night. He mentioned the Museum reception, but not that he'd gotten drunk and spent the night at my place.

Last time, I'd taken Eric to the gala, and he'd been on his best behavior. Though he wasn't terrific at socializing either, he'd tried. I blinked again. I hoped I'd never see him again. I hadn't seen him since the grocery store, but he'd been around. I shook my head. Thoughts of Eric were unwelcomed and intrusive.

"I won't be here tomorrow," Christopher told his brother. "I'm going out of town. Something unexpected, but I'll be here Monday."

We stopped at the nurses' station on the way back to the elevator. Christopher wanted to let them know that while they could reach him on his cell, he wouldn't be around. While he spoke to the head nurse, I spied two men stepping off the elevator. One was tall and thin, and the other was short and stout. They wore trench coats and fedoras, which was odd and like something from a stereotypical detective movie. They should have just worn signs that said, *"Hired goon."* It was a sunny September morning and felt like summer. They didn't belong, and I couldn't imagine anyone looking more suspicious.

They strolled toward us while Christopher rambled and I overheard the tall man say, "The boss told him human trials needed to start. Nobody thought he'd take it upon himself to be the trial."

I froze at his words, my ears straining to catch every syllable while I almost stopped breathing.

His companion said, "It puts us in a dangerous position. The boss isn't known for his patience. We're lucky he's preoccupied with another project."

I'd been right. Someone else was involved in this, someone who'd pressured Brandon. My back to the men, I pretended to be absorbed in my phone. I didn't want to attract their attention.

"Winters screwed us." The tall, crane-like man set his face in a scowl. "He's set the company back months, maybe longer, unless the boss can replace him or replicate his work."

Christopher finished, and we strode past the men and got on the elevator. Christopher pushed the button for the lobby, but I tapped the one to hold the doors open. He shot me a querying look with his eyebrows, in all likelihood wondering what I was doing. I wanted to hear more of the Brandon conversation. The mismatched men stopped at the nurse's desk and I tried to imprint their features on my brain. One looked like a crane, the other like a bulldog.

"What room is Dr. Brandon Winters in?" said the stout man.

"Oh, he's popular today," said the nurse. "It's smart of you to take shifts to see him."

I jammed the button to close the door, suddenly worried the men would look back or the nurse would point us out. I stabbed it twice more, willing it to hurry.

The short man glanced over his shoulder as the elevator closed.

I breathed a sigh of relief. I didn't think they had seen us.

"What was that?" said Christopher.

"They were talking about Brandon and know about his research. They said something about the boss not liking what he did."

Christopher's eyes narrowed, but he said nothing else until we were in his car. I glanced over my shoulder several times to see if they had followed us.

"Do you think it's safe to leave Brandon?" His voice was too loud.

"They want him to wake up and share his research. They won't hurt him. The sooner we help, the sooner these guys leave him alone. They wanted to confirm his condition for their boss."

He took a deep breath and changed the subject.

"Did you know Reno is at least a nine-hour drive? I looked it up."

I nodded and bit my lip. *"You still willing?"*

I expected him to change his mind. It was too far. I met his gaze. Up close, his icy blue eyes were more intense than I remembered. It was hard to breathe with his scent surrounding us in the car.

"I am. You think this will help Brandon? I trust you."

Relief flooded through me. I wouldn't have to make this trip alone.

He started the car. "You don't drive at all, do you?"

I shook my head as he backed out of his parking spot and we headed for the exit.

"Did you drive before the accident? Were you a comfortable driver?" He glanced sideways to see my answer.

I waggled my hand back and forth to indicate so-so. The lines by his eyes crinkled and some of his tension eased.

Christopher took a deep breath. "I haven't changed my mind. You're off-limits. I feel shitty about sleeping with you then ending things. I'm not a one-night-stand kind of guy. I was interested in more and you deserve better. It sounds silly, because we only spent a few days together, but I miss you. I've never told my secret to anyone else. It was satisfying to not hide who I am or what I can do. Can we try being friends?"

I nodded, thankful that he'd addressed the issue. It made my heart ache that we were nothing more than friends, but this was better than not seeing him. It would have been an endless road trip with nothing but bad radio or silence.

The drive could have been awkward with the one-sided conversation, but once the ice was broken, it wasn't. Christopher chatted about how much he liked my exhibit and what he'd learned from the display. He'd never heard of several of the hominids like Ardipithecus ramidus, Australopithecus anamnesis, Kenyanthropus platyops, and the various species of Paranthropus. I was impressed with his memory. His job focused on methods of preserving artifacts, not the displays themselves.

His driving was smooth and comfortable, and the trip was uncomplicated. I forgot to be nervous about not talking. Being with him was the same as before—he put me at ease. I'd never had to work so hard to maintain the image of a rigid brick wall for so long. I rubbed my temples, hoping to ease the tension.

We stopped at a McDonald's for lunch.

"This ok?" he said. "We can be quick and get back on the road, but I need to stretch."

I nodded.

Before Christopher stepped out, he took a breath. "I know what you're trying to do. To keep me from hearing your thoughts and what you're feeling." He glanced at my face to see how I was taking his comments.

I wanted to hear what he had to say, so I kept a neutral expression.

"It works, but it's too much. It's a strain. You won't be able to continue all day. You don't need to. We're going to be together all weekend and while I don't know your exact thoughts, I know you. Your thoughts won't hurt me. Besides, I can guess most of them."

I raised an eyebrow in query. Daring him to tell me.

"You missed me too, and your feelings haven't changed." His face was kind as he spoke. "Mine haven't either, but we're adults and we just have to cope. If you admire my ass again when we walk inside, I'll know from the expression on your lovely face, not because I read your filthy mind." His eyes twinkled and his dimple flashed.

I blushed. I'd admired his ass at the hospital but thought I'd been discreet.

"I'm your friend. I won't ravish you, even if I admire the way your skin glows in a certain light or the look in your beautiful brown eyes when you're teasing me. Please Lizzie, just be yourself. Can you do that?"

I released the image of the bricks with relief. I kept only the small mound at the heart of my mind that I never opened. Christopher spoke his mind like no one else. Even if we were just friends, this was something I appreciated. I wasn't good with empty talk or social situations. I liked his straightforward honesty.

"You talk a lot."

He laughed out loud, the first genuine one I'd heard in forever.

His laugh warmed me inside. I hopped out of the car and texted him my usual order, knowing he wouldn't mind. I inhaled the aroma of the parking lot, a crispy deep-fried smell that meant one thing. My mouth watered at the thought of the salty fries.

As predicted, lunch was quick, and we got back on the road. My headache dissipated with the lowered shields and food. It wasn't long before I fell asleep.

Chapter 10

It was late afternoon when I woke, my heart racing. I was sweaty and my stomach clenched with sharp pains. I'd dreamt about Eric and the first time he'd hit me. We'd been married for a month. I'd been late, as usual, for dinner downtown after work. He'd simmered and been abrupt at the restaurant, but waited until we arrived at home to release his anger.

He'd smacked my face without warning and split my lip—the sharp sound, the sting of my mouth, and the coppery taste of blood. Nobody had assaulted me before, and I hadn't known what to do. In my dream, Eric and Brandon had merged into the same person. He looked like Brandon, but Eric lurked beneath his skin, staring from his eyes—watching my every move. When he'd shoved me into the bedroom, forcing me to apologize from my knees, it had been Eric's voice coming from Brandon's mouth.

"Need me to pull over?" Christopher said with a sideways glance.

His mouth flattened in concern, and his worry radiated over me.

I shook my head and opened my window, feeling the wash of fresh air.

"He was an asshole," he said.

He confirmed that he'd sensed something from my dream.

"You don't need to see him. If you do, tell me. I promise I won't let him hurt you."

I considered texting my daily concern about being followed and the home invasions, but I still had no proof. I didn't want Christopher to think I was making up reasons for him to be nearby. I shoved my concerns aside, but without the bricks, Christopher had questions.

"You saw him again. Where?"

I held up a finger to show once. Shopping was the only time I'd seen him.

"Did he threaten you?" Christopher's voice growled.

I shrugged, then shook my head. I'd interpreted Eric's words as a threat, to someone else they might seem innocuous. Christopher didn't answer right away. I stared out the window.

Another few minutes passed as we drove and exited the interstate toward Reno.

"Why didn't you tell anyone?" He kept his eyes on the road.

"Who?" I said. *"Now or before?"*

He glanced at his phone when it buzzed. "Ever. Your friends, your family?"

"I don't have many friends. Even before I lost my voice, I was socially awkward, if you remember. I was too embarrassed to tell my family. He made me feel like I deserved it."

"That's not what you deserve," he said.

It looked like he had a lot more to stay, but he stopped himself.

He rubbed the back of his neck. "I'm stopping for coffee. Want something?"

"Tea with stevia, please."

He parked at a Starbucks and we got out.

While we were stopped, I sent him Benny's address—so he could get directions—and the list of questions to ask, so we were prepared. This was better than me handing the list to Benny Jacobs and not being able to speak. Meeting Eric at the party, then the store, had made me more aware that without a voice, I was vulnerable. Christopher was more than a driver or moral support. He was protection.

When we arrived in downtown Reno, the streets were packed. Several were blocked to traffic, and crowds of people filled the streets. I hadn't considered that it would be busy this weekend, given that summer was over. We circled several blocks before Christopher parked.

We sauntered the last few blocks, the smell of roasting meat in the air. There were *"Ribs"* signs in the windows of many of the restaurants, and a huge banner proclaiming this weekend: *"Best in the West Rib Cook-off"*. Jewelry tables, street vendors, and food trucks of all varieties lined the streets. Most advertised different ribs. Hot ribs, Buffalo ribs, spicy ribs, smoked ribs, and a multitude of sauces. I hoped it wouldn't be too long until dinner.

"Dinner is my treat afterward. Thanks for driving."

"This isn't a favor. Brandon's my brother. It's good to have a plan with action. I hate sitting and waiting, doing nothing but watching him in that bed."

From the distance floated the sounds of live entertainment, a keyboard and someone singing a haunting cover of *"See You Again."* The rap portion came in with a different voice. At the end of the block, I glimpsed a street performer juggling aboard a unicycle, riding backward and forward in a dizzying motion. It was a whole busy street fair downtown. I became concerned about where we'd stay the night. I hadn't made a reservation, figuring we could be spontaneous and get rooms somewhere. The trip was too long. We couldn't drive back today. It wasn't realistic.

"We don't have hotel reservations." A tight band circled my chest. I didn't like to make people mad. Christopher wasn't like that. He wouldn't hurt me, but I hated that fear was my first reaction.

"We can head back out of town, where it's quieter." He spoke with a gentle voice. "I'm not angry with you, Lizzie. We'll find something, don't worry."

I was grateful he understood, both the problem and the fear.

Benny's collection was advertised as: *"The Biggest Little Collection of Venomous Creatures."* The sign on the door read, *"Open 10-5 daily. Closed Sunday."* It was just after five, so I rang the bell as instructed.

Footsteps thumped inside as they descended a flight of stairs. Benny turned out to be about forty, with medium brown hair that begged to be cut. His bangs hung over his face, though it was short on top and long and shaggy in the back. His glasses swung on a lanyard around his neck. He wore gloves on his hands and carried a gun in a holster on his belt. I hoped it wasn't for dealing with his creatures. He hadn't shaved in a few days. On my own, Benny would have been intimidating. With Christopher here, I was unconcerned.

Benny peered out the glass of the door. When he saw us, he unlocked it.

"You must be Elizabeth." He peeled off his gloves, looking Christopher up and down.

I nodded and shook his hand.

Christopher stretched out his hand. "I'm Christopher. I work with Elizabeth. She has severe laryngitis, so she asked me to do the talking. I hope that's all right."

"Sure," said Benny with a shrug. "Nice to meet you, folks. Come on up."

He held the door open, and we started up the stairs while he relocked the door below and followed. The air inside was warm and filled with a musty smell I disliked, much like the reptile house at the Seattle Zoo. To me, the smell meant snake.

Terrariums lined three walls, while larger floor tanks with lids divided the rooms into sections. The fourth wall had a desk and several windows with natural light. In one tank, seven or eight large rattlesnakes slithered over each other, their patterned scales creating an optical illusion that was mesmerizing to watch.

I recognized Gila monsters on one side. Smaller terrariums contained a variety of spiders, according to the signs. I couldn't see the arachnids from this distance. The odor was stronger here. It was easy to imagine pokey little spider feet crawling on my skin. I shivered and stayed as far from the walls and tanks as possible.

"You asked about the Arizona bark scorpion," Benny said. "I've got seven. They're rare these days. They collected too many in the name of science in the past."

We peered into the indicated enclosures. The yellowish-brown bark scorpions varied in size. Two were less than an inch in length, while the largest was as long as my hand. I shuddered. Insects or arachnids that size were terrifying, more like monsters than bugs. I looked to my left, where more large glass tanks contained snakes. They were labeled cottonmouths, copperheads, and coral snakes. Nearby were the Gila monsters and Mexican beaded lizards with their slow alien movements, and claws splayed out in the sand. I tried to look away, but there was nowhere that was creature-free.

They'd filled the far wall with shelves containing smaller terrariums, each one housing spiders, mostly tarantulas. Spiders like these starred in the horror movies in my mind, though I avoided actual scary movies.

These tarantulas were behind glass. I was safe, but I hated it here. It was too warm and made me feel sticky. And it stunk. I couldn't help but imagine what would happen if the creatures got loose. My eyes darted from place to place, scanning for creatures that might have escaped on their own. Christopher shot me an amused glance. Right now, the inside of my head was probably a riot.

Christopher had memorized the questions and asked them through conversation.

"This is quite a collection. I've never seen so many venomous creatures in one place before. How deadly are the snakes to handle? I remember seeing TV shows that made it look like they're more docile than we think."

"Most people, like me, who handle snakes keep antivenom nearby—as do hikers in the desert or swampy areas where corals and cottonmouths live," said Benny. "I'm careful, but you don't take chances."

"I've never heard of cottonmouths." Christopher looked at the tank where several swam in the water and another twined around a branch in the corner, half in and half out of the water. Its tongue flicked out, tasting the air in my direction.

I suppressed a shudder.

"Another name is the water moccasin." Benn lifted one from the water with a metal hook and the snake twined around his arm.

I couldn't stand to watch and looked away.

"Could it kill you?" said Christopher. "If it bites?"

His blue eyes watched the snake, intent on keeping out of its striking range. He didn't step back, but I did. I wouldn't take chances. My sweat glands were working overtime.

"Their venom keeps blood from clotting, right?" said Christopher.

His questions were close to the ones on my list, but reworded when necessary. The anti-clotting was something I'd wondered about from a book called *The Yearling* that I'd read as a teen.

"That's right." Benny deposited the snake back in the water, where it glided away in the tank. "I'm careful. I've got antivenom. Different for each species."

"Does anyone have a use for venomous snakes?" said Christopher. "Besides zoos and displays or collections like yours."

"Not really," said Benny. "Unless you count the Pentecosts."

"Who?" said Christopher.

This was news to me. I'd heard about the "Shakers" in the seventeenth and eighteenth century and figured that snake-handling religious groups were a thing of the past. Made sense that they mostly died out. Since they'd let venomous snakes bite them on purpose.

"Pentecosts. Religious groups who handle snakes, usually copperheads. They're mostly in the Appalachian region, but there's a chapter in this area. Their Church has been accused of mistreating the snakes, not watering them, so they dehydrate and become more docile, less likely to strike. Makes their venom weaker. Handling snakes is supposed to prove their faith in God that they won't be harmed."

Benny curled his mouth when he talked about them. He wasn't a fan. That spoke well for how he believed snakes should be treated. For all I didn't like them, I didn't believe in animal cruelty.

"How long do snakes live in captivity?" said Christopher.

"About twenty years," said Benny. "The article said Pentecost snakes only last three to four months. I won't sell to them."

"How serious are the bites without antivenom?" Christopher circled back to what I wanted to learn from an expert. Information online was varied and often contradictory.

"Painful," said Benny. "Sometimes fatal if not treated. Depends on the size and age of the individual. There's a reason they make antivenom."

"What about the spiders?" Christopher waved his hand toward the tarantulas.

My eyes followed one, and its slow movement across its heated tank. Its fur looked redder than the ones I'd seen before. They could be quick when hunting. I remembered camping and playing Jenga at the picnic table in the dark when I was young. When the tower fell, pieces fell under the table. Dad moved the light so I could collect them, and seven or eight tarantulas had been under the table. They'd been there all along. Seeing so many tarantulas brought back the memory.

"With the smaller spiders, often people don't know they've been bit," said Benny. "Varies from itching, swelling, and pain, to occasionally death if untreated."

"No radioactive spider bites, though."

Christopher looked relaxed, in his element talking to someone. He leaned in to listen to Benny, his body loose and comfortable. I envied that ability. I'd always had trouble talking to strangers.

Benny laughed. "Yeah, no Spiderman."

This was closer to the truth. It hadn't been on my list, but it wasn't far from what Brandon may have been trying to create. Using venom to give someone abilities. Christopher was smart to lead the conversation in this direction, just to gauge Benny's reaction.

"For the scorpions, how long does the venom effect usually last?"

"About seventy-two hours," said Benny. "But it depends on the concentration, the size of the sting, and the victim. For an adult human, they'd have numbness, tingling in affected regions, vomiting.

If the victim had a powerful reaction, like an allergy, they could lose consciousness, maybe permanently."

Benny's words stuck with me. Perhaps Brandon was having an allergic reaction to the venom in his serum. I wanted to interrupt in my excitement, but Christopher was on a roll.

"Why collect these?" Christopher indicated the surrounding room. "No offense intended. I'm just curious. It's an impressive collection and I can tell you take care of your creatures."

Benny, who'd started to hackle at the question, settled with Christopher's final statement.

"I've always thought they were cool and misunderstood. They get a bad rap." Benny glanced around the room and nodded.

His pride in his collection was apparent. He'd wanted us to see them because he was proud and he wanted to share his interest.

"Is there still a market for their venom?" said Christopher, "And if so, what outfits buy it? Labs? Universities?"

"Pretty select now. Mostly companies doing medical research, though they can synthesize their own from DNA coding. They like to have authentic samples from time to time. Maybe to compare it to the fake stuff?"

"They make synthetic venom?" said Christopher, pretending this was news.

"Yeah, it's pretty new, ground-breaking," said Benny. "Lots of medical research uses venom."

"That's interesting," said Christopher. "Could someone inject venom into a human and cause a permanent change to their nervous system?"

"No way." Benny laughed. "Just in science fiction. We're back to Spiderman territory. Even in comics, it was accidental. As far as I know, all the research is medical. Now that they can make the fake venom, they're experimenting on treatment for diseases like cancer."

Unless he was a convincing liar, he knew no more than we did about the lab tests for the military.

"We appreciate you answering our questions," said Christopher. "Any idea where we could buy antivenom?"

Benny narrowed his eyes, looking between us. "Who did you say you work for?"

We hadn't discussed it, but Christopher told a portion of the truth.

"We work for the Portland Museum of Science and we're thinking of putting together a display. Nothing living, of course," he said. "We wanted to see a bunch of the venomous reptiles, spiders, and scorpions that are native to North America. Ask an expert some things we'll get asked by our boss or include on the display plaques."

His ability to ad-lib his answers amazed me.

"If you make the exhibit, let me know. I would come to see that." Benny walked to the counter and collected one of his business cards. He wrote something on the back and removed a different card from inside his desk.

"That's my cell phone," he said, pointing to what he had written. "So we don't have to trade emails. In case you want advice on that display. The second card is for a supplier that sells antivenom. You can order online. It can take a while for him to fill orders."

"Thanks for your time. We'll call if we have more questions."

"Go ahead. I like you better than the other guys from Portland who came a few months ago. From some lab. Tall guy and a short one. They wanted to buy all my scorpions and I wouldn't sell. Too hard to get more, they're rare.

Christopher and I glanced at each other at the description.

Benny handed the cards to Christopher. "But you two are all right, even if she hates my beauties."

I shrugged with a smile to show I couldn't help it. They both laughed.

Benny showed us out and locked the door behind us.

Out of the musty snake air, I took several deep breaths to clear my lungs.

"Want to walk? Get ribs for dinner?" Christopher jammed his hands into his pockets. "You were thinking about a Jenga game. Care to share that story over dinner?"

I nodded and smiled.

We wandered downtown Reno for about half an hour. It was pleasant to stretch my legs after all day in the car, though there wasn't much of a view. We found a place we could sit on the patio and enjoy the late summer evening. We ordered a variety of ribs and sauces to compare and rate, equivalent to ordering a flight of beer. Christopher ordered a pint of craft beer but was content to nurse it through dinner and didn't order another. Counting drinks went back to my childhood—it was involuntary.

While we waited for our food, I looked up hotels near the highway that led home and after several minutes of searching, found one with vacancy. I booked two rooms online and breathed a sigh of relief. With that settled, I enjoyed dinner when it arrived.

It was comfortable around Christopher. He did most of the talking, but encouraged me to text and explain from time to time. He didn't treat me like that was strange and pushed me to participate.

"Time for Buffy, then sleep?" he said. The sun had set while we'd finished dinner.

I nodded. I liked that our evening wasn't over.

Chapter 11

Christopher and I found our hotel on the outskirts of Reno. I was relieved I'd booked something, though it had been last minute. All the places we passed had bright neon *"No Vacancy"* signs lit, as did this one. Who knew ribs were so popular? Or perhaps gambling was a regular draw that kept the town busy.

It was a standard chain hotel with the faint scent of lemon cleaner and a hint of old smoke in the air when we entered. They'd decorated the lobby in shades of burgundy and yellow-gold, a generic look reminding me of other hotels where I'd stayed. We brought our bags with us as we'd limited our luggage to one small bag each.

Christopher sauntered up to the counter and said, "We reserved two rooms. Under the name Elizabeth Bergstrom."

"Oh," the clerk said with a blush. "I have some bad news."

I didn't like where this was going. He avoided looking at me, but his eyes twitched in my direction as he spoke.

"You see, it's my first solo shift, and I made a tiny mistake. I gave one of your rooms away, just after you booked online. The system said 'Pending' and I didn't know what that meant. I hit override. The other couple has already checked in. One room is still reserved. You can have that one. I'm so sorry." He took a deep breath.

"What kind of room is left?" Christopher's voice was flat, without inflection. Not like his usual friendly sound. The look on his face made the young man squirm. Christopher glanced in my direction. His eyes looked harried, panicked.

I could relate.

"A Queen single," the young man swallowed. "One bed," he clarified.

I wouldn't mind rooming with Christopher if necessary, but sharing a bed was unacceptable.

"Is there anything else?" said Christopher. "A king or a suite or a fold-out couch? A cot you can send to our room? We're colleagues. This is awkward."

The poor clerk shook his head. He looked miserable. "We're totally full with travelers for Rib Fest. I tried to fix it. I called around, but everybody was full. The rooms were only available because we had a last-minute cancellation." His voice broke a little. "I have coupons. I can give each of you a free two-night stay this year at any of our locations. Please don't tell my manager."

He produced the vouchers. We didn't take them, so he set them on the counter. The kid looked like he might cry. I didn't want to feel sorry for him, but he was just a kid who'd made a mistake. I clenched my teeth and took a few deep breaths. No point in showing anger.

Christopher turned to me. "I can't drive back tonight. I'm beat. I haven't been sleeping."

I picked up the coupons, but they didn't solve our current problem.

It wasn't fair to be a jerk about staying. Christopher had done all the driving—it was his call. *"We should stay."*

I paid with my credit card and tried not to worry about the sleeping arrangements.

Christopher put out his hand. "Keys please."

"Room 315." The clerk pointed to the elevator nearby.

The young man looked relieved we hadn't made more of a fuss. He passed Christopher the key cards in an envelope with the Wi-Fi password.

"Breakfast is down here from six am until ten every day. Just down the hall."

In the elevator, I said, *"I'm sorry. I should have booked something from home."*

"Not your fault," he said. "Next fact-finding mission, we'll be sure and check accommodations. It didn't occur to me it would be so busy, either."

It was kind of him to let me off the hook. I smiled a nervous smile.

The room was standard. Nothing fancy, but at least it was clean.

"You're tied in knots." Christopher sat on the edge of the bed and kicked off his shoes. He leaned back, stretched, and groaned. "That feels amazing."

"I could sleep on the floor," I said, looking around the room for a likely spot.

He glanced at his phone. "Don't be stupid. Hotel floors are gross. Notice I'm not offering to sleep there. I won't bite."

As I wiggled my toes, I raised an eyebrow and kicked off my sneakers.

"I won't touch you. You're safe with me." He sat up.

"That's not what I'm afraid of." I was worried about what I might do. Not him.

He doubled over, laughing until his eyes watered.

It seemed more release than mirth.

"You don't think you're funny, Lizzie, but you're hilarious."

My eyes narrowed, but I couldn't be angry at his good humor. I liked that he was seldom down or moody. He exuded positivity.

"I love that you're worried about taking advantage of me. I'm twice your size. If I can resist temptation, so can you."

He sounded like he was trying to convince himself.

"Temptation?"

"Don't bother fishing for compliments. I'll give them freely, but I can control myself."

I said nothing. Could I?

"C'mere." He patted the bed beside him and scooted back. "Come sit. Relax. Watch TV. Friends can sit together. You can even lean on me, and I won't think you're seducing me. I'll even let you massage my feet," he said with a wink.

I grimaced but sat beside him, trying to leave a little space. He was right. It felt fantastic to stretch my legs on the comfortable bed and relax. We propped ourselves up with the extra pillows and leaned back. Christopher draped his arm across the top and pulled me against him. Tears filled my eyes at his touch. He remembered how much I craved physical contact. Perhaps he did too. I lived apart from most people, keeping them at arm's length, even my family to a certain extent. He was the exception, but it meant that even at the cellular level, I was lonely.

When I glanced upward, he looked down.

He kissed my forehead. "Me too." He picked up the remote, found Netflix, and signed in. "Did you watch any more?"

I shook my head. I hadn't wanted to watch without him. It had been better with his company. Tonight, we watched four episodes of Buffy: Amends, Gingerbread, Helpless, and a hilarious episode, called The Zeppo, which was told from a unique character's point of view and had a quirky soundtrack.

At its conclusion, we took turns getting ready for bed. I was nervous and uncomfortable with restless energy. I hadn't brought pajamas for sleeping because at home I slept wearing nothing. Tonight, I wore a T-shirt and underwear. Christopher stripped down to his boxers, ones with red hearts. I raised an eyebrow.

"Brandon's idea of a Valentine gift," he said, looking down. "Not a woman."

"*I wasn't jealous.*" I looked away as my face warmed. They left little to my imagination.

"Yes, you are," he said, "But it's cute."

He moved his pillows and settled in, and I tried to do the same. We left as much space as possible between us on the bed, an uncrossable chasm.

I didn't fall asleep at first, and from his breathing, neither did he. After an hour of silence, I faked falling asleep, making my breathing slow and even. I drifted off, Christopher awake beside me. Within arm's reach, but far away.

• • •

When I woke sometime later, I wasn't sure why. Most nights, once asleep, I was a deep sleeper. Once as a child, a migration of red ants had marched in a swath a couple of feet wide through the house, covering surfaces as they went, creating an orb of glowing red as they crossed the globe of my basketball-sized night light. In the morning, I'd thought it a dream until I found scattered miniature corpses, scorched by the heat.

This feeling of unease was similar. The brain's primary job is to keep us alive, and it remains aware, even when we sleep. I woke, because something was wrong. It took me a minute to realize what. Christopher must have felt me awaken and was pretending to sleep, but he was crying. My heart went out to him. Somehow it seemed worse when a man cried, though it shouldn't. Crying was private, and he probably didn't want me to know. Perhaps he didn't want me to think less of him, though of course tears couldn't affect my opinion of him. I wasn't sure what to do, but I considered what I'd want if it was me, crying alone in the night.

With our phones away, I couldn't communicate. Dim light from the clock radio and from under the door in the hall made the room gray instead of pitch black. As an experiment, I reached across no-man's-land, finding Christopher's smooth, warm skin.

He stiffened at my touch, then apologized, his voice a rough whisper that shredded me.

"I didn't mean to wake you. Sorry to be a bother."

"You aren't a bother," I said in my head, hoping he heard. I sensed his pain when I concentrated. He was distraught. I didn't know how that happened—perhaps it related to his abilities. I slid closer and wrapped my arms around him. I wasn't a hugger, but he needed one.

"Tell me." When I didn't receive an answer, I put my mouth near his ear and whispered in my softest voice, a sound only for him. They

were the first words I'd chosen to say to another person in over two years. "Tell me."

"I'm scared." His voice cracked. "Scared to be alone. My mother and father—the Winters—moved to Florida, and now Brandon could be gone. I'm an adult and shouldn't care, but I'm alone."

I hated his birth parents for scarring a little boy, for leaving him and making him believe he wasn't worthy of love. "I won't leave you." Once more a whisper just for him.

"I can't have you." His voice was quiet, but thick with emotion. "Brandon means too much. I can't risk it. I just can't."

I rested my hands on either side of his face and kissed him. The softest kiss I could, not sexual, but filled with love. He was a kind man and a wonderful brother. He deserved more.

"I promise not to leave you," I whispered on his lips as I had once before. "I'll make you a deal. Until Brandon is awake, I am yours. I'll never be his, but he'll never know it's you I want." It would play with fire, but I wanted us to have the happiness we could.

When Christopher's lips claimed mine, it wasn't gentle. He left me breathless and rocked me to my toes. My skin tingled everywhere.

"Deal." He rolled on top of me, pinning me to the mattress with his solid weight. "I need you." He ground his hips against me and I ached for him.

"Please," I whispered. "I'm yours."

I expected more hard kisses, our mutual attraction taking over an inferno of our heat, but his fingers were tender as he caressed my face, his lips soft as we kissed, his tongue gentle as it met mine. His hand slipped under my T-shirt, sending shivers throughout my body, warmth at my core. My body arched toward him, his hands leaving a trail of fire. He removed my shirt and traced circles on the sensitive skin of my breasts. I wanted to claw him apart, satisfy myself at once. Instead, I followed his lead. Everything was slow, patient, and thorough. I became drenched and whimpered. My body craved his and I couldn't hold still.

Our underwear did nothing to prevent me from feeling his arousal. His kisses were slow, but deep, and caused flashes of heat throughout my body, desire igniting my passion. I couldn't feel anything but him and time passed without me being aware. I wanted to do this forever.

"I can't wait longer. I ache for you. I've thought about this a million times." His voice brought me back to an awareness of more than his touch.

There was a ripping sound I hadn't expected. A surge of victory washed through me. He'd brought condoms. He hadn't been so sure he could resist me after all. He growled and slid off my underwear and flipped me onto my stomach with a gentle swat at my naughty thoughts. When he touched me from behind, I gasped as his fingers slid into my swollen wetness. First one, then two, sliding in to the hilt. It was electric.

"Still delicious," he said, sliding his fingers inside again.

He'd tasted me and I trembled all over. When he entered me, it was exquisite. Each slow, powerful stroke made me cry out, not with pain but pleasure. I was on the brink from the first thrust and when his release came, I came with him, our bodies and minds in perfect accord. Shaking even when it was over, he kissed my cheek and jaw.

"What am I going to do with you, Lizzie?" He nuzzled my neck and kissed its nape.

He sounded less sad.

"Whatever you want." I flipped over and kissed him again. We fell into an exhausted sleep, tangled together in the middle.

● ● ●

We woke early the next morning. I would have liked to linger in bed, marveling at Christopher's hard muscles and how nice it was to touch him, but we had to get back on the road in order to make dinner with my family. It seemed odd to be up so early when we didn't have work. The sky was a sea of orange and pink clouds through the window.

At breakfast, I said, *"Will you come to Sunday dinner?"* In the light of day, I was back to texting instead of talking. Whispers in the dark were progress. Dr. Maeve would have been encouraged.

At his hesitation, I said, *"They invited you before. I promised to go. I need to pick up Ember."* He adored my kitten, so mentioning her was a dirty trick.

"What do they know?" He looked down.

"That you backed off because of your brother. I told them about the ring. You're honorable, not mean. They don't know how hard it's been." I looked down at the table. Tears pricked at the back of my eyes, but I willed them away.

"You shouldn't shut them out," he said. "You have family, they care."

I nodded. I didn't want to hurt them and push them away. They deserved better. I was trying to be better than before, but it was difficult when I couldn't tell them the whole truth.

"Maybe Andrew can help investigate. He has contacts. We can ask about Brandon's work and about the men from the hospital."

"It might be dangerous. Should we involve anyone else?"

"He's the police. His job is already dangerous."

Christopher nodded. "What about us? How should I act? Like a friend? Or can I hold your hand around your family?" He traced circles on the back of my hand.

"Be yourself. We're together now. They won't judge."

"Like hell. They will, but I don't want to keep my hands off you or pretend we're not together. Now that I've started, I can't stop. I've wasted three months of groping."

I laughed and took a last swig of my tea, grimacing at the taste of bitter hotel tea. Christopher had turned up his nose at their coffee, saying he'd get one on the road.

"I understand, you know. I want to touch you all the time, too."

"I know. You're as bad as I am, but I have to admit, it impressed me how well you shut me out. I couldn't feel you at work. Less than ever before. I don't want to see those damn bricks again. I hated them, but I was proud of you."

My hand tingled where he touched it, and I leaned forward to kiss him.

"Will you stay with me tonight?"

His thumb stroked my bottom lip, and I trembled. "You couldn't make me leave."

He stood up. "Let's get better coffee and tea and hit the road. We need to leave now to make it in time for family dinner. If we don't check out, I'll have to take you back to bed."

I got up to follow, feeling warm inside at his words.

The car ride felt faster on the return trip, though I stayed awake. Christopher talked about his favorite movies and I communicated with head shakes and hand signals, except when we stopped for lunch. I rated movies with my fingers. The Princess Bride was a ten. We agreed The Empire Strikes Back was also practically perfect. We liked many of the same movies and decided we needed to have a Star Wars marathon. Making plans was exciting.

It was just after five when we pulled in at my dad's house. I'd texted Dad and Meghan in advance to let them know to expect Christopher.

Meghan had replied, *"I hope you know what you're doing."*

When we got to the door, I hesitated, about to knock. I hadn't brought someone to Sunday dinner in years. Eric hadn't wanted to come. Neither had Brandon, though he hadn't minded when I came alone. Maybe I should just go in. Before my hand touched the door, Meghan solved my dilemma by flinging the door open.

"Thank goodness you're here. We need you to solve an argument."

She grabbed my arm and towed us inside.

"Nice to see you again, Christopher. It's been a while. The nice thing about someone else being in charge of time is that my sister isn't late." She looked pointedly at our joined hands. With a bright smile, she said, "You break her heart, I'll break your face."

At five foot three, it wasn't likely, but she meant what she said and I appreciated the sentiment.

"What if she breaks mine?" he said, stepping into the kitchen.

That stopped her for a second. She glanced at me with a slight frown.

"You're both crazy. You want my advice? Keep it simple, stay together. You adore each other. That way, everyone is happy."

We looked at each other. I watched Christopher's eyes. She amused him.

"If Brandon has any sense, he'll see that in one second," she said.

A cloud darkened Christopher's face, but he didn't release my hand. Instead, he tightened his grip.

"What's the argument? The one you need me to solve."

"Right. Dad says we went to the beach for the summer of 1997. I say he's wrong. We went camping in California that year."

"You're both wrong. We stayed home. Too soon after mom died. We went to the coast in 1998 and went camping the next summer. I have photos upstairs if you need proof."

"I'm going to tell Dad I was right." She winked as we reached the kitchen.

Dad turned from slicing tomatoes. "What's the verdict? Coast or camping? How's the throat?"

"She's still having trouble, sir." Christopher released my hand and went forward and shook my dad's. When done, he stepped back and rested his hand on the familiar position of my lower back. It belonged.

"Elizabeth looks smug, so I assume she knows the answer to Meghan's question."

"She can't remember," said Meghan.

"Liar. We stayed home that year."

I held my phone up for Dad to read the explanation. Meghan stuck out her tongue. She hated when I was right. Time stood still here. It felt easy and familiar.

Dad laughed. "You girls never stop. Andrew should be here any minute. He was working. He'll be glad for a new referee."

We talked in the kitchen while Dad trotted back and forth to the grill outside, bringing it up to the optimal temperature. Sunday dinner was his favorite, and we weren't allowed to help. He hadn't cooked when I was young, but after mom died, he'd learned. He discovered he enjoyed it. Tonight's menu looked like steak, baked potatoes, grilled vegetables, and green salad.

"*At dinner, will you help me explain?*" I said to Christopher.

He nodded and kissed my temple.

"You're just talking to Christopher," said Meghan with a pout. "You need to have a group chat and share with us, too."

"*It'll be a lot faster if Christopher explains. If he's wrong, I'll interrupt.*"

"Too bad you didn't get laryngitis years ago," she said.

A scowl crossed my face.

"You've always hated talking to people. Not us," she corrected, "but people." She waved her hand to indicate the public.

She had a point, but this hadn't started by choice. A car door slammed out front.

"Andrew's here," she said, running for the door.

After all these years, I had yet to see my sister slow down. She was a whirlwind of energy. It made me tired to watch her in action. In 2022, my three-year-old nephew Drew kept her on her toes, but she loved it. We hadn't talked, but she'd sent photos every few days.

Andrew wore his police uniform as he'd come straight from work. "Hey Pop, hey Elizabeth." He nodded at Christopher. "We've missed you at dinner these last few months. Meghan was about to send me with the squad car to pick you up."

Meghan swatted his shoulder and handed him cutlery to set the table. "Make yourself useful."

Andrew didn't move, but kept talking.

"Sorry we didn't see you at the reception the other night," he said.

He'd seen Christopher at the bar. They hadn't spoken.

Despite his friendly words, Andrew's manner was cooler than at the engagement party, and his eyes cut to us holding hands. I didn't need his protective big brother act. I knew what I was doing, I hoped.

Christopher said, "I can see some explanation is in order. I don't want there to be hard feelings. I talked to my brother the Sunday after we were here for your party. He'd broken up with Elizabeth. I thought they were finished, or I never would have moved so fast. That's on me." He shook his head.

Dad stopped chopping to listen.

"Brandon had an engagement ring on his desk. Said he planned to get back together with Elizabeth when his project was done."

Christopher glanced down at me and I shook my head. I wouldn't have said yes. I knew better now. Brandon wasn't the man for me. With him, I'd always be alone, and I needed more.

"I ended things with Elizabeth. He's my brother. I couldn't get in the way."

"What changed in three months?" said Meghan. "She hasn't heard from either of you. Doesn't seem like you or Brandon are that interested in a relationship."

Christopher and I exchanged looks. We'd agreed to talk to Andrew, not my whole family. I shrugged and showed with my head that he could proceed.

"Brandon's in a coma. Elizabeth and I are working together to find out why. He was involved in something dangerous at work and was pressured to perform human trials with something unproven and unsafe. We believe he injected himself and had an adverse reaction. The doctors aren't sure he's going to wake up."

"I'm so sorry, son," said Dad.

Most of the time, Dad stayed on the fringes of the conversation. For Christopher's sake, I was grateful for his words.

"What happens if your brother wakes up?" said Meghan. "What about you two, then?"

I wished she'd let it go. I wanted to talk about the venom, not my love life.

"We don't know if he will," Christopher said. "I know this might not make sense to you, but Brandon being in a coma, made me re-evaluate what's important in my life. If Lizzie and I can be happy, I want to try." He turned to me. "If he wakes up, I'll talk straight with him, tell him how I feel. He'll have to understand."

This was news to me. My heart swelled. He would talk to his brother about us?

"I can understand that," said Dad. "You can't help who you love."

He was thinking about mom. Dad had loved her, though she was a negligent mother and an emotional mess. He'd known her before alcohol ruled her life.

"Me too," said Meghan. "You only live once."

Or in my case, twice.

I sent a separate message to Andrew. *"Can Christopher and I talk to you about something after dinner?"*

Meghan watched me send and Andrew receive my message. She snatched Andrew's phone from his hand and read the message aloud.

"What the hell do you need to talk to him about that I can't hear? I'm the one you're related to. Sometimes I think you like Andrew better than you like me."

Sometimes I did, but I didn't dare reply.

"It's about the coma. Maybe he can help with some background information," said Christopher.

"About what?" said Meghan. "You may as well tell. I'll just nag until I find out."

Christopher and I traded glances again. I was trying to protect her. It wasn't my fault that she insisted on being in the middle of everything.

"We're looking into what happened to Brandon. Lizzie suggested Andrew might help. She suspects there are men after his research. It could be dangerous for us to investigate without more information."

Andrew had been quiet, listening until now. He looked casual, leaning on the island in the middle of the kitchen, stealing potato chips from a bowl. "What makes you think this is something more than an accidental drug overdose?"

My head shot up. He'd already investigated. He'd known about the coma.

My sharp look registered. "I did some digging. When you wouldn't tell your sister what happened with Brandon, she badgered until I looked into him. Did you know about the drugs?"

I rocked my head violently. *"He didn't do drugs."*

"My brother never touched drugs a day in his life," said Christopher. "I don't believe for a second that he'd start now, no matter what the official report says. It's a cover-up."

He held up his hand when Andrew would have interrupted.

"Elizabeth overheard him on the phone a few months ago talking to someone about the human trials. She believes they threatened him. He may have pushed her away to protect her. I would have."

He looked down at me, his icy blue eyes warming me with their chill fire. I hadn't considered that reason. It made me feel better about Brandon disappearing. A little. It didn't make me want to renew our relationship, but I was less angry.

"This weekend we went to Reno to investigate a lead about Brandon's research into scorpion venom. Elizabeth found an expert there," said Christopher. "We're going to make an antidote for his creation, give it to him, and hope he'll wake up."

"What if he wakes up and is mad you've stolen his girl?" Andrew crunched another handful of chips while Dad excused himself and hurried to the grill to rescue the steaks.

"We'll see," said Christopher. "I'd rather have him alive and angry than fading away in a hospital bed, never to wake again."

We stood near each other, his arm wrapped around me, his hand warm on my hip.

"I think this is moving too fast," said Meghan. "First, you're with Brandon, then Christopher, then nobody. Now back to Christopher. You're saying Brandon might still be mad and wreck the whole thing? That's stupid."

"I'm done with Brandon. You can't blame this mess on Christopher. Being together is my idea. If I get hurt, it's my fault." I held my phone up for the others to read.

"She didn't do this on her own." Christopher tightened his grip, his fingers digging into my side possessively.

"If someone threatened Brandon, they could be dangerous," said Andrew.

He was in police mode and had returned to the investigation. From his eyes, it seemed Christopher had passed some kind of test.

"How can I help? Do you have names or descriptions?" said Andrew.

"We have a few pieces of information. Elizabeth heard two men at the hospital yesterday talking about Brandon. Someone matching their description went to Reno, trying to buy scorpions. Brandon's company is called Real Tech. We need to find out what else they are involved in. We think they're trying to use synthetic scorpion venom to create soldiers that don't feel pain. They could sell to the military and make a fortune."

"Money makes people dangerous," said Andrew.

"Dinner's ready," said Dad. "We can eat and talk."

The rest of the dinner was pleasant. We talked to my family about the venomous snakes, lizards, and spiders that we'd seen. Meghan told the Jenga tarantula story and re-enacted my hysterics. She'd collected the pieces off the ground. She was braver than I was, even if she was younger.

"Maybe I should get a tarantula." Meghan's eyes danced. "They're cool."

"No way." Andrew crossed his arms, a stubborn set to his jaw.

"I'm with Andrew. They're creepy."

Meghan might stop arguing when it was two against one, but that didn't mean she wouldn't get one if she wanted to.

They spent the rest of the evening bickering and comparing the worst pets they'd had growing up. Meghan's had been her stinky turtles. Christopher had a three-legged dog that farted all the time, and Andrew had owned a rat that bit his toes.

Before we left, Meghan took me aside for a chat.

"You're falling for Christopher," she said. "This is really soon to be all in. Your heart isn't just on your sleeve, you've served it up on a silver platter. Do you know what you're doing?"

"Thank you for looking after Ember." I didn't want to talk about Christopher. I'd already addressed everything, including her worries.

I smiled to let Meghan know I wasn't angry and hugged her. She seemed surprised at the affection, but squeezed me in return. Collecting my kitten from the couch where she'd snoozed since dinner, I put her in her carrier. Christopher held the case while I hugged the others to say goodbye. It sounded like Andrew would help, so we had a place to start.

Chapter 12

Tuesday night, Christopher and I went to Brandon's and retrieved his laptop. Christopher knew someone who could hack in, no password required. Soon after, we had access to his files, at least some of them. I also ordered the antivenom using the card Benny had given us. Benny had warned us it would take a couple of months. The expected delivery date was late November, around Thanksgiving. I waded through Brandon's formulas and research to develop my understanding while we waited. We were impatient for the antivenom's arrival, but the timing was out of our control.

After we collected the laptop, a black SUV appeared outside my house several days in a row. At the wheel was the tall, bird-like man from the hospital. After that, when we exercised, we left together. We ran a route that took us to the hospital and I waited downstairs while Christopher talked to Brandon. I didn't want to return home alone.

The next several weeks fell into a rhythm. I went to karate while Christopher went to the gym. We spent most nights together and got up several mornings a week to run before work. We weren't together every minute, but spent time together every day.

With Christopher's return to my life, I hoped my stalker had been foiled. None of my missing items reappeared, but nothing else disappeared. Eric had been in my house over the summer, but now he'd stopped. I relaxed and let my guard down at home. The Real Tech-related SUV was a separate issue. We must have alerted someone that we were interested in Brandon's research when we went to his townhouse. I hoped they'd searched my house too and come up empty. I'd rather believe that people being in my house related to business and wasn't personal.

"Maybe we missed something at Brandon's and so did Real Tech. We have to assume they've been back. Has anyone checked his place for break-ins?"

"I'll go," said Christopher. "Nobody's been there for almost a month. Not since we got the laptop in September. I had his mail forwarded."

"Not without me," I said. He raised an eyebrow. His expression told me I'd have to make my case. *"We're in this together."*

I couldn't stay shackled to Christopher forever, but I also wanted to be involved.

Christopher grinned.

We drove toward his place, as though we were going home. When he determined we hadn't been followed, he doubled back to Brandon's. We parked in the alley and entered through the back door with Christopher's key. The back door frame was splintered, but the door had closed.

Inside was a disaster. Brandon's place had been ransacked.

We stepped over junk strewn across the floor. The air smelled stale with a hint of garbage. My guess was this had happened weeks ago, as a fine coating of dust sat on his scattered belongings.

"Touch nothing." Christopher surveyed the destruction and let out a deep breath. "I'll let Andrew know. He should bring a team here. I'll take pictures. I hope my brother has insurance."

"They would have used gloves," I said. *"I'm certain they didn't find what they were looking for, which is why they've been following us. They think we have something they need. We have to look in places they missed."*

Christopher surveyed the apartment. "They didn't miss much. Don't touch the mess."

They'd left nothing undisturbed in the living room—tipped the furniture, slit the cushions, and emptied the bookshelves. I wandered into the kitchen while he headed down the hall toward the office and the bedroom. Food lay scattered in piles on the counter and someone had dumped cereal and dry pasta on the floor. A couple of cans of baked beans had rolled against the baseboards and a tin of sardines was wedged under the front of the fridge as though kicked. The cupboards were open, though Brandon's dishes were intact. I spun and took in the kitchen and suddenly felt a lightbulb flash in my brain. The fridge.

I opened the refrigerator door. The smell of rotten vegetables permeated the air, and I wrinkled my nose in distaste. It might not have been searched thoroughly because of the foul aroma. His fridge was almost as empty as mine had been in 2022. The sign of a true workaholic. Other than a bag of slimy lettuce and the plastic-coated liquid remnants of a former cucumber, the sole contents were the condiments in the door. He owned five kinds of mustard, a practically empty ketchup bottle, chipotle and moldy hot sauces of a variety of vintages, and a small glass jar of crushed garlic.

I was about to close the fridge in disappointment, when I remembered Brandon despised garlic. He avoided it because it gave him severe heartburn. The jar of garlic didn't belong in his fridge and was the type of thing I was searching for. I opened the jar and peeked inside. It wasn't garlic. I replaced the lid and stuck it in my purse. It was a long shot, but I thought perhaps Brandon's apartment was bugged. I didn't want anyone else to know we'd found what they'd missed.

I sent Christopher a text. *"Found something. Pretend you give up. Come get me."*

He reappeared a minute later. "Lizzie, this is a wild goose chase. They've searched this place from top to bottom. We couldn't have missed anything important. We have to let the police know and let the professionals handle this."

I nodded, and he took my hand. We returned to his car and Christopher sent photos of the mess to Andrew.

We sat in the car, but he hadn't started the engine. "What did you find?"

I looked around. Nobody was near us and I hadn't seen the Real Tech black SUV. I removed the glass jar from my purse and set it on my lap.

"Garlic?" said Christopher with a frown. "Brandon hates garlic."

I unscrewed the lid and tipped the contents in his direction. Three small vials sat in the jar and clinked against the side. Mini test tubes, labeled A, B, and C.

Christopher slid them out one at a time, keeping them lower than the window level.

A was empty, while B contained a gray solution, and C a pale blue one. We'd found what Brandon may have injected himself with. It meant I needed to look for information about A, B, and C in the folders on his computer. I hadn't known what to read, so narrowing the search would be helpful. It also meant he may have injected himself at home and not the lab. Perhaps before work. He'd collapsed at work so initially, they would have searched the lab, not his house. They'd injected him with drugs to make it look like an overdose for the authorities.

"When the antivenom arrives, let's try that. I still think the coma is due to anaphylactic shock. If that doesn't reverse it, we can try again with these."

"You know you're brilliant," Christopher leaned over to kiss me.

I warmed inside at his compliment as I closed the jar and returned it to my bag.

"Let's go put that in my fridge, in case it needs to stay cold," he said. "Have I ever told you how much smart girls turn me on?"

One phrase, one look, and I was wet again. All thoughts of the investigation slipped away. He had an adverse effect on me because now all I wanted was to get him home so we could be naked. He excelled at changing the subject and my focus.

"Take me home." He gave me a knowing glance, started the car, and revved the engine.

•   •   •

November sped by as we waited for the antivenom to arrive. A few weeks after checking Brandon's place, I arrived home from karate and jumped in the shower, expecting Christopher any minute. He'd planned to pick up Mexican after his workout. I'd given him a key, just like I had one for his house, as we spent an even amount of time at the two houses.

Through the noise of the streaming water, came the sound of the front door closing.

The thick bank of steam inhibited my vision as I'd forgotten to turn on the fan.

There were no further noises. I half expected Christopher to join me in the shower like he'd done earlier that week, but he didn't. Maybe the door had been my neighbor's or my imagination. I hurried and jumped out to dry off. If he wasn't here, he would be soon.

I looked up. Someone had drawn a large heart in the condensation on the mirror. I smiled because Christopher must be here.

I walked into the bedroom and dressed in clean clothes, all the while expecting to hear Christopher's voice. While putting on my jeans, I glanced at the bed. A single red rose rested against my pillow. I picked it up and went looking for Christopher. To my consternation, he wasn't in the kitchen or the living room. The house was quiet, and he wasn't there.

My forehead tightened in a frown. Maybe he'd left the food in the car and gone outside to collect it. My palms grew sweaty when I checked outside and his car wasn't in sight. As I watched, he drove up to the curb. He was just arriving. Light-headed, my legs became rubbery, and I wasn't sure they would hold me up. I sat down at the table, trying not to be sick.

Christopher came in carrying takeout bags. He took one look at my face and dropped them to the floor. He crouched beside me and put his hand on my jaw. When he touched my skin, he read my mind better.

"What's wrong?"

I didn't answer. My eyes flicked toward the crimson rose.

"What the fuck? Eric was here? How did he get in?"

I shook my head, not in denial, but because I didn't know. I was glad Christopher could read my mind because I hadn't wanted to type Eric's name. It would be too real. The rose was the first physical piece of evidence. Something tangible, concrete. It was there, not in my imagination. The blood rushed from my face. The note after the gala about the black dress. The familiar handwriting wasn't Christopher's. It was Eric's. He must have been in the house while I slept—months ago. The flower meant he hadn't given up. How many times had he been here, and I hadn't known? My blood chilled.

My icy hands shook as I picked up my phone. *"Didn't see him. I was in the shower. Left this in the bedroom."* He'd watched me shower. The heart on the mirror. I wanted to throw up.

Christopher grabbed my hands. His hands felt hot compared to mine.

"Has he been here before?"

His voice was too loud. Anger rolled off him in waves and filled the room.

A tear escaped. It rolled down my cheek and splattered on my pants. I slipped my hands free and picked up my phone.

"I think so." I bit my cheek and waited for Christopher to yell.

"This is going to take too long." He grabbed my phone. "Let's try an experiment." He hauled me to my feet and led me to the bedroom door.

I wasn't sure what he had planned.

"Tell Ember what happened. You talk to her when nobody is here."

It was true. Had he heard, or was he guessing? He pushed ahead into my room.

"After I check the closets, under the bed, and the windows."

I paled further as I watched. Eric might still be here. I'd assumed the sound of the door had been his departure.

"If he's here, this time I'll kill him."

One look at Christopher's face convinced me of the truth. He was irate, but not with me. His temper was contained, if barely.

After checking every conceivable hiding place, he said, "We're alone. You can do this. I need to know everything. Texting will take too long and leave too much out. I want every detail. There's so much emotion in your head and mine I can't get information. I need to know."

My heart thumped against my ribs, reminding me I was too scared to speak.

"Why didn't you tell me?" Christopher's mouth flattened as he handed back my phone.

"It was before we were back together. I didn't want to talk about it and hoped it was over. I was also scared that you wouldn't believe me. Meghan didn't. Her disbelief made me wonder if it was real." It was hard to meet his blazing eyes.

"I'm not mad at you. But you have to trust me." His eyes searched mine.

Christopher must have been satisfied with what he saw, because he squeezed my arm and closed the door. Ember and I were on one side, he was on the other. A loud curse broke the silence as he saw the now-faded remnants of the heart. I expected him to come charging back, but he didn't. I stood near the door, looked at my kitty, and spoke.

"I don't know how to begin. It started months ago. Soon after the day at the park when we decided we couldn't be together. I went grocery shopping at the store just down the street. Eric was there, even though he didn't live in this neighborhood. He cornered me and taunted me. It wasn't a coincidence, but I didn't tell anyone. Soon after, things disappeared from my house. I was scared and almost called you, but you weren't my boyfriend." My voice got stronger as I progressed.

"I couldn't figure out how anyone was getting in, but I had a feeling deep down that it was Eric, that he'd been here. It was never when I was home, always when I was at work. My intruder kept eating my apples. My pink underwear disappeared and my fuzzy purple socks, the ones I like to wear around the house after work. I found my book in a different place and the bookmark had disappeared. I checked the windows and locks over and over. Nothing was broken or forced. When I was alone, I checked them every hour. Meghan had the only spare key, but it wasn't her."

I took another deep breath and started again. My hands still shook.

"I tried to tell my family, but Meghan laughed. She didn't believe me, made me feel stupid or forgetful. I didn't know what to do. I found a note the morning after the exhibit reception, about looking fantastic in black, but I thought it was from you. But that means Eric watched me sleep. At least once. Probably more." I stopped to catch my ragged breath.

There was more cursing from the hallway. The shadow from Christopher's feet stretched in front of the door. Christopher was right there. I turned back to the bed, speaking only to Ember.

"Sometimes he followed when I walked to and from work. I thought I saw him waiting outside my karate class just before the trip to Reno, but I couldn't be sure. Tonight, while I was in the shower, the front door closed and I thought it was you arriving with dinner." I glanced at the door. Christopher was still there. I moved closer to Ember.

"I sensed his eyes all the time, watching me. He stays away when you're with me, but it's even happened at work, but only when I'm alone."

I cried while I talked. It was such a release to speak. I petted Ember's silky fur and traced the black stripes on her head with one finger. Her fur was so soft.

"Pack a bag." Christopher had opened the door without me noticing.

His jaw was clenched and his eyes blazed brighter than lasers.

"I let Andrew know. Took a picture of your mirror. He's going to meet someone who will change your locks and install an alarm this weekend. He's going to dust for fingerprints. Until that's done, you're staying with me. I won't let you be here alone for another minute."

He opened the closet and yanked out my suitcases. He looked at me and dropped them to the floor with a thud.

I wrapped my arms around myself as I trembled.

"Lizzie, I'm not mad at you. I'm incensed that I didn't notice. I can read minds, but I missed this, thinking all your fear was from the past. You don't have to deal with everything on your own. Remember, we're a team. I want you to trust me."

He took a deep breath and blew the air out while he stared at the ceiling. He crossed the room and took my hand. Sitting on the edge of the bed, he tugged me into his lap and wrapped his powerful arms around me. Some of my tension left as I breathed in his familiar chocolate smell. I buried my nose against his neck and shoulder.

"I'm scared for you, Sweetheart. Will you please pack clothes and anything you'll need for a week or two? Stay with me. I'd like you to." His voice was quiet and even. "I have an alarm system, and I want you to be safe. A stalker is serious. I believe you. I'm sorry you're scared. You don't have to deal with it on your own. I promise to help."

His arms and calm words helped more than anything. Relief flooded through me at his decisive action and his firm belief.

"He's escalated to notes and flowers. He's watched you sleep. This is fucked."

Fifteen minutes later, we'd packed everything for myself and Ember for an extended trip. I took the Real Tech notes, both computers, and clothes for at least two weeks, so I'd have options. At the last minute, I added my red dress and heels. Christopher's favorites.

Christopher cleared out a large dresser drawer and half the closet at his place and I unpacked. It didn't feel temporary.

Andrew and I texted the next day.

"I'll meet the locksmith Saturday morning. Safest for you to stay away."

"Thank you." I was grateful for a brother-in-law who was also the law. Sometimes I forgot that in this time, he and Meghan weren't married yet. He seemed like family.

"Your sister feels horrible. We both do."

"It isn't your fault. He's sick." Texting didn't have enough emotion, and they'd missed how upset I'd been. Perhaps if I'd spoken out loud, they would have listened.

I told Andrew about Eric's words at the party. That he'd spouted something about instant attraction and our chemistry.

"I didn't realize he was dangerous. He seemed like a normal neighbor. I had no idea."

Andrew texted again half an hour later.

"If we find prints or DNA at your place and prove he's been in your house, you need to press charges. Anywhere, in particular, I should look?"

"Closet doors, the black garment bag, my dresser drawers, my bedside table, the doors." I hesitated. *"I doubt there's anything."* He was smart and would've been careful, but I couldn't share how I knew that.

The next day Andrew called Christopher, who put him on speaker so I could listen.

"I didn't want to call you back to the house, but when I arrived this morning to meet the locksmith, the house had been ransacked. There's property damage. We'll need you to see if you can pinpoint anything that might be missing."

"We'll be there." Christopher was careful to set his alarm before we left.

"Who has keys to your place?" It was less than ten minutes between our houses. I wanted reassurance that nobody else could get into his

house, the only place I felt safe. *"Nobody can get in here without setting off the alarm."*

"Brandon had one. I got it back from the hospital with his personal effects."

"Anybody else? An old girlfriend, a neighbor?"

"You and I have the only keys. I changed the alarm code. Nobody knows it except us."

Relieved, I accepted his words.

At my house, Andrew met us on the sidewalk. "They broke in through the back door. The window was smashed. Was that how Eric gained entry before?"

"I don't know how he got in. Never left a trace." Why had the method changed?

"This won't be easy," said Andrew. "It never is." His face pinched into a frown. He looked like Officer Jennings, not Meghan's fiancé. "It's more personal than the other break-in."

I nodded, wondering what he meant. Eric had a penchant for the dramatic and violent. I steeled myself and slipped my hand into Christopher's.

At the front door, an appalling sight greeted me. Everything I owned had been moved or destroyed. The bookshelves had been dumped, and the covers ripped from several novels. Like at Brandon's, the kitchen cupboards had been emptied, the couch cushions slit open, and their stuffing scattered around the room. The pungent scent of strong cleaner filled the air. We found empty containers from half a dozen cleaning products emptied in the hallway—their contents staining the floor.

My old room, the empty master bedroom, had been left virtually untouched, but the room where I slept was the worst. Painted on the walls in blood red, foot-high letters, was, *"It's destiny. You're supposed to be mine, Bitch."*

The room smelled like paint, which was still tacky to the touch. He'd splashed everywhere with splotches of paint. It looked like once he'd finished his message, he'd emptied the rest of the paint can around the room. The carpet was ruined. Paint splattered the furniture, my clothes from my dresser, the bedding, and the floor. It looked like a murder scene, with everything saturated with paint the color of blood. I shivered despite the warmth of the house. We'd made him angry. I couldn't live here ever again. I'd pay someone to repaint, then I'd sell. My insurance should pay for replacing my belongings and the damage.

We salvaged some of my clothes from the closet, but the rest were ruined. I wanted nothing else from my bedroom. Eric had smashed my dishes all over the kitchen floor—bits of them crunched underfoot as we walked. He'd smashed them as additional malicious mayhem. My plants had been overturned, their dirt in messy puddles. I was relieved that I hadn't been home, and that Ember had been with me. Christopher and I took pictures of the destruction for my insurance claim. My storage room was intact, and we removed a few boxes of memorabilia, my winter boots, and Christmas decorations. I'd get the rest later.

Eric was sick to have done this. In this timeline, I'd met Eric twice and never spoken to him. Why was he interested in tormenting me? It made little sense. I considered the broken door. He'd gotten into my place without breaking glass for months. Why now? My blood ran cold and shivers trailed down my spine. What if it wasn't just him? What if I'd had two sets of intruders? I looked for the papers I'd printed with Brandon's messages and research. They were gone, as was my key card for work. They planned to search my office.

"What if Real Tech searched my place after we left with suitcases? They broke the window. They tossed my place AND later, Eric painted his message and added to the destruction?" I shuddered at the memory of the hateful words. After Eric died, I'd done research into behavior like his. He'd been a classic narcissist. He needed to make others small, so he felt important. He'd never thought he was wrong and never apologized. Every violence was justified.

"What do you mean?" Christopher looked up from the ruination of the living room where he was gathering and straightening my battered books. It looked like a lost cause.

"Real Tech is looking for Brandon's serum. They took the research."

"I'm tired of all this intrigue," said Christopher. "We need a vacation. We have to wait for the antivenom anyway, so maybe we take the entire week at Thanksgiving. We'll have to arrange it with work, but we need to get away." He grinned. "I know just the place."

Chapter 13

Christopher and I made arrangements to leave town for the week of Thanksgiving. The Museum owed each of us vacation time before the year-end. I needed to forget Eric. The break-in had left me uncomfortable, knowing that people had looked through my belongings. It was a violation. Late November was a good time to be away from the museum. Work was quiet in the fall, at least until the Christmas break, when we got busier with families looking for holiday activities.

We were both on edge leading up to Thanksgiving. Real Tech and Eric knew where Christopher lived and where we worked, and the black SUV followed us a few times, always at a distance. There'd been no more home invasions. We suspected they were waiting for us to make progress with Brandon's notes.

We'd seen no sign of Eric, which left me feeling on edge. We hadn't seen the last of him. He would wait and make his next move when I'd least expect it. To make it easier to leave town incognito, we rented a vehicle, an unremarkable white SUV that neither of our stalkers would recognize. It was indistinguishable from half the vehicles on the road.

Christopher's perfect place was his family's cabin. It had once belonged to his grandfather. It sounded remote and like a perfect getaway. Well, perfect for somewhere cold. I preferred the idea of lying on a beach somewhere, but this wasn't that kind of vacation. We were still working on how to wake up Brandon.

Meghan and Andrew took Ember for the week, and we dropped her off Friday after leaving work early. Andrew promised to leave a squad car stationed outside Christopher's place while we were away. The cabin was located outside of town, a four-hour drive into the mountains. Christopher assured me that once there, you were in a different world.

We turned off the main highway, onto a smaller, older one that was smooth, and almost deserted. Since turning onto this road, we'd only seen one other car. Yellow and orange-leafed trees still wearing their finest fall colors lined the side of the mountain road. In places, the trees arched over the road, creating a yellow-gold tunnel. It seemed like we'd wandered into a fall painting. It was too stunning to be real. In the distance, the mountain peaks were covered with a dusting of snow that completed the storybook feel.

"Brandon and I haven't been up here together for a couple of years, since before he started dating you," said Christopher. "Not your fault. He was just too busy. Some of our best summer holidays were here with our grandfather. We were such city kids. This was the perfect escape. It was like a dream come true, to come to the mountains where it's quiet. I love it because it's a break for my brain. Nobody's thoughts interrupt or bombard me.

I shot him a look, wondering if that's how he considered my thoughts. An invasion.

"Sweetheart," he said. "Your thoughts aren't intrusive. They're welcome, but I get as much from the expressions on your face. I love being around you. I'm hoping that I hear your voice more one day. It'll happen when you're ready, but until then, hearing your thoughts helps me to know you."

My heart flip-flopped. His words made me crazier about him than ever. We'd been together only two and a half months, but I'd known no one as well as I knew him, or let anyone know me either.

The homemade cabin nestled at the end of a long driveway, beneath a canopy of trees. It was cold here—the air temperature had plummeted on the mountain.

"It's going to freeze tonight," he said as we parked. "I'll build a fire right away."

The air was crisp and smelled like snow. I wouldn't be surprised if we woke up to snow on the ground. We took our bags inside and Christopher started a fire in the woodstove while I ferried the remainder of our belongings inside. From the cabin's porch, an ocean of trees and the mountain rose above us. The cabin was completely private. I looked at Christopher and my heart danced. We had the same thought from his naughty grin. We were free to be uninhibited.

The slow burn of anticipation began as he collected more firewood from the woodshed around back and turned the water on from an outbuilding. I stowed our groceries in the small kitchen. He'd stocked the cabin with enough canned food for months, though we'd brought a week's supply of food. If there was ever an apocalypse, this should be our destination.

The cabin had electricity for lights, a fridge, and a stove. There was no Wi-Fi and no cable. No cell service either; we were off the grid. The TV was hooked up to a DVD player, old-school style. An extensive video library filled the shelves nearby. Upon examination, it looked like Christopher kept it up to date.

He came in, stomping to warm his feet. He held his hands to the wood stove, then tossed more firewood into the blaze inside. The iron lids on the stovetop rattled. "Brrr. I should dig out my gloves."

"Who eats all this?" I said, pointing to the pantry. His phone didn't buzz.

With no cell service, I wouldn't be able to talk my usual way. To get his attention. I shook my phone by my ear as if it was broken. I could text and show him the screen if I had to, but it was inconvenient.

"Oh, right," he said. "I forgot to mention that, didn't I?" The smile lines around his eyes looked amused. "You're going to have to find a different way to talk to me."

I raised my eyebrows and pointed to the cupboards and to the now empty grocery bags. I picked up a can of tomato soup in the cupboard and one we'd just brought, balancing them back and forth as though trying to choose between them.

"Every time I come, I bring extra and eat the older stuff. My grandfather told stories about being snowed in here. More than once he had to melt snow for water and live on canned food. I keep the wood pile stocked and plenty of emergency supplies on hand. There's also a backup generator."

I moved the newer cans to the back of the cupboard and rotated others forward.

I hadn't heard Christopher come up behind me. He swung me around, taking my breath away.

"I'm going to ravish you tonight," he said, as he returned me to my feet. "I've dreamt of bringing you here. It's my favorite place."

He took my face in his hands, then bent to kiss me. It always amazed me how he could be so much bigger than I was, yet we were a perfect fit. He was warm already and his lips were soft and teasing. I wasn't hungry for dinner anymore.

"You're going to have to tell me what you want," he said. "I remember a conversation in Reno. Your words on my skin bewitched me. I want more." His pale blue eyes seemed to see inside me. How did he always make every situation better?

"You promised to make love to me one day." I spoke against his throat as I kissed the sensitive place behind his ear. "I want slow, agonizing hours of us. To forget our worries. I want the outside world to disappear."

He made a sound somewhere between a growl and a groan.

"That's going to have to be the second round." His large hands slid down to cup my ass. "Later, I'll take as much time as you want, but I need you now. I can't wait that long to have you."

A hot rush shot through me. His words excited me beyond belief.

In less than a second, he had my bra unfastened and had removed my sweater.

The cool air brought goosebumps to my bare flesh.

I undressed for him, taking off everything. He watched every motion. The cabin was chilly, but the air in the living room near the wood stove was the warmest. The only sound was the crackle of the fire when Christopher led me to the couch. He'd undressed too and sat at the edge and leaned back.

"Do your worst." His icy blue eyes looked almost silver with desire. I loved how they changed color with his moods. "When it's my turn, I won't hold back."

I knelt between his knees and took him into my mouth, shuddering at his silken hardness. The defined muscles of his abs begged for my fingers. He sucked in a breath when I touched him. When he couldn't take any more without unraveling, I slid up and kissed him. With one hand he stroked himself, with the other he touched me, playing with me, swirling closer and closer to the button of nerves where I was most sensitive, but never quite reaching it. I craved more, though I held myself together.

"I love you," he said.

His eyes held the truth.

At that moment, I came hot and wet with a rush. We'd never said those words to each other. I still shook when he pulled me to my feet and leaned me over the back of the couch, facing into the living room while he grabbed my hips and entered me from behind.

"You're mine," he said. One hand reached around to cup my slippery wetness.

His first three thrusts were slow and torturous, tantalizing us both, but he built the momentum afterward, leaving me barely able to hold on while he rocked from behind, pressure from within, and his fingers giving me pleasure at the same time. He was huge and strong and incredible. I shuddered and cried out my pleasure.

I tried to stifle my noise, but he said, "Don't you dare. One of these days you'll scream and I want to hear."

He rested one hand on my back and pushed me lower, arching my back. I trembled all over and when I came, I seized, squeezing him. I took him with me when I tipped over the edge into bliss.

"Fuck, damn, and hell." He punctuated each curse with an additional thrust. "Never stop. Damn Lizzie. The things you let me do and do to me return."

He shuddered again. "I'm never letting you go."

The words hung in the air between us.

I turned and stepped into his arms.

"I don't want to be without you again. We only just found each other, but you're my dream girl." His lips found mine, sealing a new deal.

I wanted to tell him I loved him too, but let my body, lips, and thoughts speak for my heart.

• • •

Though it was only dinner time, we put on pajamas and cooked together. Outside, lazy snowflakes drifted down from the night sky. When the dishes were done, by mutual agreement, we started our Star Wars marathon. In this time, they'd released Rogue One the previous year. The Last Jedi, or Episode VIII, was due to be released soon. I spoiled nothing about the future movies but we agreed to watch them with each other. It made me feel warm inside to think about a future together.

After the Phantom Menace, Christopher took me to bed and lived up to his promise for round two, making me cry out time and time again, while he used his mouth, fingers, and other parts, to find all of my nerve endings. When at last we fell asleep, my entire body thrummed. Every part of me had been worshipped, cataloged, and loved. I ached and had sore muscles, but couldn't imagine better sex.

On our last night, I told him my darkest secret. I wished I'd been able to find my proper voice, but whispers sufficed. I couldn't share this via text. It would lose too much of the emotion that made it important. I curled up next to him on the couch, my feet tucked under my body. We'd be going back to the real world soon, and I wanted him to understand more about what had happened with Eric.

"Why do you torment yourself?" he said. "Why do you let that monster matter so much? He deserved the broken nose. He beat you, marked your beautiful skin, and made you ashamed. If I get my hands on that creep again, I'll snap his neck."

He saw my face. "Well, if I thought I could get away with it. I won't go to jail over that asshole. Anyway, what happened wasn't murder. I'd call it justice."

Leaning close to Christopher so he would hear me over the crackle of the flames, I whispered, "It wasn't just about his nose. I didn't want to be a bully like him. We got in the car so I could drive to the hospital. There was a car swerving, rushing toward us. I froze. I let it hit us. I didn't know where to go. I thought we might both die. I didn't want to, but I resigned myself to the idea." Once more, I relived that moment in the blinding lights and took Christopher with me.

When I looked up, tears coursed down my cheeks. "That's why I'm a murderer. I did nothing to prevent the accident."

"You couldn't have avoided that accident." He wrapped his arms around me.

"I put us there," I said as he kissed my jaw.

"You weren't the drunk driver who would have hit anyone on the road that night. You were there because your husband beat the shit out of you. It was Eric's fault you were there. You are not a murderer. I need you to say it and to believe it."

He waited while I processed his words.

"Tell me you're not a murderer." He held both my hands in his, tracing circles with his thumbs on the back.

I hadn't looked at it quite like that before. Maybe it had been just an accident. I'd had good luck and Eric's had been terrible.

"Tell me," Christopher said.

"I'm not a murderer," I whispered.

He patted the spot in front of him on the couch and I moved from beside him to sit there and he wrapped himself around me. Our hearts beat in sync. I'd never felt closer to anyone. I'd come clean. He saw inside my head and believed in my innocence. The part of me that had believed I was guilty for so long, healed.

When we had sex that night, I cried out Christopher's name, as I shuddered with repeated orgasms that left me weak and exhausted. Unburdening myself had been liberating.

Chapter 14

Christopher and I cleaned the cabin and left on Sunday after a quick lunch. We'd restocked the wood supply, and changed the sheets and towels, leaving everything ready for the next time. If the roads were clear, we planned to come for another getaway between Christmas and New Years. I considered turning on my phone to check my messages to let my family know our arrival time, but I didn't want to interrupt the last of our alone time. To my surprise, I'd enjoyed being off the grid. I hadn't had trouble communicating.

It was five o'clock when we arrived at my dad's house, hungry for Thanksgiving dinner. There was a police cruiser parked by the curb, so I guessed Andrew must have come straight from work. Sometimes a fellow officer dropped him off. Officers sat in the car, but I paid little attention. We stepped out of the SUV and Christopher squeezed my hand as we walked toward the house.

We got as far as the top of the front steps when there was activity from the police car and I glanced over my shoulder. Two officers in navy blue uniforms stepped out. I didn't recognize either of them.

"Christopher Winters?" said the officer, who was closest to us.

"I'm Christopher Winters." Christopher turned to face them.

He raked his hand through his hair and his shoulders tensed. I hoped this wasn't about his brother and that nothing had happened to Brandon while we'd been gone. Christopher wouldn't forgive himself if there'd been a problem. Or had someone broken into his house? Scenarios ran through my mind.

I hadn't knocked on the door, but Meghan flung it open and yanked me inside, tearing my hand from Christopher's grasp.

What had gotten into her? Her behavior was odd, but I was more concerned about the police. Meghan was a brief distraction.

Looking back outside, the officer had pulled her gun. To my horror, she pointed it at Christopher. My heart leapt to my throat, and I froze. This had to be a mistake.

"Christopher Winters, you have the right to remain silent. Walk toward the sidewalk. When you get there, drop to your knees and put your hands behind your head," said the other officer.

I didn't understand. I could tell from Christopher's face that he too was confused, though he complied with their orders.

"May I ask what this is regarding?" he said from his knees.

He sounded calm. I was upset for him and tried to follow, but Meghan held my arm in a firm grip. I yanked several times, but she stood in the doorway to block me and was immovable. I couldn't get past without hurting her.

"It's okay, Lizzie," Christopher said, noticing my struggle. "There must be a mistake. I'll get it sorted out and come back to get you in a few hours."

Meghan stepped forward on the porch. In her distraction, I shot past her and ran down the stairs.

"There's no mistake, you sick bastard," Meghan spat.

I stumbled as I whipped my head around, shocked at her tone.

"Miss, stay back," shouted the first officer.

I swallowed and stopped in my tracks, midway between the police and the house. Torn between following orders and getting to Christopher.

The second officer read Christopher his rights.

"What am I charged with?" Christopher said when he'd finished.

"As if you don't know." Meghan stomped down the stairs and grabbed my arm again, but I refused to budge.

I needed an explanation.

"They found work gloves with red paint and your missing socks and underwear," said Meghan. "In his desk. At work." She hissed the final words.

Meghan had it wrong. Eric must have planted the evidence. That explained the missing security card. Christopher was innocent. A tight band formed around my chest. I wanted to explain what must have happened. Tears gathered in my eyes. I clenched my jaw to keep them from falling. I couldn't find my voice.

Christopher shook his head. His beautiful blue eyes trained on me. "Lizzie, I promise it wasn't me. You know who it was. We'll figure this out."

I nodded to reassure him, though I was scared. This was all wrong.

The taller officer handcuffed Christopher, who didn't resist.

"Mr. Winters, you're coming with us," said the first officer. "Ladies, please return to the house."

She still trained her gun on my boyfriend. As he turned toward the police car, she holstered her gun. I shook like a leaf. It hadn't been Christopher in my house, moving things, taking things. Eric had framed him.

I jerked away from Meghan again and tried to get to Christopher so I could say goodbye. My voice wouldn't work. I tried to scream, but it was only the sound of air, not his name. I needed him to know that I believed him.

The officer blocked my attempts to get to Christopher.

"Calm down, Miss. He can't hurt you anymore."

The dam burst as tears of frustration broke free. I wanted to explain that it couldn't have been Christopher. At the time of the break-ins and paint, we'd been together at his house. I could vouch for his innocence.

"Lizzie," Christopher said, "You know it wasn't me."

His voice soothed me, and I nodded. I focused on his eyes. He was telling the truth. Every fibre of my being believed him.

"I'll call a lawyer, don't worry. I promise we'll sort it out."

He radiated calm, but I didn't know how he managed. Tears streamed down my face as they guided him to the back seat of the navy blue and white police cruiser, slammed the doors, and drove away. I wrapped my arms around myself and squeezed.

Meghan tried to comfort me by putting her arm around me. I shoved her away and took out my phone, turning it on with shaking hands. I had five missed phone calls. Four from her today and one from Andrew yesterday. They'd tried to warn me. We hadn't told them where we were going in case the goons from Real Tech became desperate for our location. My family couldn't give us away if they didn't know. We'd said we were going on a retreat and that we wouldn't regularly check our phones. I had twenty-seven messages from her I didn't have time to read.

"What the hell?" I shook with fury, making it hard to text.

"Come inside and I'll explain. It's cold out here."

Once more, she tried to wrap her arm around me. I threw it off.

"Don't touch me." My face burned and now that the tears had stopped, my blood boiled. I stalked into the house. I wanted an explanation.

The scents of roasting turkey and the cinnamon of sweet apple pie filled the house, but I wasn't interested in either. Andrew and Dad stood in the kitchen by the table. They'd watched from inside. Cowards.

"Meghan and I ran into Eric on Tuesday." Andrew held up his hands. "No, I didn't run him over with my car."

It was supposed to be a joke, but I wasn't amused. I was so irate that I couldn't see straight. My heart pounded like I'd run a marathon and it was all I could do not to grab him by the shoulders and shake his words loose.

"I can see you're upset, but let me explain," he said.

Anger blazed from my eyes, and he stepped back. I took a deep breath. When nobody spoke, I tapped my toe on the laminate floor, standing with my arms crossed while I waited to hear what he had to say.

"I was rude to Eric and pissed off about the engagement party incident," he said. "Eric said he was upset and remorseful. He felt horrible about that miscommunication. He said he took off when Christopher attacked him for no reason."

My eyebrows shot up. Eric felt bad. No reason? Ha. I shouldn't be surprised that he'd put his own spin on the events.

"It wasn't for no reason," I said to the family group chat. *"He tried to rape me. He held me down, flipped up my skirt, and fondled me. He'd backed me into the corner crying when Christopher burst in. There was no mistake. His actions were deliberate."*

"I stuck up for you. I know you'd never make up that kind of accusation," said Andrew after he checked his phone.

"He's a liar." My hands still shook, and I blinked to clear the tears from my eyes. *"He's been stalking me for months and wrecked my house. You saw what he did. I've seen him outside my dojo, in my grocery store, and near my work. For three months, he followed me everywhere. He only took a break when I got involved with Christopher because I was never alone. You saw a picture of the heart in the steam. That freak watched me shower."*

There was a pause while they all read my words.

"Maybe Christopher did that to scare you," said Meghan. "To make you move in with him. It worked."

Andrews's eyes looked unconvinced at my arguments. How could he believe that bully instead of me?

"Remember how upset Christopher was when we asked for your help? He's sweet, and patient, and gentle. It wasn't him."

"Eric's been out of the country on business," said Andrew. "He has an alibi for the break-in. He gave me his card, and I checked with his company. He was gone this summer and most of the fall. Before Eric left in July, he saw Christopher hanging around outside his place. While he was away, someone broke in, but he didn't find anything missing. Eric was intimidated. Christopher's a big guy, or Eric says he would have gone to the cops then. Since he's been back, he hasn't seen Christopher, so he let it go. He chose not to press charges."

"That makes no sense. Eric is a liar. An accomplished one. He made everything up to separate Christopher from me. You did what he wanted and are leaving me vulnerable. You took away the only person who makes me feel safe. Andrew, you need to undo this."

My pleas fell on deaf ears. As usual, Dad said nothing. My heart broke that he didn't believe me.

Meghan rejoined the argument. "They found Christopher's prints in Eric's house. Your stuff was in his office. Christopher is the liar. How well do you know him? Couldn't you be mistaken?"

Eric's lies had been well-planned, and he'd convinced my family. He'd taken the facts but twisted them, making Christopher look guilty. He was adept at manipulation. I had no other choice but to tell them the truth.

"I need to tell you my secret." I couldn't think of another way to show them what Eric was capable of. *"I didn't tell you before because I didn't think you'd believe me. I worried you'd think I was unstable, but I need you to trust me. I know it was Eric."*

I looked up to gauge their reactions and took a deep breath. All six eyes watched me, expectant. They were waiting. It was time.

"I'm from the future."

They looked up from their screens. All three faces remained blank. Nobody believed me. Hell, if I'd heard someone say they'd come from the future, I wouldn't believe either. This was why I hadn't bothered to explain until now. Seeing their reserved expressions, it dawned on me that I had said nothing that made them think I was unwell. They already thought that. How could I blame them?

I hadn't spoken in six months. I'd complained about a stalker they'd believed was imaginary. Meghan had mocked my fear and paranoia to tease me out of it and hadn't taken it seriously. She believed Eric's version of the attempted rape—that I'd overreacted. They'd been convinced that Christopher was violent and had taken advantage of me. To top it off, I'd just announced I'd time traveled from the future. I'd expected too much. This was not going well. In fact, it was horrible. I couldn't make it worse, so I gave them more information.

"I realize it's difficult to believe, but it's a long story," I said. *"I'm from 2022 and traveled back in time five years after I made a wish. Five years ago, I met Eric at your engagement party. We got married six months later. He was an abusive asshole and a liar. He beat me, gave me scars, but I was too scared to tell anyone. I know better than anyone what he's capable of. He terrifies me. He sees me as powerless, a victim. Eric is my stalker. He's framed Christopher. I'm scared he's going to hurt me. He's violent and dangerous."*

I watched Andrew. He reread my messages. He looked up with a frown, then scrolled back to read them again. Maybe he was listening, thinking. He was my best hope. He knew some things just couldn't be explained. I didn't see how this differed from his belief in UFOs.

"So, you're saying Eric is your husband?" Meghan's eyebrows remained high, her voice strained, her tone incredulous. One hand was on her hip. She remained unconvinced. She preferred concrete facts and explanations. Black and white answers. Good and bad. No shades of gray or supernatural hocus pocus. To be fair, if it hadn't happened to me, I'd find the story unbelievable.

"We were married at City Hall on December 3rd, 2017. We were in a car accident that killed him on April 30th, 2020. That's when I lost my voice. Trauma-induced selective mutism. That's why I can't talk. I was miserable and alone for two years. One night, I wished I could redo my life. The next morning, I woke up, and I'd traveled back in time five years. Ember was a kitten again. That was in May. I still have no voice, but my scars are gone, and I remember the other time. That's how I know Eric is evil."

Meghan shot Andrew a look, and he shrugged. Perhaps he didn't know what to believe. She nodded again, and he looked away. Her mouth was a flat line of disapproval. I didn't understand their silent communication, but when he looked back, he nodded and looked resigned. What decision had they made? They didn't believe me. My tears threatened to return. I was on my own.

"Elizabeth, this doesn't make sense," said Dad, looking up.

He looked tired. These were his first words since I'd arrived.

"Have you been drinking? Do you need help?" His expression showed him at a loss. He didn't know what to think and was reaching. He wanted a reason.

I flinched at his cruelty. Was he saying I was like my mother? A drunk who didn't know delusion from reality. That's what he thought of me? My heart felt bruised.

Andrew stared out the window in the direction the police car had driven. The electric kettle turned off and Meghan poured hot water over the waiting tea. Nobody spoke for several minutes while the tea steeped and they reread what I'd written. There were more strange glances back and forth. They weren't sharing their thoughts, but the silent messages flying around the room left me with a sense of unease.

Meghan handed me a cup of steaming tea. "Drink this. You need to calm down. You're overwrought."

Her words were insulting, but I tried to view things from her perspective. Maybe she just needed time to accept my difficult revelation.

The tea was bitter and perfumed, like earl grey. I preferred it to be sweet and less fragrant, but I humored Meghan and drank it, anyway. It wouldn't make me calm. I was too agitated about Christopher's arrest and Eric's web of lies.

"None of you believe me." I blew on the hot beverage and took another sip.

I sat down at the table with a deep breath. What could I say? Without a voice, it was difficult to explain. I had to find another way to convince them. I had an idea about how I could reach Andrew at least.

"They will release the next Star Wars movie in less than a month," I said. *"I've seen The Last Jedi."* I used a Star Wars example because I'd just watched our marathon and thought about the next movie. Andrew was also an avid fan. He had advance tickets for the new one

in a few weeks. He might not believe me today, but when he watched Episode Eight, he might remember my words and change his mind.

"It had surprises, like new characters using the force. The movie ends the debate about Rey's parents, at least for now. They weren't anyone special. They were nobodies, which was a disappointment. I wanted her to connect to Obi-Wan or Leia." It took forever to text when my hands shook with the intensity of my conviction.

"You've watched the trailers too many times," said Meghan with a dismissive sniff.

"When it comes out next month, you'll see."

She turned her head away, drumming her fingers on the tabletop. I needed to clinch it with a fact that couldn't be written off as a simple guess.

"Luke Skywalker dies."

"Now you're just making stuff up," said Meghan. "Just stop."

She looked like she might cry and her mouth turned down at the corners. She wasn't considering my words. Red colored my vision.

I gulped my cooling tea. I didn't want to stay here, thankful Christopher had helped me remember how to drive. I wouldn't have to stay. It was almost dark, but I was mad enough to leave, anyway. To hell with Thanksgiving dinner.

"Get my cat. I'm leaving. When you're ready to listen, I'll be at Christopher's, since I can't go home. I have to see about getting him out on bail."

I stood up, and my legs wobbled. A wave of heat rushed through me. I grabbed the edge of the table as my vision blurred. I couldn't type. The room spun, and I crumpled to the floor. The bright light hurt my eyes, and the tile was cold and hard. A timer went off on the oven.

"The tea," I mumbled under my breath. She'd put something in it.

From a long way away, Meghan said, "Dad, it's for her own protection. I'm worried she'll harm herself. Her delusions are dangerous. We can have her held for seventy-two hours while they do an independent assessment. We have to go on record saying we're worried she'll harm herself. Aren't you worried too? She's involved with a violent stalker, defending him. She thinks she's a time traveler. There will be a hearing with the doctor's report and our testimony. We need her to be taken care of by professionals. We waited too long to help Mom. I won't make that mistake with Elizabeth."

Her words stopped being coherent as the room faded.

I returned to consciousness as they jolted me onto something hard and wheeled me from the house. I fluttered my heavy eyelids, but couldn't get them to stay open, so I saw only flashes. Meghan was at my side. She meant well, but this damage would be difficult to overcome.

"I'm so sorry," she said. "It's for your own good."

I didn't agree, but I couldn't say so. I tried to get up, but was strapped down and couldn't move. They stowed me in the back of a vehicle and the doors slammed, leaving me alone. As we drove away, everything faded once more to black.

Chapter 15

I woke to pale light entering the top window cut into the stark white walls. Nothing looked familiar, and the chemical smell had a horrifying familiarity. My heart raced in an erratic fashion while I tried not to panic. I was sweaty, and I felt as if I might throw up. My stomach churned. My first thought was that Eric had done this. I endeavored to move, but found my wrists strapped to the metal bars at the side of the bed. Fear swirled through my veins and my chest constricted like something heavy was pressing the air from my lungs.

Memories came flooding back. Meghan had had me committed to the psych ward. I screamed and couldn't stop. With my brain clouded, this time my scream had volume. I didn't want to be here. I couldn't believe my family would do this to me. Someone dressed in blue scrubs injected me with something in the arm. Everything became foggy again, remote. I floated above myself, watching my struggle to regain control. My screams cut off, and I closed my eyes. My muscles relaxed though my thoughts whirled.

They'd taken Christopher. Eric would hurt me. I was alone. Even in this place, I could be in danger.

I regretted mentioning time travel. I'd known my family would never accept that as a possibility. It must have been the last straw for Meghan, who'd already been concerned about my mental health. I'd ignored many of her texts, suggesting I take time off work, and her repeated questions about my laryngitis. Nobody believed me. A tear leaked a cold track down my face. That wasn't true. Christopher believed.

For a moment, I'd thought I might sway Andrew to my side, but he'd gone along with Meghan's plan. They'd drugged my tea and called an ambulance. I had vague recollections of my arrival at the hospital. They'd taken my phone, causing me to kick and scream. I'd fought when they'd taken my lifeline because, without it, it was impossible to find out what had happened to Christopher. He was in jail and I was worried about him. I'd have to trust that his lawyer would contact his alibis. The problem was, I was one of them and I was in the psych ward. I hoped the others would be more convincing.

Meghan had said the authorities could hold me for seventy-two hours. She would have called her workplace, so I was certain I'd be here the maximum time, as a favor to her, but there were limits to her power. She'd need to work within the law.

Was it like jail, where I'd be entitled to a phone call? With Christopher in jail and my family's betrayal, I didn't know who I could call, even if I could talk. My feelings sank lower. How long had I been here? I didn't know if I'd be left alone the entire stay or what to expect. I didn't want to spend the next three days drugged and fogged. I needed to be calm, follow orders, and be on my best behavior so I could be lucid when a doctor interviewed me. That seemed reasonable. It was hard to stay awake.

The next time I woke, it was bright outside and light streamed in the barred window. There was another bed in my barren white room, but it was unoccupied. Only the best private accommodation for Meghan's sister. I estimated that I'd been here for over twelve hours. I'd spent the night drugged and sleeping. There was nothing to do but wait.

It was sometime later when a nurse arrived with a tray. Thankfully, it wasn't my sister. I didn't want to see her right now because she would make it difficult to remain calm. She believed Eric instead of me, her sister. She'd also compared me to our mother, which was unforgivable. I swallowed so I wouldn't cry.

"You look better," said the nurse, wearing a fake smile.

She looked familiar. She waited to set the tray down while she gauged my reaction.

"If I loosen your restraints, are you going to try to get away?"

I shook my head.

"That's right," she said, "You don't talk."

She swung a hospital table from the side of the bed into position and deposited the tray. My lunch consisted of a tuna sandwich on white bread, a small bunch of bleached-looking grapes, and a mini cup of butterscotch pudding. It looked like plastic, but I was hungry. I'd missed turkey dinner and apparently breakfast.

The nurse released the velcro holding my right arm. She watched me with an intent gaze as I picked up the sandwich and took a bite. The bread was dry, but otherwise, it was okay. I wanted to make a positive impression, so I did nothing alarming and made no sudden movements. She released my other wrist and poured me water in a plastic cup.

At the end of the meal, she handed me a list of patient regulations and a schedule, which she gave me time to read. I'd missed group therapy this morning, which was a relief, though it looked like I'd have to attend tomorrow and the next day. I didn't know what I'd get out of it since I didn't talk.

"Do you have questions?"

I pointed to my inner elbow, where it hurt.

"Standard procedure. We draw blood from everyone when they're admitted. To make sure you have nothing you shouldn't in your bloodstream."

I raised my eyebrows.

"Your sister mentioned she'd sedated you while you waited for the ambulance, so we know that wasn't your choice," she said. "You were clean. No drugs or alcohol."

Sedated wasn't quite accurate. I mimed using my phone, but she shook her head.

"No cell phones and no outside contact for seventy-two hours. If you stay longer than that, there is a supervised area for short phone calls from a landline. No visitors for the same time. After that, there's a visitors' room and specified hours."

I tapped the top of my wrist and shrugged, hoping she understood my question.

"You've been here about eighteen hours, though you were asleep for most of it. They've assigned a doctor to your case who will speak with you the day after tomorrow. If you stay longer, you will speak with them at least once a week. I advise you to tell the doctor the truth, otherwise they won't be able to help you."

I rolled my fingers, as though to say, "After that...."

"If you convince the doctor that you aren't dangerous to yourself, or to others, they may write a favorable report and release you."

Her tone and her eyes showed she didn't think I would leave in the minimum time. She may have spoken with Meghan and heard my claim about time travel. I didn't like her attitude, but I appreciated her information.

"I have to take your vitals. We missed that this morning when you were sleeping."

Sleeping? Ha! More like drugged. They could call it what they wanted. I cooperated while she took my temperature and blood pressure, making note that they were normal. When she finished, she passed me a pile of folded clothes. To my surprise, they were ordinary clothes, not a hospital gown or scrubs. She added a white towel and a toiletries bag. The clothing was Meghan's, not mine. Everything I had was in the rental car or at Christopher's. Eric had ruined the rest.

"You can freshen up in there." She pointed to a door on the left.

My legs wobbled when I first got out of bed, but I regained my strength after a few steps. The bathroom was spartan and smelled like bleach. It contained only a sink, a tube-like shower stall, and a toilet. Once clean, I became marginally more optimistic. I needed to maintain appearances and look together. The biggest strike against me was my inability to speak. Well, that and claiming to be from the future.

The clothing was a reasonable fit, though loose, as Meghan had a fuller figure than I did. I'd always been athletic and slim. I kept my bra and rinsed my underwear so I wouldn't have to wear hers tomorrow. As I walked back to my room, I hitched up the pants. My sneakers, which I found tucked under the bottom of my bed, were also loose, as they had removed my laces. I hadn't been given a belt.

With my phone confiscated, I had no easy way to communicate. I hoped I could make myself understood by the doctor on Wednesday. I didn't want to stay here past the seventy-two-hour hold, though I had little hope for release.

Had Christopher been formally charged? If they needed me to press charges, I wouldn't. The police had read him his rights, but they hadn't searched the vehicle and they hadn't stated specific charges. They might have taken him as a favor to Andrew. It had been Meghan who'd told me what the police had found at the Museum in Christopher's office. Eric hadn't pressed charges as part of his act to look like a nice guy. Eric must have lifted prints from Christopher's office when he'd set him up, then transferred them to his place.

I was pretty sure they could also hold Christopher up to seventy-two hours without formal charges. I hoped he knew an excellent lawyer.

The nurse returned after I stacked the pillows behind me so I could sit upright on top of the straightened covers. It was weird not to have my phone or laptop. I wasn't sure what to do with myself.

"Would you like to join the others and watch TV?"

I shook my head and pantomimed reading a book.

"I'll see what I can scare up," she said. "Shouldn't take long."

Ten minutes later, she returned with three battered paperbacks. Fluffy escapist fiction. Perfect for forgetting you were on a psych hold and your boyfriend was in jail, accused of a crime he didn't commit.

I disappeared into the books until they brought me dinner, then again until I was bored. I changed into the pajamas that Meghan had sent. Climbing into bed, I picked up the novel again when the lights clicked off. I remembered from the regulations that I was required to sleep for a minimum of eight hours per day. They must regulate this quiet-time to encourage rest. I couldn't read, but neither could I sleep, though I tried to appear calm. I didn't know if I was being watched. Tomorrow, I'd have to take part in outdoor exercise and group therapy, probably the following morning too. I wasn't looking forward to being social, especially with strangers. I wasn't in the mood.

With nothing else to do but eat, sleep, and read, the days crawled. My exercise involved supervised walking time outside, but it was cold and not enjoyable. Boring flat walks that were nothing like my recent hikes with spectacular views. I missed Christopher and the mountains. Group therapy was unproductive. They placed me with eight others, and while most of them clamored for attention and wished to talk, I remained mute. I didn't want to be here, but I did my best to remain calm and pass the time.

The third morning was identical, other than minor substitutions to healthy uninspired food. I was relieved that I hadn't seen Meghan, even from a distance. She would have thrown off my even keel. Had she taken time off, or was it policy because I was family, or was it her choice to be scarce? She may not wish to see me either. I'd also done my best to put Christopher and Eric from my mind. I needed to stay focused on getting out.

The nurse from the first day collected me after lunch. This time, I recalled where I'd seen her before. She was one of Meghan's friends and had been at the engagement party. I spied her tag and recognized her name, Chloe.

"The doctor is ready for you now."

Nurse Chloe escorted me down a long hallway, her shoes squeaking on the shiny floor with every step. We passed more than a dozen doors like mine on either side. A couple were ajar, a few were closed with the lights on, the way mine had been. Most were quiet. From one came the sound of tears and another, screaming.

In the common room that I'd avoided, the TV played one of those raucous talk-shows. The volume seemed too loud, especially after the quiet of my room. It seemed like it was yelling at the four patients who sat on plastic chairs. They appeared engrossed in the drama and paid no attention to us. On the other side of the lounge, stretched another hallway with the doctor's offices.

"Remember," Chloe said when she opened an office door. "Be honest with the doctor so she can help. After your meeting, I'll take you back.

I stepped inside and sat in a wooden chair in front of the desk to wait. I tensed and untensed my muscles to loosen them and wiped my sweaty hands on the faded jeans I wore. It became harder to breathe as my anxiety increased. Behind me came the clicking footsteps of high heels in the hallway.

"We aren't in the habit of providing computers for patients," said Chloe.

A familiar voice said, "I realize it's unconventional, but I'd like my patient to have the means to communicate."

The first genuine hope I'd had in days rose as the doctor walked into the room. The scent of cinnamon and goat cheese followed her. What did she get for lunch? Probably something better than processed deli meat on dry white bread.

Dr. Maeve placed a laptop in front of me on the desk.

"Isn't this a mess you've gotten yourself into, Elizabeth?"

Chapter 16

Incredulous to find Dr. Maeve here, it was difficult not to burst into tears of relief. I took a deep breath and flipped open the laptop. I logged in as a guest with a single click—no password required. Sensing my powerful emotions, she rested her hand with its long purple nails on my shoulder for a couple of seconds before she sat behind her desk. The constricted feeling in my chest dissipated. I'd found someone that would believe me, no matter how odd my story. She'd seen the scars and understood what Eric was capable of. Somehow, she'd orchestrated my time travel as therapy.

My nurse stood at the door, so I waited to start our session. My eyes cut to her. I didn't want her to listen and report back to my sister.

"I've got this, Chloe. Please close the door on the way out. Conversations with patients are confidential. Elizabeth isn't dangerous, and I know where the alarm is if I need assistance."

Dr. Maeve's voice was crisp and professional.

I could have hugged my eccentric doctor as the door closed.

She waited a few seconds, listening to the nurse's squeaky footsteps as she departed.

"Elizabeth, you've been naughty. I haven't heard from you in months, despite letting me think you'd stay in touch." She wagged a finger at me. "How is our experiment going to work if you don't keep me apprised of your life? Hmmm? I doubt being locked in here is part of your plan for a better life. You're going to need to catch me up on the details."

I took another deep breath and nodded. I'd tell her the short version, but at least I could be honest.

"Log in through Zoom and use the chat like usual." Her bright blue lips pursed as her finger tapped them while she gave instructions.

My fingers flew over the keyboard while I explained about Brandon's coma and falling for Christopher. She nodded her head when she heard about the deal with Christopher and his more recent declaration that made it null and void.

"That's more like it," she said. "Taking control of your life is excellent. More karate and a new boyfriend. Wonderful to hear you haven't been passive and avoiding everything this whole time."

I told her about Sunday dinners and staying in contact with my family, the engagement party, and its aftermath. I summarized Eric's stalking, while she stopped me several times for clarification and details. When I got to the part about the note, she asked if I still had it. I'd saved it initially, but it had since disappeared. She asked that I forward the photo of the heart in the steam when I had a chance.

When I got to the break-ins, I mentioned Real Tech as well. I explained about returning from out to town to Christopher's arrest, though he was innocent. She shook her head when I said I'd tried to convince my family about the time travel, in order to make them see Eric as the villain, but they'd had me committed.

"Your sister is a nice enough girl and a skilled nurse," Dr. Maeve said. "But she has no imagination."

Coming from Dr. Maeve—a sixty-year-old grandma with dyed, flame-colored locks, her rainbow yarn sweater, and knee-high lace-up red leather boots—this was a critical flaw, a harsh indictment.

My surprise at her criticism of my sister must have shown, because she said, "You and Meghan are very different. You've always seen possibilities about your work and your life. She prefers everything to be safe and predictable. She needs to be in control."

It sounded like Dr. Maeve preferred someone like me, which made me feel valued. The only secret I held back was about Christopher's mind-reading. It wasn't my secret.

"You've been busy," was her comment when I finished. "You're still very tense."

"Christopher. I can't relax with him in jail."

"We need to get you some information," she said, tapping her lip again.

My eyebrows shot up my forehead, surprised that she could help with this too. Of course, what was a little computer hacking when she could facilitate time travel? My heart skipped with excitement while my stomach churned. What if he was still in jail? Where would I go? I didn't want to be alone.

She tapped several keys on her computer and used her mouse to navigate the pages she found, though I couldn't see what she was looking at.

"Does this mean your report will be favorable?"

"You aren't a danger to yourself or others. That's the criteria for a continued psych hold." She waved away the idea.

I breathed a deep sigh of relief at her dismissal of further incarceration. I hadn't realized I'd been holding my breath for the last three days. I wanted to leave. The air here compressed my lungs and made it difficult to breathe.

"I worry that you've gotten involved in something dubious, but for the right reasons," said Dr. Maeve. "It's wonderful therapy to help someone for whom you used to harbor resentment."

It was true I felt different about Brandon now. I felt sorry for him instead of angry. When he woke up, he was the one who would be alone.

She paused. "Do you want to return to 2022? Or are you happier here, despite the setbacks? I notice you still cannot speak in front of people."

"I whisper to Christopher." My cheeks burned. They were usually intimate, naked whispers.

"Oh, that is progress, my dear." Reading my discomfort, she laughed, clapping in delight as I turned even redder. "Fantastic progress. Good for you. Let's continue your therapy. At last, we seem to be on the right track."

She typed a password. "I'm in. What's your Christopher's last name?"

"Winters."

"They released Christopher Winters an hour ago. They brought no formal charges, as all evidence was circumstantial. Even the fingerprints were dismissed."

"He'll be worried when he gets home and finds I haven't been there."

"Borrow my phone." Dr. Maeve slid her desk phone toward me. "Dial nine first."

My hands shook as I did as instructed. I handed the receiver to Dr. Maeve and wrote my comments in our chat.

"I'm calling for Elizabeth," she said when he answered. "Hold on. She's fine."

"She wants to know where you are." There was a pause.

"You just arrived at her father's in an Uber."

He must have thought that I was there. I typed instructions on the screen.

"Elizabeth says not to go in. She isn't there. Ember will be fine and can stay a little longer. The rental car is still there with your stuff."

"Yes, Elizabeth is here with me right now, but she doesn't have her phone back yet. This is the landline phone in my office."

"I'm Elizabeth's therapist, a doctor. I've worked with her off and on for years. Her family had her put on a psych hold for the last three days and she hasn't been to the house."

"Yes, I agree that's extreme. She's at the Providence Portland Medical Center. I'll have her released within the hour if you'd like to collect her."

She paused. "Elizabeth would like to know if you're alright."

She cackled with delight. "I can see why she likes you."

Dr. Maeve didn't repeat his words, so I didn't know what he'd said. Probably something witty or charming. Either that or lots of swearing. That was more probable. His language could be quite colorful. I seldom noticed his cursing anymore unless it was exceptional. Jittery, I couldn't sit still. I couldn't wait to see him. To feel his arms around me. That's when I'd know I was safe.

"Yes, I'll start her paperwork immediately." She laughed. "That you can tell her yourself."

I held up my finger. One more thing. I typed, "HURRY" in all caps.

Dr. Maeve chortled again, amusement sparkling in her emerald eyes. "She says to hurry. I don't think she enjoyed her stay, though she's fine. It was lovely talking to you, Christopher. See you soon."

She hung up the phone.

"Let's get started." Her manner turned professional once again.

She loaded my file onto her computer and filled in the relevant sections. She showed me she was recommending out-patient therapy sessions every two weeks. Under her supervision, I chose times for our next four online sessions.

When I finished, she winked. "I knew something good would happen today."

"I don't know how to thank you. The last few days showed me how important it is to have people who believe you. My family loves me, but they don't know me and I can't count on them to trust me. I'm not avoiding them, but am going to take a break."

"It's my job, dear," she said, patting my hand. "Also, my pleasure. I'm looking forward to meeting your young man. Someone wonderful enough to melt your reserve."

Dr. Maeve came around the desk and gave me a hug. Her spicy smell was stronger up close, but pleasant. She buzzed for a nurse, and Chloe returned.

"Elizabeth will be leaving us. Please locate her street clothes and her belongings. I've filed my report and her ride is on the way," said Dr. Maeve. "Please walk her through the discharge process. I'll meet you both at reception in thirty minutes."

Chloe's eyebrows shot up. Her mouth flopped open and closed fishlike, at a loss for words. A tiny rush of victory zipped through me, but I kept it contained.

"Dr. Maeve," the nurse said at last. "Elizabeth can't talk. It's been six months."

Chloe had more to say, and I didn't think it would be in my favor, despite my best behavior and her friendly manner. She was Meghan's friend and would have heard a different story.

Dr. Maeve stopped in her tracks. "Yes."

"I thought for sure Elizabeth would be staying. Remember what Meghan said?"

"I'm aware of what her sister said. Which was extremely unprofessional of her to share information about my patient. Meghan is not a doctor last I checked. Elizabeth is under my care, and I see no reason for her to remain with us on the ward. She isn't a danger to herself or anyone else. You'd be wise to remember who has the authority to decide the particulars for patients if you'd like to continue working here. If Meghan doesn't like my decision, she should speak to me herself. I'll tell her the same thing. Do you have a problem completing the discharge? Shall I find someone else?"

"No problem, Doctor Maeve," said Chloe. Head down, she shuffled her feet in place. "I'm sorry."

Chloe's eyes shot daggers at me.

"Apology accepted," said Dr. Maeve. "See you in twenty-seven minutes."

I wanted to jump for joy and fist-pump the air. Take that Meghan. Instead, I stayed calm and nodded my thanks with a smile for Chloe.

Back in my room, I didn't have long to wait for my original clothes to arrive. They'd been laundered and smelled like floral detergent that made me sneeze, but I was relieved to wear my clothes that fit. I folded the borrowed clothes, leaving them in a pile on the bed. They weren't mine, and I wouldn't take them. The ill-fitting garments reminded me of my family's betrayal.

The discharge at the reception counter was smooth and on time. Chloe cut off my hospital wristband and returned my phone. The battery had run down, so it wouldn't turn on. Even with it dead, I enjoyed having it in my pocket. I could soon communicate. I threaded my belt into my jeans and replaced the laces in my purple Converse sneakers.

Christopher half ran into the building as I looked up. He must have stopped at home to shave and change first, as he wore different clothes than when he'd been arrested. I had nothing to carry. I ran toward him and he scooped me up in a hug, my feet dangling.

"Thank god you're ok," he said into my hair. "If I'd known they might have done that, I'd have skipped Thanksgiving dinner. If you want to avoid them forever, we can."

I kissed him, wrapping myself around him. I didn't care who was watching. I'd never missed anyone so much in my life. Tears of relief flooded my eyes. He tightened his hold and kissed me in return.

When at last he broke it off, he said, "I take it you missed me, too."

With a dorky grin on my face, I nodded, and he set me down.

"Ready?" he asked as he took my hand.

"Before you leave, Elizabeth, I'd like to meet your young man," said Dr. Maeve from across the room. A faint smile played about her colorful lips.

I switched my hold to Christopher's left hand. I didn't want to let go. When we turned back toward the Doctor, I glimpsed a furtive movement as someone ducked into a nearby office. Had Meghan been watching?

"Dr. Maeve." He shook hands with the doctor. "I'm Christopher. I appreciate you looking out for my Lizzie."

"I haven't heard her called Lizzie before." Dr. Maeve turned her thoughtful look on me. "I'll remember that. She probably hates it." She winked.

I shrugged. Only Christopher called me by that name. From anyone else, it would be wrong. I used to hate it, but now it was special.

"She has appointments every two weeks. Please make sure she logs in on time. They're on Zoom and she has no excuse to skip them."

He squeezed my hand as I nodded. I wouldn't skip them. Dr. Maeve had done me a favor in accepting everything I said and tracking down Christopher. She'd spared both of us worry.

"Be careful, you two," she said as we left.

When we got to the car, Christopher still had the white SUV. He must have used this one because it was harder to follow.

"Your dad was home. I picked up Ember but didn't tell him anything about your release. I was angry, and he was pretty sheepish." We drove out of the lot and headed for home. "I wasn't sure he was going to give me the cat, but I insisted. You said she could stay, but I'd rather we have her, so we don't have to go back."

I squeezed his arm in thanks.

"You must have questions," he said. "Because I sure as hell do."

I nodded and held up my phone to show him it was dead.

"That's okay. I'll go first, if that's alright with you."

It was preferred. I'd been so worried about him. I nodded.

"They had nothing on me, but they weren't talking at first. They stuck me in a cell and said they'd be back to let me make my phone call, but it took all night. In the morning, they stalled again. It took my lawyer most of the next two days to get access and permission to view the security footage of the Museum. He had to find someone with the authority to have me released, and that seemed harder than it should. Turns out, someone used your missing key card to plant your belongings in my office. The person kept their backs to the camera the whole time, but was too small to be me and was too big to be you. I'm betting it was Eric or someone he hired."

We were on the mountain and on vacation at the time my card was used.

"We paid for gas and groceries on the way to the cabin, and coffee on the way back with my credit card, placing us far from the scene. I made a fuss about your security card being stolen in your break-in. It was on record with the Museum's security that you had to have it replaced. They should have deactivated the old one. I'm reporting that in the morning. Once we had that, they had to release me, even if they stalled until this afternoon. They had nothing."

He stopped at a red light and tapped his fingers on the steering wheel in time to the Foo Fighters' song on the radio. "Even their so-called fingerprints consisted of a partial, smudged set. My lawyer had them thrown out in a minute. It was easy to show that they could have been transferred from somewhere else. He did a trick with tape as proof."

He glanced at me. "The whole time, I worried about you on your own. I was afraid that sick bastard would come after you, which was the whole reason he framed me. He wanted me in jail so he could get to you. He's probably fuming that you ended up out of his reach. I don't know where Eric lives, or I'd kick his ass."

Christopher's knuckles gripped the wheel, and when he turned, he stomped on the brakes.

He glanced at my face. "I won't do anything stupid. I just hate that asshole. I've been angry and unable to show it for days. I kept it bottled up, so I didn't get in more trouble."

I could relate. I'd been livid, but also on my best behavior.

"Let me guess," said Christopher. "You told your family about the time travel and they didn't believe you." He rested his hand on my leg.

I looked out the window and blinked back tears. I couldn't fool Christopher, nor did I want to. I just wanted to get control of my emotions.

"They could have said they didn't believe you and left it at that." He sent me a sideways glance. "They didn't have to have you put in the psych ward. That's pretty cold."

He would have seen glimpses of the scene in Dad's kitchen from my thoughts.

That had been what I'd considered my worst-case scenario. Until they'd drugged me and had me sent to the psych ward, which gave a whole new meaning to worst.

He stopped in a drive-through for coffee and ordered tea for me before the conversation resumed.

"Was it because of your mother?"

I tipped my hand back and forth. Partly. From the outside, I might not look like the picture of mental health but I was stable. Sure, I couldn't speak, but I wasn't dangerous. I needed to work harder to find my voice.

"The house is fine. The alarm company didn't call and the windows, doors, and locks are intact. Before I went to get the rental car, I checked when I changed. I'd called the company, and they said you hadn't returned the SUV. I thought perhaps you'd stayed with your family to be safe. No sign of Horace and Jasper."

We'd named our watchers Horace and Jasper, after the secondary antagonists in 101 Dalmatians. We called their unknown boss Cruella. Giving them Disney names made them seem less frightening.

"They may have been thrown by the unfamiliar vehicle or spooked by the police if they were watching your family. The upside of you being in the hospital is that Eric was stymied."

That was true, but I couldn't forgive Meghan, even if she'd disrupted Eric's plan. My whole family was complicit, but she'd been the driving force. I'd noticed the looks back and forth between her and the others. She had them under her thumb.

Christopher joked about his time in jail, trying to show the humorous side of the situation. "I can't wait for actual food. I'll find something for us in the freezer, so we can shop tomorrow. Tonight, I just want to be home with you."

He stopped at the post office to check the post box. After Real Tech had hung around, we hadn't wanted our mail searched and had rented the box. He ran inside and came back with a yellow packet, which he tossed to me as he got back in the car. I tore open the end and removed a small white box.

"The antivenom?" he said.

At my nod, he said, "I called the hospital about Brandon. There's been no change. He won't notice if I don't visit tonight. I'll stop by tomorrow morning. Today's Wednesday, and we both have work tomorrow and Friday after unplanned absences. Saturday, we can stay all day. Let's try then?"

I nodded. What would they say at work about our absences?

"I got my lawyer to call the Museum," he said. "Said we had car trouble in the mountains and needed a couple more days."

I wondered if the hospital was required to tell my sister that they had released me, though she might have seen for herself. Dr. Maeve wouldn't say anything, but Chloe would've called right after I left. If Meghan phoned, I wasn't planning to answer.

Chapter 17

Saturday morning, Christopher and I prepared ourselves for both positive and negative outcomes. We subscribed to my theory that Brandon's coma wasn't caused by the serum he'd created, but by an allergic reaction. We weren't sure what Serum A's intended effects were, but had determined it was phase one of the experimental treatment he'd developed. We learned that Serum B was supposed to be the second phase, the pain-blocking formula, and Serum C was the antidote for both A and B. Both serums and the antidote required either real or synthetic venom to create.

The doctors said that Brandon hadn't suffered neurological damage, other than the coma itself. Brandon's sense organs and nerves appeared to function and his body reacted normally to physical stimuli. But as long as he was unconscious, we had no way of knowing the extent to which he felt pain.

We gambled on the antivenom as our first treatment. After our research, we'd concluded that it wouldn't cause additional harm. At worst, it caused nausea. Injecting Brandon's concoctions came with more risk. That would only be undertaken if our first trial failed. Without a source of venom, we couldn't make more of the antidote.

We hadn't been able to replicate Brandon's experiments. His written reports left out too many details and the practical aspects were beyond our realm of expertise. His notes documented things for himself, leaving out key pieces of procedure that were a given. We suspected he'd been vague deliberately to keep others from stealing his research. It made him indispensable, an incentive for his boss to keep him unharmed. Smart thinking, but annoying.

At the hospital, the surveillance vehicle used by the Real Tech henchmen sat in the lot with a single occupant, Horace, again. He was easier to spot, as his profile was more distinctive than Jasper, who watched less often.

Christopher and I entered the building hand in hand. The entire way across the lot, I'd felt everyone watching, like we were conspicuous. But when I looked around, no one had paid attention to us, except Horace. Christopher was a frequent visitor and the girl at the front desk smiled at him.

All the way to the eighth floor, I worried about breaking the hospital rules. My mouth was dry and sweat gathered on my palms. Christopher seemed cooler, though he'd mentioned he had qualms about potential complications. After my recent stint in the psych ward, I liked the hospital even less than before. Its combination of smells of disinfectant, stale coffee, and underlying tangy scents of copper and urine reminded me of sickness, disappointment, and pain.

Was this nervousness how it felt to do a heist?

"We aren't doing a bank job," said Christopher as the elevator stopped on Brandon's floor. He wore an amused smile and his eyes crinkled at the corners. If it had been anyone else, I'd have felt mocked or laughed at, but Christopher had a way of making me feel part of the fun. He enjoyed my company and made me laugh. I couldn't believe I'd ever tried to convince myself that what I felt for him was dislike. More like denial about our mutual attraction.

We waved to the nurses and continued to Brandon's room at the end of the hall. Christopher was well-known here too. My heart rate sped up. We were about to try something illicit. We needed to give Brandon the injection of antivenom with no one knowing or there would be consequences. The medical staff wouldn't understand and we'd never be allowed to inject a patient with their knowledge. They still believed he'd suffered a drug overdose.

Christopher would inject him, and I would be the lookout. I seldom entered Brandon's room, so it wouldn't be unusual for me to stand in the hall. Being in the hospital dredged up old memories that made my stomach churn.

We'd timed our visit just before lunch to avoid the bustle of rounds in the morning and the probability of running into Brandon's doctor. Because it was Saturday, we had time to wait nearby in case it worked. If Brandon woke, the first call from the hospital would be to Christopher. We'd go for lunch and a walk in the neighborhood.

Brandon's room was the same, sterile and quiet, except for the sound of the machines. I stood in the doorway, my body blocking the view of Brandon's IV stand from the hallway. It was best to do it right away. If there was an immediate reaction, we could call for help.

Christopher took the vial of antivenom from his pocket and loaded the injector with a quick glance at me. I flashed him a nervous smile and checked the hall. Nobody was there, so I nodded. He stepped to the IV and injected the tube where he'd watched doctors and nurses administer medication. When he finished, he pocketed the empty injector. He waited a few minutes and closed the valve, returning it to its original position.

We didn't know how effective the antivenom would be to counteract Brandon's serum, which was only partly composed of scorpion venom. We didn't know if it would have any effect after three months in this state, as antivenom was usually administered within four hours of the scorpion sting. There were so many unknowns.

Christopher sat on his usual chair beside the hospital bed and told Brandon about our vacation at the cabin, focusing on the hiking and our Star Wars Marathon, not our relationship. It seemed odd to listen to Christopher while I watched Brandon for signs of movement. I didn't want to wait here until lunch. I worried that my watching presence was intrusive and left, giving Christopher alone time with his brother.

While Christopher talked, I slipped out and went downstairs to the cafeteria for hot drinks. While I sat at the table, I let my tea steep. I allowed it to cool to the perfect drinking temperature before I collected hot coffee for Christopher. I'd been gone twenty minutes and thought he'd be ready to leave. He seldom stayed longer than that. Today's visit should appear normal.

As soon as the elevator opened on Brandon's floor, I noticed the difference. There was an unusual hubbub on the eighth floor, instead of its usual quiet. The hive of activity was centered at the end of the hall. My heart and feet sped up as I hurried down the hall, drinks in hand. Christopher stood outside Brandon's room, hovering on the edge of the action but staying out of the way.

"He's awake." His blue eyes sparkled, though there was a crease on his forehead.

I handed him the cup of coffee.

"What happened?" I'd missed a message from Christopher saying, *"He's awake."*

His face split into a grin. "Almost as soon as you went downstairs, he opened his eyes. It took him a few minutes to get oriented while I called for the nurse. They called the doctor up here right away. They don't know why he woke up today as there have been no changes in routine or his physiology. Right now, they're testing his brain function."

He kissed me. "Thank you for giving me back my brother."

Christopher had too much energy and couldn't stand still while we waited for more information. His pacing drove put me on edge.

Several minutes later, Brandon's door opened, and two nurses exited.

One held the door and said, "Mr. Winters, the doctor would like to speak to you."

I smiled in encouragement and he gave me a quick look I interpreted as excitement. The door closed behind him and I couldn't make out words, just the faint buzz of conversation. I was okay with being excluded. I was here for Christopher. He'd share everything in due time.

The door opened again, and a nurse poked her head out.

"Ms. Bergstrom, can you join us, please?"

Curious why I was needed, I entered the crowded hospital room.

They'd pushed the ventilator against the wall, the tubing and mask removed from Brandon's face. He sat in bed, with better color than he'd had in months, despite his three-month coma.

Christopher stood beside him, his arms crossed and his smile gone.

"I don't know her either," said Brandon.

My eyes narrowed as I examined Brandon again.

"What do you remember?" said the doctor.

"I've supposedly been in a coma for three months. I remember many things, but few people, other than colleagues. I remember my job. I'm a toxinologist and work for Real Tech and have for several years. One day, my research will make rattlesnake venom a cure for cancer."

The doctor looked at us for confirmation, and we nodded.

Brandon continued his list. "I know my social security number, my banking information, and my computer password. My full name is Dr. Brandon Franklin Winters. I attended Yale University and completed my PhD at Stanford. My birthday is November 20th, 1985."

I'd forgotten his birthday in the excitement of our vacation. He was a Scorpio, somewhat appropriate for someone who now studied scorpions. Of everything he'd said, I latched onto the one fact he'd stated that was incorrect. He no longer worked with rattlesnakes.

"Ask him the date," I said to Christopher. *"What year?"*

"Can you tell me what year it is?" Christopher said.

"It's 2014," Brandon said. His eyes flicked toward his brother before he answered.

His tone bordered on rude. He straightened the covers on his bed, smoothing them to perfection. Something bothered me about his voice. It was like he was discussing the most boring of subjects, like the flavor of a fluoride treatment or the weather, not his memories.

His belief that it was 2014 explained why he didn't know me. We'd met in 2015. It didn't explain how he'd forgotten his brother, adopted or not. They'd been family since they were seven years old. Something else was wrong that I couldn't put my finger on.

Brandon recited his address, his locker combination from high school, and listed a dozen presidents, moving backward in chronological order. He'd never believe who the current president was, but that was a separate matter. Very few people had seen Donald Trump coming. That was something you had to live in order to believe. There was nothing wrong with Brandon's long-term memory, except that he didn't know his brother. Then it clicked.

"Ask about your parents. Where they live."

"What about Mom and Dad?" said Christopher. "Where do they live?"

This was a trick question. In 2014, they'd lived in the house that was now Christopher's. They moved to Florida in 2015, though I'd never met them. I'd never been "meet the parents" material. I'd thought Brandon, and I had been serious, but that was another sign that we hadn't been close.

"Who?" Brandon said.

His face had no expression, and his voice was flat. He looked around the room bored, like he was watching paint dry.

That's when I realized the piece that I'd been missing. Brandon didn't feel emotion. He remembered facts, but nothing with emotional attachments. No former girlfriend, no brother, no parents. The antivenom had countered the anaphylactic-like reaction to the serum itself, but the serum had been successful at removing the emotional component from his working memory. It inhibited memories. Brandon had become an emotional blank slate. The scientist version of a super soldier.

Christopher's arms remained crossed, and he looked like he wanted to argue, but he kept his mouth shut. He'd rant later. There was a cost to staying quiet and it would eat him alive. Normally, he was a yeller, expressing his thoughts as needed. He wasn't one to bottle them up. I needed to talk to him, to help him understand my latest theory. The serum took detachment to a whole different level.

"Tell him it isn't 2014," I said, since it didn't appear anyone else was going to tell Brandon.

Christopher did as I suggested and included the current date. Brandon had no reaction.

We'd just told him he was missing three years of his life and he acted like he was bored or impatient.

"How long will I have to remain in the hospital?" said Brandon. "I don't feel sick, just hungry. I have important work that has been neglected while I've been here."

"You'll need to stay at least another forty-eight hours," said the doctor. "I'm concerned about the loss of time you've experienced and we have several standard tests for recovering coma patients. We need to evaluate your motor skills, memory, and physical status. We need to determine if there will be lasting effects on your brain function from the coma."

"My brain function is fine," said Brandon, still without inflection. "I'd appreciate it if you two would leave," he said to us. "My medical matters are none of your concern."

I understood, but Christopher flinched, struggling with the words of rejection.

"I don't know you," Brandon said. "You don't belong here. If I have questions about my life that I can't answer, I'll call after your identity has been verified. What did you say your names are?"

"This is Elizabeth Bergstrom and I'm Christopher Winters, your brother."

I rested my hand on Christopher's arm. It was rock hard with tension and he was shaking.

"Right. I trust if you're my brother, your number will be on my phone. I'll call if I need something." Brandon looked away, dismissing us without another glance.

I stood on tiptoe and whispered, "Let's go." I took Christopher's hand and led him from the room.

He stayed silent only until the door was closed.

"What the hell happened? What went wrong?"

"I'll explain outside. I have a theory."

"Of course, you do." He took a ragged breath. "Ok, let's go. At least he's awake and alive, right? That's what's most important."

We headed for the exit, passing the nurse behind the desk

"I'm so happy for you that your brother woke up." Her kind gray eyes were warm and sympathetic. "Would it be possible to drop your brother's personal effects back around later today or tomorrow? I'm sure once he gets his bearings, he'll be thrilled to get his stuff."

"We'll bring him some clothes, his keys, and his phone and charger. We're going for lunch, but we'll drop it by this afternoon," said Christopher.

We would also need to return his computer. I'd already copied all the relevant files.

The nurse had been in Brandon's room and knew he hadn't remembered his brother. As a regular visitor, Christopher was popular and sympathetic.

Christopher was quiet in the car, but we didn't go far, just a couple of blocks to a sushi place. Once we'd ordered our usual way, we talked about what had happened at the hospital.

"Out with it," he said. "What went wrong?"

"I think it went right."

Christopher's face told me he thought otherwise, but he didn't interrupt.

"It's his serum. I think he designed it to inhibit emotions. It suppresses any memory tied to strong emotion. He figured out what part of the brain was targeted by the scorpion venom and used that knowledge."

"Do you think it's permanent?" Christopher furrowed his brow.

I shrugged. *"We'll have to wait and see."*

"He sent us away. He won't put up with us hanging around or calling to check on him." Christopher separated his chopsticks and rubbed them together, the sound both annoying and soothing. "What will I tell Mom and Dad?"

Christopher had a point. We would only know Brandon was better if he contacted us.

"If it doesn't wear off, we could ambush him and inject him with his antidote."

"Desperate times…" I imagined us following Brandon into a parking garage, Christopher wrestling him into a darkened corner, while I injected him with the antidote.

"I wasn't a criminal until I met you," Christopher said, leaning over to take my face in his large, gentle hands. "Not even an imaginary one. What would I do without you, Lizzie?"

"Let's not find out."

His answer was a very thorough kiss that drew looks from the other diners.

"Maybe we should go out to the car and make out like teenagers."

He threw back his head and laughed. It wasn't that funny, but laughing helped relieve his tension.

For all that our gamble with the antivenom had worked and Brandon was awake, his emotional amnesia was a problem. After three months with the serum in his system, I was afraid the effects were permanent.

Chapter 18

The next Friday, the eighth of December, was the office Christmas party and our first work event as a couple. I hated parties and social gatherings, but Christopher was a force to be reckoned with. He was the life of any party. The part I looked forward to was dressing up. Most days I wore jeans, but I liked to wear skirts and dresses on occasions as they made me feel desirable.

"I won't drink like last time," he said. "I was miserable, worried sick, and an idiot."

Christopher wore black dress pants and a white shirt with a striped red and green tie as a nod to Christmas. His crisp white shirt looked like it had come fresh from the dry cleaner. I loved a man that could iron.

I'd taken my insurance money and bought another black dress. Association with Eric and his creepy note spoiled the original. We hadn't seen Eric and while I hoped we'd seen the last of him, I didn't believe it. I hated the feeling of waiting, looking over my shoulder. I'd done enough of that for a lifetime, but he was out there somewhere.

"You look good enough to eat," Christopher said, as I twirled for him, the full skirt swirling around my knees.

I liked the swishy sound it made. *"Maybe we should stay home instead."*

"You're not getting out of wearing your sexy clothes," he said with a wink.

"I'm going to stick to you like glue," I warned.

"Please do. It'll make up for me being such an ass at the last party."

"What did you do besides get rip-roaring drunk, threaten to drive, and follow me home?"

"I might have hit on the boss's wife," he said with a grimace.

I laughed. *"Mrs. Brown? This is the first I'm hearing of this."*

"I just flirted," he said. "I had no intention of it going anywhere, but when it got late, I sobered up just enough to realize that she was interested. She didn't seem concerned about her husband, but I don't know where Jake was. We danced, and she was all hands, clinging like an octopus. When I got away, I hid upstairs."

I bit my lip to prevent my smile.

"I came down when I thought the coast was clear, which is when I bumped into you in the elevator."

"I see. Is she going to be a problem tonight?"

"No way. If she so much as tries to talk to me, I'll make out with you. That should scare her away. My gorgeous girlfriend is a perfect human shield."

I pictured him twisting me to block him from her unwanted advances, throwing me between them. My tiny frame protecting his great big one. I grinned.

"Now I almost want her to try," I said, amused at the image.

I finished putting in my sparkliest earrings. *"Eric's note said he liked me in black. Could he have been at the last party? I didn't see him, but I was so busy avoiding you, you're all I saw. He could have been anywhere and I wouldn't have noticed."*

"Eric probably saw you dressed up when you left your house," Christopher said. "He'd better not try anything tonight." He spun me toward him and into his arms. Tipping my chin upward, he kissed me, soft at first, then deeper, leaving me breathless. "You are stunning."

I'd never thought I was beautiful. My whole life, I'd felt plain, but Christopher's sincerity made me believe I could be. Around him, I was pretty.

Christopher's words almost chased away my belief that Eric would ruin the night; and if not tonight, another one.

"Practicing for later," he said, grabbing the keys and my hand as we left for the party.

Sometimes being with Christopher was all I thought about; he was as addictive as any drug. He was in my system, yet I always wanted more. It seemed Eric was the same about me and I didn't understand why. In this timeline, we'd only met twice, and I'd never encouraged his obsession.

They held the party in the main reception area of the Portland Museum of Science, which had been holiday-decorated for the public since mid-November. They festooned it with silver and blue ornaments, lights, and garland. Our Christmas tree at home wasn't color-coordinated, but a hodgepodge of special ornaments that was a history of our lives. Putting up the Christmas tree had been a walk down memory lane.

I missed my family, but I was still angry, and we hadn't spoken. What would they think when they watched the new Star Wars movie next week? I might call my dad over the holidays.

We danced and nibbled at food. Christopher held my hand or stood with his arm around me while he chatted with our colleagues. I let my guard down as the evening wore on. He thrived in social situations and it took the pressure off me. I was happy to discover I was having a good time.

The boss's fifty-something wife looked put out both times she'd tried to cut in while we danced. Christopher had done as promised, twirling me closer and kissing me. She got the message after her second attempt. I was tempted to pretend to see her approach again when the music stopped and the lights came on.

It was time for the boss's traditional Christmas speech. Mr. Brown was a nice enough man, almost too nice, in fact. It seemed petty to dislike him. One of his worst qualities, other than his tendency to micromanage, was that he enjoyed hearing himself talk. Once he got the mic, it would go on for a while. He was a less comic but equally loquacious version of the genie from Aladdin. His voice grated on my nerves, though he'd done nothing wrong. I stuck it out for a few minutes, but the monologue continued. I needed a break.

"Back in a minute," I whispered to Christopher, my lips near his ear. A hint of unease about Eric stole over me as I left his side. Taking Dr. Maeve's advice, I distracted myself by looking for five things I saw as I departed and four things I heard. The calming strategy was enough to allay most of my fear. It was silly to be nervous on my own for two minutes with the party so close. I ducked down the long hallway at the far side of the Museum lobby listening to the bubbling voices ahead. The restroom was crowded with others taking an opportune break—others who'd paid attention and bolted sooner. My phone chimed after I'd been gone longer than expected.

"Everything okay?" said Christopher.

It was sweet that he was checking on me. Our lives had been tense for months, leaving us on edge with the break-ins, stalking, and the creepy surveillance. We were seldom apart.

"Just a line," I said. *"There's always a line for the women's washroom."*

There was also an interminable line for the sink and the hand dryer. When I was done, I was one of the last to leave the restroom. When I stepped out into the dim hall, Mr. Brown was finished. His speech hadn't been short. I'd just been gone too long. I paused in the hallway to text Christopher and let him know I was on my way back, when Mrs. Brown slammed into me from behind and bowled me over.

Unstable on my high-heeled shoes, I toppled sideways, rolling my ankle and my left heel snapped with a crack. I caught myself on the wall, but my ankle throbbed, hot and painful. Something inside had popped. A sprain? The hallway lights seemed to dim for a second with my dizziness. Heat washed over me with a sudden burst of anger. Mrs. Brown hadn't stopped or said, "Excuse me." She just shot me a dirty look before she headed back to the party, leaving me on my own at the far end of the long hallway.

If I could have spoken or called out, I would have said something rude. In my head, I cursed her out as I returned to an upright position. The pain in my ankle made me see red. Removing my heels, I hobbled down the hall, shoes in hand. At each step, my left ankle sent shooting pains throughout my foot and up my leg. My dancing was over for the night.

I reached the mouth of the hall and searched for Christopher at the far side of the lobby, scanning the food tables first. I couldn't see him. He wasn't at the bar either. The lights dimmed in the main area as a video montage of our year played on a large screen at the front. Loud music blared from the speakers. I winced, tempted to cover my ears.

I took out my phone, intending to finish the text asking where he was, when a hand clamped onto my elbow. Christopher was a lifesaver and I could use a rescue. But it wasn't him. It was Eric, with his beady eyes and sweaty hands. My resigned good humor vanished, and the bottom dropped out of my stomach. My efforts to stay close to Christopher for safety had failed.

I tried to yank away from Eric's grasp, using self-defense techniques to break his hold. But it was no use, as my heart pounded in my ears. He grabbed my other arm and wrested it behind my back. Tears welled in my eyes, though I clenched my jaw. I didn't want him to see me cry. My twisted shoulder turned numb as he forced me down the hallway to a side door. With my throat closed, I was rendered voiceless, as usual. I struggled, but to no avail.

"I just want to talk. Calm down."

I took a deep breath, trying to scream, but no sound emerged. He shoved me through a side door that exited outside. I stumbled on my injured foot and pain shot up my leg. My shoes dropped in the doorway and I grabbed the doorjamb. He pushed again, prying my fingers loose. He yanked away my phone and tossed it to the floor, where it slid like a hockey puck toward the restrooms. He followed me out the emergency exit into the night, pulling the door closed. We were alone and nobody knew I was missing; a recipe for disaster. Hot tears leaked as I tried to maintain some composure. Panicking wouldn't solve anything.

Though he'd said he wanted to talk, Eric flung me against the cold cement wall. My pulse raced out of control. I clenched my jaw to keep the tears from getting worse. With an arm on either side of me, he trapped me in his personal space. I wanted to turn away, but there was nowhere to go. He leaned in, his face in mine, his hot breath struck my face. Confronted with him, I froze. My limbs wouldn't obey as my heart drummed against my ribs. The wind brought goosebumps to my bare arms. I shivered, though the rain had stopped.

"I've been waiting all night to talk to you. That creep you're with needs to keep his hands to himself. I just need a minute."

He wasn't sane. I tried to knee him and get away, but he blocked my attempt and slammed me against the wall. My vision swam as my head throbbed from the impact, a painful heat on the back of my skull. My mouth was dry as my former husband berated me about Christopher. His voice came from a distance as though he were yelling through a tube. I had trouble concentrating on his words. My stockinged feet were wet and cold as icicles. The pain in my ankle and head warred with each other. I kept my weight on the other foot, but it left me unsteady.

"We have to get out of here," Eric said. "You'll listen when we're alone with fewer distractions."

I was dazed, and though I fought, he towed me into the darkness. He held my hair in one hand and my arm with the other. My struggle was ineffective, useless. Any self-defense I'd learned, now forgotten. My feet couldn't grip the slick pavement behind the Museum as he dragged me deeper into the blackness of the alley.

"Stop fighting, Elizabeth. We want to be together. Don't you feel our connection? I'm saving you from that asshole."

He was so much crazier than I remembered. Unstable and delusional. I tugged in the opposite direction, making him earn every yard of ground he gained, scraping my feet. He removed his keys from his pocket and pressed a button on the fob. A trunk opened on the black car parked nearby. He wrestled me into the trunk while I struggled in silence. My breath came in gasps as I scratched his neck and face, but he didn't let go, though I'd bloodied his face with three long scratches. I tried everything to get away. Everywhere he gripped, bruised my flesh. He was too strong. I sobbed and my chest hurt with the effort to breathe.

It wasn't until he closed the lid of the trunk that I found my voice and screamed—too little, too late. It was after midnight and dark, the back alley deserted. The streets, too, would be empty this time of night. Any noise I made was covered by the blaring music of the Christmas party that had resumed.

The engine started, and the car moved. I beat at the roof of the trunk from inside, but it was ineffective. I needed to think. I took a deep breath and closed my eyes. In movies, people were locked in trunks and abducted all the time. I'd been skeptical about the likelihood of that and Googled it years ago. All cars made in the US since 2002 were required by law to have a trunk release in the car.

When I opened my eyes, I searched for a glow-in-the-dark sticker that should be on the release. I was in luck. It was near the latch of the trunk. I pushed the lever, and the latch released. I eased the trunk open and peeked out. The car picked up speed. I couldn't escape from a moving vehicle. Not far away, police sirens wailed. If I got out, I could run toward help.

I waited for an opportunity and one came sooner than expected. The car slowed, then stopped for a red light. I lifted the lid and slipped out, leaving the trunk ajar, not wanting to close it fully and make either noise or a sudden movement that would alert Eric to my escape. I hoped that the poor light would hide the lid's movement.

The deserted streets remained quiet, but I was only a few blocks from work. We'd circled around from the rear on one-way streets. The tires of Eric's car dug into the gritty sand on the surface as the car advanced when the traffic light changed to green. I didn't care about my bare feet or sprained ankle. I ran toward safety. Adrenaline must have kept the pain at bay. I had a head start and was fit from running the last few months. Brakes screeched behind me and I risked a backward glance.

Eric parked in the middle of the street. He flung open his door and checked the trunk. The lid had risen with the motion of the car. He must have seen it in the rear-view mirror. My feet slapped the pavement and my chest burned from running in the wintery air. My stockings had holes and provided no protection for my feet. The gritty sidewalk scraped my soles, but I couldn't stop. Footfalls thundered behind me. Eric must have abandoned the car to pursue on foot. I pushed harder, my breath loud in my ears as I fled toward the Museum, thankful he wasn't using the car for the chase. On foot, I had a chance.

I passed the homeless couple I'd given change to on several occasions, lying in sleeping bags at the edge of the boulevard park that ran the length of several blocks in this part of Portland. They were park regulars.

"You need help, Miss," the man called as I ran past.

I pointed to Eric behind, filled with desperate hope they could slow him down. I was a block from the Museum stairs; he wasn't far behind and gaining. A crash and curses sounded in my wake, but I didn't stop until I reached the steps. Eric lay sprawled on the sidewalk, tangled in a borrowed shopping cart—the contents strewn everywhere. They'd pushed the cart into his path. I'd thank the couple later for their timely assistance.

I raced on, leaping the stairs three at a time until I reached the front door of the building. I didn't stop until I was inside and at the edge of the party. Everyone here was oblivious to what I'd just gone through. My heart thumped double-time and my chest heaved as I gasped for breath. I needed to find Christopher or hide. Eric might still follow. He'd found me once and would again.

Chapter 19

With the adrenaline fading, the throbbing of my swollen ankle resumed. I ignored it and looked around. Christopher's voice rose above the chatter of the guests and the music. I limped toward the restroom hallway and followed the shouting. He was berating a security guard who shifted his feet and kept his head down in the face of my boyfriend's wrath. Christopher brandished my phone in the poor man's face and gestured to my shoes as he yelled.

"Where the hell is she? Don't tell me she stepped out for a fucking breath of air barefoot. Her shoes are broken and her phone's on the floor. Get a security team down here."

The security guard pointed at me, his hand quivering as he said, "Is that her?"

Christopher broke off mid-rant and turned. The worry left his face, but not the anger. He ran to me, grabbing me into a hug. I yelped, off-balance, my weight shifting onto my injured foot. He was tense and shaking all over.

"Are you okay? Was it Eric?"

His voice was too loud and hurt my ears with its volume.

I nodded. My trembling legs couldn't hold me any longer. When he let go, I collapsed onto the floor and burst into tears.

Christopher must have taken a deeper look at the condition I was in as his tone of voice changed, becoming more controlled. "Call the cops. Is there somewhere I can take her to clean up?"

The security guard opened a door just beyond the emergency exit. He flicked the light switch on inside.

"This will be private, Dr. Winters. It's the security break room, but nobody will bother you. I'll call the police and direct them here when they arrive."

"Thanks," Christopher said.

He took a deep breath as I tried to compose myself, too.

"I'm sorry I yelled. Thank you for your help. I panicked. We need a few minutes of quiet before we make a statement."

"Ms. Bergstrom doesn't talk, does she?" said the security man. He looked concerned.

Christopher held up my phone. It was a miracle that it was still intact. "She can tell me what happened. We'll share the details with you and the police when they arrive."

He helped me to my feet. I'd stopped crying, but my nose was running. I sniffled, embarrassed about my outburst. I must look a fright. Bedraggled hair, mascara down my face, ripped stockings, and barefoot. I was like Cinderella after her stepsisters had gotten through with her, the stage before the fairy godmother arrived. Was Christopher my fairy godmother? Or was it Dr. Maeve? Either of them was an unlikely visual in a ballgown which made me chuckle despite my fading terror. Dr. Maeve and I had another online therapy appointment in a few days, and our conversation would be about tonight's attempted abduction.

At my first limping step, Christopher scooped me into his arms and carried me into the lunchroom. He placed me on a brown fuzzy couch on the far side and sat beside me. The guard closed the door, leaving us alone.

"What happened?" Christopher's blue eyes were as cold as ice, but his voice was gentle. "I lost my shit. I was terrified when I found your phone, but couldn't find you."

He pulled me onto his lap. It felt safe there; he was warm, and my shivering stopped. I leaned into him, his heart pounding like a racehorse. Tension leached out of us both at the physical contact. At first, I said nothing, taking time to calm myself. I held out my trembling hand for my phone and wrote.

"Can you talk?" He pressed a kiss to my temple.

I shook my head.

"Whisper."

My tears threatened again and my throat felt too thick for words, but I wanted Eric caught. I trusted Christopher, and I needed him to speak to the police. Speaking out loud for them tonight was out of the question. For him to tell my story, I had to share. I told myself to breathe.

"There was a line for the bathroom," I whispered. "It took so long. I stopped to ask where you were when Mrs. Brown knocked me over. My shoe broke, and I sprained my ankle. I'd been at the end of the line and I was alone in the hallway. When I stood up, Eric grabbed my elbow and twisted my arm behind my back. He forced me out the emergency exit. When I fought, he slammed me against the wall." I reached up and touched the lump on the back of my head. Christopher's careful fingers found it, too. His face was a storm cloud, but he said nothing and let me continue.

I summarized what had happened after Mrs. Brown bowled me over until I had escaped and was running. I finished with, "A homeless couple in the park pushed their cart into the path and he tripped." I stopped to take a breath. "He acted like you're the one who has abducted me. He said he was saving me."

"There's something wrong with him," said Christopher with a squeeze.

"He left his car in the middle of the street. There should be traffic cam footage. I want him put in jail. He scares me, and I'm not sure how much more of this I can take. Every time I'm not in the room with you, I feel like he's watching, waiting. As soon as I let my guard down, like tonight, he reminds me he's dangerous."

As I finished talking, there was a knock at the door. Keys jangled as the security guard let in two police officers. It was Andrew and his usual partner, Officer Park. Andrew looked uncomfortable and wouldn't look me in the eye. The last time I'd seen him, I'd been on my dad's kitchen floor.

"Ms. Bergstrom," said his partner.

I nodded in recognition. We'd met several times in the years he'd been Andrew's partner.

"We'd like to get a statement," he said.

I slid off Christopher's lap, but took his hand.

"Elizabeth has stress-induced selective mutism," said Andrew. "She's complained for months about a stalker. Her house was invaded several times, and she was followed. It looks like it's escalated."

"Selective what?" said his partner, arching an eyebrow.

"She's unable to speak," said Andrew. "She was in an accident and witnessed something horrible. Her voice doesn't work most of the time. She texts and she whispers."

Andrew hadn't believed me a couple of weeks ago, but tonight he was on my side. Hot tears filled my eyes. It was almost enough to make me cry again, but I held myself together.

"Can you tell us what happened?" Andrew grabbed a chair and sat near me. I texted him. *"I told Christopher."*

He looked at his phone. "Dr. Winters will speak for you. Then we're going to ask you some questions. Can we do that?"

I nodded.

Christopher repeated my story, stressing that from the beginning I'd known my attacker was Eric Dahl. That he'd been stalking me since June and I lived in terror of him, though nobody else believed, not even family.

Andrew blanched at Christopher's choice of words.

As Christopher finished the account, he held up my right foot for the officers to see. It bled from cuts and scrapes on the bottom. My left was in the same condition, but he didn't touch it. My left ankle was swollen and turning purple. Maybe a sprain, but it could be broken.

"She has a massive lump on the back of her head. She needs medical attention. We'll cooperate with your questions, but then you need to let us go, so we can go to the hospital."

"We'll make this quick," said Officer Park.

"What kind of car did he drive?" said Andrew.

"A black Audi," I said. *"Normally he drives a red Corvette."*

Andrew received the text and held it up for his partner to read.

"Where did you get out of the trunk?"

"11th and Mill. Check the traffic cams. He left the car to chase me."

"Did he say where he was taking you?"

I shook my head.

"Did he say what he wanted?"

"That we belonged together. Said he was saving me from that asshole." I looked at Christopher. He winked.

"Did you know this man before your first encounter in June 2017?"

I appreciated his careful wording that used the year.

I shook my head.

"Since that time, have you spoken to Mr. Dahl, dated him, or given him any encouragement regarding your relationship?"

I shook my head.

"Do you believe he is the same person who broke into your house in November?"

I nodded. It annoyed me I had to repeat this, but understood that it was standard procedure. Officer Park wrote everything in a notebook.

"Is there anything else you'd like to add for the record?"

I whispered into Christopher's ear, "I want him stopped so I can sleep again."

"She wants him arrested so she can sleep again."

"Can you show me the emergency exit and where the car was parked?" said Andrew.

Christopher's eyebrows shot up his forehead. "Do you see the condition of her feet?" His voice was loud, almost yelling. He was a hair away from an explosion. Some of his anger was because of his worry for me. He directed the rest at Eric.

I put a hand on his arm.

"Carry me. I'll do it."

Christopher scooped me into his arms and I threw an arm around his shoulders.

Andrew's partner jumped to the door and held it open. Across the hall was the Emergency Exit, and I pointed. My broken and discarded shoes lay on the floor by the wall. Andrew picked them up and handed them to Officer Park. He put on gloves and we went outside. I pointed to the wall and touched the back of my head. Andrew felt the lump.

"Elizabeth," he said, his voice ragged.

This wasn't Officer Jennings speaking—for a moment, it was Andrew.

"I'm so sorry. We thought we were helping. Your sister will be a wreck when she hears. She'll want to apologize."

I didn't want to talk about it, shook my head and pointed down the lane. I wasn't ready to talk to Meghan. About thirty yards away was a dry patch on the pavement where a car had been parked during the rain earlier tonight.

"When he put you in the trunk, did you scratch him?"

I nodded. I'd caught the side of his face at least once. I hoped this wouldn't take much longer. Any movement of my ankle sent shooting pains through my foot up my leg. It throbbed and felt hot. My jaw remained clenched to deal with the extreme discomfort.

"Is there anything else you need from her tonight?" said Christopher.

He'd picked up on my pain, plus I was probably getting heavy.

"If you have more questions, you have her email. Text her, or call my place. I'm taking her to the hospital. Her ankle needs to be treated."

"Make sure they collect DNA from under her nails," said Andrew. "Hopefully, they can get a good sample. I'd love to get the bastard this time."

He clenched his jaw. It looked like he took it personally that Eric had duped him.

We left as the officers called in on their radio, telling the station to put out an alert for a black Audi and to order the traffic cam footage for the area. Eric would be long gone, and I doubted he'd dare to go home after tonight. He may have planned to take me somewhere else and had gone there. This time, he'd left too much evidence to pin it on anyone else. It wouldn't just be my word against his. While relieved they were searching, I didn't expect immediate results. They still needed to locate him.

It wasn't until we were in the house after the trip to the hospital and x-rays, with the lights down, the house secure and locked, Ember on one side and Christopher on the other, that I let myself cry again. Christopher held me and stroked my hair. I fell asleep in his arms, grateful for every second we were together. I couldn't imagine my life without him.

Chapter 20

The next couple of weeks as Christmas approached were slow in the lab, even if other parts of the Museum were busy. I stayed off my sprained ankle and worked on my computer or from a stool. The police hadn't found Eric at his home, and the address for his office turned out to be false. The police were looking into leads about where he worked but had been unsuccessful. The number Andrew had called before was disconnected. Knowing Eric was out there put a damper on the Christmas season.

Eric Dahl hadn't existed prior to three years ago. He'd used a false name. That information was something I hadn't known and hadn't expected. Instead of knowing everything about Eric, he turned out to be a mystery. I'd never known what his job was—he'd told me it was classified. Now even his name was a lie.

On December fifteenth, The Last Jedi opened at movie theaters. Christopher and I went two days later with the tickets I'd purchased in advance. I liked the movie better the second time around. I chuckled when I received a text from Andrew.

"You were right about the movie. I can't believe Rey was nobody important."

"Wait until Rise of Skywalker. We revisit her lineage. Do you believe me now?"

"I don't think you're lying," he said. *"Not sure I believe in time travel, but I admit you know things that don't have a logical or reasonable explanation."*

That was the best I was going to get, and it was better than a trip to the psych ward.

"*Meghan?*" I hadn't responded to her texts. After the incident at the Christmas party, she tried to apologize for not believing I had a stalker. She'd been quiet since.

"*She didn't watch. I went with your dad. You should call him. He misses you.*"

I promised nothing. The anger was still too fresh.

Christopher and I had time off between Christmas and New Year's. The forecast for Christmas day was clear, so we decided to go to the cabin after presents and breakfast.

Remembering Andrew's words, I sent Meghan a Merry Christmas text. Christopher did the same for Brandon. Neither replied. I called my dad on FaceTime. I wasn't sure what to expect after a month of silence, but Christopher talked for a minute and broke the ice. He shared our plan about the cabin and then handed the phone to me so Dad could talk.

"Merry Christmas." Dad looked pleased that I'd called.

I put my hand on my heart and nodded.

"It's pretty quiet here this year," he said, "But Meghan and Andrew will be here after lunch and are staying for dinner. I hear you're headed to Christopher's cabin for a few days. You guys kept the location secret, but I trust you'll be safe. If I don't know where it is, I doubt this creep Eric does, either. Next Sunday is New Year's Eve, and I'd like you two to consider coming here. It'll be low-key, just dinner with your old man. Maybe stay for a movie."

When I hesitated, he said, "Andrew and your sister have a fancy party to go to, but I'd like to see you. Just dinner. You don't have to decide now. Just text me your answer later. Even that day is fine. I'm glad you called. I miss you."

My eyes filled with tears, but I smiled. I missed him, too. I'd talk to Christopher to confirm, but I was pretty sure he'd think dinner was a good idea. We'd leave before it was too late and have time for our plans as well.

Before I ended the call, Dad said, "I know you're angry with us, especially your sister. And you have every right, but she's the only sister you've got. I hope you forgive her one of these days. She thought she was doing the right thing, looking out for you."

My anger swelled. My chin lifted, and I clenched my jaw.

Dad must have noticed too because he said, "I know, you don't need that much looking after. You are not and have never been like your mother. I never should have said that. I'm sorry."

I appreciated his apology. Being compared to my mother had hurt.

"Merry Christmas, Dad," I whispered and then hung up. I didn't know if he'd heard me.

"You good with dinner there?" Christopher said.

I nodded and sent Dad a text. *"Yes, to dinner. Raincheck on the movie."*

Christopher squeezed my hand, then called his parents the same way. He talked to them weekly, but not on FaceTime. His parents had been kind to him, but they were closer to Brandon. They knew Brandon had woken up and were hopeful of his continued recovery. They'd considered flying up for Christmas, but Brandon hadn't returned their calls, except for the first time when he'd asked for time and space.

I'd been surprised this morning when Christopher pulled an extra present from the Winters from under the tree. The card said, *"Elizabeth, we've always wanted to meet you. Take care of our Christopher, Merry Christmas."*

Their thoughtfulness had blown me away, as I had expected nothing.

Today, Christopher tugged me into the camera frame with him and introduced us. It wasn't quite the same as an in-person introduction, but it meant a lot. Christopher had put my name on the gift he'd sent and they thanked me. They'd been friendly and knew that I didn't speak, so it wasn't awkward. Christopher had prepared them well and, as always, he was happy to fill any silence with chatter.

When the call finished, I picked up their card and pointed to the word *"Always."*

"Mom knows I kicked myself for introducing you to Brandon." He scooped me up and kissed me. "Maybe she feels like you're with the right brother this time."

His eyes were serious, with the icy blue that seared my soul.

"No more pining," I whispered, partly in jest.

His answer was another kiss.

"I wasn't pining," he said at last. "I was biding my time for you to come to your senses."

"Thank you for waiting."

I texted when I talked to Christopher if we were out, but alone in our home, I whispered. Dr. Maeve was thrilled with my progress, calling it "Astounding" and said she was a genius. She took all the credit, but I owed a lot to Christopher.

This time, we took Ember to the cabin. She roamed the car for a few minutes, then settled in by my feet and slept. We would have to be careful with the cabin door to ensure she stayed inside, but I didn't think she would want to escape into the cold outdoors.

We left after a quick lunch at home. The journey started clear and glorious as we left Portland, and the roads were quiet because of the holiday. I saw no sign of Eric or anyone from Real Tech, though we watched to see if they followed our vehicle. The landscape rolled by, snowy, but magical where it had been undisturbed. A blanket of snow made the world feel clean and new.

We hadn't gone far up the mountain highway when the weather changed. An angry blackish-gray mass engulfed the sky. The blue disappeared, as did the daylight. It was dark before we expected and the air had a strange yellow cast. Forty minutes from the cabin, the sky turned white and small flakes twirled through our line of sight, melting on the road before us.

The further up the mountain we drove, the larger the snowflakes and the slower Christopher drove. The road became icy and there'd been no sign of the snowplow or sand trucks. We'd rented the SUV again, and he put it in four-wheel drive and slowed our pace to a crawl. The last leg of the drive took an hour instead of half that because of the treacherous conditions and poor visibility. The driveway hadn't been plowed and was slippery underneath the new snow, but somehow, we got to the top.

"We're going to be stuck for a few days if this doesn't let up soon," said Christopher as he parked. He squinted into the whiteness above. The view was gone. "Good thing we don't need to be anywhere for a week."

I smiled. I didn't mind the idea of being stranded with him.

Like last time, we separated to do different jobs for the sake of efficiency. He turned on the cabin electricity and the water in the shed and carried stacks of additional firewood to the back porch, while I took Ember in her carrier, then the suitcases and the groceries inside. Gusts of wind blew my hair in my face so I couldn't see. Broken branches scudded past on the frozen ground while cold snow stung my face and hands where they were exposed. The wind was stronger here where it was open. The mountain above had disappeared in a cloud of white, and it was as though we were alone in the storm.

Christopher had shown me how to start a fire in November and once inside, I did my best to remember his lesson. I was proud when my small fire grew large enough to consume first the kindling, then the larger firewood. The storm should have worried me, but it made me feel safe. Though we were snowed in until they cleared the roads, it meant we wouldn't be bothered. In the back of my mind, I was always aware that Eric hadn't been apprehended, but I had confidence that we would have seen him on the empty highway.

Christopher and I talked more about our past. I told him about my mom and he talked about his dad. We had emotional scars from their bad parenting. My dad had been in denial about my mom's problems until her accident. I didn't think about her accident very often, but the one I'd been in with Eric hadn't been my first.

"When I was ten, we were on the way back from a mid-afternoon playdate. My mom had been drinking in the kitchen with my friend's mom. They'd had several glasses of wine while we played. I was nervous about getting in the car and tried to protest. I wasn't brave enough to refuse a ride home. I was a kid and powerless."

My throat thickened as I continued my story. "She lost control of the car in the rain and hit a cement median. It crushed my side, but the car spun as though in slow motion, water cascading higher than the windows. A big truck hit us afterward. I was okay, but it killed her on impact."

Christopher squeezed my hand.

"That was my first visit to the hospital. It was also the first time I saw an adult's tears. Dad crying was almost harder than the news that my mom had died. It scared me."

"I don't remember my mother," said Christopher, his thumb circling on the back of my hand. "I was too young when she split and I can't picture my father's face anymore, just his grating voice and his sour smell." He stared into the distance for a moment while he collected his thoughts. "He went out for smokes one night and didn't come home."

I remembered the rest of this story. Brandon and the Winters had rescued him. It broke my heart more than ever, though a flame of anger burned inside me at his horrible biological parents. He'd been a resourceful kid to overcome those odds and make something of himself.

We'd brought a few new movies to add to the collection and started a Marvel movie marathon. Eighteen Marvel movies were available on DVD and Christopher owned all of them. I'd seen all twenty-three in the future and knew how the saga ended, but was excited to watch them again. They'd be better with his company. My favorite character was Captain America and his was the Hulk.

Christopher was as gigantic a movie nerd as I was, and we'd brought ice cream and popcorn for movie nights. We wouldn't be able to finish that many movies in our time up here, storm or no storm, but planned to watch them in chronological order. We could continue on subsequent trips, giving us something to look forward to. I'd never thought I'd be with someone who was so fun to hang out and do nothing with. He made me laugh with his ridiculous comments; we liked each other's company.

Outside, the snow piled up, and the wind howled, but inside was safe and warm.

The first night, after Christopher and I had exhausted ourselves and fallen into blissful slumber, something startled me awake. It was well after two in the morning. I tried to remain motionless, as I wasn't sure what had woken me. As I lay in the dark cabin, the howling of the wind carried the same sound as the car I'd driven in the accident, the same jarring noise that used to haunt my nights. I hadn't had the dream in months. Sleeping with Christopher had cured most of my sleepless nights. If I had a difficult time sleeping, all I had to do was reach out and feel him and know I wasn't alone.

I listened to the wind whistle through the walls and thin gaps around the windows where it sucked out warm air, stealing it for the storm. The wind tore around the building and rattled the chimney pipe over the wood stove in the living room. It was quite the snowstorm.

Goosebumps rose on my arms as I turned over my edge of the cover and exposed my skin to the cold air. The cabin was freezing, our stove's heat stolen by the wind. Once I was awake, unless I got up and went to the bathroom and got a drink, I wouldn't fall asleep again. My bare feet touched the wooden floor and shocked me further awake. I was so cold that I couldn't believe we'd slept on, blissfully unaware and warm in the island of our bed. Christopher didn't move as I slid out into the frigid darkness. I tucked the covers back in to preserve his heat.

When I returned, I was an icicle. Christopher's heat radiated through the blankets—he generated enough for both of us. I slipped back into bed, trying not to touch him so I wouldn't disturb his slumber. My side of the bed was cold and the sheets frigid on my bare skin. I hadn't thought he was awake, but he turned and wrapped his red-hot body around my icy one. He put his hand on my chest and tucked me into him. He kissed the side of neck and let me steal his body heat without complaint. It should have been a small thing, but it wasn't.

"You're freezing," he said. "Stay with me. I'll keep you warm."

He was more awake than I expected. He didn't seem bothered about my shivering body.

"I love you," I whispered. Though quiet, my words were audible. It was the first time I'd said those words. He should know, but until now, they hadn't been spoken aloud.

He tightened his grip and kissed my shoulder. "You're pretty okay too. Go back to sleep."

• • •

The storm's fury lasted three days before it blew itself out. In flat places, there were two feet of fluffy snow and the trees looked like misshapen marshmallow people. On the morning of New Year's Eve, the road had been cleared, and we used snow shovels to dig a track on the driveway. Christopher had dug out the SUV a couple of days earlier. As we finished and trudged back up the hill with aching muscles, he pushed me into a snowbank. Snow slid up the cuffs of my jacket and I retaliated, forcing him into the snow up to his knees. He made me feel young and alive.

Ember had enjoyed the cabin and had even caught a small mouse on the second day. Any other rodents had made themselves scarce. We packed up and left by lunchtime, giving ourselves extra time in case the roads were icy. If we arrived at Dad's early, he wouldn't mind. I checked my messages and texted him once we had cell service. I didn't want to be blind-sided like the last time we'd stopped in after the cabin.

It was approaching five when we pulled up to the curb. No cop cars in sight. The yellow house I'd grown up in looked the same as it always had. Cheerful lights shone through the living room and kitchen windows. Red and green Christmas lights lit the eaves and around the windows. I wondered what my dad had made for dinner. Hopefully not turkey. Since Thanksgiving, the scent carried negative associations. I'd been nervous about coming, but was glad to make up with Dad. I decided to try harder to talk to Meghan, too. Dr. Maeve had encouraged me to try again.

Dad wasn't wrong when he said holding a grudge was bad for my emotional well-being. I missed my sister. I wasn't one for New Year's resolutions, but fixing things with Meghan seemed like a reasonable one.

"I agree," said Christopher.

He seldom did that. Most of the time he waited for me to tell him what I was thinking, but I'd long since stopped building brick walls in my mind when he was near.

My palms grew sweaty standing on the porch. I shouldn't be nervous; it was just Dad. I rang the doorbell, and it chimed. I hadn't rung the bell since I was a kid and had gotten my own key. After the way I'd left last time, strapped to a stretcher, I hadn't been sure I would be back.

Dad answered the door with a huge grin on his normally calm face. He waited until we were inside and our boots and coats were off before hugging me. He had tears in his grayish-blue eyes when he said, "We missed you at Christmas. It wasn't the same without you. Your sister feels awful. Knowing your stalker was real. Please forgive us. Forgive her."

I nodded. *"I'm trying."*

He glanced at his phone and smiled.

"Happy New Year's, Christopher," he said.

They shook hands again, and we followed Dad into the warm kitchen. I freed Ember, and she went to inspect the Christmas tree, then the couch. The kitchen was warm and smelled of pot roast. Dad had set the small kitchen table, rather than the dining room, with red and green cloth napkins and Christmas crackers. We settled in for a cozy family dinner wearing cheap paper crowns and reading the lame jokes they came with. We stayed until eight, not wanting to leave too soon, but also eager to get home and our own festivities.

"Are you sure you don't mind us leaving?" I said as we stood by the door.

"I'm happy you came for dinner," Dad said. "My plan is to be in bed by ten. I'm not much for New Year's Eve celebrations. You two go, enjoy the rest of your evening."

Chapter 21

After dinner with Dad, Christopher and I headed home for New Year's Eve. It surprised me how much I was looking forward to being at the house and having a hot bath. We'd had quick showers to conserve water and power at the cabin while the main bathroom at Christopher's was luxurious, with a two-person steam shower and a deep tub with a reclining back, perfect for reading.

Christopher's house felt like home. We hadn't planned on living together yet, but that's what we'd done the last two months while I'd stayed with him.

"Thank you for making me feel safe," I said as we drove up to the house. It didn't sound glamorous, but it was a sincere compliment.

"I always want you to feel safe. I know what it feels like to be unsafe."

After his childhood, he understood the importance of security.

"I want to check my messages, return a few calls," he said. "Meet in an hour?"

"Perfect." I wrapped my arms around him, kissed him. "Thanks for a lovely vacation."

He smiled. "Don't drown."

He winked as I dumped my suitcase in the bedroom and fished out my latest romance novel. My soak was everything I'd wanted, and I got out when my timer went. I didn't like to make Christopher wait.

Christopher called down the hall into the bedroom where I was putting on lounging pajamas.

"Buffy and ice cream?"

"Sounds perfect," I sent. I wasn't up to yelling or even regular speaking volume yet, but it wouldn't be long. Walking into the living room a minute later, I felt underdressed. Christopher wore a pale blue dress shirt that matched his eyes and his good jeans. He must have showered upstairs. He was so gorgeous he took my breath away.

"Want me to change?" I glanced down at my comfy pajamas and bit my lip.

"Never," he said with a flash of his dimple.

"Are you dressed up because it's New Year's? I can put on a dress."

He smiled and his eyes scorched me with their heat.

"I love your kitty pajamas. Go sit, I'll get dessert."

I sat on the couch, grabbed the remote, and pulled up our show while he dished up our favorite salted caramel gelato. My mouth watered at the thought. Dinner had been excellent, but I'd saved room for a treat.

Christopher carried in two bowls of dessert in his fancy dishes. The blue glass ones from the china cabinet in the other room that his mother had collected but left behind. He set his down on the coffee table before he got down on one knee.

At first, I didn't understand what was going on. My hand flew to my mouth. Tears flooded my eyes and my heart skipped several beats. An engagement ring stuck out of the top of my ice cream, which he held before him like an offering. He smiled while I took it all in, but his eyes were vulnerable, begging me not to stomp on his heart. My pulse raced erratically, like my heart had forgotten how to behave, and my hands trembled.

"Lizzie, you mean more to me than I ever imagined anyone could. You fill a void in my soul. You're my other half. Since we've been together, even if there have been some rough experiences, this has been the best time of my life, and I owe it to you."

My heart thumped so hard against my ribs, I worried it would jump out. I hadn't expected his proposal and was floored.

"Will you marry me?"

Overwhelmed with joy, I tried to express what I wanted to say. Even whispers eluded me and my mind was swept blank.

Christopher misinterpreted my silence and set the ice cream down on the coffee table.

"You don't need to decide right away. I just want you to know how much you mean."

I couldn't bear the thought that he might doubt my answer, and it prodded me into action. I slid onto the floor in front of him and plucked the icy ring from the ice cream and sucked off the ice cream while my eyes didn't leave his. His sudden grin told me I'd done the right thing. I warmed the white gold in my mouth and passed it to him.

Like all my important declarations, I answered, my lips against his. "See if it fits."

The cold band slid onto my finger as though made for me. Christopher took my face in his hands, reducing my insides to jelly. His thumb stroked my jaw, sending currents through me everywhere. His lips were gentle as we kissed. My heart might burst. I'd never been more in love.

"Tell me again," he said, leaning back, so I saw his entire face.

"I love you." I had no doubts.

This time, our kiss led to more than kissing.

By the time we finished, he'd satisfied me in every way, though our ice cream had melted into sticky caramel puddles. I stirred mine, forming a soft-serve pyramid, which I swirled and licked from my chilly spoon. We cuddled on the sectional couch, our feet in front of us while we watched our show. I stole happy glances at him, trying to make it feel real.

Just before midnight, we turned off the TV and Christopher whisked me off to bed for a second round of love-making. A perfect start for 2018.

• • •

On New Year's Day, in the afternoon, we strolled around the neighborhood, enjoying the crisp winter weather. There was less snow than the mountains with only a skiff remaining on the ground, and it wasn't as cold, but it was brisk enough that we returned with rosy cheeks. We didn't discuss a date for our wedding, but I was content to be engaged for a while—to enjoy the feeling. There was no need to rush. Maybe we could get married next year at New Year's. We'd be able to refer to each other as "my fiancé".

When I'd gotten married before, Eric had planned everything and had chosen a date less than a month away. Everything had been rushed. We'd been married at City Hall and kept it secret until afterward. The day had been flat and unreal without family.

I didn't want a huge fancy wedding, but this time I wanted something that Christopher and I could make special. The other benefit of waiting was that it gave us time to smooth things over with my sister and his brother.

When we got back to the house, Christopher had a voicemail from Brandon. We'd shared our joyous news with family this morning—calls to parents, Brandon via voicemail, and Meghan by text. Christopher's eyes lit up and his face became more animated than I'd seen all day. As he listened to the message, his good humor faded and his fist clenched.

"His memory seems to be caught up." Christopher placed his phone on the counter. He glared at it with suspicion, or like it was poisonous.

"What do you mean?" I came around the table so he could hear my quiet voice.

"It means his research is up to date. He knows it's 2018. Scorpion venom instead of rattlesnake. He asked if we'd taken anything from his place, specifically a jar from the fridge. He'd better not start experimenting on himself again."

"Look at the positive side. He remembers more." Interpreting the closed look on Christopher's face, I said, "He didn't mention our news. At all?"

He shook his head. His mouth remained flat, and I read his disappointment.

"What are you going to tell him about the jar?"

"Nothing."

"It might be our chance to inject him with the antidote."

"Don't think he cares about the antidote. Says his mind has never been clearer." Christopher's jaw tightened. "He enjoys being... unemotional."

"It sucks that he didn't call to congratulate us, or even to talk to you. Just to say that he wants his stuff back. That's thoughtless. That part of him hasn't improved. Remind him about the break-in last fall. He can draw his own conclusion."

"I thought he'd improve," he said. "I thought maybe by now he'd want to try hanging out, get to know me again. Come for dinner or go for beers. Some sign that I matter."

My heart went out to Christopher. He sounded defeated. I hugged him, hard. I couldn't make up for his brother's insensitive actions or how his brain had been compromised, but at least I was here. We'd get through this together.

"We have nothing to cook for dinner tonight." He squeezed and let go. He reached for his phone and keys on the counter. "I'm going out."

"We were going to order pizza. We can shop tomorrow. It's a holiday, lots of places are closed."

"I need something to do. When I'm around you, I don't like being angry. I need to blow off steam. Loud music in the car, slam the doors, buy red meat. I'll be fine." He tried to smile, but his heart wasn't in it.

I nodded. Christopher spent all his time with me. He was gentle and sweet, but he missed his brother and he needed time alone. Now that we were home, we could pursue our regular hobbies, like my reading and his video games in his office. In the cabin, we'd been together even more than usual. It wasn't a problem, but he needed a break.

An unreasonable spike of fear ran through me and, for the first time in ages, I imagined the brick wall. Christopher didn't seem to notice. I didn't want to be alone, but it was silly to feel unsafe in the house. Something bad could happen if he left home, though that was silly. He referred to it as our house and had treated it like it was our place for months. I still owned my townhouse, but planned to sell it soon. It was scheduled to be repainted and re-carpeted. We'd salvaged more of my belongings, but I didn't want to live there and Christopher understood.

After the surprise proposal, this was my home in truth and I wouldn't need to find a new place. Here, there hadn't been problems with Eric or Real Tech. I was safe.

"You go. Blast the stereo. Go for a drive. Buy giant steaks. I'll be fine."

"Thanks for understanding, Lizzie." He kissed me. "I don't know what to do about my brother, and I need to clear my head. I'll be back in about an hour. Anything special you want me to pick up?"

"More ice cream," I said, arching one eyebrow.

He attempted a better smile. "Of course."

The car engine roared to life outside. From the window, I watched the rosy glow of his taillights as he left.

Ember and I rattled around inside the quiet house. Christopher was substantial and talkative and took up space. His laugh made the house warm and lived in. Without him, it seemed cavernous. I turned on the stereo for background noise, grabbed a book, and took a hot bath. I didn't pay attention to the time, but emerged when my water got cold. Hunger prompted my stomach to investigate. How much longer would Christopher be gone? To keep busy, I finished unpacking and started the vacation laundry I'd avoided earlier by going for a walk.

I made tea, grabbed a snack, and fed Ember her dinner. It was dark outside. I checked out the windows time after time, watching for Christopher's return, hoping to see the glow of his headlights turn into the driveway. But he didn't. I hated waiting and chewed my lip. He'd been gone longer than expected. As I was someone with a poor sense of time, I gave him the benefit of the doubt. He'd be home soon.

Time passed, and my imagination invented scenarios to explain his absence. He'd run out of gas. He'd run into an old friend and they were caught up talking. He'd gone to Brandon's to confront him. The car got a flat tire. He'd had trouble finding a store that was open. I made reasonable guesses and less reasonable ones. In any of these scenarios, he would have called or would soon. I tried not to consider ones where he could be injured, like car accidents. My worry mounted. It wasn't like him to be missing or careless of time.

After three hours, when he still wasn't home and hadn't called, I texted.

"Home soon? Should I figure out my own dinner?"

At eight p.m., I still hadn't heard from him, so I heated a can of chicken noodle soup for dinner. My unease had grown and tied my stomach into knots. His absence was out of character. He was punctual and considerate about letting me know when he was running late. When the doorbell rang, I forgot my usual caution and ran to the entrance, hoping that he'd returned with his hands full and needed help with the door. My hands trembled as I opened it, afraid it could be different news.

A delivery man handed me a long rectangular box with a white ribbon tied on top.

My brow furrowed. I'd ordered nothing, but it was addressed to me. Not Christopher or us.

I checked my phone. Still nothing. Curious, I took the box. After the delivery man drove away, I opened it. Inside lay a dozen blood-red roses in a nest of snow-white tissue. I hadn't received flowers in years. My hand shook as I reached for the card. Maybe Christopher had planned this, knowing he'd been gone longer than expected.

'I miss you. We belong together, Love Eric.'

The blood drained from my face and I dropped the box as though scalded. It hit the floor and bounced, roses scattering on the floor. I backed away. My stomach churned. There'd been no sign of Eric since the night of the Christmas party. I broke out in a cold sweat. Did he have something to do with Christopher's absence? The timing of the flowers couldn't be random.

Christopher hadn't answered my last text, so I sent another. *"Roses arrived from Eric. WTF. Are you ok?"*

A creeping sense of anxiety mounted with each second of silence. I waited another fifteen minutes, trying not to watch the clock despite my panic. My throat was dry. I wanted to be wrong, to give Christopher a chance to reply. Still no response. Something must have happened. I needed help.

With shaking hands, I called Christopher's phone, hoping he'd pick up, even if I hadn't tried speaking on the phone. I dreaded each ring, as it meant he couldn't answer. What if he was injured? Dead? It was easy to visualize a scene of a roadside accident caused by the icy, treacherous roads. Whether or not I could speak was moot. He didn't answer. His phone rang four times, then went to voicemail. I couldn't leave a message. I sent a final text.

"Please let me know you're ok."

I told myself it was the last message and that he'd be home soon, then we could laugh about how silly I was to panic.

The silence became deafening. An old clock ticked on the wall by the kitchen and Ember crunched her kibbles. Even the hum of the refrigerator hurt my ears.

By ten, I was a nervous wreck, my chest tight with each breath. I'd lowered all the curtains and blinds and double-checked the locks. I checked and rechecked that the alarm was armed. I couldn't sit still or concentrate. I tried several TV shows, but nothing held my interest. I reread the same page several times before I gave up on reading. Going to sleep was out of the question, though it was getting late.

I might be over-reacting, but he'd been gone five hours instead of one. It was time for the cavalry. I texted Andrew.

"Sorry it's late, but I need help. Christopher went for groceries five hours ago. Hasn't come back. They delivered flowers from Eric tonight. Coincidence? Please advise."

Less than a minute later, Andrew called. My ringtone echoed in the empty house.

With trembling hands, I answered the FaceTime call.

Andrew had a deep furrow in his brow when he appeared on my screen. He was in pajamas and probably was on his way to bed.

"You okay?"

I shrugged, then shook my head.

"Eric sent flowers. Was there a card?"

I nodded as he went into police mode.

"Show me."

I found the card on the floor where I'd dropped it and showed Andrew. I kicked the box of flowers.

"Where would Christopher have gone for the groceries?"

I wasn't sure how to answer. I took a deep breath and closed my eyes.

I pretended Andrew was Christopher and whispered. "Albertsons is closest. The one on Twelfth, but they closed at nine. He got an upsetting call from Brandon before he went out. Maybe he went to talk, but I have a bad feeling. He hasn't answered his phone or texts. It's not like him. Something's happened. I feel it in my gut."

"It's late enough and after all the trouble you've had, I understand why you'd be worried," Andrew said.

His voice was even and projected calm. Relief flooded through me that my concern was being taken seriously.

"I'll call someone at the station, have them send a car to swing by the grocery store and his brother's. Send me Brandon's address. Is there anywhere else he might have gone? A bar or pub he might have gone for a drink?"

I shook my head. I didn't know. He'd done nothing like that in the four months we'd been together. When he used to have beers on Thursday nights with Brandon, I didn't think they had a usual place. They'd tried different places, so I didn't know where to start. I took a deep breath to keep from crying.

"With the joyous news you shared this morning, I agree it's troublesome for him to be gone so long with no word."

"Thank you." My voice shook. I hated to seem like a clingy girlfriend, but this was something more. The flowers had been a taunt, a message.

"What was he driving? His sports car?"

I nodded.

"Do you know the license plate?"

I sent the letters and numbers to Andrew.

"Are you without a vehicle? You have work tomorrow. With your stalker on the scene again, I'd feel better if you didn't bus or walk alone."

I shook my head. "Rental SUV. We took it to the cabin and kept it because of the snow."

"Good. At least you're not stranded."

I took a deep breath that made my constricted chest ache. The fear wouldn't dissipate and the tight band remained.

"Congratulations on the other news. We texted, but it's better to say it when I can see your face. Meghan and I are happy for you two. You deserve something wonderful."

I blinked my eyes to keep the tears back. It felt like a car had parked on my chest, making it hard to breathe.

My brother-in-law's face held sympathy. I hated to feel so helpless. So much for regaining strength and confidence. One evening alone shouldn't leave me a pathetic wretch.

"We'll find him. I'll let you know as soon as I hear something. I'm calling this in."

"Thank you," I whispered.

After checking the locks for the dozenth time, I got ready for bed. I gripped my phone, even in bed, hoping Christopher might call.

Forty-five sleepless minutes later, my phone rang. I jumped at the noise and answered, my heart racing.

It was Andrew again, still wearing Officer Jennings' face and a navy-blue robe over his pajamas. I'd kept him up.

"I don't want to alarm you," he said.

My heart stopped and my blood froze. It hurt to swallow and my hands turned ice cold.

"It was good you called this in," he said. "They found his car outside the grocery store with all four tires slashed. His phone was under the car on the ice. The notifications are your calls and texts. He didn't see them, but it gives us a timeline. We've sent a team to do forensics. He's only been gone a few hours. We'll find him."

Chapter 22

I survived the next week in a daze, sleepwalking from one meeting or a job to the next. Co-workers came up to me at work to express their sympathy and concern. Everyone liked Christopher. I showed them my engagement ring and tried to be positive, but my smiles were forced. Everyone was kind, but it made it harder to pretend that I was okay, because I wasn't. I was terrified. Friday night, I looked in the mirror and didn't recognize myself.

I resembled a version of myself I hadn't seen since the days when I was married to Eric. My eyes were bloodshot and rimmed with red, though I'd refused to cry. My cheeks were hollow, though I tried to eat. Nothing tasted right. Christopher and I had enjoyed eating together. Food had been our first common ground and meals without him were strange. It wasn't the same alone, night after night, in our house. It was no longer safe and inviting. Just empty.

If they didn't find him, what would I do? I hadn't heard from Christopher's parents, though I expected to soon. I didn't have their number and he couldn't answer his phone, which was at the police station. Perhaps they hadn't noticed his disappearance yet. After all, they'd talked on New Year's Day. I dreaded their call, not knowing what I'd say or how.

After five days, the police had no leads. It was as though he'd vanished. I lived in a perpetual state of fear that I might be next. I waited to hear from Eric, expecting his involvement and demands. I was frustrated that though the police worked hard, they had learned little beyond an approximate time for his disappearance. I needed more help to get results. I wanted Christopher.

I sent a message to Andrew

"Can you recommend an investigator? There've been no leads in almost a week."

"These things take time." He video called, sympathy in his eyes.

I chewed my thumbnail, which was bitten to the quick.

"We don't have time. He's been gone too long. Weird stuff is going on. I don't want the police to think I've lost my mind. But I can't do this alone." I was getting used to whispering to Andrew, too.

"Time travel weird?"

"I need someone who would believe me if I said that was a reason."

"I'll get back to you." He ended the conversation thoughtful, rather than annoyed.

Saturday morning, Andrew sent a photo of a business card. 'Wilson Detective Agency.' Then he called on FaceTime.

"I asked around. The Wilsons are a husband-and-wife team, Luke and Ella. They specialize in unusual or unexplained cases. Even though I haven't worked with them, I've heard they're terrific. They've gotten results in situations that were mysterious and unsolvable."

"Thank you. You're the best almost-brother-in-law ever."

"Will you come to dinner Sunday | ? Meghan needs to talk to you."

"I can't drive in the dark." It sounded idiotic out loud, even delivered as a whisper to someone I trusted. "I'm scared." Thanks to Christopher, I now drove in the daytime. I left for home before dark, even if that meant at this time of year, I was leaving work by four-thirty in the afternoon and taking an Uber when I had karate.

Andrew didn't bat an eyelash. "We'll come to your place and bring the food. All you have to do is open the door and provide plates."

I suspected he was worried that I wasn't eating, but I wanted to see my family. I needed a hug, though my muscles were so tense I might break if they squeezed too hard.

I nodded. "Six?"

When I got off my call, I considered my next move. I couldn't speak on the phone to strangers. Texts wouldn't provide enough information. I sent the investigators an email.

Luke and Ella Wilson,

I was given your card by my brother-in-law, a police officer in the Portland PD He says you specialize in unusual cases. I'm not sure how unusual my case is, but I need help. My fiancé has disappeared without a trace, one day after our engagement. The odd part is my circumstance, which may or may not be related. If you take the case, I will explain more. One complication is that I have selective mutism and cannot speak over the phone. I would like to meet in person if possible. Between texting and gestures, communication will be easier than over the phone. Alternatively, I can meet online via Zoom and use the chat function.

If you are interested in my case and are available ASAP, please contact me at 555-899-2411.

Sincerely,

Elizabeth Bergstrom

I didn't expect a reply this weekend. It was Saturday, and Sunday was a day off for many businesses. An hour later, I received a text from an unknown number.

With my heart pounding, I read.

Elizabeth, we'd be happy to hear the details of your case this afternoon. Come to our office on Ninth. Address on our card. Two p.m.? -Ella Wilson.

For the first time in days, I latched onto a shred of hope. It was noon, only two hours away. Knowing how poor I was with time management, I ate a tuna sandwich and left by one. I'd arrive downtown early, but I couldn't be late. Not for this.

I waited in the car until ten minutes before my appointment, my head swiveling while I kept watch for Eric, then went to meet the Wilsons. Their office was in an older three-story building off the beaten path, but close to work. As I climbed the narrow staircase to their office, it didn't impress me. The place was run down and smelled like old smoke. Upstairs, the carpets were threadbare, and the walls were scraped and in need of fresh paint. They'd stenciled their names onto the window of a door at the end of the dingy hall. The next surprise was their ages—they were younger than I expected. Ella was petite, blonde, and wore designer clothing. She also couldn't be over twenty-five.

Luke wasn't much older. He was tall and dark with the bluest eyes I'd ever seen. My first impression was that he was like a quiet Christopher. He had some of the same air of practicality, but I sensed he watched more than he talked. He reminded me of that scene where Jason Bourne had no memories but could describe what he'd noticed coming into a diner—threats, weapons, and exits. Luke's eyes were like that—they missed nothing.

The Wilsons made a striking couple, though I was a little put off by their youth. I tried not to be disappointed. Andrew wouldn't have sent me if they weren't excellent investigators.

"Ella," she said with a disarming smile. "He's Luke. You must be Elizabeth."

I nodded.

"Take a seat," she said, indicating what looked like her desk, with a jar of purple pens.

"You can type on my computer," she said. "I've got a chat program open. I'll sit with Luke so we can both see your answers."

"Coffee or tea?" she said, waving to a kettle of boiling water and a coffee maker with fresh coffee.

I sat and typed, *"Tea, please."*

She fixed tea for the two of us and set out a tray with sweeteners, so I helped myself. She poured coffee for her husband and gave him a stunning smile when she placed it beside him.

His thank you to her was as personal as a kiss. They looked so in love. What was their story?

Impressed with her thoughtfulness, I leaned back in the comfortable black leather chair. Their preparedness elevated my opinion of their competence.

"I read about selective mutism," Ella said once we were ready. "I don't expect you to talk, but the more information we get, the more likely we are to help."

I nodded.

"Tell us about your case," she said.

"It's weird," I typed, *"Which makes me nervous about explaining. Last time I told someone, I spent seventy-two hours in the psych ward."* For a second, I wished I hadn't shared that, but if they investigated me, it might come up.

Luke said little. He let Ella take the lead, but he was watching at me. Analyzing.

My eyes flicked in his direction.

"Shoot," he said. "We can handle it."

"Last May, I made a wish and traveled back in time five years to this time. I'm from the future. I don't plan to go back. I can't do it at will. I've made different choices, fallen in love with someone new, and gotten engaged."

I glanced up to see how they'd taken 'time travel' and 'future.'

No reaction. Their faces were impassive as they read the screen. I wasn't sure if that was a positive sign or not. At least they weren't mocking.

I took a deep breath and told them the short version of my time in 2017.

"Has your former-late-husband-turned-stalker hurt you?" said Ella as I finished.

She made a note on a notepad.

I shook my head. *"Christopher interrupted him the first time in June. He abducted me from my office Christmas party in early December, but I escaped. We haven't seen him since. I'd hoped he was gone. It's hard to live looking over your shoulder all the time."*

Luke and Ella exchanged glances, making me wonder anew about their story.

"On the first, Christopher received a call from his estranged brother. He got upset and went for a drive. Five hours later, his car was found with

all four tires slashed. He was gone. There have been no leads. It's like he vanished."

"Have they traced his phone?" said Ella as she made another note.

"It was under his car on the ground, with my texts unread. That gave the police the time of disappearance as between five and six p.m. Nobody at the grocery store saw anything unusual. A tub of ice cream and a tray with steaks were on the backseat."

I'd put both in the freezer to enjoy when he came home.

"You think your stalker had something to do with his disappearance," she said.

"He sent flowers that night while I was waiting for Christopher."

"Any contact from him since? Demands?"

I shook my head.

"Besides your future-late-husband, named...?"

"Eric Dahl."

"Besides Eric, who might have a problem with Christopher?" said Ella.

"Nobody." I paused and bit my lip. That wasn't exactly true. *"There's Real Tech."*

"You also mentioned an estranged brother." Luke leaned back in his chair and took a drink of his coffee, watching me over the rim of his mug.

"This is weird too." I explained about the coma and the venom, and how Christopher and I had woken Brandon up, but that he was different.

Neither investigator was easy to read. They just asked more questions. I told them about Horace and Jasper, Real Tech, and the break-ins and Brandon's garlic jar with the three serums.

At the end of the meeting, I said, *"Do you believe me? Can you help?"*

"We have no reason not to believe," said Ella. "If I got stuck in a fairytale, you can time travel with a wish."

My glance startled upward. She'd been in a fairytale? Someday I'd have to hear that story.

"The science the brother was working on sounds interesting," said Luke. "It gives Real Tech motive if they think you have something they want or need for their valuable research."

I breathed a sigh of relief that they believed me with so little effort or explanation. I suspected they would verify some of my information before continuing and was glad I'd been upfront with my issues.

"We'll look into the people you mentioned and get back to you in a couple of days. Where does Eric work?"

I frowned and shook my head. *"He said it was classified when we were married. I've never known. As far as the police can tell, Eric Dahl didn't exist before 2016."*

Chapter 23

At six that night, a car parked in my snow-covered driveway. It was Andrew and Meghan.

I sent Dad a quick text. *"You aren't coming for dinner?"*

"You and your sister should make up on your own. Andrew is there to referee if needed. We'll see each other soon."

Turning off the alarm, I let Andrew and Meghan in. Once they were inside, I reset the alarm and locked the door. Standard precautions these days. My family hadn't been here before and they looked around with interest. Christopher's parents had taken most of their belongings, leaving only a few items of artwork and the china cabinet behind. Christopher had decorated the rest with local art and repainted in warm, earth tones. I pointed to a coat rack and accepted a bag from my sister while they hung their jackets. Without Dad as a buffer, I prepared for it to be awkward.

Andrew took the food as I led them to the kitchen. Emanating from the pan was the smell of roasted meat.

I tried to see the room how they would. The Winters had updated the kitchen a few years before they'd moved. It had new stainless-steel appliances, new handles on the cupboards, and LED pot lights in the ceiling. The wooden cupboards were a soft cherry color that gave the kitchen a warm, comfortable feeling. Andrew set the warm bag of food on the counter.

"Dad didn't come this time." Meghan burst into tears.

I hadn't seen my sister cry since I'd moved home from university. Any lingering resentment flew out the window. The intensity of her reaction took me aback.

Andrew indicated with a jerk of his head that I should go to her.

"Washroom's this way?" he said, starting down the hall. "I'll just look for it."

With a ball of nerves in my stomach, I wrapped my arms around Meghan. Her sobs grew louder, great gulping sounds as she tried to speak. Her whole body shook, and she squeezed harder while I held on. When her tears slowed, I retrieved a box of tissues from the island.

"Elizabeth," she said with a sniff. She blew her nose. "I'm so sorry I didn't believe you about your stalker; he could have really hurt you. I hope you don't blame me for what happened. I feel responsible."

It had never occurred to me it was anyone's fault except Eric's.

"It wasn't your fault." I was so upset that I forgot to text. I whisper-shouted my replies. "It annoyed me you didn't believe me about Eric. Then I was irate when you had Christopher sent to jail. You didn't trust my judgment, drugged me, and sent me to the psych ward. But I didn't blame you for what happened later."

"Your story was far-fetched." She looked up, her dark eyes ringed with red. This wasn't the first bout of crying.

"You could have chosen not to believe without trying to have me committed."

She stared at me as though she didn't recognize me. Maybe because I'd defended myself.

"Just because I can't talk, doesn't mean I'm mentally ill or incapable of recognizing when I'm being stalked, or that someone tried to rape me. I can tell the difference between a creep and someone I love."

"I know." She looked down. "Andrew and Dad already let me have it. They're pro-Christopher."

"Good."

"I'm sorry for all of it," she said. "The whole mess."

"Whispering is progress," said Andrew as he rejoined us in the kitchen. "Not everything in the world has a reasonable explanation. Some things we have to take on faith, even when we don't agree or understand. That's how I'm choosing to look at it." He unpacked dinner onto the counter and opened the lids to the containers of hot food.

"Thank you," I said, giving him a hug.

"Your house is lovely," Meghan said, trying to change the subject.

"It isn't my house yet," I said, my eyes feeling wet. There'd been enough tears already.

"You know, you're still whispering," said Andrew, stepping around the island to give me a hug. "I'm glad you're doing better. Christopher has been good for you."

I had forgotten, but they weren't strangers.

He smiled. "Where are the plates? I promised food."

I set the table, and we sat and ate. Over dinner, I told them about my meeting with the Wilsons.

"That's great that they met with you so soon," Andrew said. "They're motivated."

At the end of the meal, Andrew and Meghan packed up and left with more hugs. Dinner hadn't been tense once we'd cleared the air. They'd been a welcome distraction and made the house feel lived in again. They agreed to talk Dad into coming next week and volunteered him to cook the dinner. I would host again. I wouldn't be alone, but wouldn't have to drive in the dark. I appreciated their company and their accommodation.

• • •

Tuesday at lunch, I checked my messages, surprised to see a text from Ella suggesting I stop in after work. My pulse quickened at the idea that they might already have news. I couldn't believe how fast they worked. Their office was just around the corner, so I walked. It made me nervous to be outside alone, but I stopped outside at the bottom of the stairs, planning to give money to my favorite homeless couple, the ones who'd foiled Eric at the Christmas party. The woman was alone.

"Frank disappeared over a week ago," she said in answer to my question. "Maybe aliens. He and four others from the park are all missing."

That was close to the same time Christopher had disappeared. I dropped a couple of dollars in her money tin and kept walking. Maybe this was something bigger than myself and Christopher. Maybe it was Real Tech, and they needed subjects for their human trials. I didn't feel well. I hurried to hear what the Wilsons had to say.

"Yesterday, I tailed the black SUV that followed you to work," said Ella, once I was seated at her desk in front of her laptop and she'd moved to sit on the arm of Luke's chair.

Horace and Jasper had followed me, even though I hadn't known. I seldom saw them anymore. I hadn't noticed Ella in my neighborhood or near my work. She excelled at blending in.

"After you arrived at the Museum, they didn't wait, but drove to the Real Tech lab. That didn't surprise us, but we wanted to be certain where they reported."

"I snooped at Real Tech last night," said Luke.

He may as well have said he'd wandered around the White House at night and evaded security. They'd built the place like Fort Knox and I'd never made it past reception.

"How did you get past security?"

"Invisibility cloak."

"Seriously?"

He shrugged. "You're from the future. A witch gave me an enchanted cloak. We all have secrets. Sometimes they're an advantage."

It was easy to believe when explained that way.

"Tell her what you found," said his wife with a warm smile, resting her hand on his shoulder.

"I borrowed a security card and followed the guard in from the front desk to an elevator. When he returned to the lobby, I checked each floor and poked around. On the third floor, I found a series of rooms, holding cells big enough for people. Several were occupied. You mentioned human trials. I think they've started."

I related my new information about the people missing from the park. Luke nodded, and Ella wrote something in her notepad.

"*Did you see Brandon?*" I said.

"Fourth-floor lab. I overheard two phone calls and recorded them. You should listen."

Luke placed a device on the table.

"Mom, Dad," Brandon said in the recording.

There were brief pauses for his parents to reply, but it was his voice that was important.

"Christopher's fine. Remember, he lost his phone. I'll remind him he shouldn't work so hard and that he needs to get another one. No, he's fine. His medical procedure went according to plan. Elizabeth is taking good care of him and I'll see him Thursday. I can get him to call you in a couple of days if you haven't heard from him by then."

I gasped, covering my mouth.

"*Christopher didn't have a procedure. If he's there, it's against his will.*"

Luke shut off the device. "I agree. It's shady. There was someone unconscious, strapped to a hospital bed in a secure room behind Brandon. I caught a glimpse, and the patient matched Christopher's description. A tall man with dark hair. I waited to get through the door, but Brandon didn't leave."

"*Why is Brandon covering up Christopher's disappearance? Why is he at the lab?*" Now it made sense why his parents hadn't called the house. The other son was lying. I'd blamed Eric, not Real Tech. Brandon and his company were responsible for Christopher's disappearance. I didn't understand how or why. How could Brandon do that to his brother?

"There was a second call," said Luke. "This might not be easy to hear."

I looked up, worried. My icy hands gripped the chair, and I broke out in a cold sweat, knowing this must be worse.

Luke hit play on the recording.

Brandon answered his phone again. Luke watched while I listened. His sympathetic expression made me struggle to breathe normally. He was worried about how I would take the call.

"Hi Boss," Brandon said. "It's too soon to tell. He didn't have an adverse reaction or an outright rejection. Not like the last one."

There was a pause while his boss spoke, though we couldn't hear that voice.

"He should be asleep for another forty-eight hours to sixty hours. I'll have him moved downstairs for observation." There was another pause. "I don't think that will be a problem, sir. After Christopher wakes up, I will update you."

I gasped in horror. I'd been expecting to hear they'd done something to him, but it was worse to have it confirmed. I'd prepared for the worst, but it wasn't enough. My stomach churned.

"We have to get him out." My fingers shook so hard I spelled every word wrong on the first attempt. I took a deep breath and retyped my message.

"Sounds like they've injected him with the serum that removed Brandon's emotional responses," said Luke. "If it follows the pattern, Christopher won't know who you are."

His blue eyes held pity.

"I can't leave him. They've experimented on him." My stomach lurched again, and I fought the urge to vomit. What if he wanted nothing to do with me? He wouldn't remember that we were in love.

"What about the cops? Could your brother-in-law get a warrant?" said Ella.

My heart sank. Real Tech wouldn't let the police search. They'd need a warrant, and I didn't know if we had enough legal evidence to get one. It would take more than suspicion, some missing homeless people, and their stalker-like surveillance. We had no legit proof to tie any of the missing to Real Tech. It was possible Real Tech and Brandon could hide what they were doing. All they'd have to do was move Christopher to a different location and the police would find nothing incriminating.

"How much will it cost to rescue him? Can you do that? Not just investigate?"

The Wilsons looked at each other and Luke nodded. He wouldn't say he could if it was impossible. I had to trust he could do this.

"We'll get him out." Ella's eyes were kind, and she looked apologetic. "It won't take as long if you and your brother-in-law help. We'll write up an invoice afterward."

I didn't care about the money—I'd pay. Getting Christopher back would be worth every cent.

"Done."

"We need a solid plan," said Ella. "Give us a couple of days. Day after tomorrow at the earliest for his retrieval. Probably Friday."

"What can I do?"

"Be ready with a security distraction and an unfamiliar vehicle in case we have to separate. Our cars need to look the same. Rent a black CRV to match ours," said Luke.

I nodded and gave them the address to the house. There were so many ways this could go wrong, but I didn't see that I had other options. I couldn't leave Christopher there.

"I have the antidote at home," I said. *"If he wakes up wrong, I'll use it."*

I had concerns I might need help to restrain him long enough to inject him. If Brandon and Real Tech had made him super strong or impervious to pain, we'd have to sedate him, not overpower him. He might not want to be rescued once he woke in the lab. Brandon enjoyed feeling emotionless, but Christopher wouldn't. I hated to leave him there for days, knowing he'd wake up, trapped and alone.

Luke's second investigation confirmed that Christopher had been moved to one of the holding cells on the third floor. There were cameras in each room, in the hall, and in the elevator. Luke and Ella planned how to compromise the security system. They took video in the empty halls and the lobby. They hacked the security feed to download footage of Christopher sleeping. Their security loop would make it appear that Christopher was in his room and that the hallways were empty while we moved him. Luke could enter unseen, but Christopher wouldn't be invisible. They'd have to resort to ordinary ways to escape instead of magic.

I called Andrew for additional muscle. He got a warrant from a judge that owed him a favor. It wouldn't give us full access to everything at Real Tech, but it would get him, Officer Park, and invisible Luke upstairs into the lab to question Brandon. Luke would sneak away to extract Christopher. My job was to provide a distraction in the lobby and compromise the security feed. Luke called a friend and asked him to make untraceable sedatives to administer to the security guard so we could move Christopher out the front door. It would also give us time to get the vehicles out through the security gate.

We didn't know how to contact the head of Real Tech, though Luke and Ella continued to follow leads, searching for the boss's identity. There were layers of ownership companies, one owned by another, owned by another and so on, but each level always led to someone else in the cycle.

The days crawled by, until at last, on Friday night, we waited outside the lab. The Wilsons and I went in their car, behind Andrew and his partner in my new rental. Security at the gate waved us through together when Andrew flashed his badge and the warrant.

I turned away so the cameras wouldn't see my face. I was the only one that security, including Horace and Jasper, might recognize. At eight o'clock it was dark and there were few cars in the lot, the familiar SUV that often followed us, Brandon's car, and another older sedan. In the distance sat an expensive Audi parked all by itself. I peeked in the windows of the building and saw Paul, the security guard, inside. At least the person I was supposed to distract wouldn't consider me a threat.

Andrew and Officer Park headed for the door. Luke was with them, but there was no sign of his presence. Since he was supposed to be invisible, that was a relief.

I clutched the flashdrive from Luke in my sweaty hand. We watched through the floor-to-ceiling windows as Andrew presented his warrant and Paul made a call. The security man wasn't on the phone long. He used his security card and swiped the police officers into the back hall to escort them up the elevator. Once they were out of sight, I jumped from the car and entered the building. Luke had ensured that the outer door hadn't latched. I ducked behind the security desk, my heart racing.

My eyes scanned the console, searching for the USB port Luke had described. Breathing fast, I jammed it in and watched the closed-circuit TV screens change. The hallway cam showed an empty hall instead of Paul chatting with the cops at the top of the elevator. Luke and Ella had created footage that would change the security feed for an hour. The lobby camera showed Paul at his desk. After we had Christopher, I would have to retrieve the drive.

I slid out from behind the desk and unloaded my props while I waited for Paul's return. My chosen weapons were a thermos of hot chocolate and two disposable coffee cups.

Seconds later, Paul returned. I was just in time. His friendly face lit up to see me and guilt flashed through me. This wasn't his fault and he might get in trouble.

"Miss Elizabeth," he said. "What a lovely surprise. We haven't seen you here in months."

"Brandon's been working so hard since he got out of the hospital," I said. I'd practiced saying this aloud several times today. It was just a loud whisper, but it was audible. I hadn't been sure I'd be able to talk, but I'd do anything for Christopher. "I thought I'd wait. He said he'd be down soon."

"What's this?" Paul said, nodding at cups on the counter.

"I brought hot chocolate." I poured from the thermos, the steam carrying the rich scent of chocolate and sugar. "A treat."

"I shouldn't." His eyes didn't leave the cups as he breathed in the delicious aroma.

"I brought it especially for you. It must be boring and cold out here, night after night."

I grabbed my cup and sat on the chairs by the window where I'd always waited for Brandon. I trusted Paul didn't know Brandon, and I were no longer together.

Every second seemed too long, and my pulse raced. This wouldn't work. Trying not to be obvious, I watched Paul. He checked the camera behind him and blocked the view of the hot chocolate. He winked at me, took a flask from inside his jacket, and poured a generous dollop into his steaming drink. I breathed a quiet sigh of relief. We had a backup plan in case he wouldn't drink the hot chocolate, but it was riskier. He took a long drink.

"That's nice, Miss Elizabeth. Thanks."

The cup I'd given Paul had a special coating inside. His drink should have him on the floor in fifteen minutes or fewer, if it worked as advertised.

I sent Luke and Ella a text. *"Fifteen minutes."*

I pretended to be engrossed in a romance novel like the old days while I waited. Paul yawned several times and leaned back in his chair. Before the fifteen minutes was up, the older man fell asleep. He snored softly, his head resting on the back of the chair. He didn't look comfortable, but he looked like he wouldn't wake anytime soon.

I dropped my book on the floor to see if he'd flinch. He didn't move. *"He's out."* I packed up the evidence, returning it to my bag, including the cup of hot chocolate, which I poured back into the thermos to dispose of at home.

Ella came inside and stationed herself by the inner door with the security card from Paul's desk. There was a sharp rap from inside the door and I jumped, my nerves on edge. Ella opened the door and Christopher emerged, leaning on an invisible Luke. Luke had warned me that if Christopher saw him wearing the cloak without a hood, when it went back up, Christopher would be immune to the magic.

Christopher would see him, but we wouldn't. I'd believed him, but it was disconcerting to see Christopher leaning against something I couldn't see.

"I didn't sedate him." Luke's voice came from Christopher's left. "He's groggy from whatever they've given him, but he wanted to leave."

"I want to go home," said Christopher. "I don't like it here."

He mumbled, as though half asleep, but the meaning was clear.

He didn't pay any particular attention to me. His eyes flicked over both Ella and me with no sign of recognition. I blinked back my tears. I had to keep it together. No crying during the rescue mission. I'd told myself I was prepared for an indifferent reaction, but feeling it was worse than expected. My heart ached and I couldn't help but be disappointed. He needed to be different. I'd hoped the serum wouldn't be effective on him, that his feelings would be too strong and it would fail. Maybe it had only worked in part, and he was fighting the effects.

Luke guided Christopher outside and Ella opened the doors while I texted Andrew. I grabbed the security loop memory stick. I had thirty seconds to exit without being seen. We hid Luke in the backseat of one of the SUV's and I sat beside him.

"Were you in the lab experiments, too?" His voice was quiet.

"We came to get you," I said in a whisper.

"I have to get home. I can't remember why, but it's important." He turned his icy blue eyes on me. "You look familiar. Do I know you?"

"You do," I said. "We'll explain when we get you home."

He nodded and closed his eyes. "I don't feel well. I just want to sleep."

"Just keep lying down," I said as I smoothed his hair from his forehead.

Ella and Luke climbed into the front seats.

"You okay?" Luke lowered his hood and appeared in the seat right in front of me. He looked back at Christopher, but I suspected he was talking to me.

I nodded.

Andrew and Officer Park exited the building and climbed into the other SUV. We left, following their lead. We might have a problem with the gate if Christopher's absence had been discovered, but it swung open as we drove up. The drive to our house didn't take long, about twenty minutes. Everyone was silent.

When we arrived at the house, the porch light was off. In my excitement, I must have forgotten to turn it on. The bad habit had returned, as until recently, I'd felt safer here. Walking up to the house, shards of glass lay on the porch where the bulb had shattered. Neighborhood kids could have taken it out with a rock, but it had been Eric. He must have been lurking.

I pushed the bits aside and unlocked the door with shaking hands. Inside, the alarm wasn't set. I must have forgotten that too, in my worry about the rescue. I stopped in the doorway, my unease almost palpable. I expected Eric to attack, but no one was there. The interior remained dark and quiet.

"This is my house," said Christopher. "I remember it. I've lived here a long time."

He forged ahead and stepped inside.

"Just a second." I checked for signs of an intruder, but nothing was out of place.

Christopher looked at me for confirmation, and I nodded. He continued inside.

"You going to be, okay?" Luke took me aside. "He doesn't seem upset about you being here. He just doesn't know who you are."

"He's calm. We'll be okay." In my house, I was comfortable whispering.

"Want us to wait?"

I shook my head. "Thanks for your help. I can take it from here."

"Andrew said they're going back to the station, but that he's close if you need something. Make sure you fix that light in the morning," said Luke. "The police are going back to Real Tech with warrants tomorrow for the other prisoners."

I nodded. "I couldn't have done this alone. What do I owe you?"

"We'll send the bill in a few days," said Ella. "You were brilliant tonight."

She gave me a hug and took Luke's hand as they walked back to their car. I'd like to get to know them better. Maybe we could have them over for dinner once things were back to normal. I didn't always like strangers, but I liked them. We'd been a job, but they treated me like we were friends.

I set the alarm, took a deep breath, and went to look for Christopher.

I'd readied the antidote but hadn't dared to carry it with me, thinking it should remain refrigerated. The needle was loaded and ready in a Tupperware container.

I couldn't find Christopher at first. He wasn't in the kitchen, living room, or his office. I went down the hall to our bedroom. He stood in the middle of the room.

"Is this your house too?" he said.

His brow was wrinkled, and he wrung his hands while he spoke. It was disconcerting to see him confused and without a smile. He was still gorgeous, but he seemed muted, less vibrant.

"It is." I erected the brick wall in my mind to keep my thoughts from intruding on his recovering brain. "There's another bit of medicine to help you feel better. It should help your memory. Can I give it to you?"

He nodded. "I don't like not knowing anything. I'd like to remember someone as beautiful as you are."

His sad smile tugged at my heart.

"You smell nice too," he said as I took his hand and led him to the kitchen.

He sat on the bar stool at the counter where I showed. I injected the antidote into Christopher's shoulder and hoped for the best. There was no immediate reaction. Maybe it took several hours to be effective. Serum A could take up to three days.

"I'm tired." Christopher rubbed his eyes and his face split in an enormous yawn. "Can I go to my room and sleep? Maybe I'll remember you in the morning."

His smile was slight, but genuine.

I nodded, too disappointed to speak. Alone, tears filled my eyes. I tried not to let them fall, to look at the bright side. Christopher was out of the lab and home, which is what mattered right now. I wanted to kiss him and for him to wrap me in his arms, but he would only be bewildered. I hated the wall in my mind that was necessary not to hurt him. Deep down, I'd hoped the antidote would fix everything.

"I'll see you in the morning," I said as he shuffled down the hall toward our room.

As much as I wanted to, I shouldn't sleep with him tonight. That would be more confusing. The little-used upstairs consisted of two bedrooms, a bathroom, and the stairs to the attic. I made up a bed in my choice of spare room. I'd only been up here a few times. Ember followed me upstairs, curious at the change in our usual location. She jumped on a cushioned chair by the window and kneaded the fuzzy blanket folded over the back and seat before settling in a tight ball. Before bed, I went downstairs and checked the doors, windows, and the alarm. Everything looked secure.

The room was cold, but I took comfort that growing up, this had been Christopher's room. Some of his old books sat on the shelf above his desk and there was a box of his childhood treasures in the closet. In my exploration, I discovered a much-loved brown teddy bear with one eye. I set it on the bed next to the second pillow. His threadbare bear could sleep with me.

I sent a text to Andrew. *"Injection went well. Christopher has gone to sleep. No way to tell if it worked. Talk in the morning."*

"Squad car posted on your street in case the Real Tech goons show up."

"Thanks." It eased my mind to know that the authorities were watching the house. I didn't know if I'd be able to sleep, but that wasn't Andrew's problem.

For a long time, I lay sleepless in the cold, unfamiliar bed, hoping the antidote worked and that Christopher would be himself tomorrow. The emotional week caught up to me and I fell into an exhausted slumber.

Chapter 24

A creak of the wooden floor awakened me. The room was pitch black, and I'd left my phone downstairs in the kitchen charging. What time was it?

"Christopher?" I whispered, wondering if he'd woken on his own. Perhaps he'd come looking for me.

A weight settled at the end of the bed and I sat up, my eyes straining at the darkness, willing my night vision to work.

"It's me, Baby Doll," said Eric.

My blood ran cold and my heart pounded against my ribs so loud I feared he would hear and know that I was terrified. Despite the chill in the air, I broke out in a sweat. How could he be here?

"Didn't you think it odd when you got home and the alarm was off? I've been waiting for you to slip up and forget to set it." His creepy smile was audible in the dark.

I'd been caught up with injecting Christopher and my disappointment that he wasn't cured right away. The alarm had slipped my mind.

"I can get into any house without breaking a thing. I'm an expert at picking locks of all kinds. I'd have come for you sooner if it wasn't for the damn alarm."

I leaned away from where he sat, repulsed by his words. His voice brought goosebumps to my arms and my throat was too dry to speak. He slid closer, though I couldn't see anything.

"I knew you'd forget eventually," he said. "I've spent months watching this place. Too bad you've been all alone this week. I could've kept you company."

"Get out," I whispered. It was barely more than a breath and he laughed.

"That's the best you can do?" He moved closer and stroked my cheek. At the touch of his slimy hands, I cringed.

I slithered off the side of the bed. He lunged and caught me. I twisted and landed hard on the floor. I got up and ran toward the faint gray outline that must be the doorway. He caught my foot and pulled me to the floor, half in the room, half in the hall. The moon shone through the window at the end of the hall, and I was no longer blind.

I kicked and struggled, trying to dislodge his hand from my ankle. I banged on the wall with my fists, hoping Christopher would hear, but I couldn't free myself. Eric and I were making enough noise that on a regular night, Christopher would have heard the disturbance, but he wasn't himself. The serums had compromised his body. Downstairs remained silent.

"I thought I'd solved the boyfriend problem." Eric's eyes gleamed above me.

Something sharp jabbed my arm where he must have injected me with something. Despair washed over me.

"You're coming to my lab."

His lab?

"Those incompetent idiots who work for me should have brought you to Real Tech months ago. I could have shown you how a real man treats a woman."

Real Tech was his lab? The insidious pieces clicked together. He was Brandon's mystery boss. He'd always worked there, even the first time we'd met. At the engagement party, he'd come looking for me, an easy victim. He'd known I'd just been dumped. He'd been interested in taking me from Brandon and had orchestrated our first meeting, both times. Had he injected me with one of Brandon's serums? I didn't want to be an emotionless zombie. Bile rose in the back of my throat.

My eyes widened and my breath became ragged. I couldn't get up, but I needed to fight him now. Soon it would be too late as the strength leached from my muscles, stolen by whatever he'd injected. I didn't know what he'd given me, but it was a problem.

"What was that?" I said, my voice almost too quiet to call a murmur.

"Something to relax your muscles," he said. "You're too tense. Don't fight it. You've secretly wanted to be with me for months."

"I don't. You're disgusting."

He stroked my face again, and I tried not to gag.

"Hush, Baby Doll. I'm going to take you back to bed first. When I'm done, I'll take you away where nobody can ever find you again."

His hand stroked my bare hip. Christopher's T-shirt barely covered me. I'd worn it to bed because it smelled like him.

My hands and feet grew numb, heavy. I would only have one more chance. I let myself go limp—that's what he expected. He bent down to kiss me and I smashed the heel of my hand upward and crushed his nose. Like 2020, it was a direct hit. His nose broke with a familiar sickening sound. I'd sworn not to hurt anyone, but I had to protect myself. I kicked him and he fell back against the wall.

"Bitch!" he yelled, covering his face with his hands.

His nose gushed dark blood. I scooted away from him, half rolling, half crawling. I wouldn't get far, but I had to get away. A tight band constricted my chest as I struggled to breathe. I had to get to my phone or to Christopher. I needed help. The phone was closer. Eric's moaning came closer as he got to his feet.

"You're going to regret this." His voice was an angry growl.

His foot connected with my back as he shoved me down the stairs. I hit the stairs and smashed into the wall with my head. Agonizing pain shot through my body despite the relaxant. I stopped on the landing, my arm bent under me in an awkward position. It had cracked when I stopped and my chest heaved with pain.

I tried to slither down the remaining stairs, but fell and rolled instead. I hit the floor. My arm exploded with heat and pain. It must have broken. I crawled across the floor, tucking my injured arm against my side. My phone lay on the kitchen counter, tantalizingly close, but I couldn't get to my feet. The torment in my arm was excruciating when I tried to pull myself up using a stool. Eric's steps thunked on the floor as he followed.

"You can't get away from me."

He grabbed me by my hair and my injured arm and dragged me toward the door.

I screamed. The sound reverberated in the dark, empty house as he dropped me to the floor with a thud.

From our bedroom, there came a crash. A flicker of hope surged through me. Eric stood over me, blood dripping from his face. He kicked me twice in the ribs and again in the head. He wore boots, so each kick felt like a Mack truck.

"Christopher." I could barely whisper. It was hard to remain conscious with all the pain coursing through me.

Eric laughed, a hideous mocking sound as he grabbed my arm again. "You're a pathetic little bird that can't even squawk." He towed me toward the door, dragging me across the tile.

"Christopher," I said again, louder.

From a distance, Christopher roared, and a light snapped on.

"Brandon said you'd be a perfect candidate because you're so cold inside, but I want to break through that reserve. It'll be quite the challenge."

I screamed in agony as he attempted to haul me outside. If he got me out of the house, I'd disappear. Nobody would know what happened.

There was another thump and Eric looked up.

"Lizzie!" Christopher lurched into sight.

Eric dropped my broken arm. I screamed at the inferno, burning my arm from the inside. Pain blurred my vision. My eyelids were too heavy and I hurt in so many places. He threw open the front door. The alarm sounded and then faded from my awareness. I lay on the cold tile floor—the door opened to the January night as Eric fled and the world disappeared.

Chapter 25

When I came to, everything was muffled, and the light was too bright. I panicked and struggled at first, but I was too tired to fight, so I drifted. It was easier to sleep. When I came to again, faces blurred above me. Bland walls and the faces of doctors and nurses filed in and out. I was in the hospital, not in a lab. I searched for Christopher's face, but couldn't find him.

"Where's Christopher?" I pleaded with those around me.

I don't know how long I existed in that state, a fog of morphine and misery. It could have been a few days; it could have been a week. There was no way to guess. It was painless to sleep, but my mind couldn't rest. Fevered nightmares plagued me with monsters and shadowy attackers. I searched for Christopher, knowing he'd make everything better. Where was he?

When I opened my eyes, this time the light was muted. Meghan's tear-streaked face was the first I saw.

"Meghan?" I whispered.

My sister yelped and grabbed my hand, squeezing so tight it hurt.

"We've been so worried. Thank goodness you know me, this time. You're awake."

"What's wrong with me?" It hurt to talk and my throat was dry as sand.

"You were attacked." Fresh tears fell from her eyes. "Your shoulder was dislocated and your ulna and radius were both broken. You had surgery a couple of days ago. Your head injury and bruised ribs had us worried. The doctors didn't know why you wouldn't wake up." Meghan's voice broke as she finished her account.

"Where's Christopher?" My lips were cracked and dry. I wet them with my tongue and whispered again, worried that she hadn't heard when she didn't answer. "Where's Christopher?"

Meghan covered her face with her hands and sobbed. She didn't answer my question and ran from the room. Had Eric hurt him, too? I couldn't remember past Christopher's entry to the kitchen when he'd called my name. I'd blacked out just as he'd yelled his nickname for me, 'Lizzie'. He was himself again; the antidote had worked.

Andrew was the next visitor.

"Hey, you're awake. We were worried."

"Did they get him?" I forced my voice to be audible.

Andrew's eyes were bloodshot, and he had several days' worth of stubble on his face. He dropped to the chair beside my hospital bed and took my hand. He looked so worried; I must look awful if it scared him to talk to me.

"Christopher? Is he here?"

Andrew shook his head and turned away, perhaps so I wouldn't see the wetness in his eyes.

Was Christopher hurt? Is that why he wasn't here?

Meghan returned to the doorway. "I let the nurses know you're awake."

She attempted a smile. She looked different, younger, without makeup. Meghan and Andrew were freaking me out. What were they hiding?

The doctor and a nurse came in and shooed my family out. Other than the tight ball of fear in my chest, I was much improved. The staff checked me over and talked to me about my arm and caring for the cast, but I wasn't listening.

Dr. Maeve strode into the room accompanied by billows of something spicy, like curry with a hint of sandalwood. She appeared prepared to do battle as the doctors left.

"Elizabeth, my dear." She took my hand in hers and squeezed. "This isn't what I had in mind when I sent you here. Would you like to return to 2022?"

I opened my eyes wider.

"I can send you back and this can be like a bad dream."

Tears welled up in my eyes. Her words scared me. Why would I not want to stay? Unless... No. It couldn't be. It scared me to ask the question that tumbled around my head. It was hard to breathe as I swiped at my eyes. "Did something happen to Christopher?"

She looked at me with a keen eye and a thoughtful expression. I stared into her emerald-green eyes. They seemed to expand, and she pursed her lips in disapproval. "Your family is well-meaning. They're trying to protect you by keeping painful information from you. They don't believe it was him, but the evidence is stacked against him. Their hearts are in the right place, but you need to know. You asked about Christopher time and again when you'd slip in and out of consciousness. They've left you in the dark about why he isn't at your side."

A feeling of horror niggled at my foggy brain as I tried to absorb what she was saying.

"Someone else was there that night, weren't they? Besides Christopher."

That got my attention. I sat up straighter. My heart lurched onward; my eyes widened. What did she mean besides Christopher? Didn't they know?

"Eric was in the house." My throat ached as I forced myself to speak.

"Eric got away. Again. He's out there and nobody has been searching for him."

I shook my head. That wasn't possible. "Where's Christopher?"

"He confessed to attacking you, so the authorities had no choice."

I shook my head again to clear the cobwebs. This was all wrong. Eric was supposed to be in jail. The bottom dropped out of my world as I realized what had happened.

"Christopher." My hand covered my mouth in horror. This was why he hadn't come to the hospital. Christopher had confessed to hurting me. I painted a new picture in my mind as this knowledge rushed into my brain. He'd been startled awake, confused and disoriented. Half awake, he'd staggered into the kitchen. He'd seen the blood, found me broken on the floor. He thought he'd hurt me because he hadn't seen Eric. The alarm had sounded and the cops from the nearby car would have rushed inside. They'd found Christopher beside me on the floor. When he couldn't explain, they'd arrested him. He'd gone with them, convinced my injuries were his fault. He must be in jail, tormenting himself, worried sick.

"Yes," Dr. Maeve said. "Your love is in jail. He thinks he attacked you. I spoke with him this morning and let him know you were awake. But he can't forgive himself."

She pursed her lips. "Christopher didn't do this to you."

"Eric hid in the house and attacked me." My heart hurt, but I could feel it again, healing with every second. The shards fit back together like a three-dimensional puzzle.

"I know," she said. "I met your Christopher once before today, and I know what kind of person he is. When we called him from my office, I heard it in his voice. You're his world and he's yours. You need to decide because you're running out of time."

I could go back to the future and this never would have happened. Christopher wouldn't be in jail and Eric would be dead. The offer was tempting, the easy way to solve my problems. But Christopher would be alone and I'd promised him I'd never leave.

Or I could stay, help get Christopher released. Someone would have to find Eric. My money was on Luke and Ella. I might have to face Eric again.

"If you want to help Christopher, it has to be now. He won't make it much longer thinking he hurt you. It's destroying him. He looks as bad as you do."

"Did the injection work? Is he himself again?"

"Does it matter?" She got to her feet. "Make your decision."

"Stay. Eric needs to be stopped."

"I hoped that's what you'd decide. Christopher's court hearing is in less than an hour. Convince him and the judge that he didn't do it. You can't use email or texts. This time, you're going to have to speak. Can you do that?"

I swallowed. For Christopher, I could. I nodded.

Dr. Maeve handed me a backpack. Inside were my clothes, a toothbrush, toothpaste, and a comb. I shuddered to think what I looked like. She taped plastic around my cast.

"Go on. Clean up. Be fast. I'll drive."

I was ready in record time, the fastest shower of my life. I was unsteady on my feet and my arm ached, but I was on a mission. A quick glance in the mirror showed fading eggplant-like bruises in a sea of mottled yellow. At the bottom of the bag was a chocolate bar, a Clif bar, and a bottle of water. Protein and quick energy. I'd need both. I ate as I dressed and we walked out together.

Dr. Maeve led me toward the exit and her car. Nobody looked twice as we left, two women in street clothes. If I'd been in a hospital gown, they would have tried to prevent my departure.

We raced across town, parked outside the courthouse, and bounded up the concrete stairs. Dr. Maeve might be over sixty, but she was quick.

"They'll be starting any minute, Courtroom Four."

Our feet echoed on the slippery floor as we ran toward the proper courtroom. People stared as we ran past, skidding to a stop in front of the door.

"Let me start. I know the judge." Dr. Maeve opened the heavy door with a nod to the guard while I trailed in her wake.

As we entered the courtroom, the judge said, "Dr. Maeve Fossey, you're late."

"I had to collect an important piece of evidence from the hospital," she said.

All eyes turned toward us. My family sat in the front row, wearing confused expressions. Dad looked old and beaten down. His face crumpled at the sight of me and Meghan put her arm around him. I stared at the other side of the room. Christopher sat at a table with a man in a black suit. His lawyer. Christopher's head hung low, his hands on his face. He hadn't looked up at our entrance. Had he given up? Was he ashamed to look at me? I needed to fix this. There were no bricks in my mind, it was wide open.

I'm here, I love you.

He didn't look up.

"Dr. Maeve, you know that's not how this works," said the judge. "You've taken part in enough of these hearings."

"I know," my red-headed therapist said, towing me forward, "but a grave miscarriage of justice is about to occur."

The judge's eyebrows shot up her forehead. "You've got my attention. Who's this you dragged out of the hospital? A strong breeze could knock her over."

"Elizabeth Bergstrom, the woman the accused has confessed to assaulting. The police haven't questioned her about what happened that night. If everyone had done their job, we wouldn't be here."

"Is that correct, Miss?" said the judge.

I nodded. The lump in my throat wouldn't prevent me from speaking today. I needed to help Christopher since he wouldn't help himself.

"Yes, Your Honor." My voice wasn't loud, but she heard.

"Bailiff, swear her in. We'll hear her side of the story. I'll ask the questions."

Before I knew it, I swore to tell the truth, the whole truth, and nothing but the truth, and sat on the chair in the box beside the judge. I pretended the others in the courtroom weren't here. There was just me, the judge, and Christopher. I had to be smart and tell the right part of the truth. Not time travel.

"I want the facts," said the judge. "Help me understand what's happened."

"Your Honor," I said. "My fiancé, Christopher Winters, was abducted and was gone for two weeks. Private investigators removed him from where he was being held captive and brought him home."

"What happened after he came home?" said the judge.

"The abductors had drugged Christopher, leaving him tired and disoriented so, I sent him to bed. I went upstairs to sleep on my own. Sometime in the night, Eric Dahl attacked me. He'd hidden in the house, waiting for me to be alone."

"Who's this Eric person?" The judge's voice conveyed a sense that her patience was wearing thin as she scanned her documents. "Does anyone know? His name isn't in the brief."

Both lawyers shrugged. The prosecutor flipped several pages, wearing a confused expression on his face.

"Your honor, if I may." Andrew stood, wearing his Portland City Police uniform.

"You are?" said the Judge.

"Officer Andrew Jennings. I've handled several incidents with Elizabeth Bergstrom's stalker, Eric Dahl, who has eluded the police for several months."

"The police want him and he is on record as her stalker?" said the judge.

"Yes, Your Honor," said Andrew. "We couldn't ascertain if that is his real identity or determine his whereabouts, but he has tormented Elizabeth for months."

"You may continue," the judge said to me. "What happened upstairs?"

"Eric assaulted me. I fought my way free. He caught me and injected me with something that made me dizzy and weak. He didn't expect me to fight. I bloodied his nose, but he shoved me down the stairs. I hit my head and broke my arm. He tried to drag me out the door, but my screams woke Christopher. Eric ran. I passed out and woke up in the hospital. Until an hour ago, I didn't know that they had arrested Christopher. I came as fast as I could." I begged his forgiveness with my eyes.

"Your family didn't tell you about Christopher's arrest?" said the judge. "And you didn't tell them about Eric." Her sharp gaze met mine.

"I didn't get a chance, but Christopher would never hurt me. I'm sorry I took so long." I said the last as I stared at him, not the judge.

He'd looked up during my retelling of the evening, his eyes riveted on my face. His expression, at last, was hopeful.

"Dr. Winters, case dismissed." The judge banged her gavel. "You're free to go."

The bailiff released him, and his lawyer shook his hand. Christopher looked at me throughout.

Everyone else in the courtroom disappeared as I ran to him. He scooped me into his arms and buried his face in my shoulder.

"Oh, Lizzie." His whole body shook with emotion. "I thought the lab techs had done something to me and that I'd hurt you. I thought I'd lost you forever."

I squeezed tighter. "Do you forgive me for not coming sooner?"

He kissed me, my face in his trembling hands. It was more than forgiveness. I sensed love and almost overwhelming relief.

"I remember nothing after I bought ice cream. My tires were slashed, and I tried to call you. Horace and Jasper knocked me out. My next memory is you unconscious in my arms. Your arm was crooked. There was blood all over the floor and I didn't know how I got there."

"We rescued you from the lab." I wrapped my arms around him and looked into his tearful eyes. They were the palest I'd seen them, reminding me of glacial pools with dark rings. "I'll tell you about it later." My throat hurt. I wasn't used to talking so much at once.

His thumb stroked my bottom lip with his promise. My heart reminded me it had pieced itself back together by fluttering at his touch.

Somebody cleared their throat, reminding me we weren't alone.

Meghan, Dad, and Andrew stood nearby. All three wore smiles to see Christopher exonerated and me out of the hospital.

"If you've been in the hospital and I've been in jail, where's Ember?"

"I've got your cat," said Dad. "Andrew brought her the first day. I hope that's okay."

I nodded. Tears threatened again, and my gut clenched. I wanted to go home, but wasn't sure it was safe. Eric had bragged that locks couldn't keep him out, but alarms could.

"I forgot to set the alarm when I went to the lab with the private investigators. Eric waited inside for me to return. We'll be safe at home with the alarm on." Once I would have tried to take the blame for what had happened, but the attack wasn't my fault. It was Eric's.

"Has anyone been back to Real Tech?" I turned to face the others, though I rested my back against Christopher. He wrapped his arms around me. We weren't going to be able to stop touching each other. We needed physical contact.

Andrew nodded. "The human trials have been shut down, but they have manipulated the men who were taken to be without emotions—phase one of the experiments. We don't think they injected anyone with the second compound."

"Oh," I said, realizing that the other revelations from that night had been lost. "Eric is the mystery boss at Real Tech. He referred to it as his lab."

Andrew's jaw dropped. "When?"

"He boasted about it that night in the house. Brandon worked for him under duress, at least before his injection."

"How are we going to find Eric?" said Andrew. "Nothing we've done so far has worked. We don't know his real name or where he is. The boss has cleared out of Real Tech, so we won't find him there. He's a horrible human, but brilliant. He's always a step ahead."

"Hire Luke and Ella. If anyone can find him, they can."

He nodded. "I'll call them tomorrow."

Christopher checked in at the courthouse office to collect his personal belongings on the way out. As they'd arrested him in his pajamas, there wasn't much.

"I'll give you two a ride," said Andrew. "Glad you're both okay."

Christopher laced his fingers through mine. "Let's go home."

Chapter 26

The first thing Christopher and I did upon entry at home was to set the alarm. We searched the house together, from top to bottom, to ensure that we were alone. The pool of blood in the entryway had been scrubbed away. If they'd taken samples, they would have Eric's DNA to match when he was caught. They might not have tested it because Christopher had confessed.

Holding hands, we checked room to room. Upstairs, where I'd slept the last night, the teddy bear lay upside down on the floor beside the bed. Christopher picked up his old bear.

He tightened his grip on my hand and we continued our search, checking Brandon's old room next door. The second room was also empty. Christopher lowered the stairs to the attic and completed a thorough inspection. I suspected Eric had hidden there, but he wasn't there now. When we finished searching the house, we double-checked the locks on the doors and windows. Our home was one place where we would be safe.

Christopher lifted me to the kitchen counter, spread my knees, and stepped in for a long hug. I closed my eyes and breathed in his mocha scent that made me feel safe and loved. With Eric at large, I could only relax when Christopher and I were together. I leaned in and enjoyed this moment. We'd almost lost each other, and it was a relief to touch and feel each other breathe.

Christopher cried while I held on. I'd cry later—this was his turn. He was a private person and wouldn't want to share these feelings with anyone else. I was honored that he trusted me. When he finished, we sat perpendicular to each other on the couch, with my legs across his lap. I leaned on him and the arm of the couch, my cast in front. My arm was painful, but it was overshadowed by the love surrounding me.

We had so much to talk about, but I didn't know where to start. I wanted to hear about his time away, but the time was lost. I didn't want to share too much at once, but in bits and pieces, I explained what had happened. I couldn't stop looking at him, noticing subtle differences. His cheekbones looked more defined, his cheeks hollower. He needed to eat.

"The house didn't feel the same without you. It didn't feel like my home."

"I want to add you to the title of the house—even before we get married. If anything happens to me, I need to know that you have a place that's safe, a home. I worried about that when I was in the lab."

"You didn't eat enough," I said as I stroked his cheek.

"I lost my appetite."

My finger traced the lines of his face. His lawyer had made him shave before court. I held his smooth jaw in my hand. He caught my hand and kissed my palm, electricity in his touch.

"You didn't eat enough either. When I hug you, I swear I feel every rib. I'm worried you'll break."

"I'm not that fragile. We can take turns cooking our favorite dinners. I've missed eating with you."

"You were brave today," Christopher said. "I know talking in court wasn't easy. I'd given up until you and Dr. Maeve arrived. That was the first time I'd allowed myself to hope."

"You didn't look at me."

"I was scared, but the second you walked in, I sensed your crystal-clear thoughts. You were on a mission." He paused. "Thank you for being on time."

He traced circles by my collar bones. I swallowed. I'd missed him in so many ways, and my pulse quickened. I hadn't known if we'd want sex tonight, but now, I hoped.

"My brother visited when I was in jail. He sounded shaken. They'd brought in him for questioning and he has a court hearing for his part in the human trials next month."

"Maybe he can prove he was a victim and not a villain."

"He injected himself, so we need proof they coerced him, at least in the beginning," he said, raking a hand through his hair.

"Maybe Eric threatened him," I said with a shrug, thinking back to the original call I'd overheard.

"Maybe we can help him," Christopher said. "But he says he likes the clarity of his mind. Emotions are distractions."

"I don't want to talk about Eric or Brandon tonight."

"What should we talk about?" Christopher's voice lowered.

His heart sped up beneath my hand and he touched my face again. His laser beam gaze turned to me. "What would you like to do?"

I answered by pulling his mouth to mine.

His lips were soft, but his hands were demanding as they found bare skin under my sweater. "I'll try to be gentle, but I won't feel like myself until I'm deep inside you and feel you come around me."

As always, his words shot through me and quickened my breathing.

I parted my lips, and his tongue found mine. I shifted to straddle his lap. As I stroked him through his jeans, he became as hard as a rock. He tangled his hand in my hair and eased my head back to kiss my throat and neck, taking his time. One hand unclasped my bra, and he played with my sensitive breasts as I squirmed against him. He bit the side of my neck. My breath became ragged as my need to be naked grew.

"Take my clothes off," I said.

I raised my arms, and he lifted off my bra and sweater in one move, other than over my cast where it caught briefly. His shirt followed. I slid my hands across his chest and toned muscles. He lay back on the couch with me on top of him, his lips on mine. We were like teenagers, half-clothed, making out on the couch. He caught my face in his strong but gentle hands and cradled it as he kissed me until my toes curled.

Breaking off our kiss, we removed the rest of my clothes. He watched, but made no move to undress. I tugged him to his feet and unbuckled his belt while I kissed his chest and down his solid abs. His ribs were prominent, too. I kissed each one. When we were both naked, I had a moment of shyness, but when his arm wrapped around me and tugged me against him, it was both intense and comfortable.

I stopped feeling self-conscious about my battered body. We kissed again for a long time, our hands exploring each other for every familiar favorite place, cataloging every change as he learned where was sensitive. He touched my bruised ribs with gentle fingertips.

I pushed him to a sitting position on the edge of the couch and knelt between his knees.

"Can I please?" I looked up at him.

"God yes," he said with a grin.

With one hand, he held my hair back to keep it out of the way. A stream of curses erupted as I started. I'd even missed his foul language. After teasing him long enough that we were both focused only on pleasure, he spread a blanket on the floor.

As he wound me tighter and tighter, I became frantic for him, more frenzied than usual. I ached for him all over. Every part of me needed his touch. My breasts pushed against him in desperation, and so did my hips. My fingers dug into him, encouraging him to need me the way I needed him. His eyes and mouth and hands showed me we agreed. At last, I broke away and lay back on the floor. I cried out with our love-making's perfection. Our kiss matched the rhythm of our hips as we unraveled together.

I'd missed this closeness. I'd missed Christopher. Our worries disappeared in our ecstasy. There came a point where we no longer felt like two separate beings, but became one. I didn't know where he started and I finished. With my mind wide open, I sensed his wonder and joy at us being together.

After a quiet evening with our food delivered, we watched a movie, a normal evening. When it was time for sleep, we curled up in our bed, wrapped in each other's arms. Our problems weren't solved, but when we had each other, it was easier to believe we'd get through them. This was a respite, a chance to heal and regroup. Eric was still at large, and Brandon needed the antidote. But tonight, we were with each other and safe.

•   •   •

We had a week to recuperate. On Friday morning, Andrew video called.

"You're looking better. I wanted to let you know we took your advice and hired the Wilsons to find Eric. The department was desperate to get this solved and had to admit we were at a standstill."

"They should have results when nobody else could." The sound of my voice almost surprised me.

"They want more information from you," said Andrew. "Even if you haven't spent time with Eric here, you know him better than anyone else. They're compiling questions for you. Everyone wanted to give you two a few days to recover. It's been tough lately. I called to see if you'd be up for their questions. You don't love talking to strangers, but I hoped that this wouldn't be a problem."

"They aren't strangers anymore. I like Luke and Ella," I said. "I'll help, especially if it puts Eric behind bars."

Christopher was quiet while we ate breakfast. He must have something on his mind, and I didn't think it was Luke and Ella. We'd talked about the Wilsons and he wanted to meet them. He didn't remember them from the night of the rescue, but from his questions, the invisibility cloak intrigued him.

"There's something I need to do this weekend," he said as we cleaned up.

He looked more like himself this morning than he had all week. Regular meals and proper sleep had filled out his face, so it wasn't so sharp. We'd taken the time to eat, sleep, and exercise; trying to return to a normal regimen.

"What's that?" I said. From the way he set his mouth in a line, it was something unpleasant.

"I need to talk to my brother," he said. "Whether he's interested in talking to me or not. They shut Real Tech down, but he needs to make more of the antidote. Brandon can probably get equipment, but not supplies, so I'm going to force the issue."

"He'll need real venom; he no longer has access to the synthetic kind. It's the key ingredient of the antidote. I'd learned that much from his research notes."

Christopher grinned as he shoveled another massive piece of maple syrup-drenched buttery pancake into his mouth. He held up the hotel vouchers from Reno for a free stay. I hadn't seen them in months.

"We wouldn't want these to expire, would we? Road trip anyone?"

I laughed. "Have you talked to Mr. Jacobs?"

"Oh yes. My friend Benny was thrilled to hear from me. We talked for half an hour. When I asked if we could ask more questions, he suggested we come in person. He has a new two-foot-long Gila monster he's sure we'll love."

I shuddered. I wouldn't, but as we had a favor to ask, it was important to be polite.

"Can we work in a road trip and the conversation with your brother?"

"Brandon today and Reno tomorrow?" he said. "Book a room. One with a king-size bed and a soaker tub."

He flashed his grin and dimple, and my heart skipped a beat. It made me feel warm inside that he was more like himself. He'd been subdued all week.

I went online to see if our vouchers were valid for a luxury room and discovered that they were, so I booked a room for the following night.

Christopher texted his brother and asked if he could stop by later today. The answer was short and affirmative. We decided to talk to Brandon together. He wouldn't be bothered seeing the two of us together because he didn't know or care that I'd been his girlfriend. We drove past the front of Brandon's place but didn't stop, because sitting at the end of the block was a familiar black SUV with tinted windows. I'd bet that Horace and or Jasper were inside even though they'd disappeared when Eric had. We turned left down the alley before we reached them and I called Andrew.

"The Real Tech goons are in their SUV outside Brandon's." There was a hitch in my voice. I'd guessed Horace and Jasper, but it could have been Eric. We hadn't been able to see through the windows.

"I'll send someone right away," he said.

We stayed in the car. Less than five minutes later, I received a text from Andrew.

"Must have spooked them. They're gone."

"Either way, Brandon's on his own," said Christopher. "Let's go."

We parked in the alley and walked hand in hand to Brandon's front door.

"I didn't expect you to bring your girlfriend," he said when he opened the door.

His manners hadn't improved since he'd awakened from his coma.

"Can we come in, talk to you inside?" said Christopher.

Brandon shrugged and opened the door wider, inviting us in. He didn't ask us to sit, so we stood in an awkward huddle just inside the door.

"I heard you got out of jail," he said, looking at Christopher.

Brandon should look uncomfortable about what he'd done to Christopher at the lab, but he didn't show it. He may have been curious about why we'd come, but not in an emotional way. His lack of reaction was unsettling, and it hurt my stomach to talk to him when he was so flat and detached.

"Look," said Christopher, "I was rude when you came to see me in jail. I'm sorry about that. I'm not sorry for telling you what I thought, just how things came out. I yell too much."

He hadn't told me that part.

"You aren't angry now?" said Brandon, his eyes narrowing.

He didn't understand emotions. Christopher was furious—for all he was being polite. His muscles were granite-like with tension.

"I've been angry since you injected yourself last August. After I got out of jail, I learned you lied to our parents. Told them I was fine and looked after. That Elizabeth was taking care of me. That's fucking unacceptable. It's total shit. When you're like this, not only are you not my brother, but that's not something you should do to anyone. Science shouldn't always come first. You should know right from wrong."

Christopher's fists were clenched and his eyes blazed. Brandon wasn't in danger. Christopher wouldn't hit him, even if he was justified.

Brandon stepped back, unable to meet Christopher's eyes.

"You're probably right," said Brandon. "The law seems clear. I should not have put science before the law, and I know now that it was unacceptable."

It wasn't an apology, but it was an admittance of guilt. Perhaps that was as much as Brandon was capable of right now. It was a start.

"The thing is," said Christopher, "I want you to make and take the antidote."

"I can't make more." Brandon shrugged. "No more lab."

"Hypothetically speaking, if you had the supplies, would you be able to?"

"Hypothetically speaking? I could."

"You need to," said Christopher. "The others you injected need it and so do you."

"I don't think I do. I'm fine."

"Look," I interrupted. "You were always kind of cold and distant, but Christopher mattered to you more than anyone. You weren't detached with him. He knows the real you, the pre-injection you. You should listen to him."

"You're his girlfriend," said Brandon, turning to look at me. "I found lots of pictures of you on my phone. Were we friends?"

"We dated for a while, but you were never serious about me," I said. Once those words would have stung, but now they were simply the truth.

"Did you love me?" said Brandon.

He tilted his head and seemed to have a genuine interest in my answer.

"I cared about you," I said. "Not love. We weren't that close. We didn't talk about important things, never discussed the future, and we liked scientific conversations over dinner."

"I see," said Brandon. "Do you think I should take this antidote?"

"I do."

"I like my head being free of distractions," he said. "You sound like you were an emotional distraction."

"Maybe I was, which is why we didn't work out and could've been why you broke up with me. That happened months before you experimented on yourself."

"I'm curious," said Christopher. "Do you remember your reasons for injecting yourself with a dangerous serum that killed all the test animals? Was it fear, intimidation, thirst for knowledge, or unbridled ambition? Did you ever consider what might happen or how your family might feel if you died?"

Brandon's jaw dropped at Christopher's vehement tone and he shook his head. "I don't recall." His face looked thoughtful, with a small crease between his eyes. He glanced out the window, then turned back.

"If I said yes, how would you get scorpion venom as a base? I need it to make the antidote. My boss supplied me with the means to synthesize venom. He's missing, so I can't create more."

"You haven't heard from him?" said Christopher.

I liked how he slid that into the conversation. It would be fantastic if that information came into our possession.

Christopher kept the question casual, but his tell of the tightening around his eyes, showed me how tense he was. He jammed his hands in his pockets as he waited for the answer.

Brandon shook his head.

"He stationed his men outside, watching," I said. "Today, just before we came in."

"I don't think I like that," said Brandon, his frown deepening.

"We called the cops. The goons must have seen us too and guessed we'd report them because they split."

"If we can get the venom, you'll do it?" said Christopher.

"I'll make it. I don't know if I'll take it."

"How much would you need for six doses?"

"Six milliliters," said Brandon. "That's a lot of real venom. Scorpions produce minute quantities at a time."

"We'll try to get it," said Christopher. "You start work on the rest. Get whatever equipment and supplies you require. We could have some of the venom soon."

"You going to tell me your source?" said Brandon.

"Nope. You look like my brother, but until you're yourself again and have taken the antidote, I don't trust you."

Brandon nodded. "I understand."

He should have looked sad. It was like talking to a robot version of Brandon. He was missing what made him human.

We turned to leave and Brandon said, "Elizabeth, I'm sorry I don't remember you and I'm sorry if I hurt your feelings."

"Thank you." As we left, I felt a sense of closure. I didn't know how much of this conversation Brandon would remember if he took the antidote, but it had been right to speak. I wasn't angry about how our relationship had ended anymore, just how he'd treated Christopher.

• • •

I had invited Luke and Ella to the house on Friday night for dinner so they could ask their questions about Eric.

I'd dressed in jeans and a soft pink sweater and was determined to speak tonight. I'd spoken to Brandon and in court, I could speak to them. Christopher had faith in my success.

The Wilsons arrived on time in a new white Civic. Had they brought the invoice for their work, as I had yet to receive a bill?

"Come in, come in," said Christopher after they rang the doorbell and he'd opened the door. I hung back as they entered. I let him be his charming, extroverted self.

"We've met," he said, extending his hand to first Luke, then to Ella, "But I wasn't at my best. I don't remember much from that night."

Ella handed me a bouquet with a friendly smile. "Thanks for having us here. Much nicer than at the office."

Luke and Christopher chatted about house maintenance and their favorite BBQ methods and sauces.

"I've been meaning to ask," I said. "I don't want unpaid bills. You said you'd send me the fee for your work, but you haven't."

Luke extracted a white envelope from his back pocket and handed it to me.

Christopher led them into the kitchen while I trailed behind and opened the invoice. I had some money saved and hoped it would be enough. I couldn't have gotten Christopher back without their help. Whatever price they'd charged was worth it to have him home and whole again.

"Is this a joke?" My voice wasn't very loud, but Luke turned.

"Nope," he said, turning to face me. His eyes were serious.

"My first big case brought in a lot of money, and we've made it last. We keep our expenses down by paying low rent for that crappy office. We work as much as we want. Contract jobs for corporations or the police, we charge a substantial fee. A regular citizen like you, expenses only. All we ask is good references or referrals, and you've already hooked us up with the Portland PD. We'll get more contracts with them if we find this creep."

"You charged me for two cups of coffee and a tank of gas," I said. "I owe you $87.25? That's it? You said getting him from the lab would cost extra."

"It was free before that," said Ella with a smile. "It's the least we could do."

I was speechless with their generosity. They'd donated their time and energy. They'd taken risks. Tears swam in my eyes.

"Hey," said Ella, stepping forwards and hugging me. "We were happy to help."

"We heard about your day in court," said Luke. "Seems to have helped get your voice back." He put his arm around his wife as she stepped back, and they smiled at each other.

I nodded. "My therapist was right. She said I needed to find the right incentive."

I smiled at Christopher. He kissed me.

To my surprise, dinner was fun.

After we devoured the strawberry rhubarb crumble with vanilla ice cream, we got down to business at the round wooden kitchen table. Christopher held my hand.

"Did you ever hear Eric called by any other names?" said Luke.

I shook my head. I'd wracked my brain all week, trying to think of anything that might help. I had an exceptional memory, but I'd spent a lot of time the last few years repressing the memories of my time with Eric.

"He used to get mail addressed to him as Eric with a 'k' instead of a 'c'. When I asked him about it, he ranted about how people were stupid. It was odd. He said he cared, but did nothing about it. That seemed out of character."

"That's something," said Ella as she wrote that down.

"What about phone calls for other names?"

I shook my head. "We didn't have a house phone, and he didn't like it when I answered his cell. He was very possessive about it."

"We want to follow the money," said Luke. "See if we can trace him that way. You know anything about his finances?"

"He received a lot of mail from businesses, statements or something. They had thin envelopes." I listed some of the company names that I remembered. "Real Tech wasn't one of them, but some others sounded like tech companies."

Ella wrote the names I remembered.

"What about his job?" said Ella. "Andrew mentioned you learned Eric was the boss at Real Tech."

"The whole time we were involved, he didn't share what his job was. Ever. When I asked what he did, he said it was classified. I can't believe I married someone who kept so many secrets. The first I heard he was the head of Real Tech was when he attacked me. He bragged about it."

Christopher squeezed my hand.

"So, Eric targeted you from the beginning," said Luke.

He'd figured that out faster than I had. I nodded.

"How did Eric dress when he went to work?" said Luke.

"Suits," I said. "He mentioned once that the boss needed to set a professional tone in the office, so I always thought it was an office job. He criticized me for not dressing up more for the Museum and said I looked unprofessional." My voice wavered on the last word. Eric had put me down in a hundred tiny ways, chipping away at my soul and self-esteem, eroding my confidence and personality.

"What about money?" Luke dished himself another scoop of dessert.

"He had money, but was tight fisted with it. I opened one of his bank statements by accident and saw hundreds of thousands of dollars. That's when I realized it couldn't be mine. He insisted we kept separate accounts. He paid a share of the mortgage payment and household expenses, not a dime more."

"Which bank?" said Luke. "If you opened it by accident, was it your bank?"

I nodded. "Umpqua Securities. But he received statements from several big banks."

"That gives us a start," said Ella. "The spelling of his name and the name of a bank might help us get his real name."

"We have electronic surveillance outside his home address. The night before last was the first time he's been home in weeks. He spent seven minutes in his house but was gone before the police arrived. Can you think of anything that he wouldn't want to leave behind if he went on the run?" said Ella.

"A steel lockbox," I said. "It wasn't heavy and was about this big." I showed them with my hands. It was about a foot high, a foot wide, and slightly longer. My voice caught, but I continued. "He gave me a black eye when I asked what was inside." I didn't enjoy telling them that, but they took it in stride. Christopher squeezed my hand again.

"When he traveled for work, he'd get something from the box. Probably his passport. Or cash? I never saw his birth certificate or other personal documents. He kept them somewhere."

"If the box is there, I'll see if I can look inside," said Luke. "He didn't retrieve anything that size. Perhaps he needed something from inside the box."

After their questions, Luke and Ella thanked us for dinner and promised to have us over when the case was finished. It wasn't often I made new friends. I liked them both.

When they'd gone, they left me with the feeling that they'd break this case; it was only a matter of time.

Chapter 27

Saturday dawned cold and clear as we hit the road for Reno. Though I could talk, Christopher dominated the conversation. He was in the mood to talk about his brother and shared some of their silly boyhood stories and escapades. I enjoyed seeing him so relaxed and hearing about the pleasant part of his childhood.

It was after five when we arrived in Reno. The downtown was much quieter than in September. We found parking on the same block as Benny's building. The air was chilly, but there was only a dusting of snow. Open areas had been scoured by the wind and were dotted with patches of ice.

Christopher texted Benny to let him know we'd arrived. Rather than wait outside with the brisk wind, we waited for his reply in the SUV with the heated seats. We'd returned the white SUV we'd leased and insured my red one from my garage at the townhouse. It had sat undriven since last May, when I'd arrived in 2017. There was no reason to ignore it, even though it was a relic from my old life. It was the vehicle I'd been driving when I crashed with Eric in a future that wouldn't happen.

After fifteen minutes with no answer, Christopher said, "Fuck this. He said he's here whenever and knows we're coming. It's cold. Let's go."

We stepped onto the icy sidewalk and skated our way to Benny's door. The glass in the door at the bottom of the stairs was broken.

Pieces littered the ground, blending into the bits of ice and the fine snow that covered everything like powder.

"There's no way that happened very long ago," Christopher said, showing me the broken window. "That's from today. He kept his room up there warm. The heat is leaking out." He held his hand up to feel the waft of warm air. "He'd have covered it or boarded it up if he was aware."

"Agreed."

"Benny," Christopher called through the hole and up the stairs. His voice was loud and echoed in the staircase. "It's Christopher and Elizabeth from Portland. You up there?"

There was no answer.

"Benny?" He spoke through the hole again. "We're coming up."

The door wasn't locked and Christopher led the way. The familiar musty odor filled the air as we ascended, though it wasn't as hot as the last time we'd come. I glanced back toward the sidewalk several times as we climbed the stairs, biting my lip. I didn't know what I expected to find, but I had a creeping sense of unease.

We were almost at the top of the stairs when a low moan sounded from above. My eyes met Christopher's.

"Mr. Jacobs, are you here?" Christopher's booming voice echoed through the stairwell.

There was no reply.

I took a deep breath, preparing myself for conflict. We bounded up the final two stairs and around the corner. I stopped and Christopher sprinted forward, his body in motion before I realized the reason.

Benny lay on his back on the floor near the snake tanks in the middle of the room. His skin glistened with sweat while his skin looked pale, though his cheeks were flushed. He appeared unconscious. They'd rolled his left sleeve up past his elbow, exposing his flesh where he had two double sets of puncture marks in his forearm. A thin trickle of blood ran from each hole in his wet arm and stained the cheap linoleum. I couldn't wrest my gaze from the injury.

"Benny, what bit you?" Christopher crouched beside Benny's prone form and gave him a gentle shake.

There was no answer, just another faint moan.

"I'll bet it was the cottonmouths. He's right by their tank," I said, bustling into the room. "Call 911. I'll look for his antivenom. He said he keeps it handy." I remained alert for a snake that could be loose, but saw nothing.

The shelves behind his desk held only office supplies and books about venomous creatures. Benny kept a bar fridge in the corner. Inside were over a dozen white rectangular packages. He'd left the ends opened for easy access. He'd labeled them in black marker with big writing over the original packaging: scorpion, Gila monster, tarantula, black widow, coral snake, rattlesnake, etc. I fumbled to locate the correct package. At first, I didn't see one for cottonmouths, but then I remembered they were called water moccasins. I grabbed a box from the top shelf.

My ears roared, and my heart chugged like a freight train. In the background, Christopher spoke on his phone. My hands shook, and I almost dropped the antivenom kit. Everything became slow motion as I scampered across the room to join Christopher. I didn't know how to inject Benny with the antivenom. I was out of my depth. My hands trembled.

I met Christopher's scared eyes, and he asked the person on the other end of the line about the antivenom. His hand covered my icy one.

"911 said to wait. They'll have someone here in two to three minutes. They've dispatched the police and an ambulance."

I took a deep breath to steady myself and nodded. A lump formed in my throat. I wouldn't be much help with the explanation. Benny's forehead was hot beneath the back of my hand. How long had he lain on the floor before we'd discovered him? What if we'd gone for dinner when he hadn't answered?

"It's better with an IV and a professional to make sure he doesn't have an allergic reaction," said Christopher, relaying information from the voice on the other end of the line.

My ears strained as I listened for the ambulance. Sirens. In the distance, but coming.

"The door was open at the bottom of the stairs," said Christopher into the phone. "It was unlocked, the window broken at the bottom."

Outside, the siren wail stopped and feet pounded up the wooden stairs. Red lights flashed through the window facing the street. Two paramedics in navy blue jackets rushed in and we backed away. Christopher put his arm around me. One put in an IV right away while the other checked Benny's vitals.

"Breathing is shallow, heartbeat is erratic."

"How long since you found him?" The paramedics spoke to each other or us without taking their attention from Benny.

"Seven minutes," Christopher said, checking the time.

I wiped my sweaty palms on my jeans.

"Was he conscious when you found him?" asked one paramedic.

"We heard a couple of moans, but that's it," Christopher jammed his hands in his front pockets. He rocked back and forth on the balls of his feet. "This happened a while ago."

"How can you tell?" said a uniformed police officer who joined us upstairs.

"The room's been losing heat out the broken window at the bottom for a while. It's noticeably cooler up here than the last time we visited Benny."

"Good catch," said the officer. "How do you know this man?"

I watched the paramedic monitoring his heart while the other injected the antivenom slowly into the IV bag.

"We met last September," said Christopher. "We had questions about scorpions. He's an expert. We're back in town and arranged to meet him this evening, but he didn't answer our text when we got here."

"You'll have to wait to speak with him until morning," said one paramedic.

"What hospital are you taking him to?" Christopher said.

"Reno General," said the second paramedic as they loaded him onto a stretcher.

"Officer Aaron Quinn," said the police officer. "I would like to get your full statement. You're from out of town, so I'd like to know where you're staying and for how long, as well as how you can be reached after you go home."

We went through what had happened again and how we'd found Benny. Christopher did the talking, gave our names and numbers, and produced his card from the Portland Museum. Now that some of the excitement had died down, I couldn't help but scan around the room. The creatures still gave me the creeps. Upon closer examination, there was a gap where a couple of small tanks were missing in the back corner. As I walked toward them, I had a sinking feeling about what I'd find was missing. I was correct. The adult Arizona bark scorpions were gone.

I sent quick texts to Andrew and the Wilsons, updating them on what we'd found.

"Benny is unconscious and bitten by snakes. Going to the hospital. Scorpions have been stolen. If Eric was in Reno today. It should be a good time to check inside his house."

Eric had been here earlier today. Horace and Jasper hadn't done this on their own. Maybe he wanted the scorpions for further research purposes or to keep us from getting venom to make the antidote. I ground down on my teeth. Either way, he was a step ahead of us. Again.

While the officer finished speaking with Christopher, his partner boarded up the broken window below. He'd also swept up the broken glass. We strolled out while he finished and they secured the scene with yellow tape.

"Just to be certain, what do you remember touching?" said Officer Quinn. "We're going to lift fingerprints."

"The door, the knob, the handrail, the fridge," said Christopher. "Not sure if I touched the tank beside Benny or not when I was on the phone."

"If we need your prints for reference, would you come to the police station and give them voluntarily?" said the officer. "Maybe in the morning."

"Of course," said Christopher. "We're headed to dinner and will be in town overnight. After that, you can reach me on my cell."

"Have a nice evening. We'll be in touch," said Officer Quinn as we walked to my car.

I hoped Benny's creatures would survive without him for a few days. Maybe he had a friend or assistant who could feed them and check that they were warm enough. I wasn't about to volunteer.

"We'll go see Benny tomorrow at the hospital," said Christopher as we got in the car. "I still have questions for him, if he's up to answering."

"The adult scorpions are missing. I texted the others."

Christopher cursed. I was glad we were back in the car.

"How did I miss that?"

"Do you think this was Eric?" I said, biting my lip.

His eyes hardened, and his jaw clenched at the name. "I do. He can't stay ahead of us forever, though. We're catching up. This was recent." He started the car. "Let's eat."

• • •

The next morning after breakfast, we went to the Reno police station and left our fingerprints for reference. We looked up the hospital visiting hours and confirmed Benny's room number at the front desk. He was conscious and available. He'd told the nurses he wanted to see us and to send us in if we stopped by.

The hospital was smaller than the one in Portland, but it had the same distinct smell inside that triggered negative memories. I took a few deep breaths near the door as I steadied myself. Benny was on the third floor.

Benny's homely face lit up when he saw us.

"Christopher and Elizabeth from Portland," he said. "I'm glad you stopped by."

His color was better, the hectic flush was gone from his cheeks, and he was no longer chalky and sweaty.

"I'm lucky you two showed up when you did. I understand you're the ones who found me and called 911."

"You've already spoken to the police," said Christopher, "But, do you mind telling us what happened?"

"It's weird," said Benny. "Remember how I mentioned the Portland lab with the two goons who wanted my scorpions last summer?"

We nodded.

"Turns out they came back yesterday with their boss. They demanded I sell the adult bark scorpions. I refused. They said if I didn't sell them, they'd take them, anyway."

"Was the boss about five foot ten, kind of stocky, green eyes with a buzz cut?"

"Yeah, that's him. You know him? He was a pushy asshole. The tall man called him Fengdahl."

"You mean 'Dahl'? That's his last name."

"Nope, they said 'Fengdahl.' I remember because my cousin married a Fengdahl, and I thought what an unusual name. Never expected to hear it again unless I visited Norway or something."

"*Erik Fengdahl,*" I sent to the Wilsons. "*Try that.*" Hope surged at the clue. We were making progress.

"What are the odds they showed up right around the same time as you? You don't work with them too?"

"We do not. We wanted to talk to you about them because we've had problems with Mr. Fengdahl and his men."

Christopher filled in Benny about the last few months, including Brandon and the experiments. We might catch up to Eric by pooling our knowledge.

"As you can see," said Christopher, "We hoped to buy scorpion venom so my brother could make the antidote."

"I thought you two worked for the Portland Museum." Benny looked back and forth between us with a furrowed brow.

"We do," I said. "But the boss from Real Tech is my ex-husband, so this is personal. The cops haven't been able to find him and the name we knew him by is fake."

"He's a jerk." Benny shook his head. "When I said I wouldn't sell, he got his minions to hold my arm into the tank with the cottonmouths and he slapped the tank to get the snakes agitated. After two of my snakes bit me, they took the scorpions and knocked me out. I came to at some point, but was too weak to get to a phone and call for help. I didn't think anyone would find me in time. They probably thought so too, as I don't get a lot of business this time of year. The doctor said I only had another hour before it would have been too late."

"We were just lucky," said Christopher.

"If there's anything I can do, let me know," said Benny. "I owe you."

"We need to buy scorpion venom. My brother is going to make the antidote for the people that were experimented on. Guess that's out of the question now."

A strange expression crossed Benny's face. He sat up straighter, leaned forward, and spoke in a conspiratorial tone.

"They took my scorpions, but not my insurance supply. I've stockpiled over ten milliliters of bark scorpion venom. I extract it regularly and sell just enough to pay my rent. My creature collection isn't exactly a top tourist attraction."

The tension in Christopher's shoulders lessened. We wouldn't fail. Hope surged through me that Brandon could be cured.

Benny said. "You saved my life. You can have it."

"We don't need that much," I said.

Christopher's eyes hadn't left Benny's. "Are you sure? The hospital can be expensive. We could buy six milliliters. That's enough for six doses of the antidote."

"It's yours, no cost," said Benny. "But I can't get it while I'm in the hospital."

"We have to get back to Portland for work tomorrow."

"When I get out in a couple of days, I'll courier it to you. Send me the address and I'll let you know when it's on its way."

Christopher shook Benny's hand. "I can't tell you how much I appreciate this. I just want my brother back."

"You two saved my life. Let's call it even," said Benny with a toothy smile.

I sent him the address of our P.O. box and said our thanks.

When we left Benny and the hospital, we headed home. We'd accomplished a lot in Reno. We didn't know where Eric had gone, but as long as Benny followed through on his promise, we'd have the supplies we needed. The information about Eric's name was lucky. If it wasn't his real name, at least we had another alias we could use to track him.

While we'd been gone, Luke had gone to search for Eric's lockbox. I hoped we'd get to hear about his mission.

I didn't have long to wait. That afternoon while we were on the road, Andrew texted with the result of Luke's investigation.

"Lockbox located. Contents include over twenty thousand in cash, two unregistered handguns, several sets of identification documents, and four passports, including Eric Johnson, Eric Dahl, and Erik Fengdahl. New passport with a recent issue date for Magnus Bergstrom with Eric's picture."

I gasped as I read the messages aloud to Christopher.

"Your dad's name?"

"Probably his new identity if he's preparing to run again. No idea why he hasn't disappeared yet."

Another message came through an hour later.

"We got a warrant. Taking the box as official evidence. Will get legal photos of the contents. I'll keep you posted."

When we were a couple of blocks from home, Andrew sent a picture of himself with the metal box that I remembered. The police had it in their possession and with it had enough evidence to send Eric, or whoever he was, to jail for a long time. He just needed to be caught.

Chapter 28

Two long days passed, then a message arrived from Benny. *"Sent."*

The package with the venom was at the post office Wednesday evening for us to collect. Thursday morning, we delivered it to Brandon. His kitchen had transformed into a laboratory, with flasks, tubing, and a rack of test tubes with the tiny vials I recognized from his previous serums.

"There's enough for six doses," said Christopher. "Have you decided?"

"I've decided yes and will document it for science. I'll make a video of myself," said Brandon. "Telling myself everything important. That way, if I forget everything from the time I woke up in the hospital, I can fill in my missing time."

"Good idea," I said. What would he consider important, other than information about his research? "What if you have another allergic reaction?" Had he considered that possibility?

"Thought of that," said Brandon. "I'm going to give myself antivenom right after the reversal treatment. I have some here. Leftover from previous research. At worst, it may make me nauseous."

"Sounds like you've thought of everything this time," I said.

"I appreciate you figuring out that's what happened before, Elizabeth. I hadn't considered allergies before my trial."

"How long until you have the antidote ready?" Christopher kept his tone even.

"Three to four days," said Brandon. "Then a good night's rest to be on the safe side. I'll finish the video and inject myself before I sleep. With luck, I'll wake up the next morning with my memories intact."

"What about the doses for the others?" said Christopher.

"I'll try the antidote first. When I'm awake, I'll call you. Unless I die. Then, as my next of kin, you'll be notified when they find my body. The video will be evidence that I did this to myself."

It was shocking to hear it said in such a matter-of-fact way. The old Brandon had been cold, but not like this. This level of detachment was wrong.

"The other doses will be in the fridge. When I wake up, Officer Jennings can distribute them to the victims."

We wished him luck and left. For us, there was nothing to do but wait, though we'd be on edge until we heard from Brandon. My fingernails would be chewed to the quick this week and Christopher would need a long workout every day to burn off his excess energy.

In the meantime, information arrived from Andrew.

"Erik Fengdahl is wanted in three states for sexual assault. FBI sending a pair of agents to work with the Portland Police Department to aid in his apprehension."

• • •

On the fifth day, we still hadn't heard from Brandon. Christopher couldn't wait any longer, so we drove to Brandon's house after work. His lights were out. There was no sign of anyone from Real Tech, so we gambled Brandon was alone, if he was home at all.

Christopher rang the doorbell four times before we heard movement inside. I wasn't sure if I was disappointed or relieved when Brandon answered the door.

His eyes were bleary and his hair flattened against the side of his head with a serious case of bedhead that reminded me of an eighties pop star hairstyle. He wore plaid pajamas and was rubbing his eyes. We'd woken him, even if it was six at night.

"It's early, Christopher," he said, squinting into the dark outside. "What do you want? Couldn't you have called first? I've been working late for months. You know that."

Looking at the dark of twilight, I understood how he might be confused. I often woke up disoriented if I slept at odd hours. His face changed when he saw me standing behind Christopher. His mouth pinched in and his fists clenched.

"What the hell. You brought Elizabeth here? I told you a month ago that I'd talk to her when I was ready."

He sounded irritated, which was fantastic.

Christopher stood with his head cocked to one side. "How do you feel?"

"Well, you woke me up while it's still dark. It's six a.m. And you brought my ex to my doorstep. How do you think I feel?"

"Six p.m.," said Christopher. "You sound annoyed."

Brandon frowned at the news of the time.

"Of course, I sound annoyed. I must be coming down with something if I'm this exhausted after sleeping all day." Brandon frowned.

He'd slept over twenty hours if he'd injected himself the night before as planned.

Giving Christopher a dirty look, he trotted down the stairs in his bare feet and hugged me. He smelled like he could use a shower.

"I'm sorry I've been ignoring you," he said as he stepped back. "I shouldn't have stopped answering your calls or blocked your number. You went to my brother? I planned to explain when I wasn't so busy."

This was the real Brandon.

Tears filled my eyes, and he misinterpreted the reason.

"I know it wasn't fair to just disappear the last couple of months. I was going to call you soon and see if we could talk. I want you back. I've missed our talks."

I didn't know what to say. We'd expected Brandon's memories to be reset, but seeing it in action was difficult. My tongue twisted into knots. I shot a helpless look over his shoulder at Christopher.

"I'm glad you're okay," was my lame comment.

"What?" he said. "Course, I'm okay. Can we talk inside?"

I nodded and shrugged at Christopher. The three of us went inside together.

Christopher looked torn. He jammed his hands in his pockets; his energy level was high. We'd known this conversation was a possibility. I took a deep breath, trying not to get ahead of ourselves. We'd been disappointed before. We needed Brandon to watch his video.

A weight of unexpected responsibility settled over me. I'd hoped the video would cover how long this had been, how many months he'd been in a coma, and what had happened since. Brandon and I had broken up at the beginning of last June. It was now mid-February. We'd expected his video message to pave the way for our news. We were about to hurt him. I wanted to hold Christopher's hand for support but refrained.

"What's the last thing you remember?" Christopher said as we sat on the couch, space between us so we wouldn't touch by accident. One hand drummed on his knee; his restless energy unable to be contained.

Brandon was going to be confused and upset.

Brandon grabbed a chair from the kitchen table and sat facing us.

He took a deep breath. "Last night, I injected myself with an experimental serum made from scorpion venom. That must be why I slept all day."

He looked like he was waiting for a huge reaction.

"We know," Christopher said. "But it wasn't just last night."

Brandon furrowed his brow as he continued. "I made the serum in the lab. It's supposed to make the subject resistant to pain. It was a two-step process, but I only injected the first stage. I wanted to document the results for science. Until last week, I didn't think we were ready for human trials. My boss is a real ass and pressured me to get it done. He stands to make boatloads of money."

He looked at us and our lack of surprise. "What am I missing?"

"This isn't the first time you've woken up," said Christopher. "Your serum caused a severe allergic reaction, and you fell into a catatonic state. A coma."

"I don't remember this." Brandon looked back and forth between us for verification.

"They found you unconscious in your lab in August and you remained in a coma for three months. The hospital told us it was a drug overdose, but Elizabeth and I didn't believe them. We worked together to figure out what had happened. We went through some of your notes and guessed what you'd done. She guessed it was from a reaction, so we bought and injected you with scorpion antivenom and you woke up."

"Since then, you've been awake another two and a half months," I said. "But you were different. Your serum was successful. You were remote, detached, and unemotional."

"What are you talking about?" said Brandon.

He jumped to his feet and paced his small living room.

"You're telling me it's 2018 and that I've lost more than five months of my life?"

"I'm sorry," said Christopher. "This must be strange to hear, but we talked to you less than a week ago. We convinced you to give yourself the serum antidote. You made some for the others that were part of recent human trials. Said it would take three to four days to complete the process. Today is the fifth day. We got worried and came over to check on you."

"I don't remember any of that." Brandon sat down and grabbed his head between his hands and pressed on his temples. "Why can't I remember any of this?"

His eyes were wide open and his voice was loud.

"You were going to leave a video for yourself to watch. It should be on your phone or computer. It should explain most of this."

Christopher's voice was soothing as he tried to calm his brother.

My phone chimed. I glanced down at a message from Andrew. *"Lead on Eric outside of town, sending a car to check it out. Looks like a solid tip about where he's staying."*

Hope surged that at last Eric might be caught. The police were closing in.

"I'm going to let the two of you talk without me," I said. "There's a box of photos in my garage that the real estate agent found in the master bedroom closet. I'll walk over and get it. Let me know when you want to pick me up." Christopher nodded. He raked his hand through his hair. It would be better for the two of them to talk without me.

I hurried out and down the sidewalk. This looked like they would work it out, though Brandon needed time to adjust his worldview. It couldn't be easy if he didn't remember things well from before the coma.

The night air was crisp as I strolled. I was uneasy about being alone, but I refused to let my fear of Eric dictate everything I did. Thanks to Andrew's text, I was relaxed enough for a quick walk. There was no sign of the Real Tech goons. The sidewalk had slippery sections, but I was careful. The neighborhood was well lit and seemed safe. Inside my townhouse would be cold and not a great place to wait, but Christopher and his brother needed privacy.

Now that the contractors were finished, the heat should have been shut off in the townhouse and the water turned off so the pipes wouldn't burst if we had a sudden cold snap, but I didn't plan on staying long, but I could collect the box. Facing the place where I'd been hurt and miserable one last time might bring some closure to that piece of my life. I detoured and bought a steaming cup of tea to keep myself warm while I waited.

The porch light was on, and its light illuminated the stairs. I found it amusing that the light was on, since I didn't live there anymore. When I lived here, I'd forgotten all the time. I felt little as I opened the door. It wasn't home anymore, and I'd moved beyond the misery I'd felt living here. I wasn't planning to attend the open house.

My phone chimed again. Christopher sent, *"On my way."* He'd be here soon.

It wasn't as cold as I expected for a vacant house in February. I removed my gloves and set them on the table with the rest of my tea. Perhaps the real estate agent or the contractors had left the heat on yesterday. Curious about the repairs, I decided to check out how well they'd repainted the walls. The contractors must not be quite finished in the kitchen, though I couldn't see anything else to do besides clean up. I sighed. I'd have to send someone to deal with their mess before the open house; they'd left garbage and food containers on the counter.

I flicked on the light to my bedroom first. The room looked fantastic. Neutral eggshell-colored walls complemented the new laminate flooring which matched the new flooring in the kitchen. We'd left a few pieces of furniture to stage the house for sale. I'd hired a company to do everything. My house went on the market next weekend. It would be a relief to have it sold. Most of my memories of living here were unpleasant.

Footsteps sounded in the hallway. I must have missed hearing the door. Brandon and Christopher had finished talking sooner than I expected. I hoped their discussion had ended with few hard feelings. I was confident, given time, they'd work it out. Christopher had agonized over this for months, but had been clear that under no circumstances would he break up with me or allow me to walk away, as per our original deal.

"I'm in the back bedroom," I called. "Checking out the paint job. Must have taken five or six coats. You can't tell the wall was ruined."

"That's too bad," said Eric. "It was more work than you think getting the letters that bright and that even."

My heart stopped as I turned in the doorway, facing back toward the hall. He was supposed to be out of town.

"I worked hard to find the exact right thing to write."

His gravelly voice sent chills down my spine.

I didn't know how I'd missed it, but the hallway smelled of Eric's cologne and the door to the Master bedroom was open. He'd been inside when I arrived. Andrew's text had put me so much at ease I'd missed the obvious clues.

The takeout containers on the kitchen counter took on a whole new meaning. The contractor hadn't left them behind.

Eric had been staying at my house.

"I see you got your voice back," he said as I turned to face him.

He looked the same as he always had. Nasty and mean.

"You look fine," he said as he licked his lips.

I willed myself not to freeze up.

"What are you doing here?" The words were supposed to come out strong and confident, but they weren't much more than a whisper.

He smirked and edged closer. He kept his body between me and the exit. There was nowhere to run.

"I figured you'd show up here at some point," he said. "I've been sleeping here for a month and nobody's figured it out."

"You need to leave." My throat felt thick, but I was proud my words were audible. I'd been terrified of this man for so long. Part of me wished he was still dead, though in some ways death had cheated me of vengeance. He'd never had to pay for hurting me. Nobody had known his dirty secret or that he was an abusive creep. It hadn't affected his life, only mine.

He grabbed my wrist.

Eric was stronger than I was and knew how to hit. I'd been on the receiving end dozens of times. I remained calm while confronting him, and breathed. Our last encounter had been in the dark. I'd been terrified and drugged. This time, I was on my home turf.

I waited for my moment. It came sooner than expected. Eric jerked me toward him, trying to tow me down the hall toward the Master bedroom. I used his motion against him, breaking his hold by yanking my arm up sharply toward my head and stepping forward. I'd sworn that I wouldn't hurt anyone, but I needed to protect myself. If he got hurt, it was his fault, not mine. Now I knew better.

As I moved inward, I elbowed him as hard as I could in the chest and slammed the heel of my hand upward into his chin, smashing his chin backward. His neck snapped back and his teeth rattled. I followed up with a hard knee to the groin and he dropped to the ground. He had to be seeing stars, but for good measure, I kicked him again and ran.

I ran to the front door, but not out. If I left him here, he'd disappear again, and I'd always be looking over my shoulder. I had to finish this.

He was groaning on the floor when I called 911, my hands shaking.

"Emergency, 911."

"There's an intruder in my house. He's attacked me before. Send help to 423 Laurel Lane. Please hurry."

"Officers dispatched. Please stay on the line."

I said nothing, but clutched the phone to my chest while I waited for the police. My hands shook and my heart raced. Eric must have heard my phone call. The hallway was quiet, but I would have heard if he'd tried to open a window. He was biding his time to make a move. My knees shook as sirens neared. Eric had stopped moaning, but he was still in the house. From my vantage, I watched both the front door and the back. Each second felt like an eternity as I waited, wondering when he'd strike. When the police car arrived, I opened the front door and stepped aside. Two police officers sped past me and into the house.

Eric bolted out of the hallway and roared, head down. He charged like an enraged bull, trying to bash his way free. He got past both officers and flung himself toward the open door.

I couldn't let him get away.

Time slowed as I tripped him. He lost his balance, but his momentum kept him in motion. At the top of the stairs, he flailed his arms in a vain attempt to keep from falling. Instead, he careened down my front stairs, landing on the sidewalk on his face with a sickening thud. He lay stunned for a moment, but he wasn't dead. He twitched.

Another police car arrived, sirens on, lights flashing, and Andrew flung himself from the car. He and Officer Park ran from the street and the two officers emerged from the kitchen and converged at the bottom of the stairs, guns trained on Eric. One of his legs was bent at an impossible angle and he screamed in pain as he struggled to rise. He glared at me where I stood at the top of the stairs.

"Fucking bitch. Next time, I'll take a baseball bat to your face," he spat.

The fall had knocked out his two front teeth—lost in the impact with the concrete. Blood oozed from between his lips and drooled down his chin in two long streams as he spoke.

"Erik Fengdahl," said Andrew. "You have the right to remain silent."

Officer Park knelt and handcuffed Eric while he spewed venom and cursed in my direction. I tuned him out. I refused to listen to any more of his hateful words.

Andrew read him his Miranda Rights while a third car screeched to a halt in the street. A man and a woman, both wearing blue windbreakers with FBI in yellow lettering on the back, approached the house.

From the other direction, Christopher drove up, parking on the wrong side of the street in his haste. He sprinted past the police, the FBI, and Eric in handcuffs and bounded up the stairs, pulling me into his arms. He squeezed me hard, then checked me over to make sure I was unhurt. Besides the cast from before, I was fine.

My voice was calm. "He's been staying here, in my empty house. He came up behind me, but I kicked the shit out of him and called the cops."

Christopher took my face in his hands and kissed me, the softest, sweetest kiss I could imagine. His thumb stroked the side of my face and turned me to jelly.

"Remind me not to piss you off," he said with a wink.

My grin matched his.

He wrapped his arm around me and said, "Let's go home."

Chapter 29

Christopher and I couldn't leave the scene until I'd given my statement and had a quick once-over from a paramedic. It wasn't long before I locked the townhouse. They'd taken photos and collected prints to prove Eric had been staying there and I gave Andrew my key in case they needed anything else. I was glad to leave this place for what I hoped was the last time.

"How did it go with Brandon after I left?"

"He was confused and upset," said Christopher, "But in time, he'll understand. He asked for us to give him space, but he let me hug him and said he'd watch the video. We found it just before I left. Andrew was on his way to get the other doses when he was diverted to your townhouse. I was in my car when he texted me."

"Did Brandon say how much space or for how long?"

Christopher shook his head.

He seemed disappointed in the outcome.

"At least Brandon is himself again," I said. "He has all the shared memories you two built your whole lives. He'll come around."

"I watched the beginning of the video." He looked shocked to hear how different he sounded. His first words were, "That can't be me."

"Did you need to convince him?"

"Na, he was wearing the same clothes. He recorded it last night before he injected himself and went to sleep."

• • •

On Sunday, Christopher and I went for dinner at Dad's. Andrew and Meghan attended as well. Dad planned the menu in our honor, as it was our first time we'd gone for dinner since we'd gotten engaged. It was also the first time the family had come together since Thanksgiving. I was glad I'd made up with my family in chunks before this, or it would have been too much.

After a delicious dinner of roast beef, potatoes and gravy, and roasted vegetables, we relaxed around the table for a while, enjoying calm family time.

Meghan looked at me several times as though she had something to say. I waited for her to make the first move.

Finally, she blurted, "Elizabeth, can I talk to you about something in private?"

I was curious about what she wanted to talk to me about and followed her upstairs to her old bedroom. It held the outdated treasures of her childhood. Her bookcase contained a pink unicorn statue that she'd painted in fourth grade and half a dozen framed pictures of the family. She picked up one of all four of us. I had left none on display that included our mother when I'd tried to erase her from our past.

In the photo, Meghan was seven, and I was nine. She wore a striped bathing suit, mirrored sunglasses, and a huge grin, but it was mom that drew my eyes like a magnet. Meghan looked so much like mom did back then. My eyes misted over. She'd died when she was only thirty-five, the age I'd been before my wish. Not much older than we were now. In the picture, I held my mom's hand and was trying to pull away from her with an uncooperative scowl.

"What happened that evening? When mom died, I was just a kid, and they explained nothing. You were different from that point on. More reserved. Quieter. You preferred to read instead of playing, even if you were only ten. Sometimes it seemed like I lost you both in that accident."

I hadn't known Meghan had noticed that I'd changed. I'd assumed she was too young to remember how I'd been before.

"Mom and I had a secret." The familiar lump grew in my throat as my voice tried to quit, but I pushed past the feeling.

"Mom was mad at me," I said. "She'd been drinking at Jenny's house with Jenny's mom. We got in a fight out in their driveway. I didn't want her to drive home. She said the wine was our little secret."

"Mom crashed because of the torrential rain, that's all Dad would ever say," said Meghan, stroking mom's face in the picture.

She wasn't looking at me. To her, mom had been fun, an extra playmate. To me, she'd been a liability, unpredictable. Not wonderful traits for a parent. I'd protected my sister, making her school lunches and reading her bedtime stories.

"She did. But because she was distracted, yelling at me." My voice sounded flat, but inside, my emotions churned.

"I'm sure that's not true," Meghan said as she set the photo down on her old desk.

"She smacked my face when I wouldn't get in the car, furious that I questioned if she could still drive. She scared me and made me swear I wouldn't tell about the wine. Said Dad would be mad I'd let her drink so much. That made sense to ten-year-old logic." Of course, I know better now, but it was too late. I'd grown up believing this accident was also my fault.

I'd never told this entire story.

"I was crying. She told me to stop blubbering, but I couldn't. It made her angry. She drove too fast because she was mad. I begged for her to pull over. I wanted out. She scared me. I didn't know where I'd go or how I'd get home, but I didn't want to be in the car." My voice sounded as though it came from a distance as I remembered the water spraying up from the wheels, the bright lights over the highway flashing by, and glaring reflections on the road. The frantic swishing of the wipers as the tires hit the deeper pools of water. The motion as the car skidded from side to side.

"She hit a massive puddle pooled on the highway. We hydroplaned and spun around a hundred and eighty degrees. As we came to a rest, we hit the median and damaged my door. We stopped, facing the wrong way, but unharmed. I was relieved we weren't hurt, but she screamed at me. Said it was my fault. Asked how we would explain it to Dad. That's when the dump truck hit our car." If I closed my eyes, I could still hear the metal as it crunched and my high-pitched scream as I'd covered my face and head.

"Dad said she had a disease," said Meghan in a small voice. "When I was sixteen, I heard him defending Mom over the phone, talking with Grandma. I tried to talk to him about it, but he wouldn't. When I was older, I guessed she had mental health issues, which is why I went into psychiatric nursing. I didn't know she was an alcoholic. Last year, I was afraid you didn't know what was real and what was imagination, like what I remembered about mom. I misinterpreted her problem, too."

"Dad doesn't want to admit that she was an alcoholic," I said. "He doesn't want to hear or say anything negative about Mom. He loved her anyway."

"Is that why you stopped talking about your feelings? Why you tried to be perfect?"

"I tried to be perfect so Mom wouldn't get mad. Sometimes I forgot and fought with her when she'd been drinking. That time, I thought I got her killed. I wanted to tell Dad it was my fault, but I couldn't bear to have him hate me. I was just a kid."

"Why didn't you tell him later?"

Meghan's voice was soft. She reached out and took my hand.

"He wouldn't talk about it. He didn't want to know. He wanted to believe it was just an accident. So, I swallowed my words. It was easier to avoid it. I pretended to believe his version."

"That's where it started," she said. "Why you don't talk when you're upset?"

"I'm trying to change." It didn't feel natural, but now I forced myself to share. Christopher's ability to read minds helped. It gave us a place to start conversations. It helped that he understood so much and accepted me without looking at me like I was broken.

"I wish I'd asked before," she said. "And I'm sorry I said you were like Mom. That wasn't fair. You would never hurt the rest of us with your actions."

"I wouldn't have told you before," I said. "I've dealt with a lot of emotional baggage the last several months. Christopher helped." I stood up, intending to go back downstairs.

"Can I change the subject and ask you for a favor?" She remained on the edge of her old bed and looked up at me.

I nodded.

"I know you don't like a lot of attention or fuss, but would you be my maid of honor?"

"I thought you were trying to decide between your two best friends?" Tears pricked behind my eyes.

"I only have one sister, so it shouldn't be a choice. The job's yours if you want it."

"Will you be mine too? We're keeping the ceremony small, but I want you to be included." Meghan and I hadn't always been close, but she'd been there all my life. Maybe, for once, we were on the right path to repair things between us.

"Deal." She paused and stared out the window.

I waited to see what she was thinking.

She cocked her head to the side. "Are you ever going to explain the time travel? Was it real?"

"It was real. But I can't explain it. My therapist takes credit. It's her magic, not mine. I get to live five years of my life over again and fix some of my biggest mistakes."

"Like what?"

"I found you and Dad again, and fell in love with Christopher."

"You two are revolting." She smiled and stood up. "He's good for you, and I'm glad you're finally happy."

We hugged.

Christopher and I went home after my conversation with Meghan. On the way, I thought about the other conversation that I needed to have.

Tuesday, I left work early and drove to Brandon's. I'd sent him a message asking to meet.

When I knocked, he answered after the first tap of my knuckles. Perhaps he was curious about what I had to say.

He looked better than he had the week before. More settled. Plus, he'd showered and combed his hair.

"What do you want?" he said. "I asked Christopher for time and space. That meant from you too. I'm not impressed he started dating you so soon after you and I broke up. He knew I didn't think it was permanent."

"I know," I said. "But I have a story to tell you. You might not believe me, but I want to explain more about what happened."

"Fine," he said, opening the door wider so I could come in. He stepped back and sat on the couch. I sat on the opposite end, facing him.

I told him everything, starting with my first dinner with Christopher in 2022 and his plea for help. I talked about Eric in both times and how I'd lost my voice. Christopher's mind reading was the only thing that I left out. I told Brandon about the time travel and what I'd thought was my purpose: saving his life.

Throughout it all, he said nothing until I stopped with Eric's arrest last week.

"So, I broke up with you almost six years ago," he said, "Not eight months."

I nodded.

"I remember that dinner last spring," he said. "When you didn't speak. I didn't feel like talking to you. I was punishing you. It sounds petty, but I was mad you were late again. It seemed like time with me wasn't important to you if you were always late."

"I'm sorry. It wasn't personal. Until recently, I was late for everything. While that isn't a good excuse, it is the truth."

He shrugged. "It was annoying, but I should have realized you were different. It's clear now."

"That was my first day back in 2017. I had bought a brand-new dress and new shoes, clearing out my bank account. I planned to change your future and make sure you didn't waste away in the hospital and die."

"Thank you for not giving up on me," he said. "Contrary to what you and Christopher might think, I'm upset, but I'm not mad at my brother. He went through a lot to get me back and you did, too. I'm just jealous that you two are so perfect together."

"We stayed apart for months after you showed him the ring. He tried to walk away."

I doubted Christopher had shared that information.

"You're together now." Brandon attempted a smile.

"Saving you brought us back together. Fighting for you turned into fighting for us."

"Christopher was interested in you before I ever asked you out, so if anyone broke the bro code, it was me. He'd mentioned that he was going to ask you out. I called you the next day so I would be first."

Christopher had never mentioned the timing.

"I was an ass. You deserve better. I'm sorry I didn't treat you like you're special and get to know you better. You should be with Christopher. He's the better brother."

I was surprised at Brandon's words, but relieved. He believed in time travel with so few questions. Perhaps his work to change human evolution and create super soldiers who didn't feel pain meant he had an open mind. We don't always know what's possible, and what's not, until it happens.

Epilogue

"Hold the elevator," came the call from across the lobby.

Christopher raced toward the closing doors.

I stuck my arm into the gap to prevent the stainless-steel doors from closing and he slid in next to me.

"Thanks, Lizzie," he said, flashing the dimple in his cheek.

My heart still fluttered when he called me by that name.

"Oh Christopher," I said, batting my eyelashes at him as I put a hand on his solid chest. "I find your magnetic charm irresistible."

He grinned and awarded me with a large English Breakfast tea, which he would have sweetened to perfection. I threw my arms around his neck and we kissed until the elevator stopped on the fourth floor to let him out. My lips tingled, and I wished we were returning home, not back to work after lunch.

"Thanks for the tea," I said as he disembarked.

"Can I swing by and get you for dinner around six-thirty?"

I smiled. "Of course, I'll set a reminder. I don't want to be late."

He twirled around to blow me a kiss.

"See you after work, Dr. Winters," he said with a wink.

"Back at you, Dr. Winters." My face stretched into a familiar smile.

While change can be slow, sometimes it happens in a moment. An instant when your life is upended in a flash. In this case, the moment was as quick as the arm thrust into the elevator door. Time for infinite possibility. Time for anything to happen, even time travel and finding your true love, like I found mine, and with it, my voice.

Acknowledgments

The summer before I started seventh grade, my mom dropped a bomb. Not a literal one, but its impact had far-reaching ripples. She had enrolled me in a new school without talking to me about it. She recognized I was struggling socially at school (which I had attended since kindergarten and where she taught) and wanted to give me a fresh start. Despite her good intentions, I nearly fell apart because the idea of so much change was daunting. Even if I didn't have many friends at my old school, I knew everyone.

To get to my new elementary school, I had to take the high school bus (with dreaded high schoolers) into town to the high school and walk. It wasn't far, but without a trial run, it seemed scary. Two long-time friends, who were also going to this school, had been there a year already, but would not be in my class. One let me know she wouldn't speak to me at school because she was friends with the "cool" kids this year and I wasn't cool. I was the biggest book nerd around.

At the new school, they placed me in a class with the teacher my mom had requested, but I didn't know anyone. I'd had swimming lessons with some of the boys, but I'd never spoken to them. Another boy was a secret friend for weekends only and we didn't acknowledge each other. His mom drank with my dad while I hung out at his place and read. Sometimes we'd swim or he'd take me snowmobiling, but there was no way we would speak at school. Instead, we pretended we'd never met.

As the weeks went on, I couldn't speak to anyone at the new school. My sister and her brand-new friends spent their lunch times taunting me for reading and for my friendless state. If we were alone, I could force out a few words for my teacher, but not for my peers. It took another new student who arrived at the end of October to help me speak, just by becoming my friend. To this day, I don't understand why she chose me, but I'm thankful that she did. I want to thank Hayley Roberts, now Hayley Deveau for bringing back my voice.

Though I didn't have a name for this inability to speak, I recognized it in my daughter when she was four and attended preschool. Despite non-stop chatter at home, she didn't speak to another child for her entire six months at preschool, just the teachers. I was thankful for her wonderful kindergarten teacher that helped Laurel gain the confidence to speak at school.

I also want to acknowledge the students I have taught who have suffered from selective mutism. Most have grown out of it by the time I teach them at age nine or ten. But not all. One boy didn't speak to me either of the two years he was in my class. Sometimes he wanted to, but he couldn't. He is the reason I wrote this story. I was thankful when he learned to love writing. He wrote three or four times the amount of most students because he had so much he wanted to say but had no other outlet. He only spoke to family and whispered to a few trusted friends. Two years after he left my class, he dropped by to say hi, and he couldn't get out the words. I hope he has found his voice.

I also wanted to give a shout-out to Liza Palmer for reminding us in a SiWC (Surrey International Writer's Conference) workshop that we should write about what we love. The Wish is full of Marvel, Star Wars, and Buffy references, thanks to her.

As always, I want to thank my critique partner, friend, and editor, Tracy Thillmann, who continues to meet with me every week. Tracy understands my author's voice and lets me know when scenes don't work. Her suggestions almost always are things I can work with to improve my stories. I appreciate everything she does. The Wish was the first of five stories she has edited for me, so far, and she has been its champion ever since.

I also want to acknowledge Eileen Cook and her part in the fabulous Creative Academy for Writers, an online writing community. She's been my teacher, head cheerleader, chief blurb writer, and someone with whom I am excited to share my progress. I can never thank her enough for her support and encouragement.

Another group I wish to thank is the team at Black Rose Writing. The Wish is the second book of mine they have published, and working with them has been a terrific experience. They respond to emails and questions immediately, even on weekends, and provide clear information and instructions. Through their Facebook community, I have organized review swaps with other Black Rose authors. Thanks to Carolyn Geduld, David Buzan, Gail Ward Olmsted, Jeffery Jay Levin, Karen K. Brees, Kirsten Schuder, and Sara Fraser for reading The Wish. Reagan was also kind enough to send a digital copy of my first book cover to my husband, who had it printed and framed as a surprise Christmas present.

Last, but not least, is my family. I want to thank my mom for reading everything I send and Laurel, who weighs in on my synopses, query letters, and book blurbs. I want to thank Hayley who helped think of horrible things to torture Elizabeth with, particularly the psych hold. That was her evil mind. She also tells everyone that her mom is a published author and promotes my books to her friends and their families. And then there's Rob, my husband. I want to thank him for understanding me and loving me exactly how I am. I don't have to pretend to be anything other than myself. I hope he understands that's an incredible gift.

In case you missed *The Edge of Life* by Lena Gibson,
keep reading for an excerpt.

The Edge of Life

CHAPTER 1: KAT

Today would be a carbon copy of hundreds that had preceded it. Once, every day had seemed fresh, now each was another obstacle to overcome. Kat smothered the intrusive thoughts as she stress-bit the inside of her lower lip, a distraction while she searched the radio for something cheerful to get her through her Friday morning commute. Yesterday, she'd forgotten her phone at work and already she missed her music.

"As asteroid 2025 NR hurtles toward Earth, scientists forecast..." Kat changed the radio station. Nope. Not cheerful.

"Forest fires rage throughout the Pacific Northwest and into Canada, ahead of the summer forest fire season..." She pushed a different button.

"April temperatures break the one hundred eighty-year record..." She stabbed another button, searching for something less depressing.

"Climate change..."

"No," she said, pushing yet another.

"Riots last night in Portland and LA mirror..."

"Flooding along the Columbia..."

"Reduced snowpack and high temperatures combine..."

"The mass shooting at Snake River Elementary was the fourth shooting this..."

She wanted to scream, but fought the impulse and took a deep breath. "Last chance," she said with a final stab.

"Near miss forecasted for asteroid..."

"The umpteenth 'near miss' this year, blah blah blah," said Kat as she snapped off the radio. She forced her clenched jaw to relax. "How many million miles away for this one?" Rolling her eyes as she took in the now ominous morning sunshine. "Why can't one station play music?"

Tulips, daffodils, and heather blooms provided splashes of much-needed color as she passed the nearby houses and townhouses. Maybe flowers could help her be more positive. Spring had arrived and with it the promise of the upcoming summer vacation. Another six weeks of school until she was free. Though, with the doom and gloom predicted, there'd be nowhere left to go. The last few summers had been similar. Climate change, protests, and misery. Before that, the pandemic. She wished there was something to look forward to besides staying home.

Kat used to love her job, but now she couldn't wait for holidays, for time away from work. She kept the radio off and drove the rest of the way in silence. Arriving at the three-story stone building outside Seattle that housed the private school where she taught, she parked in the staff lot. Her sport model crimson hybrid Camry stuck out like a sore thumb in the expanse of black and white SUVs. It had been her only major purchase since Mark died two years ago. He wouldn't have liked her flashy car, but for her, its vibrant color had been the draw.

Her eyes swam with tears at the thought of her late husband. "Get a hold of yourself, Mrs. Davies. Time to be a teacher," she muttered. Collecting her book and lunch bag from the passenger seat, Kat blinked and checked her mascara in the overhead mirror. She pasted on a smile. Fake it till you make it. She might not be the same person she used to be, but she pretended.

Even when the rest of her life was difficult, this was the one place she needed to be friendly and pleasant, at least to the students. Her starring role was as her old self, the version that hadn't been widowed at twenty-eight. The parking lot filled as her colleagues arrived. Not wanting to walk in with anyone and be forced to chitchat, Kat hurried, glad that her sensible shoes made it easy to escape into the cool hallway inside.

She signed in and kept moving, not making eye contact with anyone. She bypassed the staff room and hustled upstairs, taking them two at a time to the second floor, where her classroom was located. Entering, she unpacked her tea, found the forgotten phone, and turned on her favorite playlist to block the incessant hum of the fluorescent lights.

She shifted into teacher mode and opened the window to reduce the ever-present underlying scents of dust, whiteboard marker, and stale lunches. She straightened desks, posted the schedule, and checked her email to ensure no last-minute changes were required to the day's plan.

When the students shuffled in, she greeted each by name and with a smile. Pouring energy into her performance, she ensured each student spoke at least twice that day, keeping a mental tally in her head. She called on the quiet students to ensure their inclusion and checked on the few who needed extra help. Her friendly teacher role had become automatic because she had done this for so long.

She also made side deals with two students to reduce their required homework, knowing it was a struggle. The last thing was a verbal "ticket out the door" math question. She personalized each, designed to be challenging enough to be of interest, but not so hard the student couldn't answer. Correct answers got a high five and a goodbye with their name that let each student know she valued them. The routine also kept the kids from giving her unwanted hugs.

She'd sorted the numerous crises for the ten-year-olds in their Kelly green and crisp white uniforms, pretending she was doing more than going through the motions. Her performance mattered. It wasn't the students' fault that her heart was numb and encased in ice.

Sipping tea, she marked the work needed for Monday and prepped her day plans for next week. She preferred to be a week ahead, rather than the one day required by the school. You never knew when life wouldn't go according to plan. She'd learned that the hard way.

At five, Kat scurried out to her car with a vague wave toward the other fifth-grade teacher from across the hall, who was also on her way out.

"TGIF," said Tracy. "That sounded like a great lesson on the rock cycle. Maybe I could borrow some samples next week. You have any weekend plans?"

Kat smiled on cue, the last toothy one until Monday. Her cheek muscles ached from over-use. "Not really. See you Monday." She headed in the opposite direction.

Getting in her car, Kat relaxed her face, massaging the tight muscles along her jaw. Once the tension eased a bit, she turned on the radio, checking traffic for the route home. Seattle and the outlying area were gridlocked at the best of times, let alone during Friday afternoon rush hour. She had to make it home; then the weekend was hers, hers to do with as she pleased. Her hands shook as she drove. All week she'd been anticipating peace and oblivion.

One nagging doubt plagued her as she drove. She couldn't shake the idea that she'd promised someone something, but she couldn't recall what. Her brow furrowed. It wasn't a birthday or her parents' anniversary. She hadn't spoken to them in months, so that wasn't it. The sense that she'd forgotten something persisted.

She parked outside her townhouse and hurried upstairs. Kicking off her shoes with a sigh of sheer pleasure, she threw her bag inside by the door and headed straight for the cabinet over the stove with the alcohol. She needed a drink.

She opened the fresh sapphire-colored bottle of Bombay gin, took down a large glass from the cupboard, and free-poured a generous measure into the bottom. She sliced a lime from the fridge into wedges and rinsed the knife and cutting board. The tonic, pre-chilled in the fridge, fizzed when opened, the sound making her mouth water. She swallowed in anticipation. She filled the glass three-quarters full and squeezed in two lime chunks, licking the excess from her fingers because she loved the tang. Adding four ice cubes, her drink was perfect.

Taking it in both hands, she breathed deep, inhaling the bubbling citrus scent. Without thinking, Kat tipped it back and gulped down half. The bite of alcohol was strong and delicious. Her hands shook as she let the rest wash down her throat. Setting down her empty glass, she sighed. With a deep breath, she made a second, stronger drink, ignoring the nagging voice inside that told her to go slow. The ritual was calming and her hands no longer trembled as she carried it to the couch and sat, putting up her feet. It was easier not to think when she drank.

She didn't bother with the TV, but stared out the window, though she didn't pay attention to the view. Sipping, she savored her drink, noticing how each swallow slid down her throat. She didn't touch a drop Monday to Thursday, but from Friday to Sunday she could do what she liked; she was beholden to nobody.

Three drinks later, Kat wobbled to the fridge to see if she'd bother with food. Fridays, she preferred to drink her dinner because cooking seemed like too much work. Each week, she told herself to order something if she didn't want to cook, but more often than not, she didn't. The first drink wasn't a problem, but after she had a second, it was never worth the effort to do more than make another drink, despite the twinge of guilt about wasting her life. She shouldn't be this way, but she didn't have a reason to change.

Her phone rang, but she let it go to voicemail. Three minutes later, it started again, the ringtone piercing and setting her teeth on edge. She glanced at the phone where it was charging and exhaled a mouthful of air in disgust before muting the sound. Nick knew better than to call Fridays. What the hell did he want? After a hectic week, she didn't feel like talking.

Her phone chimed with a text moments later. God, he was persistent tonight. She squinted, trying to read the jumble of words on the screen, but they were difficult to read.

"Shit," she said, deciphering enough to get the idea.

"Be there in ten with pizza."

"Shit, shit, shit."

She unlocked her front door, staggered back to the couch, and sat while she waited for her best friend to arrive with dinner and a lecture. She sat up straight, trying to look sober.

Nick didn't bother ringing the bell, knowing she hated the loud noise. He entered, two large pizzas in hand. The rich scent of cheese, tomatoes, and basil filled her living room. It smelled better than anything in her fridge. Maybe this could work.

He took one look at her and set the pizzas down. His shoulders slumped.

"I'm already too late." He flipped open the top box and grabbed a slice.

"Too late?" she said, trying to focus on him while the room spun. Feeling proud for covering her inebriation so well, she lurched to her feet and tripped over her shoes lying on the floor. She crawled a few steps and got to her feet, her cheeks burning.

"Kat, you promised, remember?" said Nick, his mouth full. "One drink to relax, then we'd have pizza and watch a movie."

"Just had one," she said, concentrating on walking in a straight line. The floor buckled and swam as she made her way toward the pizza. She'd been stupid to think he wouldn't notice.

"Three drinks or four?" he said, lifting the bottle of gin. "Kat, what are we going to do with you?" His tone was concerned. "Can I help?"

"Can't do anything," she said as she chose a wedge of pizza with ham, pineapple, and bacon, her usual favorite. Her words might be flippant, but she was disappointed in herself. Nick was a trusted friend and deserved better. She wished she'd remembered their plans.

"I'm thinking that's true. You won't come to our place. You won't meet us anywhere; you don't answer your phone and as far as I can tell, all you do is work and drink."

She shrugged and took a big bite. She chewed while thinking of a reply, her brain functioning slower than usual. "I don't drink all week. I just need to blow off steam."

She scowled, feeling resentful. He had no idea.

"Kat, I'm worried about you. The only time you aren't alone is when I inflict myself upon you. You don't see anyone else. Do you?"

"Don't want to," she mumbled around another bite of pizza. The sauce was tangy, still hot, and oh so delicious. A niggling voice in her head called her a liar, but she squashed it and focused on the pizza.

"Are you looking forward to time off work, your summer holiday? What have you got planned?" He grabbed a slice and sat.

"Nothing much," she said with a shrug. She hadn't made plans because she didn't know what would help her feel more connected again. The look in his eyes made her cringe inside. He was up to something.

"We should plan something. We used to hike all the time."

The pizza stuck in her throat, and she glanced at her empty glass with longing.

"We should pick a day for hiking every weekend. Every Sunday? Start right away. No need to wait for summer. Jake can join when he's free. I have another friend who needs to get out, too. We should all go."

She didn't feel well. The pizza in her stomach had become a greasy lump. She set her half-eaten slice down in the box and walked on unsteady legs back to the couch, the room spinning.

Nick's eyes held concern as he put two slices of pizza on his plate and her partial piece on another. He carried them to the coffee table as he sat at the opposite end of the couch. At least she hadn't driven him away. Even in her foggy state, she recognized she needed to meet his effort's part way. She didn't want him to give up or think she was hopeless.

"Who else for hiking?" She didn't want to exercise, but it might be easier to agree. She could always cancel. Or hike and escape this place with all its unpleasant memories.

"A friend. You might have met him years ago at university."

"Ugh, this isn't a set-up, is it?" She wasn't ready to consider the idea.

"No way. I wouldn't do that without permission, and you don't like surprises. I want to spend time with both of you, and I don't have a lot of spare time. If I double up, I can see you twice as often." He nudged the plate in her direction.

He seemed sincere. She picked up the pizza and nibbled. "Lucky us."

"That's a resounding yes, then?" He perked up, his tone hopeful.

"I guess."

"Last week, you freaked me out."

"What happened last week?" She wracked her brain but came up empty.

"You don't remember, do you?" He slumped back on the couch.

She shrugged and shook her head. She took another bite of pizza, humoring her friend. Dinner was a good idea.

"You didn't answer your phone or your doorbell even though that morning you said you'd be here, and your car was parked out front. I wanted to tell you about my big discovery at work. You used to love to hear about comets and meteors and space dust."

"I would still like to hear." She eyed her drink where she'd left it on the counter.

"Kat, your door wasn't locked, and I came in and found you on the floor, passed out cold. I put you to bed and came back early on Sunday. We made this plan for tonight."

"I don't remember." She swallowed, her food tasting like cardboard as she touched her forehead, remembering the goose egg.

"On Sunday, you sobered up, and we talked. You admitted that you blackout every weekend. You agreed to try not to this weekend. I don't want to babysit you, but if I can help be a distraction until you break the habit, I will."

Tears leaked down her face at his words. She seemed to have no control. What was wrong with her? Maybe not remembering what she'd done was better. She was such a mess.

Nick took her hand in his. "Mark wouldn't want you to mourn him this way."

"Mark isn't here." It came out sharper than she expected. The usual filter had fallen off her mouth and emotions. "He doesn't get a vote."

"You're acting like you're dead, too." Nick squeezed her hand and let go. "I want to tell you about my cool discovery. If you forget, I'll tell you again Sunday. I want to share it with you like I used to."

"I don't want your pity time," mumbled Kat as she stared at the floor. She needed to clean. Crumbs and dusty balls of hair floated along the edge of the baseboards and she couldn't remember the last time she'd swept or washed anything other than a dish. Afraid she might have offended him, she forced herself to make eye contact and saw he was smiling. Why was he being so kind? She didn't deserve it.

"It isn't pity," said Nick. "I'm looking to get my friend back. This is purely selfish."

She didn't believe him, but got up to collect her drink. She could sip while she listened.

Nick followed her to the counter, his hands jammed in his front pockets. His eyes looked sad, and she wished she could stop hurting him. She stopped with the glass halfway to her mouth and handed it to him. He gave her a tremulous smile and emptied her gin and tonic down the sink; the ice clinking on the stainless steel.

She didn't speak, but the drink being gone came as a relief. She picked up the bottle and handed it to him with shaking hands.

He dumped the rest of the gin with a gurgling sound, the ice cubes bumping into each other as they swirled around the drain. She closed her eyes, concentrating on her breathing. It would be okay.

"You might be angry, but you need help." Nick's voice brought her back to the moment.

She looked at him and nodded. How did she explain she was empty inside?

"Can I have a hug?" Stabbing pains in her chest accompanied her request. From her, it was an unusual request. Most of the time, she preferred not to be touched. It shouldn't hurt to let herself feel.

Nick held out his arms and gave her a squeeze that loosened some of her pent-up angst and loneliness. After resting her head on his shoulder, she walked away. She needed to try harder to get her life back.

She took a deep breath and swiped the tears from her cheeks with her hands. "Let's hear about your space dust."

CHAPTER 2: RYAN

Ryan glanced at the clock. It was late enough that Nick should be awake. Dreading the task, he called his friend, who answered on the second ring.

"Hey, Ryan. What's up? You running late?"

"Nick, sorry. I have to cancel. I like the idea of hiking, but not this week. I just arrived at the office." Ryan ran his fingers through his hair, standing it on end. He didn't like to disappoint his closest friend.

On the other end of the line, Nick paused. "Again?"

Even though his friend sounded understanding, it still didn't make Ryan feel any less like a flake.

"Yeah, sorry. I'm up for a promotion soon. I'm on track to make partner in six years, so I need to keep up my hours. I could do lunch this week though, say Tuesday? My treat." He hated canceling, but he'd woken up at four and hadn't dared to wait around for a nine o'clock hike. He needed to keep his mind occupied.

"I'd like that," said Nick. "I want to talk to you about something. In-person, if that's okay. Something I found at work."

His discovery couldn't be that exceptional because Nick's excitement level seemed more muted than usual.

"Sure. We can text Monday to set up a place. Enjoy the hike." Ryan hung up and swiveled his black leather office chair to take in his cramped office. At least he had a window, as this was just about the only view he saw nowadays. More downtown office towers filled the skyline, but it was better than the cubbyhole he'd used as a junior associate his first two years at Goodrich, Singh, and Hardcastle.

Though it was Sunday, he put his head down and worked, concentrating on writing the brief a partner wanted later this week.

He wrote and rewrote it a dozen times before he could no longer ignore his stomach rumbling, reminding him he hadn't eaten yet. He'd finished ahead of schedule, priding himself on getting everything done early. Checking his phone for the first time since lunch, the time was nine-thirty. He'd been here for fourteen hours with only a sandwich, but he'd driven in because it was easier to avoid distractions here than at home. Writing his hours on his timesheet, he gathered his laptop. He'd grab a bite on the way home. He couldn't remember his last home-cooked meal. Or rather, he didn't want to. It always led to him feeling foolish, rejected, and ended with crushing regret.

He drove home, the streets dark and quiet this time of night, making it an easier commute than weekday Seattle traffic. He collected his mail from the lobby on the way up to his seventh-floor apartment, his bag of chicken tacos in hand. The apartment was quiet and smelled of unwashed laundry with a hint of garbage. He hated coming home to an empty apartment night after night. He dragged one of his two kitchen chairs into position and flicked on the TV, wishing for a comfy chair instead of the rigid remnants that had been left behind.

The wall-mounted wide-screen TV and the surround-sound speakers were the only things in the otherwise barren living room. When Heather had annihilated him last year, she'd taken the couch and loveseat, lamps, coffee table, and end tables when she moved out. She'd taken the artwork from the walls and every symbol of their life together. Including the other chairs, the table, and... his heart; leaving him as empty and hollow as his apartment.

He hadn't gotten around to replacing anything. But he wasn't here often enough. Of course, she'd left the bed, the last thing he wanted.

He slept on it because it was softer than the floor, but he should have it replaced.

When he finished dinner, he sat for half an hour, letting his food digest before he changed into workout clothes and did four reps of his exercises, each with a dozen weighted arm curls and lifts, twenty-five each of sit-ups, push-ups, and squats. After a quick shower, he set an alarm for four forty-five a.m. as Monday was a run day. He had to wake early to clean up and be at work by seven a.m. He'd have to keep the pace up to get in his eight miles.

Before he fell asleep, he remembered Nick had mentioned a discovery at the observatory. He made a mental note to be sure to ask for details on Tuesday.

•   •   •

When Tuesday morning rolled around and Ryan's alarm woke him before work, he was covered in sweat and his heart pounded against his ribs. He'd been dreaming about Heather again. This time when he'd proposed, he was naked and in front of all their watching friends. When she'd said "no" she'd pointed and laughed, joined by everyone he knew. Their cruel laughter echoed through the room. His mom had shaken her head and turned away, her lip curling in disgust. The alarm had been a game show buzzer for the wrong answer.

Despite the venue changing, the dream wasn't much different from the nightmare reality. No one else had witnessed his humiliation, but he'd caught Heather cheating. In the subsequent fight, she'd laughed and said she would have refused his proposal. She'd lived with him for two years, but it turned out she'd never loved him. He hadn't expected the words that followed and tore through his soul. "Are you kidding me? I'd never marry an unfeeling bastard like you." It had shocked him to his core. He'd worked hard to create a better life for the two of them, but she'd only felt neglected.

He hadn't trusted himself since. His perception of reality and where he fit in relation to others must not be accurate. Shouldn't he have seen it coming instead of being blindsided? Perhaps that was why he worked so hard now. It wasn't enough to think he was working long hours; they had to be excessive to impress the partners.

He hopped in the shower, determined not to think about Heather anymore or to allow lingering thoughts of her to ruin his morning. It worked because his day went as they most often did, spent writing briefs that those above him on the food chain would take credit for until he left work at eleven fifty to meet Nick, as promised. They'd agreed to meet before the downtown lunch rush.

Nick was seated when he arrived at the hole-in-the-wall sushi spot they favored. His friend looked stressed; his forehead creased more than it should be at thirty-one years of age. Did he also look that weary?

"What's up?" Ryan slid into his seat after placing his order at the counter.

"I might need new friends," said Nick. "Ones willing to spend time with me."

"We can't all be that bad," said Ryan as he sipped his ice water.

"Between you and Kat, it's a tie." Nick held his hands up as though he surrendered.

"Kat, the bubbly elementary school teacher you tried to set me up with right after university? Didn't she marry some uptight guy named Matt or Mark or something? You haven't mentioned her in years. I assumed you'd lost touch. What's she doing wrong? Working too hard, like me?" He threw that out there, knowing that was why Nick worried. Broken-hearted Ryan, who lived at the office and had no life.

"Her Mark died two years ago. A heart attack at work. A heart condition that nobody knew about. He keeled over one day. They'd been married less than a year." Nick frowned and looked out the window.

Ryan felt like shit for not remembering. He recalled hearing about the tragedy. He hadn't meant to shove his foot in his mouth. "That's horrible. How does that make her a terrible friend?" He didn't see the connection, but his heart went out to the poor girl. They might have something in common now, if they hadn't in the past. She'd seemed like someone whose life had always been perfect.

"She seemed devastated and wanted to be alone, so I gave her space. I tried to reconnect a few times, but kept getting the brush off. Nobody had seen her in ages. We hadn't spoken in forever, and I thought she might need someone to talk to or hang out with, so I tried again." Nick's voice sounded strained, and he poured himself another steaming cup of green tea.

Ryan sat up straight. Nick seldom showed this much emotion. Perhaps he needed a friend to talk to if something was troubling him.

"What happened?"

Nick hesitated before speaking. "A couple of weeks ago, I got pushy and Kat and I made plans. When she blew me off, I checked on her and found her passed out dead drunk on the floor. She'd smashed her forehead, given herself a lump the size of an egg." He swallowed and looked out the window, his eyes moist.

Ryan pretended not to notice. Finding a friend in that condition would be difficult.

"That doesn't sound like the person you tried to convince me to date," said Ryan with a frown. He hoped it wasn't a setup now. She sounded like a real mess. At least he was productive in his heartache. He'd never been in better shape and had billed an extra four hundred hours last year. "If I recall, you warned me she was almost too happy and positive, if that's a thing."

"Not the case now. It wasn't then either, but I figured that would be your first impression because that's the face she shows to the world. The thing is, that isn't even the worst."

Ryan waited.

"I went back a couple of mornings later, and we talked. What I'd seen was the tip of the iceberg. I read between the lines and became horrified. It's like she's a different person. She drinks until she blacks out every night every weekend. For two years. How could I not have noticed?"

"You have your own life," said Ryan. "We're all busy. She probably didn't want you to know. If she hid it from you, maybe she hid it from everyone." She sounded like a disaster. He grimaced to himself; to be honest, he was similar.

"She hasn't lost her job because nobody knows or cares what she does on weekends and holidays. She's kept it secret because she holds it together during the week."

"It could be worse. She might have lost her job."

Nick shrugged. "It's bad enough. We made plans for last Friday night. She forgot and was smashed by the time I got to her house an hour after she got home. She didn't remember talking to me the previous weekend. I have to do something."

"You aren't her babysitter. It's been like two years. Isn't it time she pulled up her big-girl pants and moved on with her life?" Was that advice intended for himself too, to deal with his problems and move on? Ryan flattened his mouth into a frown.

"Easier said than done. When she doesn't want me to interfere, it kinda sucks. She's trying to drink herself to death. She didn't use to drink more than the odd hard lemonade at a barbeque."

"Maybe you saw her on a bad day?" said Ryan.

"Every Friday, Saturday, and Sunday? That's a lot of bad days."

"I can't picture that," said Ryan. "Thanks," he said to the server who dropped off their orders. He poured soy sauce into a dish and separated his chopsticks.

"Will you help me?" Nick dipped his sashimi in soy. "I was hoping you would come hiking with us, make it a group thing. Jake will come too when he's free. There's two coming Sundays when I'm busy with work commitments, and I need someone who will get her out of her house, whether or not she wants to."

"Maybe she wants to wallow," said Ryan as he ate. He didn't mean to sound unsympathetic.

"It's been two years. I don't know where the hell her family has gone, but they aren't helping. She's isolated and alone. That isn't good for anyone."

"Okay." Ryan's heart wasn't in it, but he owed Nick. Nick was awesome and had taken care of everyone. Back in their university days, they used to joke, "Nick's your buddy, Nick's your pal, Nick won't make you clean it up if you puke in his car." Nick helped people, and it appeared Kat was his new project, and Ryan owed him for kicking his ass into gear when Heather left.

"Thanks," said Nick as he popped another chunk of California roll into his mouth.

"So, let's hear about this discovery," said Ryan, switching to a happier topic. He wanted to show that he was a decent friend.

"It's that asteroid they're talking about on the news. Did you notice its name?"

Ryan shook his head. "Haven't there been like six already this year?"

Nick laughed. "Nope. Three. But the recent one, the one they're talking about this week, it's my discovery. Its name is the year, cause that's when I discovered it, and my initials. It isn't far away, but nobody had seen it before because the Sun was in the way. It's called 2025 NR. I found it and they've assigned me to watch it. I have to determine its final trajectory, where it will go after it passes Earth, and if it will be back."

"Is it one that will make that Sentry list you mentioned, the one that ranks potential threats?" Ryan leaned back to listen to his friend.

Nick shifted forward with a smile. "It's over 800 meters…"

•   •   •

Findings by Nick Rhodes as of April 15, 2025
I discovered 2025 NR on April 12, 2025, using a camera mounted on a telescope.
Preliminary Findings:
Estimated diameter: 825 m +/- 100 m or 0.825 km +/- 0.100 km
Estimated speed: 23.95 km/s +/- 5.0 km/s
Initial threat assessment: Add to the Sentry Table as a precaution.

Recommended Action: Further monitoring to increase data.

Conditions affecting visibility: weather, position relative to the Sun, phase of the Moon

Assess asteroid orbit for a minimum of fourteen days.

Follow-up: Observations after the initial window to increase the accuracy of orbit determination.

Calculate if, when, and where the orbital may intersect with Earth in the future (as defined by within the next 200 years).

Conclusion: There isn't enough data to make an estimate of the probability of an impact event on Earth.

CHAPTER 3: KAT

Kat waited on her couch, her knee bouncing and worrying at her lip as she thought about today's excursion. Nick was bringing a friend. He'd explained over the phone that his buddy Ryan worked too hard and needed to get out. She remembered the name, but they hadn't met. Nick had wanted to match them up eight years ago, but she'd just met Mark and turned down the suggestion.

The first hike had been for herself and Nick. They'd been gone for most of the day, driving toward Mount Baker National Forest, and they'd hiked a trail that Nick had chosen. Afterward, they'd gone for dinner, and Kat hadn't had a drink. She supposed she could have had one with dinner, but it didn't tempt her when she was with Nick. Drinking was something she did alone. She'd returned home to a bubble bath, a luxury she hadn't indulged in for far too long, then gone to bed with sore muscles, exhausted. Monday morning had been more tolerable without a hangover.

Her phone chimed with a text from Nick. *"We're here."*

She groaned, grabbed her daypack, and collected two bottles of iced water from the counter for her pack and another from the fridge. She checked she had extra Tylenol in her pocket. After being alone so long, it seemed odd to have plans for the second weekend in a row. Often, she went months without a social commitment. This was the fourth time in nine days.

Nick had arrived Friday night, the new ritual. She smiled, thinking of their evening. It hadn't been exciting, but it had meant a lot to both of them. She'd foregone drinking that night and he'd brought dinner. After they'd eaten, they'd watched the latest Marvel movie on Netflix. Nick's boyfriend, Jake, was a firefighter and worked Friday nights, leaving Nick free.

Saturday, she was left to her own devices, and she'd had a few drinks, but hadn't finished the bottle. A small accomplishment, nevertheless, it was something. No matter how her stomach churned, Sunday was for hiking. She was determined that she wouldn't cancel; it wouldn't be fair to Nick. Sometimes Jake planned to come if he was free, as well as this Ryan, who Nick assured her wasn't a set-up, just also in need of weekend outings.

Her head throbbed from yesterday's drinking. She remembered little after late Saturday morning. She'd woken up this morning on the kitchen floor, her cheek stuck to the tile. It wasn't the first time, but it bothered her more than usual. A shower had worked wonders, and she felt almost human, despite the pounding. She downed two glasses of water to clear her head. The third water bottle was for the car. She wanted to ensure she was hydrated for hiking.

She tied her hiking shoes and locked the door as she left. Despite herself, she was curious about Ryan. He'd been Nick's long-time friend, and she'd heard of him several times over the years. He was a lawyer, but she didn't know what kind of law he practiced. That kind of job sounded tedious, but to each their own. She trotted out to the orange SUV where Nick was at the wheel.

The passenger seat was empty, for which she was thankful. She'd get motion sick in the back seat on the windy roads off the highway. Ryan sat in the back on her side, her view blocked by her seat. Her first impression was that he was tall and had short hair somewhere between blond and brown. She didn't think they'd met, but she couldn't be sure because he was looking at his phone. She didn't glance at him more than once.

"Thanks for driving." She slid in, putting on her work persona for the benefit of the stranger in the back. "I'm Kat." She spoke over her shoulder toward the back seat.

"Ryan," said the voice behind her. "Checking my emails one last time before we leave the city."

His voice was flat and disinterested. He must be clear it wasn't a set-up, too.

"How's asteroid watch?" she said to Nick, dialing back the fake cheer.

"I've got more data, but I haven't run it through the machines for analysis yet. That's my plan on Tuesday, but it's a big one." He frowned, then glanced in the mirrors and pulled out.

Sometimes she had trouble reading people, but his eyes looked strained and tired. Perhaps he didn't want to talk about work today. It had been keeping him busy all week.

"I thought we'd go toward Baker again. Got another trail marked that opened this week. First hikers of the season. Listed as hard, but we're up for it."

Kat wasn't up for a strenuous hike, but she didn't argue. After liking the outing more than expected last week, she'd enjoyed having something to look forward to this week besides a gin and tonic, or six.

They drove for a couple of hours without a lot of chatter. Ryan seemed unfriendly and Nick wasn't his usual self, choosing to be quieter, perhaps overtired from work. The equivalent time spent with her mother and sister would have been more difficult to sit in recovery mode while the Tylenol did its magic.

Once, she would have filled the silence with stories about her fifth graders and questions about the hike, but now it was more effort than she wanted to expend. Being social took a toll. She closed her eyes, sipped water, and listened to the music Nick had chosen as today's road trip playlist. He'd always liked to make a list for each excursion. She'd forgotten that until last week's upbeat driving mix. Today's selection was more mellow for which she was grateful.

It was already warm when they stopped at the end of a rocky, bumpy road filled with potholes. They parked by the side of the road at the trailhead in the pull-out next to an open area filled with baby fir, spruce trees, and leafy bushes. They got out, and she slathered herself with sunscreen, using the window as a mirror. Stowing her half-full water bottle, she put on her hat and backpack. Her pack was light, with just her phone, keys, water, and lunch.

Kat would have been happy to take the rear, but Nick said, "Lead the way. You set the pace and we'll try to keep up." She wasn't fooled. They were in better shape and if she went first, they wouldn't leave her behind.

She glanced at Ryan as he came around the back of the SUV. "You don't mind?"

He shrugged.

She examined him for the first time and felt like someone had punched her in the gut. He was gorgeous, with golden-brown hair and a body that looked hard and fit; like a trained athlete with defined muscles everywhere she could see. His eyes were startling, a mismatched pair: one blue, one hazel. It was difficult to look him in the eye without catching her breath. She felt like an idiot to have such a strong physical reaction to someone she'd just met. Her cheeks burned, but she hoped he didn't notice. She was the slightest bit disappointed Nick wasn't arranging anything date-like. She almost gave Ryan a genuine smile instead of her patented fake grin. Hoping to center herself, she turned toward the trailhead.

The mountain trail started in the clear-cut area but was soon forested and shady as they headed to the Hidden Lake Lookout. They passed a couple of other groups of hikers stopped for water breaks.

Kat set a quick pace to start, not wanting to hike with strangers or be forced to go slow. The footing was uneven as they crossed a creek and climbed up the slope. She slowed just enough to place her feet with care when the footing became rougher. Once past the forested section of conifers and alders, the terrain became rocky, and the vista opened up. She could see a long way. She liked the varied terrain and appreciated the beauty as she climbed. The mountains were peaceful and undemanding.

Though it was late April, patches of snow littered the ground and, in the shade, still piled several feet deep. Ice crystals sparkled where they were caught by the sun, and slushy bits melted into the mud. They passed through clusters of granite slabs and alpine meadows, turning emerald green with recent growth. Later in the summer, they'd be filled with a riot of bright purple, pink, red, and orange, like the alpine areas where she and Nick used to hike.

Those had been happy days, and she wasn't sure why they'd stopped, but then an onslaught of less pleasant memories swept over her, overwhelming her with shame. She and Mark had always been busy with one of his projects and there'd never been time. Why had she let him dictate who her friends were? She didn't like to think of Mark and their troubles. He'd been controlling; it had been disguised by good humor and affection, but somehow, he'd always gotten his way. Strange that it had escaped her notice.

They stopped after a few miles to admire Mount Baker from a viewpoint while Kat reached for her water. Sweat drenched her clothes since she was unaccustomed to exercise. She gulped down her icy water, her face burning. It must be rosy from the exertion of the steep climb. Her heart thumped against her ribs, a hard rhythm that matched her gasping breath. The altitude made a difference. That, and she was out of shape.

She glanced at her companions. Nick didn't seem to have broken much of a sweat, though his cheeks were pink. Ryan looked like he was out for an easy Sunday stroll in the park. He didn't have even a sheen of sweat, and his breathing was normal. He took a quick drink and looked impatient to continue, pacing up the path ten feet to wait while she caught her breath. She lifted her chin, determined to increase the pace for the second half.

They hiked onward and found a shady section where the snow and ice lay thicker across the trail, reaching down the slope like a tentacle from the mountain's glacier above. If it hadn't been for the packed, dirty footprints through the ice, Kat would have been nervous. She had to be careful on the treacherous icy piece. This section would have been impossible earlier in the season.

It was early afternoon when at last they scrambled through a saddle between two peaks and found themselves with stunning views down to Hidden Lake and from Mount Rainier to Mount Baker, with a multitude of lesser peaks between.

It had been three hours since they'd left the roadside, and she was ready for lunch. This was an out-and-back hike, rather than a loop, and should be faster going downhill on the return. Her knees and ankles might feel it tonight and her butt was already sore from the sections that had been steep.

"Let's eat." Nick parked himself on one of the flat faces of a gray boulder overlooking the incredible view.

Ryan sat on his other side, and they unpacked their food while Kat sat apart on a different rock to their right, preferring space to being crowded together. The view from her vantage was no less spectacular. Her lungs burned, her legs felt like rubber, and she was glad for a break. Perhaps she would have done better if she hadn't been hungover. She was glad she'd made the effort to come, even if she wasn't looking forward to the descent.

An inquisitive chipmunk scooted around the base of the rock the men sat on. She said nothing but observed as it advanced in small bursts of movement. She flicked a few breadcrumbs in its direction and watched as it collected the tidbits. In the distance, a trio of birds circled below. It was like she was also in the sky.

She inhaled and took in the breathtaking view as she ate. The air was chillier than expected at this elevation as she cooled down. She wished she'd worn long pants or had another layer to wear while she sat and made a note to locate her zip-off convertible pants and a light hiking shirt with long sleeves for next time. Her old motto had been: wear layers. It was always colder than expected on a mountain during a break. She was already looking forward to next time.

She adjusted her waistband; she also needed a belt. Her hiking shorts were loose, and she'd lost weight. She'd never been so thin before, the result of too many skipped meals. Being on the mountain made her feel more relaxed than she'd been in years. She would try harder to be healthy and social. If it was difficult to do for herself, at least Nick would be pleased.

She leaned forward. "Ryan, have you been here before?" She broke the silence as she finished her sandwich and started on her cut-up strawberries. She wasn't making small talk, but was interested. Nick was one of the select people with whom she'd always felt herself, like there was no need to conform to a particular ideal. She extended that to Ryan almost without thinking. She was too exhausted to put on a show or mask.

Ryan shook his head and took a bite of his second sandwich. He seemed to be a man of few words. Perhaps he wasn't enjoying the hike. It was difficult to tell what he was thinking. If she concentrated, she could read some people; perhaps his experience as a lawyer helped keep his face from showing his thoughts. Still, his nonverbal dismissiveness put her teeth on edge. If she could attempt to be friendly, why couldn't he be civil?

"Jake and I came here two or three years ago, but in September," said Nick. "The meadows were insane. We might have to return in late summer."

"Count me in," she said, taking a bite. "Remember the bright red paintbrush and different purple lupins on Mt. Rainier about ten years ago? That's one of my favorite memories." She disliked thinking about the past, but leap-frogging over the Mark years wasn't so bad. A lump formed in her throat. She'd had a full life before marrying him. Why had she fallen apart without him? She didn't want to think about Mark, but she needed to try harder to enjoy her life.

They reached the car by late afternoon, and Kat's whole body was warm and thrummed with that post-exercise feeling. Her calf muscles were tight and on fire, but in a good way. She stretched, feeling self-conscious since Ryan was watching with an amused glance. She grit her teeth so she didn't say something rude. Perhaps he thought her a wimp whose hiking was too slow for him. It was odd, but she wanted to improve his opinion of her next time out.

"Going to be stiff tomorrow?" he said with a smirk and raised eyebrow.

She clenched her jaw tighter at his tone.

He might be beautiful, fit with broad shoulders and those disconcerting eyes, but he was annoying. He was also about six foot four and in another climatic zone. Somewhere with an arctic chill. Not once had he initiated a conversation, even if they'd been together for a solid eight hours and her only attempt had been shut down.

At dinner on the road home, she ordered lemonade instead of an alcoholic drink. Nick had an iced tea and glared at Ryan when he ordered a craft beer. She didn't care if Ryan drank; it had nothing to do with her. She arrived home and didn't take down the remainder of last night's bottle of gin. Leaving it in the cupboard, she soaked in the tub with a favorite book she hadn't read in a long time. Even if Ryan had been unfriendly, her excursion had been fantastic. Tears pricked her eyes, and she couldn't keep them away. She needed more weekends like this.

● ● ●

Findings by Nick Rhodes as of April 29, 2025

2025 NR was discovered on April 12, 2025. We monitored it an additional fourteen days with a telescope-mounted camera every three hours while in range.

Findings:

Estimated diameter: 900 m +/- 25 or 0.900 km +/- 0.025 km

Estimated speed: 26.22 km/s +/- 5.0 km/s

Initial threat assessment: we have added 2025 NR to the Sentry Table as a precaution. Rank eighth in concern.

Recommended Action: Further monitoring to increase data.

Report forwarded to superiors with a recommendation to speak to the government liaison with all relevant information.

Conditions affecting visibility: weather, position relative to the Sun, phase of the moon. Orbit remains difficult to calculate with precision. Assess asteroid orbit for another fourteen days. Seems to be both larger and faster than the original estimate. Possibly increasing in measurable speed.

Priority. Continue to follow-up observations after the initial window to increase the accuracy of orbit determination.

Send information to observatories in other parts of the world for additional monitoring capability and independent analysis.

Calculations indicate orbit will intersect Earth's orbit within the next forty to fifty days. Location and number of million miles away cannot be determined.

Conclusion: There is a minor concern that there could be a near miss or an impact event on Earth.

About the Author

Lena Gibson is a storyteller as an elementary school teacher and keeper of the family lore. She holds a First Class Honors degree in Archaeology, with minors in History, Biology, Geography, and Environmental Education from Simon Fraser University.

A voracious reader from age eight onward, Lena seeks wonderful books in which to escape. Because of her passion for different genres, she combines elements of many in her writing. As an adult newly recognized with autism, she often creates characters that reflect this experience.

When Lena isn't writing, she reads, practices karate, and drinks a ton of tea. She resides in New Westminster, Canada with her family and their fuzzy overlord, Ash, the fluffiest of gray cats.

Email: lena.gibson15@gmail.com,
https://lenagibsonauthor.wordpress.com

Other Titles by Lena Gibson

"Blending romance and action/adventure, Gibson makes
the end of the world the most fun the reader will have all day."
–Eileen Cook, author of *You Owe Me a Murder*

The Edge of Life

Lena Gibson

Note from Lena Gibson

Word-of-mouth is crucial for any author to succeed. If you enjoyed *The Wish*, please leave a review online—anywhere you are able. Even if it's just a sentence or two. It would make all the difference and would be very much appreciated.

Thanks!
Lena Gibson

We hope you enjoyed reading this title from:

www.blackrosewriting.com

Subscribe to our mailing list – *The Rosevine* – and receive **FREE** books, daily deals, and stay current with news about upcoming releases and our hottest authors.
Scan the QR code below to sign up.

Already a subscriber? Please accept a sincere thank you for being a fan of Black Rose Writing authors.

View other Black Rose Writing titles at www.blackrosewriting.com/books and use promo code **PRINT** to receive a **20% discount** when purchasing.

Made in United States
Troutdale, OR
11/20/2024

25101759R00213